ENEMY PATRIOTS

RODGER CARLYLE

This is a work of fiction. The names, characters, organizations and events are products of the author's imagination and bear no relation to any living person or are used fictitiously.

ENEMY PATRIOTS. Copyright © 2020 by Rodger Carlyle. All rights reserved.

Published in the United States by Verity Books, an imprint of Comsult, LLC.

All rights reserved. Except for brief passages except quoted in newspaper, magazine, radio, television or online reviews, no portion of this book may be reproduced, distributed, or transmitted in any form or by any means, electronic or mechanical including photocopying, recording, or information storage or retrieval systems without the prior written permission of the author and/or Comsult, LLC.

First published in 2021.

ISBN 978-1-7360074-0-2 (e-book)
ISBN 978-1-7360074-5-7 (hardback)
ISBN 978-1-73600-74-1-9 (paperback)

Editing: Inventing Reality Editing Service

Cover design and formatting: Damonza

PROLOGUE

UNALASKA ISLAND, ALEUTIAN ISLANDS, ALASKA, 1931

The split bamboo fly rod whipped the air. Its woven line curled back before the forward thrust of the rod sent it shooting over the brackish pool. Reaching almost to the far bank, the red and white fly settled. The boy gave the line a tug, then a second. His rod bent double as a chrome sockeye salmon went airborne.

"Got another one!" screamed Woody Gritt.

"Let me count your fish," said Mark Ishihara, with a smirk. "One, uh, two. I don't think your brother or I have made two casts without hooking a fish."

"Woody and Stephan have been giving the fish a break," laughed Chad, Woody's brother. "Seems the kids only get the fly to the water about every ten casts."

"Don't call us kids," snapped Woody. "We're only a couple of years younger than you guys." The Ishihara and Gritt brothers' friendship went back to their fathers' friendship, one an officer in the American Army and the other a Japanese officer, who fought side by side in a war in Russia just after the Great War, a war stripped from the history books, one that the then allies lost.

Earlier, glare from the sun had made it difficult to see into the bottom of the pool. Now, a ripple stirred the water offering a glimpse of Woody's fish, tugging and twisting. Sweeping clouds occasionally blocked the sun.

"The wind's picking up. Let's clean our fish and head home," said Chad.

"Who made you king? It's my dad's boat. I'm driving," said Mark. "Let's give it another thirty minutes."

The unnamed Unalaska Island lake drained into the Pacific Ocean, a short boat ride from the Ishihara Fish Cannery that the four young fishermen called home each July.

Around the boys, grass rippled unhampered by shrubs or trees from the shore to the tops of jagged mountains. To the north, south and west there was no trace of man for a thousand miles. The Aleutian Islands prove the end of the world is not Dante's Hell, but a place pure and haunting. It is wilderness unknown even by those who crave wilderness. It is also a very dangerous place.

"Mark, I promised your dad that we would watch the weather," replied Chad.

Mark set the hook on another fish. "I'd say the weather is as good as the fishing. Look, it's still mostly sunny."

The oak framed plywood boat was partially beached by the time the boys flopped their fish over the side and stored their rods along the gunnel. Their knee-high rubber boots sank into the soft sand. It took all four to tug the heavy boat out to where Chad, manning the oars, rowed into deeper water. "I'm through rowing. It's plenty deep, get Elgin started."

Mark wrenched on the cord of the Elgin outboard motor. Nothing happened. He tugged off his heavy wool coat and rolled the sleeves of his blue flannel shirt. "Nine, ten, eleven," he mumbled as he continued to tug on the cord. Elgin finally belched smoke and a growl.

"Looks like bigger waves out around the point," commented Stephan. "How long is the run back to the cannery?"

"Maybe an hour." Mark opened up the throttle.

The eight horsepower Elgin rumbled up to full throttle, pushing the green water out of the way, wallowing up and over each wave.

To the north, the overcast was lowering. The little sunshine making its way through thickening clouds ignited a rainbow where a shower dropped from the gloom. The boat tossed more heavily as it turned southeast rounding Cape Cheerful.

The southeast wind, which had been partially blocked by the mountains, met the boat head on. The cape was ten miles from the cannery dock. The two-foot waves they had been plowing were replaced by combers twice the size. Wind lifted spray from the whitecaps, adding to the surge thrown up each time the bow plunged. At first, their wool coats shed the moisture. In the distance, the cannery bay began to disappear in a rainsquall.

Chad picked up the small bucket at his feet and bailed furiously. Three more replaced each gallon of water over the side. He looked over at his brother, water streaming from his chin, his coat now soaked a dark grey.

"You have to get in closer where the wind is blocked a little," shouted Chad over the whine of the wind and the growl of the laboring outboard.

"We can't get too close," answered Mark. "On the way out, I watched. There are huge rocks running way out. We only need about three more miles! Then we will be into the outer bay."

Chad wiped the worried look off his face and replaced it with a painted on smile. "Woody, Stephan, pull off a boot and help me bail."

Elgin's throttle wide open, the boat labored up the face of an oncoming wave. A foot of water in the boat bottom flowed aft, covering Mark above his knees. Cresting the whitecap, the boat pitched down. Fifty gallons of water reversed course, its weight driving the bow into the next wave and then under it. Somehow, Mark managed to keep the motor running.

"Run'er up on the beach," called Chad. Between him and Mark, the younger boys sat, clinging to the railing around the inside of the hull, eyes the size of golf balls. Bitterly cold seawater covered their laps.

The boat wallowed toward the rocky beach only a hundred yards away. Safety seemed closer every time a wave lifted the boat. They were near enough to throw a rock onto the beach when the stern dropped onto a boulder just below the surface. The jar launched the boys from their seats, Woody smacking his head. The propeller smashed, its shaft ripped from its bearings, its brass blades folded in half. A shriek of grinding metal overwhelmed the wind, but for only a moment. Elgin was dead.

Chad pulled the two long oars from the brackets along the side of the boat and somehow managed to get them into the horseshoe shaped oarlocks. Standing in the center of the boat, he pulled with all the strength a ten-year-old boy could muster. They were only thirty feet from the beach when the boat grounded on another rock. As the huge swell ran on, the boat rolled over on its starboard side and capsized.

Chad fought his way upright, finding the bitter Alaskan water only waist deep. Just to his left, Mark and Stephan struggled toward shore, each successive wave knocking them down. "Woodrow!" he shouted. "Woody, where are you?"

Thirty yards beyond his friends, Chad watched his brother's head bob to the surface, then disappear again. Chad struggled up onto the rocky shore and began to run. His knee high boots shot water from the tops with each stride. A moment later, he splashed back into the waves and grabbed Woody's coat by the collar, dragging the boy up the beach.

Summer training at Boy Scout camp took over. He pulled his brother above the waves and rolled him onto his stomach, head downhill. He began to push on Woody's back with steady heavy strokes and was rewarded by a gush of water from his brother's mouth followed by a gagging cough and the heaving of his chest.

Chad looked up to find Mark standing over him. "Is he okay?"

"I think so. He wasn't breathing, but now he is," mumbled Chad through chattering teeth. "How are you and Stephan?"

"I think Stephan has a broken arm. I'm just freezing."

Chad leaned down. "Woodrow, are you breathing okay?"

"I think so." He began coughing; small sprays of water shot from his mouth, mixing with drops of blood from his forehead.

Chad stood, leaving his brother lying face down. "We have to get the boat up on shore. There's a tarp under the bow and a spare can of outboard oil. If we can get a fire going and some cover, we will be all right."

The older boys managed to tip the waterlogged craft wedged between two rocks on the falling tide. They pulled the canvas tarp and everything else useful from the boat then found a place partially sheltered from the wind. Mark and Chad struggled to tie the tarp over an oar jammed into the rocks. Wind tried to rip the tarp from small cold hands, and rain pounded the beach. Offshore, the clouds settled toward the ocean.

Mark scrounged for driftwood among the rocks above the high tideline, as Chad helped the younger boys from the beach. The twist in Stephan's arm made clear that it was broken. Other than the small gash in his forehead, Woody showed no signs of injury, but the shaking of his body was now uncontrollable and his walk, a stumbling shuffle.

As Mark dropped an armful of driftwood next to the shelter, Chad used trembling fingers to open his pocketknife and punch a hole into the oilcan. He poured a small amount of oil over the wood and then began to fumble in the pocket of his wool coat. He used a finger to scoop out the sand and pebbles covering what he looked for.

"Thank God," he muttered, as he unscrewed the cap of a small film canister and somehow managed to extract one match with hands shaking so hard that he had to cradle the tiny aluminum can against his chest. "Made these at scout camp last year." He scraped the wax from the head of a waterproofed wooden match. He struck the match, dropping it onto the oil-soaked wood. A fire began to smolder and then flame as the oil heated.

The four boys sat next to the roaring fire, steam rising from the front of their jackets. "You remember that old native at scout camp?" asked Chad. "What'd he say? Something about white men build big fires, sit way back, and get warm on one side." Getting words out was difficult, but at least he could speak. Woody leaned against a rock while Stephan sat next to him, the twisted arm hanging slack in his lap. Neither made a sound, the tears running down Stephan's face speaking for them.

"I am so sorry that I talked your father into letting us use the boat," said Chad to three downturned heads. "I wanted the boys to try out their new fly rods. I am so sorry."

"It isn't your fault," replied Mark. "You were right. The weather changed. We should have left earlier."

"The weather was good. The barometer hadn't changed much in two days," said Chad. He took a deep breath. He began tugging on his fingers until his knuckles cracked. "My dad used to say that if you don't like the weather in the Aleutians, wait a couple of hours."

"Just drop it," snarled Mark. After a long pause he added, "there isn't much firewood in this little cove. We will have to find more." He stripped off his wool coat and began wringing out as much water as possible.

"Maybe we should just head toward the bay. If we can get across the bay from the cannery, someone will see us. Your dad must be worried," continued Chad. They'll be looking for us pretty soon." He followed Mark's lead, twisting his heavy wool coat in his trembling hands. "Before we go, I need to warm up." He scooted closer to the fire.

Chad's head jerked up. The other three boys were asleep around the dying fire. He shook Mark awake. The others slept, even though their bodies vibrated and their lips were blue. "Mark, we need more wood."

The older boys stumbled from the crude shelter heading southeast, directly into the shrieking wind. In seconds, a shaking Chad returned. Rain ran behind his ears and down his neck. Tiny rivulets soaked his shirt. He helped Mark pull what little driftwood they found out onto the beach where they could pick it up on their way back. Mark and Chad walked a half-hour before they found themselves faced with a steep cliff that reached as far above them as they could see, dropping into deep water at its base.

"We aren't going to get to help this way," mumbled Mark. "We're going to have to go over the mountain."

"Let's take the wood back to the camp. We can leave most of it for the kids. I think we should carry enough to build a fire when we get somewhere someone can see from the cannery."

The boys gathered the wood they found, arriving at the camp just in time to stir the ashes and rekindle a blaze.

"We should build a smaller fire so that it doesn't burn up the wood so fast," suggested Chad. He reached over and shook his little brother but quit after he couldn't wake him after a minute of violent shaking. "We need to get help."

Mark sat with his arm around Stephan, who managed to respond to Mark's questions. "I am so cold, Mark, but I can go back toward the lake and get more wood. How long will you two be gone?"

"Three, maybe four hours."

The rain and air were now one, and the clouds rested only a few hundred feet above on the hillside. Chad watched the visibility drop to the length of a football field.

"Listen," mumbled Stephan, "I think I hear an engine."

Try as he would, Chad couldn't hear anything over the shrieking wind, pounding rain, and thunder of the waves.

"I really did hear something," insisted Stephan.

Chad poured half of the remaining oil from the can into the fire, the flames erupting as the oil vaporized. He tossed the oilcan and cupped his hands under the torrent of water running from the edge of the tarp, splashing the water onto his face. He turned back to his friends struggling to laugh through chattering teeth.

"You burned off your eyebrows and singed your hair," said Mark. "Does it hurt?"

"Nope," lied Chad, wiping the water from his undamaged eyes

and staring out to sea, praying for help. The boys lost track of time as they waited.

"If we don't go now, we'll be too cold to walk," said Mark. "Stephan, something is really wrong with Woody. You need to keep an eye on him. Don't let this fire die. We're going to find help."

Chad and Mark each picked up a couple of sticks of driftwood, and Chad found that while some of the oil from the cardboard can had leaked when he threw it, there was enough to start more fires.

The two started up the hillside behind camp. Remembering the huge cliff that had blocked their route along the beach, Chad led until they found themselves surrounded by clouds. He guessed at the direction to town and continued climbing. Chad led up the steep terrain torn by gullies and jumbled rocks. Between the gullies, only grass and tiny plants covered the ground on an island where wind, winter snow and ice offered no tree or large bush a chance to survive.

"Are we even heading in the right direction?" asked Mark. "With this fog and the rain, I really don't know."

"I think we are," responded his friend. The rain is right in our face still, but I can't see fifty feet in front of us. At least walking keeps me warm, but I sure am tired."

An hour later, the boys climbed out of yet another gulley filled with rushing water and found themselves in a small hollow. To their right, a crude shelter of stacked rocks with an arched roof covered by dirt and grass was built into the hillside. Mark worked his way over to the shelter. He stooped to enter, finding himself in a small dimly lit room. A wall of stacked rocks with one window and the door had been added to the front of a natural rock overhang. The shelter was at most eight feet wide and stretched back into the hillside more than ten feet. Inside it was dry and out of the wind.

"The Aleut people used to build shelters like this above the ocean where they could watch for seals and whales," offered Mark. "Some of the men who work for my father told me about the old times, before the Russians." He picked up a rock from the floor, running his hands over the surface in the dim light. "This is an old oil lamp. The Aleuts poured oil from fat into the depression in the center then lit a wick. A lamp could keep a small underground house warm."

"If I pour half of our oil in the hole and make a wick out of a stick and some cloth, maybe we can warm up for a little while," suggested Chad. "It is so foggy that we can't see well enough to go down the mountain."

"All right, but only for an hour. We need to find help."

The old native lamp warmed the small shelter in minutes, fumes from the smoke burning the boy's eyes so they closed them, the warmth welcome. Chad didn't know how long they slept, but when he awoke, the skies had cleared. The wind still left white streaks on the water, but the huge whitecaps were gone. Chad crawled from the low entrance, working around the hill toward the cannery. He kicked rocks out of his way until both feet hurt, furious at himself for falling asleep.

Mark found him standing on a huge rock. Below to their right was the bay of Dutch Harbor and at the end of the bay, the white painted cannery stood out like a beacon. Below them, four boats, most under sail were spread out along the shoreline.

Mark began to shout and wave his arms. "They are looking for us."

The boys gathered their small cache of firewood and started downhill. Around them the hillside was a sea of dark green grass, rippling with each gust. "Perfect background," said Chad. "Those men can't miss our fire."

From their vantage point, the boys could survey the hill below them and the harbor to the west. They descended to a protruding point above the beach. Mark broke up their small supply of wood. Chad used his pocketknife to cut open the cardboard oilcan, spilling what little oil remained over the wood. He worked the wax off of one of his matches, and a minute later had a fire going that stood out like a lighthouse.

Chad pointed. A powerboat turned toward the fire. They met the skiff that the boat had been towing as it reached the beach.

Michi Ishihara leaped into the surf, the water waist deep. His open raincoat billowed in the wind. At five feet-eight-inches, Michi looked like a giant as he ran ashore and lifted his eldest son into the air before pulling him tight to his chest. He reached over and tussled Chad's hair with his free hand, a huge smile on his face. "Where is your brother, where's Woody?"

"They are under a tarp with a fire a few miles from here," responded Mark. "I can show you."

"We have been up and down this beach since the storm let up. We haven't seen anything like that, so I guess you will have to be our guide."

The two boys sat in the skiff while Michi rowed the small boat toward shore, still not exactly sure where the camp was. The boat grounded; Chad and Mark ran along the narrow beach above the high tide. Back in the tiny cove where they had left Stephan and Woody, the overturned skiff was still wedged into the rocks, just a bit of bottom showing above the water. Where the camp had been, there was nothing except water where the highest tide of the year lapped at the rocks. Even the tarp was gone.

"We'll find them," said Mark.

He and Chad headed up the hillside they had climbed the night before, stopping to search in every place that might offer shelter from the storm. Only a hundred yards from where they had left their brothers, they found them bundled in the tarp. They unrolled the oiled canvas just as Michi caught up with them. He felt for pulses on each boy, finding none. His head dropped to his heaving chest.

"What am I going to tell Kiko?"

He pulled Chad close. "How am I going to tell your parents?"

Chad watched as men from the cannery loaded the bodies into a second boat. His tears and the fingers that cradled his face blurred the view. Under his breath he muttered, "I am so sorry," over and over again.

Sitting next to him, Mark stared out to sea, unwilling to watch. "I should have listened to you."

"No, this is my fault. I wanted to show your dad how much I had learned about the weather and boating."

"I was running the boat," screeched Mark, pushing Chad.

From nowhere, Chad's fist lashed out, spilling Mark onto the rocky beach. Mark rushed at Chad's legs, toppling him. He dove on top of his friend, swinging wildly.

Michi lifted Mark by the back of his coat, super-human strength born of anger and guilt filling his body. His eyes darted at Chad and then at his son, hanging in his right hand. He extended his left arm toward Chad. "Stop it, both of you. I let you go. I held off searching." He lowered Mark to his feet.

Chad took Michi's hand and struggled to his feet. "I'm so sorry Mr. Ishihara."

Mark looked at his feet. "I'm sorry too."

"Chad, I will call your parents. We planned on staying another month, but your parents company has a ship due here in a couple of days. We'll take Woody and Stephan home." He started toward the boats, then stopped. "Chad, your dad and Lisa still have you. Kiko and I… still have Mark. You two have each other."

❦

January 12, 1940

Dear Lisa,

Hello, my oldest American friend. I wanted to pass on my thoughts on spending Christmas with your son. But, first, how was your trip to Hawaii with Chad Senior? I find it exciting that Gritt Rus Am Shipping has initiated a combination freight and passenger route between your family's offices in Seattle and Honolulu. I didn't know that your husband was talking to mine about possibly building a tourist hotel in the Islands. With both boys wrapping up college, we two would be obligated to go to Hawaii and help with the design and decorating, if the project moves forward. Duty, Duty, Duty. For me it would probably be a lot more fun than fish.

Including Chad Jr. in our family's holiday in New York was a pleasure. With only ten days off from his studies at West Point, he couldn't travel back to Alaska. He has become such a fine young gentleman, you two must be very proud. He mentioned that he was going to be academically qualified to graduate in three years. With everything going on in the world today, his early commission as a junior officer would make me nervous.

He seems old beyond his years. Since the accident he and Mark have switched roles. Chad is quiet and shy while Mark is just the opposite. With the double major Mark will still graduate from USC at twenty, unless his class antics get him suspended. Chad told me that he probably would have stayed at school for the holidays if we hadn't called. I got the impression that he was well respected at the academy, but didn't have a lot of friends, at least the kind that invite a classmate home for the holidays.

Mark found friends in the city that we didn't know about. On New Year's Eve, Michi had to go down to the police station to get both boys. It wasn't Chad's fault. In fact, he tried to keep his "brother" out of trouble. Mark somehow finagled the boys way into a nightclub along with a couple of buddies. Mark started buying doubles for some Navy guy at the next table. When the guy slumped, he asked the man's date to dance. Everyone at their table thought it was hilarious. It probably was, to four kids, until the Navy guy woke up and went looking for his girl. The guy popped Mark and there would have been a real fight if Chad hadn't gotten between them. Anyway, the club called the cops. They didn't want to create any record that might hurt your son at the academy, so they let Chad call Michi.

Sometimes, I swear, Mark is someone else's son. But the

boys had fun. To appease his dad, Mark volunteered Chad and himself to serve Christmas breakfast at a soup kitchen.

 Michi and I will only get a couple of months in Alaska early next spring. He is committed to go to Japan to visit his parents. Michi's father has been under pressure since he publicly criticized the new government. His mother recently fell and broke her hip.

 If you and Chad Sr. are going to be in California this spring, please come visit.

All My Love, Kiko

CHAPTER 1

YOKOHAMA, JAPAN, JULY 1940

Michi felt fortunate to secure a second-class stateroom on the German ship *Friedrich*. The troubles between the United States and Empire of Japan meant that their planned return voyage on American President Lines was canceled. He bit his lip, momentarily glancing at Kiko next to him. She hadn't turned a page in her book in ten minutes.

Nine men dressed in cheap brown suits circulated through the room checking documents. All had identical tan fedoras pulled low on their foreheads. There seemed to be no pattern to their inquiries, just random stops among the three hundred waiting passengers. Michi tried to catch snippets of the official conversations, but the echo of voices in the windowed room and the click of heels on the marble floor made it impossible.

Michi whispered, "I love you," trying to calm Kiko. The gangway outside the double glass doors rose from the dock to the ship, but no one was boarding. The hands on the wall-clock moved past three, more than two hours after the scheduled departure time. He bit his lip even harder, drawing blood.

"Your parents are healthy," offered Kiko. "I am happy that we made this trip. It is important that we not give up our roots." Kiko checked that the pins holding her hat on her still jet-black hair were in place. She wore little makeup over her California tan, her figure reflecting a mile of swimming every other day. She continued to stare at page 118.

Michi tried to find a smile below his graying mustache. He straightened his tie, buttoning the coat of his double-breasted suit. "The company will be better after my father and I worked out our differences about entering the American market. He doesn't realize how much competition there is in the states for canned salmon." Michi watched the men in suits. He lifted Kiko's tiny hand in his; she pulled away. He dried his hand on his pants and tried again. "My mother looks better than I expected after her fall."

"You sound like a Japanese man now. So formal, so controlled."

"I'm just a little worried, and angry."

"I just wish Mark was traveling with us," said Kiko.

"Our son will be with us soon," offered her husband. "It might be for the best, that Mark is traveling on a different ship. Besides, he wanted to visit my parents' summer home in Karafuto and teach his grandfather how to fly fish."

"It will be good for him to meet his grandmother. She was disappointed that he she didn't get to meet him in Sapporo." Kiko dropped her book into a basket at her feet. She dabbed at her chin and brow with her hanky.

"You don't worry that the interview you gave to *The Times* will put him in danger?" asked Kiko.

"No, dear. Our episode with the Army police was just paranoia," he lied. "My interview stated the obvious; Japan and the United States make better friends than enemies. Both countries' economies are driven by foreign commerce. Japan can feed itself, but food like the salmon we ship here helps keep prices low. That was the point I was making."

Kiko swallowed hard as one of the men in brown suits stopped in front of them, looking down at Michi before moving across the aisle to converse with another man. He handed the man a note.

"You said more than that, husband of mine. You basically said that Japan's economy is no match for America's and that Japan had better remember that."

"I can't believe that anyone here could take issue with the truth," whispered Michi. "Japanese culture has traditions about foreigners of Japanese descent. We are Nisei, not Kibei Shimin. We are American nationals of Japanese descent, not returning citizens. Still, as people of Japanese culture, we are to be respected, and Japan expects we will always be part of Japan. Part of that is to help Japan navigate the world."

"Then why did we cut our trip short? Why are we trying so hard to get out of here? she whispered."

"Because dear, from what I see in Japan, those traditions no longer extend to the government. Regular citizens love to hear about our life in America." He closed his eyes, visualizing four separate Tokko or military "interviews." He hadn't told Kiko of the others. "I don't want to have to explain again why I am American. It's good that Mark will be on his way home by the end of July."

The loudspeaker above them crackled to life, announcing that they were ready to board first class passengers, the announcement echoing through the hall in Japanese, German and finally in English. A group rose, almost like shorebirds from a sandy beach and moved toward the doors. The gate agents began passing out umbrellas to those who asked for one. Michi smiled for the first time that day.

The short man sitting across from them rose, crossing the aisle. His brown suit was still new, his tie twisted. The man wiped his glasses before speaking, then extended his hand. Mr. and Mrs. Ishihara, I am Peter Yamai and I was planning on traveling with you all the way back to California. But I have been informed that my passage and yours has been rebooked on another ship. In the interim we have been summoned to visit an old friend of yours. I think the ship we are now booked on is the same one that your son, Mark, plans on taking.

Before Kiko could speak, Michi rose and jabbed out his hand toward the stranger who knew so much about them. He smiled at his wife, as he counted the men in suits moving toward the couple. Ten against two was lousy odds and then there was the simple fact that there was nowhere to go. "Kiko, a better answer to your earlier question is that I am just plain pissed."

"I assume that you and your friends here will be taking care of our luggage," spat Michi.

"That has all been arranged," replied Peter in a smug tone.

Michi took Kiko's hand. "This will give us some time to work on the plans for installing the new canning equipment that we shipped to my father. He wanted to put a processing plant in Karafuto to cut the waste of moving iced fish to Hokkaido." Michi pulled the hanky from his suit pocket and dabbed at the corners of his wife's eyes, then at his lip.

"Where to, Peter?"

✣

The New Grand Hotel bellboys met the small parade of blue Plymouth cars at the street. Michi waited for Peter to open the door for them, then headed to registration. Peter rushed to catch up. Two men from the following vehicle made their way to the elevator. Two more found chairs in the lobby and were fumbling with newspapers.

"I have reserved a room for Mr. and Mrs. Ishihara here," started Peter. "I believe that it is a corner room at the end of the third-floor hallway." He repeated his request in Japanese. The man behind the desk dropped a key in the hand of the bellboy before he finished. "Introduce yourselves to the two men waiting for you at the elevator. They will be in the room next to you. Your host has directed them to take care of anything you need. Within reason." He laughed, trying to calm his own nerves.

"Give me a few minutes, won't you dear?" said Michi to his wife. He took three deep breaths. "At least we have a corner room. I will be up in a few minutes."

Michi started across the lobby toward the bar. Peter, looking a bit confused, followed. The two men found a seat in the empty bar. "I'm going to have a rum and Coke," said Michi. "Under the circumstances that seems 'within reason.' Can my old friend buy you anything?"

"I'm on duty," mumbled Peter.

"I thought you might be military," responded Ishihara. He called an order to the bartender who had made no move to come to the table. "I do not drink alone, so you will have to tell my host that a drink was part of the job."

Michi stared out the window at rain dimples in the small puddles on a mostly empty sidewalk. He ran his finger around the inside of his damp collar. Michi could hear the pop of the bartender opening the bottle of Coke, then the rattle of ice in a glass. When the drinks arrived, he waived the server away after providing his room number.

He picked up his glass and stirred the brown fluid with the tiny bamboo stick. Michi leaned forward, raising his glass. "A toast to USC or is it UCLA, Peter?"

Peter leaned back. "Neither, I graduated in engineering from the University of Washington." Peter held up his right hand to show off his class ring.

"A degree probably paid for by the Army. My guess is that you studied aeronautical engineering with a special emphasis on what was going on at Boeing."

"We Kibei Shimin must all do our duty to our ancestral homeland," replied the much younger man. "My parents own a vegetable farm north of Seattle. They sent me back to Japan for high school. The U-Dub sets aside slots for foreign students. I was a two pointer for them, a United States citizen and a graduate of the Japanese school system."

"Well Peter, just what is this all about, and who the hell is my host?"

"You will meet your old friend in a couple of days; he is detained in China. I will let him introduce himself. Japan needs you to remember where you were born. You and your son will simply offer the land of your father, expertise and observations on the U.S. You are quoted in the newspapers as offering Japan your best advice. We intend to take advantage of that offer. I will pick you up at seven for dinner. We will meet with your host's America team."

"You said that you would pick me up. What about my wife?" asked Michi.

"Mr. Ishihara, Japan is not yet like America. You grew up here. Kiko will not be called on, and she will not interfere with your mission."

"After the land of my birth pulled us off from our ship, I am not going to leave her alone this evening," replied Michi.

"I will have my aunt come to the hotel when I pick you up. She will make sure that your wife finds a good meal and conversation."

"Peter, before this goes any further, you need to know that we both consider ourselves Nisei, not Kibei Shimin. We are both Americans now. We have no intention of moving back to Japan."

"Mr. Ishihara, your credentials in the states are why your family can be such an important source of information. Peter finished his rum and Coke, careful not to offend his companion. "I must report in now, I will see you later."

CHAPTER 2

MOFFETT FIELD, SUNNYVALE, CALIFORNIA, JULY 1941

Second Lieutenant Chad Gritt rolled the North American Aviation trainer into a steep left turn from the downwind leg of his landing pattern. At seven hundred feet and descending, he fed ten degrees more flaps onto the wings and reduced the power of the huge rotary engine. The propelled raindrops on the canopy made the visibility to the front of the aircraft a fraction of that to his left, where the prop sent the water past the cockpit greenhouse, instead of against it.

"Trainer two-niner Charlie, you are cleared for landing," crackled the radio in his headset. Congratulations Lieutenant, on your final solo."

"Two-niner Charlie cleared for landing," responded Gritt with a smile on his face. The runway to his left looked huge. He had learned to fly in Alaska as soon as he was old enough to reach the pedals, learning on a tiny dirt airstrip. Like his father, he had received an appointment to the U.S. Military Academy at West Point, where he was a reserve defensive back on the football team. He had finished his classwork in three years and with half the world at war in Europe, and the rest at war in Asia, he was granted a commission a year early. Already a competent pilot, Chad was able to skip the first three months of the normal nine-month cadet pilot program. *Another turn and a landing, and I will finally find out what I will be flying in the real world,* he thought.

Moffett Field had been sunny all buy one day in the previous months. Today the clouds were only a hundred feet above the canopy. He rolled the big two seat training airplane into another ninety-degree turn to the left, lining up with the runway. He rotated his head from the side window, to the windscreen in front of him. Before he could react, the front of the aircraft exploded in white and red as a flock of seagulls was sucked through the spinning propeller. To either side of him, birds slammed into the wings and the extended flaps.

A massive vibration shook the airplane as the damaged propeller began to tear the engine from the engine mounts. Chad instinctively reached down and pulled the power from the engine. "Mayday, Mayday" he spat into the microphone, "Two-niner Charlie, I hit a flock of birds. The engine is shut down. I have wing damage."

"Two-niner Charlie, can you make the runway?" came an instanta- neous response.

The airplane began to twist. *Fly the damned airplane, don't talk,* he thought. He corrected the twist with heavy rudder, but the airplane was dropping way too fast, the one drawback to a radial engine. They would fly with a piston missing, but without power, the huge flat surface at the front of the plane became an airbrake, the fuselage, a cinder block with wings.

"Two-niner Charlie you are cleared for landing."

Chad tugged on the handle that controlled the flaps, trying to reduce the drag. They moved up a bit and then jammed. He looked up at the airspeed indicator. It was flickering between the yellow and the red lines. He pushed the nose down to gain a bit more speed, avoiding a stall.

"Two-niner Charlie, this will be close," he called, as the end of the runway appeared through his blood and rain-covered windscreen. Chad managed to keep the nose of the plane toward the runway, which was disappearing into a single thin line on the horizon as the plane settled toward the ground. The lights at the end of the runway were still visible in front of him as he felt the main landing gear touch down.

On a normal day, the dirt short of the runway was baked hard, like pavement. On this day, twenty-four hours of rain had softened the ground. He felt the landing gear under the wings dragging. He pulled back on the stick with all of his strength, trying to keep the airplane in a three-point stance.

It worked until the tires, pushing through three inches of mud, hit the edge of the pavement. The plane tipped nose down and in slow motion continued tipping. He watched the landing lights slide by on either side of the cockpit, and then the plane pitched up over the prop and spinner, landing on its back, the tail smashing into the pavement. It slid another thirty feet before coming to a stop, upside down.

Chad reached out and flipped the toggle switches that shut down the electricity in the plane, killing the master and the magnetos. He closed the valve that allowed fuel to flow to the engine. The top of the greenhouse was resting on the ground; there was no way to open the canopy. The smell of aviation fuel invaded the cockpit. He instinctively released his seat belt, falling on his head. In the distance, he could hear the sirens of fire trucks. The increasing fuel fumes burned his eyes.

He rolled onto his side and bundled his legs against his chest before unleashing them against the glass and aluminum around him. The kick launched two sections of glass, and the aluminum frame that held them out onto the pavement. He rolled over to squeeze his body thorugh the opening, but could only get his neck and shoulders into it. *Damn it, Chad you are smarter than this.* He pulled back into the cockpit and released the clasps on his parachute, struggling in the cramped space to discard it. A moment later, he crawled to his feet on the runway and turned to look at the crumpled silver airplane.

Next to him a fire truck slid to a stop. Three men began to spray more water onto the plane while the fourth gently tugged Chad away from the wreck and seated him on the bumper of the truck. "You okay, Lieutenant?"

"Yeah, sure," replied Chad, still stunned. He ran his hand over his close cut hair. He looked away from the plane, trying to focus. Nothing caught his attention on the all-beige airbase, on all-flat ground, on a grey and soggy day. He took a deep breath, still trying to focus.

"What about your left leg?" asked the fireman.

Chad looked down at the torn pant leg of his flight suit, covered in blood. He slipped the small knife from its sheath on his belt and pulled at the fabric before slitting it with the honed blade. Below the fabric his leg was split open like a bratwurst on a grill, a slice more than ten inches long in his thigh. "Might take a few stitches," he mumbled.

Seconds later, he found himself on a stretcher in an ambulance on his way to the base clinic. He grimaced, clamping his blue eyes tight, as a medic leaned down with a hypodermic syringe the size of a baseball bat, pointing it at his leg. *God, I hate needles.*

❀

He watched as the prettiest nurse on the base pulled a clean sheet up around his neck. The tear from dragging his leg over a fragment of aluminum as he crawled from the crash was deep, requiring forty stitches and landing him in the hospital for observation.

She took a moment to study the blue-eyed man. He barely fit into the bed, and even under the sheet his lean body appeared coiled, ready to spring. "You have company," she offered with a smile as she turned to leave the room.

"That girl has a set of legs, just to carry around a really prime package."

"Thank you, Lieutenant," responded the nurse, as she opened the door to his room.

"Oh my God, did I say that out loud?" gasped Chad, his face turning scarlet. "I am so sorry, ma'am."

"I'll chalk it up to the pain killers, Lieutenant, but only this once," the nurse replied with a smile. She took another moment to study the light-haired man and then was out the door.

"Watch yourself hotshot," snapped Major Alvarez, as he slipped into the room behind the nurse.

"I really can't believe I said that aloud," choked Chad. He took a few minutes to calm himself before continuing. "Anyway, I guess you're here to wash me out, Sir."

"The regulations require one hundred hours of advanced training; thirty hours of solo, with one hundred take offs and landings, on the field of training. Until the wrench jockeys picked up two-niner Charlie and moved it to a hangar, it had in fact, completed a full stop landing on the field of training. You will have to wait for your wings pinning ceremony until you get out of here, Lieutenant, but welcome to the club."

"Thank you, Sir," sighed the young officer.

"You earned it. There probably isn't another cadet in the program who could have survived the damage those birds did to your plane. Now, you are only going to be here a couple of days. Is there anything I can get you?"

"Maybe the name and phone number of that nurse, Sir," quipped Chad.

Alvarez walked over to the door and leaned out into the hallway. "Hey sis, can you come here a minute, I want to formally introduce you to someone."

Chad sat frozen. His C.O. was one of his few friends in the training unit, and now he had screwed that up.

Two days later, Chad hobbled down the hospital hallway, stopping at a room where a woman sat stroking the hair of a young boy whose left side was covered in lose bandages. She looked up at the man at the door and smiled.

"Is he going to be all right?" asked Chad.

"Yeah, some scarring from where he pulled a pan of hot oil off the stove," she answered. "The doctors think he there will be no permanent damage except for where the skin is burned."

The boy opened his eyes. "How did you get hurt?" he asked Chad.

"Crashed a damaged plane trying to land."

"Someday I am going to be a pilot."

Chad stepped into the room and slid a chair up to the boy's bed. "What's your name, son?"

The boy's slurred speech telegraphed the power of the painkillers the doctors were administering. "Maxwell, Sir."

"You know Maxwell, most pilots are more afraid of burn injuries than anything else. You have already proven you are tougher than most of us. You will make a fine pilot." Chad turned to the boy's mother.

"If your mom will let me, and I am still here when the doctors release you, maybe I could take you flying."

CHAPTER 3

OTOMARI, KARAFUTO, JAPAN, JULY 1941

The Japanese crushed the Russian military in a short war in 1905, sinking most of the Russian fleet in a single battle and destroying the Russian Army in a series of engagements in southern China and along the Korean peninsula. The surrender of Russian forces protecting the harbor of Port Arthur, a city leased from the Chinese, led to a treaty that stripped Russia of islands it claimed north of Japan and opened the island the Russians called Sakhalin to joint occupation. Over the decades, the island had been divided along a line halfway between its northern and southern shoreline. The Japanese had named their half Karafuto Prefecture.

Mark Ishihara watched the sunrise from the passenger deck of the small ferry. He felt the engines reverse and the jostle as the bow pushed into its nest. A sign on one of the pilings read, WELCOME TO OTOMARI in English. The ramp dropped from the dock above. He liked Otomari. He liked Karafuto. He bounced down the gangway in a pair of Levi's and a USC sweater.

At the head of the small harbor, the neatly painted fish processing plant of his family was just coming alive. He picked up the canvas covered cardboard suitcase at his feet and hoisted a long plywood box onto his shoulder. The heavy forest surrounding the town was a welcome change from the crowded cities on the main islands of Japan.

Screeching seagulls bombarded his ears. He stopped to take it all in. The water at Otomari was blue-green, not the brown of mainland Japan, and it smelled much the same as the waters of Puget Sound or even Alaska. *You don't have to shut out the stench of sewage and chemicals like in Japan's larger ports,* he thought. At the harbor entrance, schools of salmon swirled on the surface, chased by seals.

Sturdy wooden houses flanked the short road to the cannery. Behind them, evergreens and birches covered hills that stretched into a warm blue sky.

"Watashi wa watashi no sofu Haruku o Homon suru Kokodesu," he offered to the first man he found outside the cannery. The man bowed slightly and pointed toward a small office above the building. Mark bounded up the stairs, bursting through the heavy door. The office was empty until a graying man in red striped pajamas emerged from a side room.

"Dokku no otoko ga, watashi wa koko ne watashi no sofu o mitsueru koto go dediru to nobeta," uttered Mark.

"You are Mark then," stammered the man. "I am Roku, manager. The man on dock knows grandfather usually here when he is in Otomari. He is at summerhouse now. I dress and drive you there." Roku walked over to a desk, clamping a headset over his ears. He dialed in a frequency on a radio and began speaking into a microphone. "Grandfather welcomes you to Karafuto."

The old Ford pickup purred as it wound its way north. Before reaching the small city of Toyohara Roku, it turned right, heading toward the coast. The small dirt road twisted through the hills before dropping into a beautiful valley spilling out of the highlands. Through the valley a stream grew into a short river as a dozen creeks merged. In the distance, the river flowed into the Sea of Okhotsk. Roku pulled the pickup to the side of the road and stepped out of the cab. He motioned for Mark to join him at the overlook.

Enemy Patriots

"Maybe all Japan like this once," he said. "Maybe like you Alaska?"

The valley below was filled with grassy meadows and stands of cottonwood trees. The meadows were a canvas of red, yellow and blue flowers. "It is very beautiful, like a painting," replied Mark. "Alaska is more rugged."

Roku pointed at a house near where three streams came together. A covered porch wrapped around the structure. All around the house, flower gardens added even more color. In a huge vegetable garden, a woman stood waving.

"Airi here almost all summer. Haruku comes when he can. Airi talks of you coming for a week. We go," finished Roku. As the pickup began to roll down the winding hill, a black Mitsubishi sedan rolled to a stop at the overlook.

Mark met his grandfather for the first time only a month before, when he traveled with Mark and his parents around Japan. Grandfather stopped in a half dozen villages to show his son and grandson the expanded family fishing business; places Michi had left behind as he resigned his military life in 1920's occupied Vladivostok, Russia. Mark had never met Airi, his grandmother. He wasn't really sure how to approach the woman who gardened in a silk blouse and skirt and walked with an ivory-headed cane.

Airi planted her cane in soft soil next to her left leg and ran the few feet between where she stood and where the pickup rolled to a stop. She wrapped her arms around her grandson, the top of her head barely reaching his chest. She didn't say a word. She dabbed at tears as she stepped back.

"Kangei mago," she finally managed.

"Watashi wa koko ni, saishutekini anata no sobo o mitasu tame ne ureshiku omoimasu," answered Mark.

Airi smiled at her husband.

"Your Japanese is better than my English," offered his grandfather. "It pleases your grandmother. You honor her in her own language. She worried she would not be able to talk to you."

"Anata wa watashi no teien o goran ne naritaldesu ka?" said Airi.

Mark rolled his head up, buying time to translate his grandmother's words.

"She invites you to walk through her gardens," offered Haruku. "She is very proud that after so many years away from her family farm, she still remembers how to grow things."

Mark took his grandmother's hand, as she led him into the maze of colors in front of the house. Roku turned to the older man and whispered, "We were followed. There are two men in a sedan at the overlook."

"Thank you for using English my old friend. I do not want to worry Airi," replied Haruku. "Do you think they are Tokko, policy police?"

"Maybe. One of the men was seen following your grandson off the ferry."

"You must stay for lunch," offered Haruku. "We will make a show of eating at the table in the garden before you head back."

"They will not harass me my old friend. My mother was Korean and Russian and my father, Japanese. I was born on this island. I am a bridge to everyone that the Tokko are worried about. Every week they buy me lunch and I tell them things that they would see themselves if they weren't lazy bastards."

❊

"We will bring home one salmon for your grandmother to fix for dinner," laughed Haruku. "That is, if I can ever get the hook with feathers into the water. I seem to catch only tree limbs and grass. I still do not understand why you catch a beautiful salmon just to turn it loose again."

"In the States, they call this catch and release fishing," replied Mark. "You catch them just for fun and release them so that they can continue upriver to spawn."

"I seem to catch only the trees and the end of my own pole. I struggle to throw the line behind me with this light pole and then bring it forward without wrapping the line around the tip."

A cloud swept over Mark's face.

His grandfather watched as the end of Mark's rod jerked and then jerked again without him noticing. "You are not happy to be here?" asked Haruku.

Mark snapped out of his funk. "I am very happy to be with you and grandmother," he replied. "I was just remembering the last time I tried to teach someone to fly fish."

"Your father told me about the accident, when Stephan died. He was very proud of how you tried to help the younger ones," guessed Haruku. "The ocean has given our family life for generations, but it has also taken more than one Ishihara."

"Chad and I were so cold. We found a small rock shelter and the kind of rock lamp the Ainu used a long time ago. We managed to get a small oil fire started and then we fell asleep. If we had not stopped to rest, maybe Woody and Stephan would have lived."

"If you had continued, in the fog, cold and wet along a steep cliff, Airi and I might have no grandchildren. Both your aunt Arisu and her infant daughter died in childbirth before you were born. Your father and you are the only blood family we have."

"That is why I studied business just as you and father did," replied Mark. "I am proud to be part of the family and the business. Now, one more time, bring the rod back with your elbow until you feel the line reach its full length behind you before you try to whip it forward, Grandfather. You only need a short line. Look at the line of salmon only a few feet in front of you."

The two men sat on the porch overlooking the spot they had been fishing. Airi was marinating the salmon fillets from the only fish her husband managed to land, in sesame oil, rice vinegar and herbs. She placed a tin bucket of cold Sapporo beers between the men.

"Would you still be proud of being part of the family if your grandfather goes to jail?"

"Father never told me about your secret career as a bank robber," laughed Mark. "Maybe I am going about this success thing the hard way."

Haruku began to laugh. "When your father left the Japanese Army, it was because the military was slowly strangling the elected officials who serve the emperor and the nation. He made an enemy of a senior officer who was obsessed with military power. It is much worse today. I fear that Japan is headed for war."

"Grandfather, Japan is already fighting in Manchuria, on the Chinese mainland and against a rebellion in Korea," replied Mark.

"Your American newspapers are keeping you and others well-posted on the aggression of the Japanese Army," apologized Haruku. "Many like me, speak out against the military leading our nation into overseas adventures. Many of us see a war with the United States at the end of this path."

"Grandfather, that would be a disaster for both countries. President Roosevelt is already preparing our country for a possible intervention in the European war with the Nazis. American industry and manpower is so vast that it could fight an Atlantic and a Pacific war at the same time. Japan could never win a war with the United States."

"Some of us know this, and we are trying to change the direction of the country. The problem is, Japan passed a law in 1925 that makes it illegal to oppose the Kokutai. It was not enforced for many years, but the Tokubetsu Koto Keisatsu special police are becoming very aggressive. Many who speak out are now imprisoned or forced into exile."

"I don't understand the term *Kokutai*," replied Mark.

"It means the national body, and it is being interpreted to mean anything the government says or does."

"Are you worried about this special police, Grandfather?"

"I have been interviewed at my office twice by officers of the Tokko. I've never seen them here in Otomari. Today, some men followed you and Roku."

"You and Father are both outspoken on this subject," replied

Mark. "He was detained and interviewed right after we finished our tour with you. There were a couple of other times when he was questioned. We believe that we have been followed since we arrived in Japan." Mark felt the muscles in his neck and back tighten as he visualized his father's scarlet face the last time he was confronted. "Grandfather, you are too old to go to jail. You may survive anything they can throw at you, but Grandmother is very frail."

Haruku pried the cap from another beer and handed it to his grandson. "You are only here for a few days. Let us master that silly fishing method you are so proud of and leave this political conversation for our trip back to the city."

Dinner, served in the garden was raw marinated salmon, rice balls, and pickles. Airi might have been an inquisitor, one with gray hair and an endless smile. She had waited her entire life for a grandchild, and she was bound to make for up lost time.

CHAPTER 4

CHANGSHA, CHINA, JULY 1941

The badly mauled Japanese Army was camped only three miles from the city limits of the provincial capital of Hunan province. Three times they had tried to enter the city, and three times they had been repulsed. The Chinese Nationalist Army somehow managed to kill or wound more than a quarter of the Japanese troops thrown against the city. With few planes, little artillery, and no tanks, the Chinese fought with rifles; when they ran out of ammunition, bayonets and sharpened bamboo poles.

"You are old to be a mere colonel," quipped the Japanese general to his unwelcome guest. "With combat experience in Russia and Korea, one would think you would be a general after thirty years of duty."

Colonel Haru Ito sat stiffly, unwilling to allow the insults of the man in front of him from disrupting his mission. "You were ordered to preserve your Army, Sir," replied Ito. "You threw your troops against positions that had been prepared for more than a year, expecting results different than your predecessor. But again, that is not why I am here. I need to take a look at the weapons your men captured. I need to determine if the Americans are supplying Springfield rifles and Browning machine guns to the Chinese."

"I will send you back to Tokyo with a plane load of American weapons," replied his host. "These insects should be no match for Japanese soldiers."

"I hear this all the time, General. Every time our own Army kills Chinese women and children, or slaughters Chinese prisoners, we seem to enhance the enemy's will to fight," replied Ito. "The Chinese people are inferior, but an enraged dog develops super strength. Anyway, that is between you and your superiors, I thank you for the offer of weapons. Two of each weapon you think is being supplied by the Americans is all that is needed. If you would have them loaded into a truck, I would be very grateful. I am building the case to stop American meddling. My aide and I can manage loading them into the airplane waiting to take me back to Tokyo."

"You are very smug, Colonel. You have no idea what it is like to fight a war where the enemy has an inexhaustible supply of manpower. It isn't just the Chinese Army we are fighting. There are rebels are all around us. They attack our trucks well away from the battles. They assassinate my officers while visiting comfort houses and taverns. They have even attacked ambulances. When they do, my soldiers sometimes act without orders."

"As I said, General, all of that is between you and your superiors." Ito stood to leave the ornate room that served as the general's office. "The truck you sent to bring me from the landing strip is in front of this building. I appreciate your help."

"If you will follow the Lieutenant at the back of the room, you may choose the weapons you seek yourself. He will escort you and your baggage to your plane." The general rose from his silk brocade chair. He turned on his heal and stormed through the door behind his desk, making no effort to shake hands or salute.

Ito stood, holding his salute until the general left the room.

The general was right about American-built weapons. He and the lieutenant watched as two privates loaded ten weapons into the back of the truck. Somewhere the lieutenant found transport more appropriate for a colonel. The Packard with a driver and a second guard followed the truck for the drive to the improvised airfield.

The vehicles were passing through a small village, the tails of a dozen aircraft visible across the fields a mile away when the truck slid to a stop. Four men with pistols descended on the vehicle. The driver's side door burst open, as did the passenger door. The lieutenant and his driver stumbled from a fusillade of bullets shredding the truck's cab, their bodies riddled.

The attackers walked calmly to the fallen men, laughing before they emptied their weapons into the bodies. From the houses on each side of the stranded truck people began to walk toward the truck. A dozen people, assassins and villagers swarmed onto the vehicle.

"Don't just sit there, I need the weapons in that truck!" screamed Ito, as he threw open the back door of the Packard. He pulled his pistol from its holster and began firing, joined by the driver and the guard. The small crowd around the truck scattered, never suspecting that the old Packard carried Japanese reinforcements.

Ito ran toward the truck, emptying his pistol. He paused to slip a fresh clip of bullets into the weapon as the two men behind him raced to catch up. The battle was over in less than a minute. Around the truck a dozen people lay bleeding. Two men crawled toward a ditch at the side of the village. Ito thought about his earlier conversation with the general as he calmly walked up behind the men and shot them each in the head. Among the dead and wounded were four women.

"Get the lieutenant's body and that of the private here into the back of the truck. You climb up into the cab," he ordered his driver. "The corporal and I will be right behind in the Packard."

"But Colonel, there is water coming from the radiator," replied the young private.

"We are only a mile from the airport. You will drive this truck until we get there or the engine seizes," ordered Ito.

The corporal at the wheel, the Packard pulled back onto the road, following the truck that miraculously still ran.

"What about the wounded people in the road?" asked the corporal.

"Drive over them. They should have stayed in their homes," directed Ito. "We can't wait until someone organizes a second attack. Besides, I have a dinner engagement back in Tokyo with an old friend."

"It is not polite to keep old friends waiting," agreed the corporal, as he bumped the Packard over the screaming wounded in the road. It occurred to the corporal that he had not been home in almost three years. He was envious, but the older colonel was an important man.

CHAPTER 5

SUNNYVALE, CALIFORNIA, JULY 1941

The cotton gauze wrapped around the tear in Chad's leg bulged under his Khaki trousers and the stitches itched like hell. Chad popped the cap from a beer he found in a tub of ice. In the corner of the back lawn his host was stacking dried Mesquite branches into a brick grill where flames already leaped three feet from the firebox.

"Glad you could make it," yelled Alvarez over the chatter of two-dozen people and the rattle of guitars, horns and accordion blaring from a record player on the patio. "I will put the burgers on for you gringos when this fire burns down."

"Don't make anything special for me," replied Chad.

"Trust me, Lieutenant, you and the other eleven men who just got their wings should lay off the chicken and pork I cooked earlier. My sister marinated them in a recipe that our mother used on the family ranch. The roasted chilies will stand your hair on end if you didn't grow up on the stuff."

Chad hobbled toward the fire. He stopped twice to listen to his squadron-mates conversations; moving on without joining in. He wiped his brow with his sleeve. He was sweaty and a little light-headed. *Alaska didn't prepare me for California,* he thought.

"Is your sister here, Major?"

"She is rounding up some friends. Even a Spanish girl couldn't single-handedly defend herself against a dozen newly minted pilots. She will be here in a few minutes."

"Your sister took really great care of me. She was the one who figured out the pain in my chest was a cracked rib."

"Anyway, you are out now. Next week you will get your orders for advanced training and then a couple of weeks off," responded Alvarez.

"It's not long enough to go home," replied Chad. "I would use up all of my time on a steamship trying to get back to Anchorage."

"I had forgotten that you are from Alaska," shrugged Alvarez as he began to spread out the coals with a length of steel pipe. "Where to then?"

"I had planned on visiting some old family friends, really my second family. They live parts of each summer in Alaska and have a home over in the San Francisco Bay Area. I got a telegram telling me that they were stuck in Japan. It was a really strange telegram. They're originally from Japan, but speak fluent English, way better than my Japanese, but the wording was almost pidgin English."

A graying man handed Chad a second dripping beer. "Did I hear correctly, Lieutenant, that you speak Japanese? Why don't you introduce us, Manny?"

"Captain Walter Wilson, this is Lieutenant Chad Gritt. He's the one who landed his last solo upside down. Chad, this is Navy Captain Walt Wilson. I really don't know why he has been kicking around Moffett Field the last couple of weeks, but he buys at the officers club, so he is welcome."

"I am a bit of an oddling," replied Wilson. "I was a Navy aviator. Then I spent a bit of personal time flying in China. The Navy figured out that I double majored in Japanese culture and Engineering, and brought me back. I still get some flying in, but mostly by bumming stick time from the Army. Anyway, I am curious about two of your comments Lieutenant, first about when the war is over and then about your Japanese."

"Sir, it's pretty clear to everyone in uniform that by this time next year we will be trying to kick Mr. Hitler in the nuts. As to my Japanese, when you spend a couple of months a year around a family that speaks Japanese at home, to keep their son fluent, it was easy for me to pick up."

"The Navy is thinking a bit different from the Army, Lieutenant. Please call me Walt unless some star is around. The brass in the Navy all believe that it will be Japan and not Germany that forces our hand."

"The Ishihara's have known my mother and father since they first met," Chad said. "Michi and my dad were both intelligence officers for their respective armies during the Russian conflict that no one knows about. Both of them came to the States when their tours ended. Both are outspoken critics of Japanese adventurism."

"Sounds like these two men would agree with Navy brass," continued Walt. "But how did you become close enough to a Japanese family to learn the language?"

"My family runs a transportation and trading company in Alaska. It is part of a larger family shipping company based in Boston. Michi runs a division of his Japanese family's fishing company, canning salmon and shipping the pack to Japan and cod to Europe. They almost have a monopoly on crab fishing in Alaska. It's all shipped back to Japan.

"After Mark Ishihara and I both lost our little brothers in an accident, he and I became brothers. We spent summers fishing in Alaska, and split wintertime in San Francisco and with my family in Alaska and Boston. The Ishiharas are American citizens."

"With the diplomatic posturing between the two nations, a trip to Japan might be dangerous for them," continued Walt.

"My friend Mark, his father Michi, and grandfather Haruku are all USC grads. Haruku was a politician on Hokkaido before he was pushed out for criticizing Japan's military adventures. I think the family in the states decided he needed some support. Besides, Mark had never met his grandparents."

"You are close to these folks, aren't you?"

"I am as close to the Ishiharas as anyone in my own family. I am curious, Walt, just what is this all about?"

"The Navy thinks war with Japan is only a year out. It will be an aviation war. But even more, it will be a war won by studying the enemy and reading his mail. The word is out that the Navy is building up a list of people who they can move quickly into intelligence gathering and interpretation. The problem is, the peacetime budget can't pay to bring any of those people on board. But we have a lot of money for pilots."

"I'm Army, Captain, academy like my father. If everything works out, I hope to be flying P-38s in a few months. I don't want to be responsible for anything more than keeping myself alive."

"I'm not recruiting here, Chad, just having a conversation with an interesting young man who probably flies well enough to wear gold wings instead of lead wings."

Wilson smiled at Alvarez before he could object to the oldest insult between Army and Navy pilots. He waved at the only woman in uniform, across the yard. Surrounded by four young Army pilots, she missed his wave. "I'd better save my aide from that pack of wolves," laughed Walt.

Chad watched the man opening the gate to the front yard for the tall redhead that had attracted so much attention. Only then did he notice Walt's difficulty walking.

"Training Chinese pilots to fight the Japanese requires leading them in air combat," observed Manny Alvarez. "He lost part of his left leg learning that you can't out turn a Japanese Zero with a P-39."

Chad watched Walt go, thinking about the conversation that had just occurred and wondering just what it meant. The query didn't last long as half dozen nurses he recognized from the hospital passed Wilson and his driver, headed for the party. Behind them four more women were just climbing out of a bright red convertible.

The driver sprinted for the gate, blocking the other women while she surveyed those gathered. "Take your choice, ladies," she said. "All are available except the tall, blue-eyed man standing with my brother. He has been my patient for the last three days, and he appears to need a bit of my care right now."

Carmen Alvarez was at most five feet five. Her bright red blouse was tied at the waist, accentuating her curves. Her white tennis shorts matched her white sandals. Everything not covered was lightly tanned and stunning. She caught Chad watching her and smiled and then took ten minutes stopping to talk to every guest before taking Chad's arm. "Buy a girl a cold one?" she asked.

"Yes." Chad picked a cold Miller beer from the bucket next to the grill, popped the cap, and handed it to Carmen. He stood watching the others at the party.

"You are hard to get to know, Lieutenant."

"I'm just a bit of a loner, I guess."

"You asked for my phone number, then you didn't call."

"Like you said, the drugs were talking."

"Well, Lieutenant Chad Gritt, if you won't ask me out, I'll ask you."

"Yes ma'am."

"That's it, just 'yes ma'am?'"

"I'm sorry. I am not very good at this. I grew up in Alaska, and I spent most of my time fishing or hunting or flying. Then I went to the Academy." Chad tugged on his left ear. "I don't have a car, just a motorcycle, and with the leg I can't ride."

"I'll pick you up at seven tomorrow. I'll drive. I have a favorite Japanese restaurant, if that's okay with you, Lieutenant Chad Gritt."

Chad smiled. "You've been doing your homework."

"I didn't always. But you're right, I've overheard you talking to visitors about your Japanese family."

❊

Chad awoke, the clean white sheets and the pale blue walls all too familiar. At the end of the bed, Major Alvarez sat reading. "What am I doing back here?" asked Chad.

Alvarez dog-eared his book and stood. "My sis said that you two were having a nice dinner, but that you looked a little flushed. Then you just quit talking and your head flopped forward. She got a waiter to help her and she rushed you back to the hospital. Blood poisoning of some kind, probably from your wound." He smiled. "Let me find her, and then I better get back." He stopped at the door. "Looks like you're spending your leave right here."

Carmen closed the door, and then sat on the edge of the bed. "Don't talk, let me try to explain myself."

Chad nodded.

"I married the captain of my high school football team the weekend I graduated. My mom and brothers were furious. His dad was a judge. Every one of my friends was jealous. But he was a thug. I divorced him a year later and left New Mexico to get away from him and his big deal family."

"I'm sorry, it never occurred to me that you had been married."

"Please let me finish. I like you. I like who you are and the quiet respect my brother has for you and your fellow pilots. I'm not looking to get married again, just go have some fun with a man who isn't full of himself." She got up to leave. "You're going to be here until they are sure that they have knocked out that bug that damned near killed you. Probably another week, but the doctor says you are going to be just fine. I'm still waiting for you to ask me out. If you don't before they kick you out of here, I understand."

CHAPTER 6

KARAFUTO, JAPAN, AUGUST 1941

The ten days with his grandparents raced by. The cultural differences were perhaps best signified on the day Mark gathered his courage and stopped the pretty girl who helped his grandmother with the gardening, hoping to strike up a conversation with someone closer to his own age. They had talked only a minute when his grandmother raced from the porch swinging her cane at the young woman and screaming. "Anata go shgoto ne modorimasu."

Mark stood stunned, as the girl tried to deflect the cane by covering her head. His grandfather came to the girl's rescue, as Mark stood frozen, not knowing how to respond.

"Your grandmother told the girl to go back to work. The girl is a laborer brought here from Korea, and your grandmother has shown her great favor by allowing her to live in the gardener's house instead of the women's dormitory in town."

"We have migrant labor camps in California," replied Mark. "They are not very nice either."

"The Koreans are lazy workers and do not learn like we Japanese do," replied Haruku. "Still, they are good for this kind of work. The girl should be thankful that her Japanese master takes her away from that place where Japanese soldiers go to find company. She should have asked Airi for permission to talk to you."

The day that he and his grandfather packed the old Ford sedan to drive back to Otomari was difficult. As when they first met, Mark was unsure of how to say goodbye. Again, Airi solved the problem with a hug and a huge smile. They drove up the winding road to the outlook where Mark stopped to take a final picture of the valley. Only feet from where he stood, two men sat frozen in their black sedan, staring out over the ocean.

Near the cannery, Roku waited at the ferry landing. Next to him were six trailers, their tongues propped up on blocks. On each, were four galvanized rectangular tubs filled with cleaned salmon and ice. "The catch in the last week is so large that we cannot move all of it on our own vessel. The salting room cannot handle the overflow. We will send these fish on the ferry and use the trailers to return the canning equipment that your family shipped us from America. The customs authorities finally released the shipment only yesterday."

"We will wait until the season is over to install the cannery," suggested Haruku. "If we finish in time, we may be able to process some late fish." Haruku turned to Mark. "It is too bad that the authorities held the shipment so long. I had hoped that your father could supervise the installation."

"Grandfather," responded Mark, "I know that he was looking forward to working with you. The manuals are in English. Perhaps it is better that you will start after you have shipped most of the season's catch."

"I try to keep my English current," replied Haruku. "Your mother sends me American books. When I read your Hemingway and Robert Service, I close my eyes and imagine the life you and your father live surrounded by wilderness."

"You and Grandmother have a place that Hemingway would love. Your summer home is surrounded by forests and untouched rivers. You never did tell me why you built such a large house."

"Airi always dreamed of your family coming to spend a year or two with her before she dies. Maybe it will be you and someday your wife and family," smiled Haruku. "Anyway, we will somehow install the canning equipment. Roku speaks enough English to translate for the workers while I read."

"It would have been better if Father had been able to help. Still I do not believe that there is anything that you two cannot do," answered Mark.

None of the men paid any attention to the black Mitsubishi sedan that rolled to a stop behind the trailers. The windows rolled down on the hot August afternoon, the occupants had been listening to their conversation. One of the men buttoned his collar and tugged his tie tight as he stepped from the car.

"Perhaps all is not lost," he said. "You must be Mark Ishihara," he continued, insultingly ignoring the presence of the older men. "I am Peter, and until just days ago I was with your father and mother. Their trip back is delayed. I thought I recognized you back at the outlook, from a photo they showed me. Anyway, I was asked to find you and escort you back to their hotel in Yokohama. We will get to know each other on the ferry, and then we will catch a military transport plane to Yokohama."

"What is this all about?" asked Haruku.

"Your son will contact you soon to explain," scowled Peter. "Until then, you can follow up with my friend in the car. He is with the Tokko. He will be stationed right here at the Army base north of Otomari, Kenji o tanomimasu."

Mark stood at the stern of the ferry, as it worked its way from the narrow harbor. He stood there until he could no longer see his grandfather. Then he closed his eyes. The fury in the graying man's face would be with him forever.

He found a seat on the upper deck and opened the canvas bag that his grandmother had pressed into his hand just as he was leaving. Inside were three small jars, one of marinated salmon, one of cabbage and the last of rice. He spread out the contents on a small table and laid out the linen towel and chopsticks she had included and started his dinner.

"Not quite as handy as a burger and fries," offered Peter walking up to the young man.

"I don't really know you," responded Mark. "But I admit that I dislike the circumstances around meeting you a great deal. I will let that be my guide. If you will give me some privacy, I want to enjoy my grandmothers cooking."

Peter turned to leave. "We may never be friends," he called as he walked, "but I'm confident that we will work well together."

Mark finished his meal, resealing the jars and dropping them back into the canvas bag. It was only then that he noticed the embroidery on the bag, a Haiku from Airi. Mark had never studied the ancient Japanese poetry form, but he knew that it was treasured. He struggled with the Japanese words, finally translating them:

The sun finally rises

Its light warms me

I wait patiently

For four decades

Until the long night ends

The syllables didn't work in English and the meter in Japanese, but the meaning did.

Mark closed his eyes and found his grandmother's smile and laughter, and then her frail face was replaced by that of Haruku, the fury lifting the tiny veins on the surface of his skin. Mark smiled a bitter smile. *Grandfather, I will make your anger my own and the patience of Grandmother my map of what to do. I promise.*

Mark picked up the bag and headed for the lounge to find Peter. It was time to find out just what was really happening.

CHAPTER 7

YOKOHAMA, JAPAN, AUGUST 1941

Colonel Haru Ito strode into the small conference room. His two guests sipped coffee instead of the tea they had originally been offered. Four uniformed military policemen stood at attention around the room. Mark counted another six in the hallway.

Michi leaned over to his son. "Christ, I hate that man. He's why I left the Army and moved to the states. Ito's exactly what is wrong with this country."

Peter rose as Ito entered. He snapped a salute. "Sit down you idiot," ordered Ito. "You only salute when you are in uniform. Get out of the habit; it will only tip off someone you are secretly observing. We will conduct our conversation in English, some of what we will discuss is not for unauthorized ears and none of the guards speak English. You don't seem happy to see me Lieutenant Ishihara. What has it been, twenty years?"

Michi stood. He was two inches taller than the Japanese colonel; that and his anger gave him more courage than he should have shown. "I see by your uniform, Haru, that the years have been tough on you. Was it your little adventure on the shores of Alaska that slowed your career?"

For the second time in three days, Ito fought to control his anger over an insult that was intended to infuriate him. "I chose to stay in intelligence, Lieutenant Ishihara. Promotion is slower than in combat ranks, perhaps slowed a bit more by my commanding officer, your old boss. I do not know why I now serve under General Fumi, but I serve him well and he recognizes that."

"Why are we here?" asked Mark.

"You are here because we will need your assistance providing information about what the Americans are doing in the Aleutian Islands. Your father is here to offer his homeland as much information as he can on American communications and transportation along the American west coast," replied Ito.

"I am no spy," said Mark. "I am an American citizen, born and raised."

"Did I mention," laughed Ito, "that your mother and father will be my guests until after the war with America ends? Your cooperation will determine whether they live comfortably at your grandparents' summer home in Karafuto or in some filthy prison more deserving of someone who would run away from Japan."

Michi sat down next to his son. He watched Mark's anger rise as he had seen it only once before; when he had been told that he would have to wait another year before being admitted to USC. "Let us show our pragmatic side, son."

Michi took a deep breath," I heard you use the word war, Haru."

"I prefer that you refer to me as Colonel," said Ito. "You are probably the first Americans to know for sure that there will be war between the Empire of Japan and the United States. It will happen soon, and hopefully it will end soon after it starts. Japan will show the arrogant Americans that they should stay in their corner of the world. Americans have no will to fight. Their culture will not allow them to sacrifice themselves, just to show the Chinese or the Koreans that they disagree with the policies of Japan. Their meddling is already costing Japanese lives and it must stop."

"I am not quite sure how two men who sell fish for a living can help the Empire of Japan beat America quickly," replied Michi.

"If Japan quickly destroys America's ability to fight in the Pacific and then starts to occupy American lands, the United States will quit the fight and leave Japan alone in Asia. You, Michi, will help us identify how to disrupt American communications and transportation. You, Mark, will help Japan occupy lands in the Aleutians that we will happily give back when America and her allies remove themselves from Asia."

"You know that Japan cannot defeat America in a Pacific war," said Michi.

"I read your article, Lieutenant. You were wrong. I am not included in the officer corps planning to destroy America's ability to fight. That task has been given to the Imperial Navy. The commander leading that group, like you two, was educated in the USA." Ito tugged a pack of cigarettes from his pocket. Lighting one, he blew smoke across the table. "General Fumi has been ordered to develop strategies to disrupt communications and transportation along the west coast. Our intelligence group is supporting the Navy's plan for the North Pacific. I am part of the group tasked with seizing part of the Aleutian Islands and maybe all of Alaska. After all, if America hadn't stolen it from the Russians, Japan would own it now, after the treaty that ended the Russo-Japanese war."

"I am not going to be part of any attack on America," said Mark. "You have to be out of your mind."

"He is your son, Lieutenant Ishihara. He has your same poor political senses and like you, he doesn't know when to keep his mouth shut," spat Ito.

"Mark will be reporting through Lieutenant Yami, here. Peter, it is time to make it clear that we are not asking for the cooperation of these men." Ito lifted a battered old briefcase from under the table and opened it.

He turned to two of the guards. "O ni-ri wa wakai otoko o hoji shimasu."

Two burly guards ripped Mark from his chair, pinning him against the wall.

Michi launched himself from his chair, muscles so tight that he could barely speak. "Haru, don't hurt that boy."

Ito waved to the other two guards. "Anata futari wa shikkari to rojin o daisai shite imasu." Michi was pushed down onto the table and held. Turning to Peter he continued, "Fukaro kara hasami o tori, furui man koyubi o ofu ni kiritorimasu."

Peter's face drained. He reached into the bag and extracted a pair of limb clippers. He grabbed Michi's left hand and neatly clipped off his little finger. Pulling his handkerchief from his lapel, he handed it to Michi. "I am so sorry that you were not taking the colonel seriously."

"You can see Lieutenant Ishihara, that I have no intention of hurting your boy," said Ito. "And you, Mark can now see that I am not in the mood to debate you. Any time that Peter tells me that you are not cooperating, I will take off another finger. Maybe the next one from your mother's tiny hand."

The two guards released Mark. "What do you want me to do?" he said.

"You will go back to where your family has a cannery in the Aleutians. You will track aircraft and naval movements and pass your observations on to Japan. Anything you hear about American intentions in the area will be passed on. You and Peter will figure out how you will get your information out to some place that we can set up a radio. That radio station will be manned by Peter and a couple of other men, who will resend your information to a submarine off the coast. They will rebroadcast the information to Japan.

"Peter, you will want to choose a place where you can verify at least some of the information that Mark sends you. If you even think that he may be sending you false information, you will send that observation to me, and I will visit Michi and Kiko. Mark, if Peter quits broadcasting, for any reason, I will visit your parents, and you can imagine just how angry I might be." Ito turned back to Michi, who fumbled with a shoelace trying to bind the stump of his finger. "The other side of this demonstration, Lieutenant Ishihara, is that the only casualty necessary may be one finger on one hand. We expect that the war will be short, and after we sign a treaty with the United States that removes the thorn they represent to the Japanese Army, you and your wife will be on your way home. In the interim, you will have time to help your father install the equipment that my office just released for the company plant in Otomari. Airi will get to visit with her son who ran away from his duties in Japan twenty years ago.

"Peter will work with you to develop a plan for my approval, Mark. You will leave for the States in one week. Do not waste any time."

CHAPTER 8

BURBANK, CALIFORNIA, SEPTEMBER 1941

The huge doors of the production hanger slid open, pushed by six sweating men. Lockheed Plant number six was a hive of activity as the aircraft manufacturer struggled with orders for hundreds of aircraft at a site that only a year before produced a handful of civilian aircraft and a few P-38 prototypes for testing.

The gleaming twin boom pursuit aircraft with the circled star of the U.S. Army Air Force emerged into the bright sunshine, pulled and pushed by the same six workmen. The oddly shaped plane with engines mounted in the booms to the left and right of the main cockpit looked like speed. A fueling truck pulled into position next to the new plane and began pumping hundreds of pounds of aviation gas into the wing tanks.

A workman in coveralls climbed into the cockpit setting switches and opening the valves that allowed fuel to flow to the huge Allison engines. "Clear!" he shouted, as he engaged the starter on the starboard engine, allowing the engine to settle into a rhythmic pulse, checking the gauges. Two minutes later, the other engine belched smoke and pounded into life. Chad thought he recognized Captain Walt Wilson near the airplane, but he couldn't be sure.

"Isn't she beautiful?" asked Chad to the driver of the red convertible parked across the airport from the idling plane. "I can't imagine anything faster or more lethal."

"You have never seen a Spanish girl when she is mad," replied Carmen Alvarez. "When you suggested that we take a few days to explore the area around your new base, I didn't know that we were just here to check out your new girl."

"Okay, I get it," said Chad. "I just wanted to see a P-38 in person. I am all yours for an afternoon at the beach and all night somewhere a bit more private."

"I liked the little beach house we found last night," continued Carmen. "I didn't think that cute gray-haired lady was going to rent it to you when she saw me sitting in the car."

"She liked the uniform." Chad slid into the passenger's seat. "There are more than two hundred miles of beaches along this coast. We will find another grandmother who thinks a man in uniform should be treated well before facing death to protect her bridge club."

An overweight blonde greeted Carmen at the door of the house with the VACANT sign. She shook her head no when she saw the girl in the bright red blouse and calf length white pants emerge from the car. "I don't rent to Mexicans dear," she called. Chad finished shaking the sand from his sock and retied his shoe. The back of Carmen's neck was turning red as he swung the car door shut and stretched his lanky frame before starting up the driveway.

"Oh, I am so sorry," offered the middle-aged woman. "I didn't realize that you were entertaining one of our brave young soldiers. Do you want the cottage for the whole night? I can arrange an hourly rate if you prefer," she offered in her French accent.

The woman was surprised when Chad slipped his wallet from his khaki pants and handed her a fifty for three days of rent.

"Got yourself a rich one, honey," she said. "There was a time when I was honey to the bees too."

The restaurant was only a five-minute walk from the cottage. The terrace table looked out over the Pacific, the setting sun painting the waves red, then yellow and then purple.

"That woman was downright insulting," scowled Carmen. "It's not okay to be Latina, but just fine to be a whore." She picked up her margarita and licked a bit of salt from the rim of the glass before tipping a quarter of the drink into her mouth. "Do you know what day it is?"

"No," replied Chad. "It is obviously my lucky day, but other than that, no."

"It is Cinco de Mayo."

"I speak almost no Spanish," offered Chad, "but I think that means the fifth of May, and I know it's September."

"Okay, it was almost Cinco de Mayo," smiled Carmen. "If that French witch had said just one more word, I would have had to pummel her like the Mexican Army smacked the French at the battle of Puebla."

Chad looked over the rim of the green glass, not quite sure of what to say.

"Just kidding, dear," laughed Carmen. "The Spanish have been in the southwest since long before the Americans crossed the plains to claim Spanish lands. Here in California, we seldom see her kind of prejudice. It pisses me off."

"In Alaska, it is the Native Americans who some insult. In Massachusetts, it is the Irish. People sometimes lash out at those who are different."

"But not you?"

"Nope, not me or anyone in my family. The women in my family over the last five generations include two extraordinary Native Americans, a relative of the Czar of Russia, and a Mexican from one of the landed families. Our bloodline is as far from New England blue blood as it can be. Our company employs the best people we can find, no matter where they come from or their race."

"Are you rich, Lieutenant Chad Gritt?"

"By some standards, the family is well off," answered Chad, now very uncomfortable. "We are all expected to make our own way and support the family."

"I didn't ask," continued Carmen, "because I am looking for a rich man. There is nothing wrong with money. The United States has had leaders who could devote themselves to public service because of their wealth. Look at President Roosevelt."

"My father believes that you can do real good for society by creating strong companies and providing employment. He also believes that we have a duty to help others who struggle. My mother, grandmother and great grandmother have all given everything not needed by their families to others."

"I like you, Lieutenant Chad Gritt, that's all. I am just trying to figure out whether the man I am sleeping with is the kind of man who might still interest me when the spices turn from fiery to rich." She watched Chad intently.

Chad sat carving the huge steak on his plate.

"Eat your dinner." *I guess this is the opposite of arrogant bastard,* she thought. "Then we can take a walk on the beach before a Café Diablo. That's Spanish Coffee with citrus and a lot of alcohol. My ego would not survive seducing you only to have you fall asleep."

"I am really sorry about last night," stuttered Chad. "I hadn't slept in more than twenty-four hours."

"Would you believe me if I told you that you are only the second man I have ever watched shave in the morning? Tomorrow morning, we don't have anywhere to go. I will let you make up for last night then." Carmen devoured the last four shrimp on her plate.

❦

Monday morning came too quickly for the couple. As Chad scraped away his beard with an Army issue safety razor, Carmen packed her suitcase. The couple slipped out onto the patio next to their bungalow where Carmen placed the three remaining bananas and two oranges along with the bread from their picnic the previous day, on the table.

"I hope you enjoyed your stay. Please come back as often as you can," came a voice from behind the couple. The French landlord shuffled toward the table with a pot of coffee and two porcelain cups. She handed her card to Carmen. "My phone number is on the card. When you call for reservation at Loraine's Hideaway, just let me know that you are the woman who I insulted when we first met. I will make sure you get my best cottage." The woman turned and headed back to her house without waiting for a reply.

"The girl who seated us at church yesterday told me that Loraine's husband is a Navy chief on a submarine somewhere in the Pacific," offered Chad.

"Thank you for going to church with me," smiled Carmen.

"I was raised in the church. My parents were Methodist, and my grandparents on my father's side, Catholic. I admit I was a bit uncomfortable at church. I suppose we will both have to go to confession."

Carmen laughed, a laugh that over the last few days always made Chad smile. "Why don't we hold off on confession until we see if our time together is a sin? Besides, the church and I have a couple of things to work out."

Carmen's Buick Roadster pulled up to the main gate of the air base not far from the Lockheed Burbank plant. The two military policemen stood staring as the young Army lieutenant with the silver wings slipped from the passenger door and unloaded two bags from the car's trunk. He placed them next to the driver's door as he leaned in and kissed the young woman at the wheel.

"You really willing to leave a girl like that, just to go fight your country's battles?" came a call from one of three officers who had stopped to watch.

"He knows that I will be here when he comes home," called Carmen. In a moment, her bright red Buick disappeared, a long drive back to the southern Bay Area in front of her.

"Here, let me help you with your bags," offered the Army officer who had made the cat call. "My name's Eugene Jarvis," he offered, extending his hand. "I assume you are headed for the Bachelor Officer Quarters."

Chad slipped a folded piece of paper from his lapel pocket and found the building number on his orders. "I can handle them myself, if you can just point me in the right direction." He showed the number to the man standing next to him.

"Yup, that's the BOQ," confirmed Gene. "I guess we are going to be classmates in the P-38 class. Might as well start by helping you with one of those bags."

"I'm the latest in a long line of Chad Gritts," answered Chad, shaking the other man's hand.

"Hey guys," called Gene to his friends waiting on the sidewalk. "This is the guy who lands BT-9 trainers upside down."

Chad swallowed hard, his palms becoming sweaty. "The plane was coming apart."

"I wasn't criticizing," said Gene. "The rumor is you're a pretty hot stick."

Chad dropped his bags in the tiny room in the Bachelor Officer Quarters and headed toward administration to check in. The private who thumbed through his orders called to a grizzled old sergeant in the corner of the room.

"Is there a problem?" asked Chad.

"No problem Lieutenant," answered the sergeant in a Carolina drawl. "Wait right here, Sir, the squadron commander wants to see you as soon as you check in."

Five minutes later, Chad stood holding his salute as Major Bryce Mills finished a conversation on the phone. He motioned for Chad to take one of the two chairs in front of his old oak desk. Hanging up the phone, he stood and extended his hand. "Welcome aboard Lieutenant Gritt. I need to see a man down on the flight line. Let's go for a walk."

From the Administration Building to the runway was a fifteen-minute walk, minutes that Major Mills filled with an outline of the training Chad could expect. "You have some heavyweight friends, Lieutenant," offered Mills as he stopped next to a Captain staring toward the end of the runway. The man adjusted his binoculars.

"Just curious, Sir, about just whom those heavy weights might be?" asked Chad.

"Well, Manny Alvarez says you could fly a gnat through the gut of a goose and come out with no shit on you. Manny mentioned that you really wanted fighters, not bombers. Any special reasons?"

"I love to fly, and I am willing to go kick some German ass, but I don't want to be responsible for a whole crew of men."

"Even in a fighter squadron, you are responsible for the men around you."

"I get that Sir, but someone else will be giving the orders."

"You also made a friend of a Navy captain. That's whom I was just talking to. He is looking for a pilot for some project that probably will never get funded, but it sounds like a job for someone who wants to be a lone eagle. "

"That would have to be Walt Wilson," replied Chad. "He told me to refer to him as Walt unless there is a star around." Chad nervously tugged at the single silver bar on his collar. "I'm not a loner, Sir, I just don't want people living or dying based on my judgment."

A captain with binoculars pointed at a P-38 high in the sky a few miles south of the runway. As the men watched, its pilot pushed the nose over into a dive. "God dammit, I told that idiot not to try that stunt. That's the man I called about. Thinks he is bullet proof. Thinks the problem with the P-38 losing elevator control in a dive is just poor piloting."

The men watched as the twin-engine fighter raced toward the ground. "Maybe if he pulls all of the power and gets some flaps on her," struggled the captain.

The men watched as the plane wobbled and started to skid as the pilot desperately tried to pull out of the dive. The plane slammed into a vegetable field only a mile from the airstrip. From a short way down the runway, two fire trucks emerged from a building, their sirens and lights clearing their way.

"What about an ambulance?" asked Chad, still stunned.

"If there is anything left to pick up, the firemen will take care of it," replied Major Mills. "He had to be going almost four hundred miles an hour when he hit the ground. You're supposed to be some hot shit stick yourself, right Lieutenant?" snarled Mills. "You just got a good lesson in why we spend all this money on training. That SOB just destroyed a plane that cost Uncle Sam almost $200,000. We all make decisions that mean life and death, Lieutenant. That idiot probably just died delivering a lesson so that you won't have to learn it the hard way."

The Captain wiped the shock off from his face and turned back to Chad. "We will see you tomorrow morning at seven for your first day of ground school. When you hear that the P-38 will kill you if you get into a power dive, you will believe us."

Chad headed back to the BOQ. Neither man had mentioned the dead man's name, or for that matter that a man had just died, only an airplane.

CHAPTER 9

SUBADAI, JAPAN, SEPTEMBER 1941

The drive along the Sagami River was an escape from the hustle of the urban Tokyo-Yokohama area. Where travel anywhere in the Tokyo area was difficult, this trip was almost painless over Highway 51, specifically built so that the Emperor could review the cadets at the military academy.

Michi and Mark sat stiffly in the Imperial Army staff car, both thinking of Kiko and how brave she seemed as she and three escorts departed the hotel early that morning for her forced trip to Otomari.

Kiko was frightened the night before, cradling her husband's hand against her face, begging him to tell her the real truth about how he had lost a finger. Michi stuck to his story that he had slammed it in a car door. "You will be safe with my mother," was all he said.

Before leaving the conference room the previous day, Michi had scribbled a note on a chewing gum wrapper, warning his son about hidden microphones. He had swallowed the wrapper before concentrating on the gum to block out the pain while the men waited for a promised visit to the base infirmary.

Both men found microphones hidden in their rooms. At dinner in the hotel dining room that night, Mark could feel two wires taped to the inside of the table leg. It was only when the men were walking, on the way to a meal or a car, that they found the opportunity to exchange gasps of conversation, always interrupted by nani no hanashi wa arimasen, *no talking.*

They were escorted to a quiet room in the Sobuda, the Imperial Military Academy. Their orders were to be presented in a setting designed to impress them. A uniformed Peter ushered the two men to their seats in a room filled with military memorabilia and flags.

"You will remain standing," ordered Peter.

A moment later, a tall graying gentleman in a general's uniform strode into the room, stopping in front of Michi. "I am pleased that you have prospered," whispered General Yamaguchi Fumi. "I wish we were meeting under other circumstances after two decades of separation." Mark noted a tear in the corner of the general's eye before he turned, returning Peter's salute. Fumi picked up a small brass bell and rang it. The door that he had entered from burst open as four enlisted men carried two map frames and a large chalkboard into the room. Fumi introduced two majors who would brief the men.

"You will note, gentlemen, that Japanese intelligence has identified all of the military installations in Alaska." The briefer pointed to red dots on the map over Kodiak, Anchorage, Fairbanks and at Dutch Harbor in the Aleutians. Further to the west, the map had blue dots on four islands. "The Imperial Navy has developed a two-stage plan to destroy the American fleet in the Pacific. We cannot share that plan with you, but as you can see by the blue dots, Japan is going to occupy islands in the territory of Alaska."

The second briefer uncovered a map of the west coast from British Columbia south to San Diego. "Once the American Pacific fleet is no longer a threat, Japan will begin harassing operations along the rest of the Pacific Coast. We have no intention of occupying territory outside of Alaska. Simply put, we want America to recognize that Japan can inflict serious damage to American infrastructure and make the wise decision to quit meddling in Japan's sphere of influence."

General Fumi sat, his face twisted into a grimace. Finally, he spoke. "Michi, you once served under my command just as these men do, just as Lieutenant Yami and Colonel Ito do. I have been told that you have become an American citizen, and just looking at your son, I could mistake this room for an American university. I will not ask either of you to betray that country, I know that it would do no good. What I want each of you to do is recognize that a protracted war between the United States and Japan will destroy both countries and lead to the death of hundreds of thousands or even millions of people."

Peter squirmed in his chair, recognizing for the first time that his general had a relationship with the man who he had just maimed.

Fumi continued, "Michi, you know where the transportation hubs are and where the undersea communications cables come ashore. Japan would rather destroy these places of steel and copper than cities full of people. You know which firms move fuel and the routes of their tankers to Alaska."

Fumi smiled at Mark. "After the Russian conflict, I myself toured your West Coast. I swam on your wonderful California beaches and I still cannot believe the beauty of the Grand Canyon. I even attended a seminar at UCLA. I never got to Alaska, although that is still one of my dreams."

"You know, Sir, that everyone in Alaska hunts," offered Mark. "Every home has at least one rifle and a shotgun, sometimes more. No enemy will be able to occupy Alaska's towns without first killing everyone who lives there."

"Young Mr. Ishihara, you are certainly your father's son. What you just told me worries me more than you can ever understand. That is why we plan to occupy islands with few or no inhabitants. Only if we are forced to send a stronger message is there any plan to move east. But if the field armies of Japan are forced to occupy – let's say Kodiak or Seward or Anchorage – modern firepower will make your hunting rifles little deterrent. I am sure you read the papers in the States. You have read what is written about Japanese occupation in China and in Korea. Many of my fellow officers will shed no tears if they have to empty an American city."

Michi took a deep breath. "General Fumi, I am sure you have read my comments in the American press; I have been reminded that they have been reprinted in Japan over and over since I arrived to visit my parents. If Japan starts a war, America will finish it."

"Michi, this seems like a conversation two men had twenty years ago. That is why I mentioned earlier that the sole purpose of my command is to end this war quickly. Japanese honor requires my fellow officers to fight to the death, either America's or ours. I cannot stop this war. The government has already begun movements to commence hostilities, not only against the Americans, but also the Dutch and the English in Indo-China. All I can do is to try to keep the war from destroying everything and everyone that both you and I cherish."

The general turned to Peter and smiled. "I am aware of the harsh measures that you were ordered to use with my old friend here. I want you to give me a simple report on that matter so that I can discuss it with Colonel Ito." He turned back to Michi and Mark. "Ito is far more representative of the Japanese officer corps than I myself am. He can write poetry, but it is never joyous. He can arrange flowers so that they are less beautiful. What he cannot do is fail to do his duty as he sees it.

"Lieutenant Yami, you will arrange lunch for our friends and then you will escort them to the gardens. They will want to walk together and discuss what they have learned before they return for the afternoon planning meeting."

"General Fumi, I have orders to accompany these men at all times and to keep them from talking."

"That, Lieutenant Yami, is one of the great joys in being a general, I can override orders when circumstances change. These men need to figure out how to keep America from becoming embroiled in a war that will last years. I think that I understand Americans, but these men are American and also sons of the Rising Sun."

Michi and Mark found a bench under a willow tree, next to a large pool of Koi. Mark dug two bread rolls from his coat pocket, handing one to his father. "I didn't know how long the drive would be, so I made sure I brought something to eat from breakfast."

Michi tore a bit of bread from the roll and flipped it to the waiting carp. "Both Kiko and I would die before we allowed anything to happen to you. We were very proud to take the oath of citizenship in the states. Hell, son, I don't want to die, but I am not going to help Japan kill tens of thousands like in the rape of Nanking."

"You saw their maps; they already know where most of the important installations are. There is nothing you can tell them, Father, that they don't know. As for Alaska, when Chad and I were in Anchorage last summer, we met a couple of engineers with the Army and found out that there are twice as many air strips under construction right now as appeared on that map."

Michi threw the last of his roll into the pool causing a boil as the Koi fought over the bread. "Fumi has always been a thoughtful man, but he is also a very competent intelligence officer. He knows that the only chance he has of getting our cooperation is to appeal to our humanity."

"That, and this Ito bastard's threat against you and mom and your parents," said Mark. "But that's okay, I have a plan that doesn't require me to betray the U.S. I hope that it doesn't put you and Mom at risk. In fact, we may be able to turn this into a way to keep Japan from hurting the U.S. very much."

"I only want to hear any part of the plan that I can help with. I don't know if I could be brave if Ito was threatening to torture your mother, so it is best that I don't have anything to tell him."

Mark split the last piece of bread with the carp. "Father, tell them what you can about American shipping. They already know where the communications hubs are. Hell, AT&T issues press releases every time they install a new cable. Tell them what they already know, and I will do everything I can to make it meaningless."

"I will try to do more Mark," smiled his father.

Mark stood up, contemplating his father's offer. "Did you know that Grandfather's summer place has a radio transmitter? He uses it to keep in touch with the cannery since there is no telephone at the house. Maybe there will be a time when you can use that to pass on things you learn."

"So now we go back to their pony show and let them convince us that helping them makes us patriots," suggested Michi, rising and dusting the breadcrumbs from his pants. "It will be difficult; feel free to let them see just how difficult."

"Nothing today will be as difficult as traveling with that traitor Peter," said Mark. "Perhaps there is a little Haru Ito in all of us, but I swear that someday I will kill that bastard."

"I know how you feel, son. I once had a chance to kill Ito and didn't. It's a long story. You need to get back to Alaska. I do not know their plans, but Lieutenant Yami will be close to you. When you are safe and you have a plan that will keep Ito from missing his reports, kill the bastard and keep his class ring for me. Someday, I will wear it on the finger next to the one he took." Michi popped a pain pill into his mouth.

While Michi sat with one of the intelligence majors, listening to a far-fetched scheme to send telegrams to old friends and business associates looking for more information about West Coast infrastructure, Mark sat in the next room with his stomach churning.

Peter's enthusiasm for his job shocked Mark. Finally, he found an opening to ask a question that had been bothering him since Peter's appearance at the dock in Otomari. "Who are you trying so hard to get back at?"

"I don't know what your experiences were like in college," snarled Peter, "but mine was one of constant humiliation. You ask a girl out, and she turns you down. She never says it's because you're Japanese, it's always that her father doesn't want her dating a farmer. In my senior year, even though I was in the top ten percent of my class, not a single aircraft manufacturer would interview me. I was never big enough for football or tall enough for basketball. I spent my life waiting to be the last one chosen. America is a bigoted country."

A Japanese major sat watching the exchange, a scowl on his face. "Lieutenant, you will have to control your anger," he suggested. "Fifteen years ago, I, too, was too small or too short, but I played a great third base at the University of Pennsylvania. When this conflict starts, the Americans are going to be real tough on Japanese. Do not give them any reason to arrest your parents. It will only compromise your mission."

The major turned to Mark, speaking in the carefully rehearsed tone of an uncle. "We will put a three-man team ashore somewhere on Unalaska where transmissions from the radio at your family fish plant can communicate with them. Before you leave here, I want you to mark a site where you think that team can remain hidden and still string a directional antenna to communicate with a Japanese submarine that will be stationed offshore. A new boat will replace that submarine every two months. The submarines will receive the transmissions and make sure they are alone before relaying the message." The major turned to Peter.

"Peter, would you share your code ideas with Mark?"

Peter walked over to the chalkboard and wrote the words *fighter plane, flying boat, bomber, destroyer, transport ship* and a dozen other words on the board. Next to each he wrote the name of a fish, all in English. He drew a diagram with summer at the top, fall to the right, winter at the bottom, and spring to the left. "You will watch arrivals and departures of these craft and send a nonsense message in English. For example, 'I caught three silver salmon last spring' will mean three bombers headed west." Since the transmissions will be similar to boat to boat chatter, they shouldn't create any concern. The submarine and the relay team will send only a short list of numbers with a letter between them. They will send each message twice. To send 'three bombers headed west' will take about ten seconds."

Peter looked around the room a smug smile on his face. "The relay team will have to be at least a thousand feet above sea level to communicate clearly with the submarine using only the power supplied by a small generator. Mark, as Colonel Ito warned, I will be authenticating as many of your reports as possible. I have a special code that will be added to each transmission to the submarine that assures that the message is authentic. If it stops, Colonel Ito will be notified."

"Seems like a nice plan from someone who has never spent a day clinging to a hillside in a blizzard," said Mark. "Unless you erect a tent with a stove, your team will freeze out there, and if you put up a tent, American bombers will make short work of the site."

"I will lead that team ashore," smiled Peter. "And if you don't help us find a site that will not be attacked, you will never see your parents or grandparents again."

Mark closed his eyes. "There is an ancient rock house only five miles from the cannery. It is tiny, but large enough for two to sleep at a time, with room for a small stove and a table. I spent the worst night of my life there. You will hate it, but there is no other place."

"Your ship leaves the day after tomorrow," advised the major in charge of the briefing. "Your first transmission will be due on New Year's Day. However, we will test the strength of your radio on Monday the first of December. You will send the message *what am I doing here*, every other hour that night. The U-149 will be cruising offshore. When they receive your broadcast they will send back, *waiting for Christmas*. If you have a longer or more important message, you will have to arrange to meet Peter along the coast to pass it on."

Peter wrote a radio frequency on the chalkboard. "Now write down the frequency and code and memorize it," ordered Peter. "You will check in at noon of each day and every time you see something significant."

"And I suppose you will be cranking that generator twenty-four hours a day, just waiting for my message?"

Peter never lost his smile. "The place you decide to hide us must be close enough to hear the sounds of airplanes and ships. When we do, we will be waiting."

"I will need to sleep sometime," replied Mark standing and turning toward the door. *Actually, the plan was reasonably solid, even the code is close to the one used for ship-to-ship fisheries in the Aleutians,* he thought.

"We will meet for breakfast," added Peter. "We will agree on how to communicate more complex messages."

Mark sat alone in the marine terminal waiting for the boarding announcement. He had expected Peter to escort him to the gangway, but there was no sign of him or any of the guards at the New Grand Hotel the morning of his departure.

The cab delivered him to the wharf two hours early. Just before boarding the loudspeaker echoed, calling Mark to the counter. Friends were upgrading his second-class passage to first class.

"You must be someone important," offered a tall young woman with hair to her waist. She was Japanese and something else, and she was beautiful. "My father has ordered me home, like there is some kind of danger here," she quipped. "I will be staying in Vancouver, that's home. Where are you heading?"

"If I tell you the truth, you will add crazy to important."

CHAPTER 10

BURBANK, CALIFORNIA, OCTOBER 1941

After Sunday dinner, all of the pilots in the training squadron pushed several tables together at the officer's club. "We took an unofficial vote," said Gene Jarvis. "Chad, you are unofficially the captain of this team. You're the best pilot here."

"No thanks, guys," replied Chad. "I'm not the leader type."

"Afraid you don't get a vote," said Gene. "Every one of us is struggling with one aspect or another of this training. You're the guy we trust to help get us through P-38 class."

"I'll help but knock off the team captain crap. I just want to fly."

"Then fly. But we've already set up a schedule for you to tutor. Don't worry about losing time with your girlfriend; we'll draw straws to see who helps her out."

"Thanks guys."

The group placed their drink orders, Chad ordering a beer. "I'll help anyone who needs it, but I'm not the team captain."

"Too late," repeated Gene. "Your first official act…" Gene waved at the waitress. "…give our team captain the tab."

The telegram from his parents surprised Chad. Mark had wired them from Vancouver, British Columbia, to let them know that he was taking the train to San Francisco. He hoped to see Chad before he went back to Alaska for the winter to look after the cannery in the Aleutians.

Three days after the receipt of the telegram, the long distance operator finally got an answer at the Ishihara family home. Chad caught a ride in the rear seat of a trainer, and stepped out onto the tarmac of the Sunnyvale base that he had left the previous month. He arranged to borrow Carmen's car, and two hours later found himself in the driveway of his adopted family's home.

"What do you mean your parents are detained in Japan?" laughed Chad. He and Mark sat at a table next to the empty swimming pool, sipping scotch from Michi's private stash.

Chad found the joker he had grown-up with had changed. Every question about the trip to Japan was answered in a cryptic manner. "Are you out of your mind going back to the Aleutians for the winter? Your family cannery there has been mothballed."

After three drinks, Chad finally figured out that his old friend wasn't going to volunteer very much. "I have a new girlfriend," offered Chad. "She is a nurse down in Sunnyvale, at the hospital. She's a Latin girl who stops conversations when she walks into a room. I'm having dinner with her tomorrow and I'd like for you to meet her."

"I'd like to," said Mark, "but I should head north tomorrow. I met a girl on the ship. Her mother is Japanese, and her father is a bigwig banker in Vancouver who used to be in the British Navy. I'm going to see her for a couple of days before I go back to Seattle. I'm booked on one of your family's supply ships to Alaska."

"Okay, my old buddy, that's all I find out? She's Japanese and English, that's it?

Mark started to laugh for the first time. "About an inch taller than me, really long dark hair; makes you wonder what is so attractive about leggy blondes."

"Met her on the ship, huh? It's a little hard to steal a few minutes away from her parents when there is nowhere to go," laughed Chad.

Mark's forehead turned red. "Her parents weren't with her."

"I won't ask any more," replied Gritt. "A gentleman would never answer anyway. Still, a ship and a stateroom; sounds romantic and a lot more convenient than trying to find someone willing to rent a room to a couple who can't prove they are married."

Mark burst from his chair and headed toward the kitchen, returning with a set of keys. "Give me a hundred dollars. You always have a hundred folded under the driver's license in your wallet. It has bailed us out more than once."

Chad reached for his wallet, carefully unfolding the emergency bill he had carried since his parents sent him on his first cross-country trip alone. "You are welcome to the hundred old friend, but I have never seen you broke before."

Mark started to laugh. "I'm not broke." He took the bill from Chad's hand. "I just rented you my parent's house. I will type a simple rental agreement tonight. You keep the lights on and the water flowing, and you won't have to look for a room for you and your girl."

Chad tipped the scotch and soda, emptying the glass. "Mark, just what in the hell is going on?"

"I have a dozen things that I would like to discuss with you," replied Mark. "Any one of them would put you into an impossible position right now. I am not going to lose my best friend by asking him to compromise his honor."

"You still haven't answered my question."

"And I can't, not right now. We have done so much and lost so much together. There will come a time when I will need to confide in someone who will vouch for me. I hope that is you. It is important that I know how to find you when the time comes."

"You are my brother," laughed Chad.

"And for that you also get the keys to my dad's Oldsmobile. You don't have to ride that old Indian two-wheeler you cherish or borrow your girl's car. Now let's go down to Grigio's for some Italian."

Enemy Patriots

The two men piled into the Oldsmobile the next morning and locked the house. It was still seven hours before Mark's train. An hour later they rolled to a stop in front of the hospital. Carmen tossed an overnight bag into the back seat and then crowded into the front between Mark and Chad. "I am famished," she offered. "A bunch of the wrench pullers got into a fight last night with some Navy guys. I missed both of my mealtimes putting stitches in those kids."

"Carmen, Mark," offered Chad, "Mark this is Carmen."

Mark dropped the Olds into gear and headed for the main gate. "Breakfast it is then. You were right about Carmen he added. If she was on the menu she would be listed under desert."

Chad patted Carmen's knee, still covered by the white stockings that went with her uniform. "Please forgive my friend dear, he is on his way to spend the winter in a place that has the world's worst weather. Something happened to him in Japan, he ate something that twisted his brain."

Carmen reached up and kissed Chad's cheek. "I took that as a compliment. If it wasn't, I expect you to defend my honor, friend or no friend."

The rail station was a madhouse. Nothing had prepared the trio for the number of men in uniform. "Everywhere I went in Japan is full of uniforms," stammered Mark. He slid from the seat of the Oldsmobile, opening the trunk, removing a travel trunk and two suitcases. "Thank you two for a morning of sanity. I needed this." He turned to Carmen. "You may have guessed, but Chad is normally the serious one. I am so happy that he found someone who helps him overcome his tendency to grow old right before our eyes."

Mark pressed a small folded note into Carmen's hand. "I am going someplace where it will be very hard to communicate with the world. This is the name, address and phone number of a girl I met on the ship coming back from Japan. I would appreciate you forwarding any message that I might send through Chad or his parents. It would mean a great deal to me."

"I would be happy to help," replied Carmen. "It has been a pleasure meeting you."

Chad picked up the trunk. "I'll be right back. I have the evening free if you don't already have a date."

"Remember the game my father taught us, the one where we could send each other notes without our mothers figuring out what we were really saying?" asked Mark as the men walked.

"Yeah, that crazy code your dad used when we wanted to go to a baseball game instead of piano practice. I hadn't thought about it for years. I still remember it though," laughed Chad.

"I was just thinking it might be helpful with women," chortled Mark. "Make sure you read and decode every second line, wasn't it?"

Chad dropped the trunk at the check-in. He grabbed his old friend in a bear hug. "I may be tied up a lot for the next couple of years, but I will keep you posted on how to wire me or get a letter to me." He looked at Mark, his perpetual striped shirt a bit wrinkled and his glasses crooked. "I learned how to tie a killer new trout fly." Chad turned, heading for the parking lot.

❈

"The pool man should have the pool filled by the time we get back to Ishihara's," offered Chad as he struggled to remember the route back around the bay.

"I don't have a suit with me," replied Carmen, lost in thought.

"They have a very private back yard," offered Chad.

"Maybe, I'll decide after I see the back yard. Your friend is very troubled," added Carmen. She unfolded the note. "Do you know this Victoria Roberts?"

Chad shook his head and smiled. "I've never seen him like this. Mark is always the life of the party. I tried, but he isn't ready to discuss whatever is bugging him. I feel a little helpless."

"That is the price of being your brother's keeper. You just have to be there."

"I guess."

"I was at a dinner while you were gone," started Carmen, "all military. The bets were dead-even on whether American troops would be fighting Japanese or Germans first. Your friend's parents being stuck in Japan sounds a little fishy to me."

"Their family business is all about fish," replied Chad.

Carmen punched him in the shoulder. "You know exactly what I mean."

"How about we don't talk about Mark again tonight."

Chad leaned into the seat of Carmen's convertible and kissed her on the cheek. He handed her duplicate keys to the house. "I will be really tied up for the next two months. I will probably only get up here for a couple of days in October and in November, but I should have some time after the fifth of December. Until then, maybe you and a couple of your friends might want a place to stay that's a little nicer than the base housing."

"When are Mark's folks coming back?" Carmen shifted into reverse but held in the clutch. "I don't want to move and then move again right away."

"He said that it would be at least a year," replied Chad. "I will send you enough money to cover the utilities for six months."

He watched as the red convertible backed into the street and then disappeared around the first bend. He checked the locks on the doors, locking the back door behind him and then backed the Olds out of the garage into the alley behind the house. He had twelve hours to make the drive back to Burbank.

It was well after dark as he was waived through the gate of the base with advice to get the Olds registered so that he had a proper pass. The drive had given him plenty of time to think about the visit with his friend and about Carmen. She was occupying his mind most of the time that it wasn't engaged in flying. He wasn't tired so he drove down to the flight line, climbing onto the fender of the car to watch P-38s practicing night takeoffs and landings.

I am only twenty, he thought. *Carmen is twenty-two. I guess that shouldn't make any difference. I remember my dad telling me how the military made him feel older.* He watched as one of the twin fuselage fighters cleared the fence and rolled to a stop at the far end of the runway. He smiled as the pilot reset the flaps and trim for a takeoff. In his mind, he could see every move going on inside the cockpit. The roar of the twin Allison engines set for takeoff power preceded the lights of the plane coming closer, as it gained speed.

The sleek bird lifted from the pavement using only a third of the runway in the pilot's stop-and-go training maneuver. It soared into the air, reaching a hundred feet when the sound changed. One of the engines was coughing and then it quit. The big plane rolled up onto one wing and then continued all of the way over onto its back before slamming into the grass just off from the runway. In seconds, the plane was enveloped in flames as the fuel from two ruptured tanks ignited.

Chad bailed off from the car hood racing toward the burning aircraft, arriving just as the fire trucks did. The flames were so hot that most of the water they sprayed evaporated before it hit the wreck. It was ten minutes before it finally began to dampen the conflagration. He felt a hand on his arm, pulling him away from the flames.

Major Mills stood at his side. He looked years older than just four days before.

Chad looked back at the wreck, which was now only a pile of twisted aluminum, reduced to nothing in only minutes. "Who was it?"

"Gene Jarvis," responded Mills. "He did everything by the book, I watched him, I studied every control surface. We need a new procedure for the loss of an engine on takeoff." Mills turned back toward the tower. "I have three more up there who need to land."

Chad watched the pain in his commanding officer's face. That night, he dug through his wallet for a card that Navy Captain Walter R. Wilson had given him and made a call.

CHAPTER 11

CHITOSE, JAPAN, NOVEMBER 1941

General Fumi sat glaring at his subordinate. In a room full of high-ranking officers, he was determined to keep the dispute with Ito private. He leaned over to whisper in Haru's ear. "What did you expect from Michi? He is a businessman with a home in the San Francisco area and fish canneries in Washington and Alaska. We allowed him to save face by interviewing him rather than just throwing him in jail like you originally planned."

Ito leaned over, tilting his head to get closer to the taller man's ear. "He gave us almost nothing. We learned about the new port planned on the other side of the mountains from Anchorage. We learned that most of the fuel transported around Alaska is moved by barges. That is all. He has earned nothing. I should have killed him in Alaska."

"Interesting Colonel, he said the same thing about you, yet here you are, both on the same side; at least for now. You will send him to Karafuto like I ordered."

Ito sat frozen. It seemed that every eye in the room was watching him. "What about his desire to communicate with his son over short wave radio?"

"You will agree to allow one transmission each week. You will arrange to have the radio monitored at all times and you will record all of the conversations. You will bring anything of interest and especially anything that indicates that he is a traitor to me. If there is nothing suspicious you will relax the rules."

"I do not understand why you would allow this, Sir?"

"Colonel, sometimes intelligence is not only what you hear and decipher. History has shown that often getting the wrong information into an enemy's ears is more important. If they allow the broadcast at all, do you not believe that the Americans will be listening?"

"I will send the orders to make the arrangements, Sir."

"No, Colonel, you will escort Michi to Otomari in person and arrange for the monitoring. You will make sure he knows that he is being monitored, but you will do nothing to endanger him or his family." Fumi switched to Japanese as a small man in the uniform of a Vice Admiral entered the room. "Sore wa junjodesu."

Ito acknowledged the order as the two men snapped out of their seats, along with everyone else present.

Admiral Hosogaya commanded all of the forces in northern Japan. His role as commander of the fifth fleet was mostly ceremonial, until he received orders to prepare to invade the Aleutian Islands. One at a time, he called upon the men who were planning the invasion.

Fumi took notes, always in English, a language he had immersed himself in since he was put in charge of enemy intelligence. Admiral Hosogaya would direct the operation personally. Admiral Kakuta would command two aircraft carriers that would attack the American base in Dutch Harbor and supply air support for the invasion of the islands of Attu and Kiska. Monzo Akiyama, commander of the Marines, was already assembling the actual invasion force.

Finally, it was Fumi's turn. The room sat in stunned silence, as he discussed the plan to have almost instantaneous intelligence on American ship and plane movements from the base at Dutch

Harbor. As he seated himself, there was a round of polite applause, the first of the day.

As the applause stopped, an aide for the admiral lifted a cover from a large sign in the front of the room. The date of the invasion was to be June 3, 1942.

"Now let me still two rumors," offered Hosogaya in Japanese. "First, our primary goal is to draw American forces past the Island of Midway with this attack. We want to destroy them by trapping them between the fleet that will seize Midway Island and the fleet that is supporting the Aleutian landings. Second, contrary to what you have heard, this is not just a diversionary attack. Japan will keep the two islands we capture in the Aleutians to ensure that the Americans cannot stage there for an attack on Northern Japan."

The admiral strode toward the door to the thunderous applause of those in the room. Fumi stood politely, the creases in his face growing deeper by the minute. He wondered how many men in the room had toured the United States as he had.

CHAPTER 12

SAN FRANCISCO, CALIFORNIA, DECEMBER 1941

Chad parked the Olds in front of the Ishihara home late Saturday night. The drive from Los Angeles had taken all day and he was exhausted, but disappointed when one of the other nurses answered the door, wrapped in a robe. Carmen, he learned, would be off at midnight and home an hour later.

He rummaged through the cupboard in the kitchen where he and Mark had stashed the last bottle of twelve-year-old single malt Scotch and poured himself a drink, heading for the pool area. He propped his feet up on a small stool as he collapsed into one of the oversized wooden chairs. Tilting his head, he practiced naming the constellations overhead.

He must have dozed off because he never heard Carmen's approaching footsteps before she kissed him on the cheek. "Buy a girl a drink, flyboy?"

"I am still trying to learn to appreciate Scotch," he replied. "It is a badge of being one of the boys in the officers' club."

"Personally, I prefer bourbon," quipped Carmen. "That is, when there isn't time to mix a pitcher of margaritas. I have a bottle in my room."

Chad picked up the glass in front of him and splashed the last of his drink into a potted cactus next to his chair. "I never had a drink until I graduated. I was too young to go out with the guys. With a bar on your shoulders, nobody asks for any identification. Anyway, I prefer bourbon myself. If you will tell me where your bottle is stashed, I will be happy to buy you a drink of your own whiskey."

"Sit still. I don't want you stumbling around waking either of the girls who have to be in at six."

She was back in five minutes with a small tray. She filled two small glasses with ice, adding a small amount of bourbon. "Neat or with some water?" she asked.

"Water," answered Chad.

"I am mixing them very light," added Carmen. "I want to go into the city tomorrow for brunch down on fisherman's wharf."

"It's a date my dear," laughed Chad. "I hadn't thought about privacy when I suggested you share the house with some of the girls you work with."

"I recognize that 'half here' look in your eyes, Lieutenant. I doubt that we will be waking up anyone tonight."

Chad smiled up at Carmen who was shaking out the long hair that she had kept folded up under her cap all day. "Maybe in the morning? I promise to be as quiet as a church mouse."

"We will be alone after six," laughed Carmen. "I would like to go to mass before heading into the city."

"I'll just soak you up until seven," quipped Chad dragging his tired body from the chair. "Were still not discussing our relationship in the confessional, are we?"

Carmen whacked him with one of the pillows from her chair as she rose, taking his hand.

The waiter smiled at the couple as he placed their breakfasts in front of them.

Six hours of sleep seemed like forever to the couple. The morning coffee, as they waited for a late breakfast in the waterfront restaurant, had finished the job of launching their two bodies.

"I have two weeks left, and then I am due for a month's leave," offered Chad. "I was thinking that we might drive down to the Sea of Cortez for a few days if you can get the time off. I don't know where I may be stationed. I am interviewing for something special and there are a few things I would like to discuss."

"Mexico sounds really romantic. I am very curious about the topics of these conversations. I have tomorrow off, and I am not about to lose a day with you by going in to work just to ask for leave. I will ask on Tuesday and call you as soon as I know. Even if I can't get the time, you can come up here and stay in the house." Carmen's cheeks blushed, "we'll find something to do."

Chad watched over her shoulder as the waiters began to talk excitedly just outside the kitchen. Finally, one of them pushed a small cabinet into the dining room and plugged in the cord. "May I have your attention please? There is something on the radio you all need to hear." He cranked up the volume.

"Our newsroom has just received the second confirmation of this story, ladies and gentlemen. This wire service story we have been tracking for more than an hour has been reconfirmed by sources that we cannot reveal at this time, but we are very confident that they are giving us the straight scoop. At seven this morning, Hawaiian time, naval aircraft of the Empire of Japan attacked American forces in Pearl Harbor and across the Hawaiian island of Oahu. Our sister station in Honolulu confirmed that the base at Pearl Harbor is a sea of flames with dozens of ships on fire, including at least three battleships. There are also reports of fires and explosions at the Army Air Corps base at Hickam Field. Our contact reported that Japanese planes, strafing the highways, have killed dozens of civilians. The long distance operator cut off our telephone connection, but we will continue to cover this breaking story from whatever sources we can find. Once again, the Empire of Japan has attacked the Hawaiian Islands."

Chad sat staring at the radio. Behind him, Carmen rose and wrapped her arms around his neck, placing her cheek on top of his head. Ascending from his stupor he felt her fingers stroking his cheek. "Son of a bitch," he finally mustered.

"Let's finish breakfast and steal today," she whispered. "I don't know when we will get to see each other again."

"I don't know," he answered.

The radio continued repeating the minimal information at their disposal.

Carmen found her way back to her chair and picked up her fork but could find nothing on her plate that looked appetizing. Chad sipped coffee as he continued to glare at the radio.

"This just handed to me," came a voice from the radio. "All military personnel are ordered to report to their bases immediately. All leaves and passes are cancelled. Once again, all military personnel are ordered to return to their bases. Here is a new one. All coastal defense military personnel and coastal aviation spotters are ordered to report immediately to their duty stations."

Chad stood, taking Carmen by the hand and plucking her from her chair. He started toward the cashier. A graying Italian man in a brown suit met him as he pulled his wallet from his pants. "You military young man?"

"Yes sir," replied Chad.

"He's an Army pilot," added Carmen.

The man handed Carmen a white linen napkin. "You have mascara on your face young lady. Keep it."

Turning back to Chad he continued, "Breakfast is on the house. Give them hell soldier. I wish I was young enough to join you."

CHAPTER 13

UNALASKA DUTCH HARBOR, ALASKA, DECEMBER 1941

What the Ishihara family called the cannery was a very small fish processing plant in the low white buildings across the harbor from where all of the new military activity was taking place.

Mark had arrived in Dutch Harbor before Thanksgiving on the Gritt Russ Am freighter, the *Lisa*, chartered by the fishing company to resupply tons of salt and cases of food consumed the previous season and to haul the final pack of salted cod south. The facility had a small fish canning line that hadn't been used in years. Its primary use was supporting salted cod fisheries in the Bering Sea and resupply of the family's Japanese crab boats.

The cannery's only full time employee met Mark at the dock. "What you doin' here?"

"My folks and I thought you and your wife needed a break. You haven't been off the island for five years. I sent you a letter."

"We got no letter, but this place is lonesome with the kids gone."

Mark handed the mixed Aleut and Russian man an envelope. "Here's a bonus for ten years of hard work."

Inside was two thousand dollars in hundred dollar bills. "That's almost a year's pay, Mark."

"You earned it. If you and your wife are interested, the *Lisa* will offload tomorrow and the next day. Then it's a free ride to Seattle. You can go visit your daughter's family and meet that new grandson. I'll take care of the place until next May."

"I'll help you unload and store the freight, but hell yes, we want to go. I'll get Mama packing while we work. Thanks, Mark."

Mark worked off his nerves moving freight and stacking hundreds of boxes and thousands of pounds of bags. He painted and built new shelving. He knew what was coming. Still, it was a shock when on December first his radio call, "What am I doing here?" was answered by "Waiting for Christmas." He never drank alone, but that night he was up all night, never without a drink in his hand. Even drunk, he couldn't shake off the dread that crippled his body. *Time to grow up.* By December fourth, he was back at work, whatever that meant.

The Ishihara family had remodeled a turn of the century dormitory into a spacious home and office just uphill from the cannery. It was there that Mark hosted a party for officers and officials Saturday.

"Can't y'all get that damned radio of yours tuned in any clearer? I really don't give a damn about the USC game all of you are screaming about, but I would like to hear the score of the Washington State-Texas A&M game when they read scores at the end of the half." Major Lyle Rolland was a round six-foot one. He was in charge of supply at the rapidly growing base across the bay. You would never have guessed that he had been an all-American defensive end in college. His shirt and stomach spilled over his belt, and when he talked, his cheeks flapped like a Labrador retriever.

Mark stood in the kitchen, ladling steaming chunks of deep fried Halibut from hot oil, dumping it into a large basket lined with year old newspaper. "Bitch at Captain Roads for a minute, Lyle, one of the people from his communications group rigged up the antenna. I'll get us some lunch on the table."

The community on Unalaska Island was tiny ever since the Methodist orphanage closed. Although the locals had never met

Mark, a civilian with a storeroom of beer who arrived with four cases of liquor and a gregarious nature, made him a welcome addition. When the officers learned that his radio could pick up commercial radio broadcasts from around the world under the right atmospheric conditions, he became everybody's friend.

Mark's small house was bustling with a dozen men who had gathered that morning to listen to the USC-UCLA football game and any other games that Mark could dial in. It was a rare day off for most of the men who had been working around the clock to turn the small deep-water port in the Aleutians into a military base to counter the growing threat of Japan in the Pacific.

Mark hauled the basket of fish along with another of french fries and a bowl of what he thought constituted coleslaw to the table. "Food's on," he called. "I can't believe how good the reception is today."

"You grow up here?" asked Sam Locket, an Army colonel.

"Here, Kodiak Island, Anchorage and San Francisco. I was in San Francisco before coming back up here," he added truthfully. "The Ivanoffs hadn't been off from the island in five years. I plan on going back to work on my master's next year and thought this would be a good time to give them a break. Before I left Seattle, I stopped at the university bookstore and bought most of the books I will be using. I figure I should be well ahead of most of those in my class when I go back."

"We're both from USC," continued Sam, loading his plate with fish and fries and ignoring the soggy slaw. "Why not back there for the master's?"

"This is a family business. Our primary warehouse is in Seattle. Most of our Alaska pack is cod, headed for England. I figure I can work on my degree and still coordinate with the Canadians in Vancouver to move that pack across Canada and onto ships for England. Try some of the slaw. I used two of the last six cabbages that the Ivanoffs left."

"Cabbage makes me fart," laughed Sam.

The two men continued talking as the others crowded around the table, talking about the game. "Any chance you can dial in Seattle? I mean just for the half-time on your game," asked Major Rolland. "I am sure the Seattle radio stations will be carrying it."

"Excuse me a minute, Colonel," offered Mark. He wandered over to the massive table radio and began to play with the dial. "It's weak, but I got it, I think. You may be a major, Mr. Rolland, but it's my radio. When halftime's over, we switch back."

"Don't worry about it, kid," called Sam, "I outrank him."

"You heard Mr. Ishihara, Lyle, you get fifteen minutes. I'm still not sure how a football playing Aggie made it all the way to major."

"I see you are a pilot," observed Mark, rejoining Lockett at the table before there was no food left. "My best friend is just finishing up transitioning to the P-38 down in Burbank. He's an academy guy."

"What's his name?

"Chad Gritt the fifteenth or so," laughed Mark. He spent at least a third of his life in Alaska. That was one of his family's ships I came in on. He even spent some time out here." Mark's face went dark.

"You all right?" asked Lockett.

"Yeah, I'm fine. Both Chad and I lost a brother out here in an accident about ten years ago. I was just thinking about how much fun the four of us used to have."

An older Navy captain made his way around the table. "Did I hear that you're a friend of a man called Chad Gritt?"

"I am Sir. More like a brother. I saw him just before I moved up here and visited with his folks over in Anchorage on the way. Our families are really close."

"I used to know a Chad Gritt, or rather I knew a Roosevelt Bolt who talked about a Chad Gritt." The man extended his hand. "I'm Rocky Roads. I spent a couple of years in Alaska back in the twenties working on a coal project."

"You must be the new captain in charge of engineering with the Navy construction battalion," replied Lockett extending his hand.

"Call me Lyle. I am trying to learn to fly in this God awful weather and teach a bunch of young kids to do the same."

"I'm one of those called back in," replied Roads. "Spent the last twenty years around the world with the oil industry, building infrastructure so that they can drill for oil or get it out of the oil fields. There are a bunch of us gray hairs back in the Navy, mostly doing what we did as civilians, running construction projects."

Roads stuffed a chunk of fish in his mouth and washed it down with root beer. "How you doing in getting your flyboys trained?"

"As well as can be expected," replied Lockett. "Most of these men trained down where Mark's friend Chad is training. Sunshine and eighty every day doesn't prepare them for rain and sleet and winds over thirty. We have already wrecked three airplanes and we don't have much snow yet. No one seriously hurt, so it's only sheet metal and paperwork so far."

"Maybe you can get your hands on this Gritt guy. I guarantee he is from a good family, and he has great friends," offered Roads smiling at Mark. "His knowledge of Alaska might help."

Lockett looked at his watch and then at Mark. "I'll go hold Rolland's arms behind his back while you go back to the USC game."

The party broke up at midnight. Mark decided to ignore the empty bottles scattered around the house. Just picking up the dishes with their smell of old oil made his stomach turn. He took three aspirin and stumbled toward the bedroom, knowing it would all be there in the morning.

❊

"Go away," called Mark, fighting to shake off the sleep and headache as someone continued to pound on the door. He rose, throwing on a beat up old robe and stumbled toward the noise.

Captain Roads and a young lieutenant stood at the door in a pouring rain. "What in the hell would bring you out on a morning like this, a Sunday morning at that?"

"Can we come in?"

"Sure, I am not usually this impolite. Must be my thick head, I am sorry."

"Mark," started Roads, "this is Spiff Gifford. I thought it might be a good idea if he stayed with you today."

Mark looked at Roads as if he had just stepped out of a comic book about invaders from Mars.

"The Japanese are bombing the living hell out of Honolulu and Pearl Harbor," continued Roads. "It will be a good idea for you to stay home until someone like me comes over and tells you it's okay to go out. In the interim, Spiff here is a former Golden Gloves boxing champion and probably the biggest man on the base. He is your new best friend."

"I met you last night," responded Mark, trying to find a smile. "You were USC class of '38 if I'm right."

"And you were the wiz kid that screwed up the grading curve on all the math classes," laughed Spiff. Graduated in two years or something."

"Three, it was three, like my friend Chad. "It's probably harder to do at West Point," added Mark, almost babbling now as he digested the news.

"There will be a staff meeting in a couple of hours. In the interim, everything military is on alert," offered Roads. "I am sure that the base C.O. will want to know more about the young Japanese man who mysteriously appeared only weeks before a war breaks out with Japan. I will arrange for a meeting."

"Thank you for your help, Captain," replied Mark. "Can I get a telegram to my friend Chad? You know, tell him to keep his head down. I can't stand to lose another brother."

"You write it out and tell us where to send it, and I will get it sent. Keep it short, the communications traffic will be intense for the next few days." Roads turned from the door.

"You got the makings of a greasy breakfast?" asked Spiff. "You know, the type that soaks up last night's mistakes."

Spiff finally figured it was all right to go back to supervising the crew building the seaplane hangar down at the docks on Wednesday morning. For the previous three days he had shadowed Mark as he confined his travels to the cannery and home.

Mark had been inventorying supplies when he heard the door slam. Two men stormed through the cannery into the warehouse. "Hey Jap boy, we stopped by to let you know that we are going to keep an eye on you," snapped the tall sandy-haired man. Before Mark could respond, his partner, a smaller man with wavy black hair punched him in the face, blood exploding from his nose.

"Not so tough without your bodyguard," he snarled, as he delivered a knee to Mark's stomach.

Mark came up with a right that he had been saving since his confrontation with Peter in Japan. It caught the dark-haired man in the groin, tumbling him over a stack of corned beef cases. Before he could reload, the sandy-haired man had him in a headlock. "I'll hold him while you bust him up a little Nate," he spat.

The men were only there for five minutes, but it was long enough to leave Mark's face bloody and bruised, a cut in his scalp pumping blood down his forehead and into his eyes.

"You Japs ain't so tough, only half the size of real men," spewed the dark-haired man as he hobbled out the door. "A lot of the boys have brothers in Hawaii, and from what we hear some of them are dead. If you don't want to end up the same, get off this island."

Captain Roads knocked on the door just after dark. He watched as someone inside peeked through the drawn curtains before answering. "I came to let you know that the base commander would like to see you tomorrow," he groaned, "but I better get you over to the infirmary first."

"I'm okay," spat Mark, blood from his lips leaving tiny spots on Roads' raincoat.

"Just the same, grab your coat. You need a few stitches if you aren't going to spend the rest of your life looking like a soccer ball some dog tore up. On the way, give me the short version of what happened; just the details that aren't obvious."

"Don't punish the men who did this, Captain. They are angry and afraid," begged Mark as he climbed into the waiting car.

"They are also soldiers or sailors in the service of their country," snarled Roads. "When you get through at the infirmary, it might be a good time to get that telegram to your friend through. Things are starting to quiet down."

"Thanks. About that meeting, tomorrow might not be a very good day for it."

"On the contrary, tomorrow will be the perfect day. The faster we get rid of the sloppy attitude and get on a wartime footing, the safer we all will be."

CHAPTER 14

KARAFUTO, JAPAN, DECEMBER 1941

Father and Grandfather Ishihara sat on the wharf watching the first heavy snow of the year pile up. They had finished the installation of the canning line only the night before and were celebrating with a bottle of sake warmed in hot water from the can cooker.

Heavy rubber rain pants and coats shielded them from the wet. They watched two stacks of canned cod dripping as the heat from the morning's production melted the falling snow. "We are lucky that Roku knew where to catch enough winter cod to test the line," said Michi.

"Agreed," responded Haruku, as he nursed the tiny glass of scalding sake. "I don't see much of a market for canned cod, but I am sure that someone will buy it just because it is so novel."

"When are you going back to Sapporo, father?" asked Michi.

"I will wait until this snow passes and the local government can plow the roads. Your mother and I were talking, and we agreed that it might be good if we went home for a while and left the summerhouse to you and Kiko."

"You don't need to do that. We are comfortable in the large guest room."

"Perhaps I didn't make it clear. Your mother and I have only a couple of aging sisters between us, Michi. We have never spent a lot of time with relatives. We now have two strong willed women living under one roof, from two different cultures. For the first time we understand that old Japanese proverb."

"All right, I'll bite, what proverb is that?"

"After two weeks, relatives are a lot like old fish," laughed Haruku. "It will be good for the family to separate the American girl trying so hard to be Japanese and the Japanese woman who is trying so hard to tolerate the differences."

The two men had spent a month installing the canning equipment, less than half the time they had estimated it would take. Roku had hired local plumbers and electricians to help. His natural abilities to work on anything mechanical made the translation of the instructions from English to Japanese almost unnecessary. With the snows, Roku would let the seasonal workers off for the season, leaving only himself and one maintenance man on the payroll.

Haruku would retreat to his city office, paneled in American oak, a present from his son. There, he would bargain hard to sell the season's pack at the best prices he could before May, when family tradition required that he sell what was left to the government or give it to the groups who fed the less fortunate without families to care for them.

Since arriving on the island, Michi and Kiko had been welcomed by friends of his parents and were immersing themselves in the culture of their ancestors. Every Wednesday they would check in at the small Army base just outside of Otomari. Colonel Ito would meet them grim faced, growing angrier each week at the purgatory that General Fumi had sentenced him to. The feather in Ito's cap, that Michi's return was to bring, instead brought only separation from everything important. He hated Michi for being there and alive.

Michi and Haruku finished their reward and pocketed the tiny sake cups. Michi threw the empty bottle at the gulls riding the swell below the dock hoping for a handout. They fluttered away, returning in minutes to continue their watch. "I will keep my ears open for news of Mark back in Sapporo," offered Haruku. "We Japanese are very structured. Even the military treats most of us who disagree with them with civility."

Mark's answer was drowned out by the sound of the engine of a huge Mitsubishi truck in army paint racing onto the dock. The driver, probably a draftee from Kyushu or some other southern island locked up the brakes. The truck slid across the dock and into the stacks of cooling cans, sending them across the dock like shrapnel from an exploding shell.

Haru Ito emerged from the cab of the truck, kicking spilled cans out of his way as he approached the sitting men. "You will both rise when I approach," ordered Ito.

Both men took their time getting to their feet. "I am not one of your soldiers," replied Haruku.

Ito reached under his arm and handed each of the men a large piece of folded paper. "It has started," he barked. "The Imperial Japanese Navy has delivered a blow to the arrogant Americans that they will never recover from. I brought each of you the base newspaper that offers all of the details of a magnificent victory." His speech ended; he turned and headed back to the truck. "Michi, you will continue to come to my office on Wednesdays until we need for you to do more," he called over his shoulder.

Michi stood silently as the driver somehow managed to turn the truck around without hitting the building.

His father broke the silence. "I know we both prayed that this was all some big bluff," he started, "but I also knew that the Army would never be satisfied until they provoked the United States into a fight. Those idiots really believe that they will win."

"I know, Father, and now we do our part to make this as short a war as we can," answered Michi.

"I didn't think that you were going to help these idiots with their plan any more than necessary to keep your and Kiko's heads at the end of your necks."

"America will win this war. If the warmongers destroyed California, the rest of the United States would avenge the loss." Michi unfolded the tabloid with the Japanese headline, *American Fleet Destroyed at Pearl Harbor.* "The loss of a few ships to a country that can build a ship a week means little. If the loss of life is even close to what this rag says, Japan is doomed. I don't know how, but I will do everything in my power to see that the fools are stopped before they destroy this beautiful country."

CHAPTER 15

BURBANK, CALIFORNIA, JANUARY 1942

"I'm so sorry Lieutenant Gritt," offered the private standing at attention in front of Chad. "This came in while you took a few days off. I'd planned on forwarding it as soon as I could find you, but the only address I had was in Alaska and I knew that you couldn't get there and back in a week. The communications traffic has been unbelievable. I forgot about it until I got to the bottom of my desk this morning."

Chad smiled at the private, who was no more than a year younger than him.

"No damage done, private, it's just a note from an old friend in Alaska."

"Do you have your orders yet, Lieutenant?"

"Nope, I expect them this week. I'm spending my time helping instruct until they come through. Some Navy Captain I met a few months ago will be here in the morning. Maybe he is why my orders are held up."

"They all are, Sir. No one expected the war to come so fast," replied the private, saluting as he turned to head back to the Administration Building.

Chad folded the small envelope, shoved it into his shirt pocket, and went back to the hangar where he had been watching as one of the P-38s was fitted with cameras where the five guns in the nose normally rode.

He read Mark's cryptic telegram and smiled, as he nursed bourbon in the officer's club. No one else had arrived yet and he had no one to impress by ordering Scotch that he didn't like anyway. After dinner he retreated to his small room and managed to get a phone call through to Carmen who was on duty at the hospital.

"I thought you should know," she volunteered, "I am considering giving up my civilian nursing here at Moffett Field. The Army is recruiting for nurses, and I promised that I would consider it. I would go in as a second lieutenant and could end up anywhere. I just think that with the war and all, there is a lot more I can do."

Chad couldn't comment. He was unsure of how he felt about the idea and something about Mark's telegram was nagging at him. Five minutes later, the two exchanged their "I love you and goodnight."

Chad pulled out Mark's telegram and reread it, then found a pencil and pad and rewrote part of it, skipping every other line. The message brought the hair up on the back of his neck. His meeting with Captain Walt Wilson was scheduled for nine the next morning, and Chad knew that with no sleep, he would not be at his best.

The next morning, Wilson smiled as Chad walked into the room and saluted. "I am happy to see your promotion came through First Lieutenant," started Wilson.

"Thank you, Sir. I am not being disrespectful, Sir, but I still am not very interested in considering a move to the Navy," replied Chad.

"I got that loud and clear Chad, sit down. I have to be out of the Colonel's office in an hour, but I wanted to update you on what we are doing on that culture and intelligence project. As you can surmise, we are fully funded, and we are now ramping up with the best men we can find. I already have a couple of Army officers working with me. We need to figure out what the Japanese are up to next."

Chad searched his conscience, arriving at the obvious. Mark had sent him the telegram with the hidden message because he needed help. "Let's assume, Sir, that I would like to help. Let's assume that I might be able to help steer someone to a small piece of the puzzle. Would you be the one I should discuss it with?"

Wilson laughed. "I don't know if I have ever had someone work so hard to give me information without actually spitting it out. In answer, I may not be the right one to talk to, but I just about guarantee that I know who that right one might be."

Chad smiled. Sir, do you remember me telling you about my friend who was stuck in Japan last fall? His parents are still in Japan. My family is close to a number of people in the Senate and a few in the administration. I checked and Mark Ishihara's parents are not on the exchange list between Japan and the U.S. They are not coming out on the ship that the Swedes or Norwegians, I can't remember which, is running to exchange diplomats and nationals stuck in Japan."

"Perhaps I shouldn't tell you this, Lieutenant, but I already knew that," answered Wilson.

"In for a dime, in for a dollar," gasped Chad. "I want to share a telegram that I just got from Mark. It may mean nothing, but it may mean a lot. When we were kids, Mark's father used to use a silly code to leave us messages. Often the messages were designed to – let me phrase this correctly – not tell the exact truth to Mark's mom, Kiko. He would use a code for changing numbers and dates, even places, but the key was that certain lines in his notes were to be read to mean the exact opposite of what was written."

Gritt tugged the now worn telegram from his pocket and unfolded it on the desk. "Skip the address part and go to the body of the telegram."

Wilson slid his chair around to the side of the desk and began reading:

I am angry at my father's country.

I don't know what the Japanese will do next.

Keep your head down brother.
The Japanese probably won't attack here.
Some here are angry and afraid of me.
I don't need to talk to anyone.
I can only trust old friends.
Mark

"The way the old messages worked, the first line would be the truth, but the second line would be read to mean just the opposite of the wording. The third line would be truth again and the fourth, again the opposite, and so on. If you read this telegram this way, the message is clear," concluded Chad.

"Let me make sure that you and I are on the same page, Chad," interjected Wilson. "Your friend is angry at Japan, but he thinks he knows what they will do next. He wants you safe, but he thinks that Japan may attack Dutch Harbor. The men in Dutch don't trust him, and he needs someone to talk to who will believe him. That someone is you or someone you will vouch for."

"It's either that, Captain, or the message is just a note from a harassed Japanese American who just got back from an extended trip in Japan and whose parents are now stuck on the wrong side in a war," closed Chad. "Either way I really owe that family."

"Since you mentioned your language skills and this Ishihara family, I have had a couple of those Army folks I mentioned dig into them a bit. I've been had a time or two, but this Michi fought side by side with your own father and others to repel a small invasion by a joint Russian and Japanese force that landed in Alaska back in 1921. That doesn't sound like any threat to me," closed Wilson.

"I knew there was something, but neither my dad nor Michi ever mentioned a battle," responded Chad.

"The powers to be decided it should be all hushed up. Everyone involved signed an oath to never mention it. It is one of the reasons that Michi and Kiko were granted citizenship so easily. No, I think your friend is trying to tell us something important and we need to listen," nodded Wilson.

Wilson climbed from the chair and limped toward the door. "I came here to talk to you and to take a look at a unique P-38 configuration. Why don't you tag along, and we can figure this out?"

"You are talking about the camera ship?" asked Chad.

"We still have a ways to go on security issues," said Wilson, stifling a laugh.

The men were greeted by two civilians, both balding with glasses like the ends of Coke bottles. Neither introduced themselves, and neither asked their names. The letter that Wilson produced seemed to be the only introduction necessary. "The cameras are both American made copies of units used by the British for the last year. Their resolution is fully adjustable based on the height above the target," offered one of the men. "My friend here is working to calculate the minute shift for the weight and balance of the airframe."

Wilson crawled under the plane to examine the portals installed to accommodate the lenses of the cameras. He asked for a simplified description of the operation and eventual development of the film, finishing with, "These will do nicely."

He turned to Chad. "It's in a warrior's blood to want to go into the heavens and shoot down the enemy or to fly over his bases and bomb him into oblivion. Even more important is to understand what the enemy is doing and with what resources, to get a clear picture of how we are hurting him."

He turned back to the engineers. "How much room do you still have available? I mean, if I wanted to add a radio that could listen in on what the enemy is saying during a raid, or even more importantly, what he is saying close to the ground when he thinks we are not listening, could you fit it in?"

"If it is about the same size as the radios already installed, we have plenty of room," answered the spokesman. "Anything that adds a little more weight in the nose will help with the aircraft balance issue. With a couple of tweaks to the shape of the nose, we might even be able to fit two fifty-caliber guns back into the nose, but we would have to figure out how to shield the cameras to keep the heat of the guns from ruining the film."

"Lieutenant Gritt, I need to make a couple of phone calls on the matter we discussed earlier. In the interim, how would you like to take this little baby up for a quick spin, maybe even a pass or two over the field to check the cameras?"

"I'm sorry Sir, but I don't report to you. I will have to check with my CO before flying," answered Chad.

"I took care of that when I arrived." Wilson slipped a folded note from his pocket and handed it to Chad. "The base and training squadron commanders have released you to my group, pending your assignment to a permanent billet, Lieutenant. I knew that we would need to fly this bird while I was here, and no one wants a peg leg in a one of a kind aircraft."

Wilson turned back to the two engineers. When you are ready for a test, the Lieutenant here can really fly." Wilson turned to leave. "I'm buying dinner off base this evening, Chad. In the interim, I am going all the way to Washington to get approval to follow up with your friend up north."

Dinner was at a quiet steak place only a half-hour from the field. Wilson's driver had joined them for the meal. Chad remembered her from the barbeque that seemed years ago. Her beauty was matched by a quick wit and a deeper knowledge of the Japanese threat than anyone before had discussed with Chad. On cue, she had excused herself, leaving the men alone.

"There is a P-38 squadron slated for the Aleutians," stated Wilson. "The Pentagon has assured me that her commander will be most sympathetic and cooperative to the intelligence work my group is engaged in. You were already under consideration for that unit; they can use your help in learning to stay alive in the cradle of bad weather."

"And, just what would I be doing for you?" asked Chad.

"You will be available to listen in on what the enemy is saying. You will take pictures for the Air Corps in the Aleutians but also of anything that I request. While in the air, you can monitor 'close in' radio traffic of the Japanese and let us know what you learn. You would also help your friend Mark out of a terrible dilemma. If I'm right, the Japanese are targeting the Aleutians, and he knows a great deal about the targets. My guess is that his parents are being held hostage to assure that he cooperates when called upon by the forces of the rising sun."

"Mark is no traitor. He's no spy," said Chad.

"I agree, that's why he sent you the message," smiled Wilson. "Remember, it's Walt when there are no flag rank officers around. You could be in Dutch Harbor in just over a month, doing work that most of your peers never even know is happening. This is about as lone eagle as you will find in the military."

"I don't want any command responsibility, Sir. I will make a terrible hero. But Mark is my brother." Chad finished the one drink he allowed himself. "With air transport, I could be there in four days."

"That aircraft will not be completely ready for a couple of weeks. Then we would want you to ferry it north along with other P-38s on their way to Dutch Harbor. I can even arrange for the entire group to spend a week in Anchorage before moving to the end of the earth. Your father and your mother, I think her name is Lisa, would love to see you, I am sure."

"With all respect, Sir, you seem really sure of yourself in this," quipped Chad.

"Not in me, Chad, in the man I chose for the job before you ever graduated from the academy. American soil is vulnerable to the Japanese in only four places: the Philippines territory, some South Pacific Islands in the Samoa area, Hawaii and Alaska, and of those only Alaska is within a few hundred miles of Japan. Only Alaska has a small enough population to subjugate if the Japanese decide they need its resources."

Walt downed the beer he preferred with a steak. He smiled at

Chad. "I have an old friend at Dutch now, running engineering. He once told me about you Alaskans. You want to be a state someday, but if it turned out that you became your own country that would be just fine. He has worked in the oil industry and he says you guys are worse than Texans when it comes to your attachment to the land."

"Would I be stuck in the Aleutians?" asked Chad. He caught the attention of the waitress in the almost empty restaurant and held up his empty beer. He ordered another, breaking his own discipline.

"You would only be there until we have a real grasp on that situation and then you would be on your way to the next hot spot," said Walt. "The group is only concerned with what's going on in the Pacific, so if your heart was set on authentic Italian food, you will be disappointed."

"I was more interested in sandy beaches and palm trees and maybe the chance to catch a marlin for the wall in my den."

Walt smiled, thinking about his life as a twenty something officer who knew he was bulletproof. In his mind he had already calculated that the field operatives he was recruiting probably had at best a fifty percent chance of surviving the war. "I'll see what I can do about that sandy beach. That assumes you are now one of us."

"I'm in, that is if you can arrange it with the Army. What's next?"

"You fly the bird out there hard for a couple of days before they send it back to the factory to fit the new radio and maybe a couple of guns into the nose. They will also mount some experimental drop tanks, adding two more hours of fuel. Between, let's say this Wednesday and the end of next week, you will have some leave. Use it. It will be your last for at least a year. In the interim, I will get your orders cut and your promotion approved."

"I just got my promotion," reminded Chad.

"All of the enlisted men in our group are staff sergeants and up and all of the officers are at least Captains. It wouldn't do to have the others dumping all of the shit jobs on you." Walt smiled, extending his hand, "Welcome aboard."

"What can I tell people?"

"Only that you have been assigned to a P-38 squadron in Alaska. You will test the cameras as you ferry the aircraft to Seattle and then on up the coast. You will play with the radios. I am sorry that there is no one to teach you, but this is a first time assignment."

"Got it, Walt. If there is nothing more, I am going to get out of here. I want to send a telegram back to Mark and call my girl. I doubt that she can get a week off, but she won't know until she tries."

"Maybe Carmen will surprise you," smiled Walt picking up the check. "As to the telegram, wait until we have a firm answer and date."

CHAPTER 16

DUTCH HARBOR, ALASKA, FEBRUARY 1942

The visit with the base commander had gone just as Mark had anticipated. To the CO, Mark was a distraction he didn't need. The two men who had roughed him up were spending a month on KP duty, peeling potatoes and washing dishes, nothing more. They wore the punishment like a medal and to many of their peers they were heroes.

While the officers who had attended the football party still talked to him – some even inviting him to dinner – most of the base personnel treated him like a leper. That was just as well since he'd finally received the coded message broadcast from a Japanese aircraft over the north Pacific telling him that the ground team would arrive on April 1. The stress filled him with anger that he hadn't felt since the altercation in the cannery.

He'd never believed that he could feel so alone. His appetite faded, making the clothes on his normal one hundred forty pound frame hang like a flour sack. He almost welcomed the possibility that the base CO would ship him and all of the other civilians off from the island as was rumored.

He sat that evening drinking tea in front of the window overlooking the current storm sweeping the harbor. One thought made his stomach churn was what would happen to his parents if he were shipped away. He was so deep in his thoughts that he didn't hear the rap on the door until whoever was there was pounding it.

He swung the door open to find Captain Roads and Spiff sweeping the snow from their wool overcoats with the old broom he left on the porch.

"We thought you might be dead or drunk," said Spiff.

"Neither, just trying to find the will to pick up one of my schoolbooks and get to work," answered Mark.

"Do you know what day this is?" asked Spiff.

"Honestly no, not without checking my calendar, I cross off the days every morning, but I don't even check to see what day of the week it is," replied Mark.

"It's Sunday, and over on the other side of the bay they are serving steaks. We grabbed three and some spuds and decided that you might appreciate someone's cooking other than your own." Spiff stepped into the house, taking off his coat and hanging it on the peg behind the door."

"It is also your lucky day," added Roads, slapping his hat against his leg before following Spiff.

"Oh, before I forget, here is a telegram that finally made it up here from California. Unless something is marked urgent or priority it can take two weeks to get a message through," added Roads tugging a beaten envelope from his rear pants pocket.

Mark stood, his mouth agape as both men settled into his house, Roads heading for the cooler where the sodas were kept and Spiff for the kitchen. "Sounds good to me," he finally managed.

Over dinner, the conversation slowly evolved from polite to business. "I don't know who you know back in Washington," observed Roads, "but someone wants to make sure there is no repeat of what happened last month. With that in mind, I have a proposition for you."

Mark took a deep breath, *that's all I need, more complications.* "I'm listening," he replied as he refreshed the Scotch in front of him.

"I have received authorization to lease an existing facility to do equipment sub-assembly. The shop in the cannery would fit that bill nicely. It was also recommended by an old associate, with friends in both high and low places, that I consider adding another part-time contractor to the Seabee team. He got the referral from some guy by the name of Gritt, probably the same one in that telegram you haven't read. He said that if I could find some guy by the name of Mark O'Hara who ran a cannery, he might be a good addition. As one of us, he would be immune from the relocation order we expect to come through anytime and he would also be one of the construction corps and nobody screws with anyone on our team.

"You don't have to make a decision right now, Mr. O'Hara," laughed Roads. "Hell, it's Sunday and there is no one to do any paperwork until tomorrow. I haven't even thought through what the duties would be, but I doubt that there will be much pay. Let Spiff or me know in the next couple of days."

The human sense of being alive, of being optimistic is a terrible thing to lose. It is also a joyous thing to find again, thought Mark as he dumped the dishes into the sink. They would be there in the morning. He granted himself another Scotch as he settled into a beat up easy chair and ripped the end of the envelope.

Got your message.

Not much I can do from here.

Probably end up close to home.

If so, won't be until early September.

Keep your chin up.

Chad

Mark turned the envelope over and jotted down the matrix for months in the code.

January   July

February   *August*
March   *September*
April   *October*
May   *November*
June   *December*

The visit from Roads and Spiff was the help that Chad could arrange from California and more importantly he was coming to Dutch by the end of March. Mark walked over to his calendar. Tomorrow would be the 8th of February; that meant that the Japanese plane sent to signal him would be on station at eight in the morning his time. His broadcast of *radio check* three times would set everything in motion. For the first time in weeks Mark fell asleep before his head hit the pillow.

CHAPTER 17

KARAFUTO, JAPAN, FEBRUARY 1942

Michi watched as Ito's communications team moved into the gardener's house, installing their monitoring equipment. Their small antenna was designed to pick up any transmission from the hundred-foot tower behind the summerhouse.

The corporal showed him how a transmission was detected. The system illuminated a red light. The man on duty would queue a turntable recording any transmission on a record.

Ito emphasized that only two frequencies were to be used, one for the plant and a second that Mark and Michi will use to maintain contact. "Transmissions on any other frequency will be dealt with in the strictest manner," he warned. All of the recordings would be delivered to Ito's office when one member of the monitoring crew changed each week.

Michi agreed when Kiko asked the gardener to move into the house. Both knew what would be expected of Mary if she stayed with three Japanese soldiers. What Airi had never learned was that the girl was Christian and spoke English. Kiko and Mary had become friends.

The afternoon that Ito arrived at the house, the two women were playing chess. Kiko quickly folded the tabletop over the game, careful not to move any of the pieces as Mary raced to her room for her apron.

"Meiyo gesuto o kangei shimasu," offered Mary opening the door.

"Send this creature for tea," ordered Haru as Michi appeared from his office.

"Why are we speaking English, Haru?" snarled Michi. "What do you want?"

"I bring a message from General Fumi and I don't want your Korean baishunpu listening to us," said Ito. He glared at the Korean girl.

"Mary is no whore. Her father was a minister, and she would have been in a university if the Japanese Army had not 'recruited' her."

"What she is doesn't concern me. We can never be too careful. My unit has executed two Korean spies since I came to Karafutu."

The news sent a shiver down Michi's back, but he managed to maintain his defiant smile. "Let me see the general's message."

"You do not give orders," said Ito, as he opened a leather pouch over his shoulder, handing a folded sheet to Michi.

"General Fumi wants you to keep your son informed. He would like you to send this to him while I wait," continued Ito.

"No message would stand a chance of getting through at this time of day, not with all of the radio traffic interference during the daytime. Besides, Mark is not listening now."

"How do you know? I have listened to every transmission."

"We set up a schedule before he left. We only monitor the radio twice a week; only on Sunday and Wednesday and only at a certain time of day. You think the American military is so stupid that they wouldn't find something funny about him using the radio all day, every day?"

Ito had always been capable of controlling his anger when someone presented him irrefutable logic. "When can you send this message? It is Tuesday In Alaska," arrogantly proving he'd done his homework about the International Date Line.

"At five o'clock tomorrow morning it will be nine at night in Dutch Harbor. I will try to get this through. Maybe the American Army has confiscated his radio."

"They have not. We got confirmation that he is ready to receive Peter and his team. My monitors will bring me a copy of your transmission tomorrow and any response from your son."

"Let me make sure I understand the message. General Hosogaya will leave here with nine ships the last week of May and Admiral Kakuta will command two carriers to support activities in the Aleutians. I am to tell Mark that I know of little military activity in the northern sector and expect none until next winter. I am also supposed to tell him to stay on his side of the bay during any attack. Now how in the hell am I supposed to send both of those messages? They contradict each other."

"That is your problem. I will see how well you did tomorrow."

Ito rose, and headed toward his staff car. Mary bowed to him as she opened the door. "He never touched his tea," she said as she headed for her tiny room to return the apron that she only wore when visitors were present.

The agreement with Mark was to transmit messages conversationally. Michi would wait for Mark's response to his first sentence before sending the first coded sentence.

The following afternoon, Ito sat with the record of the conversation. He had listened to every word. Michi had done just exactly what he had been asked to do. But it was impossible that Michi was following his orders precisely. Ito verified the station identifier numbers, confirming those used were the Ishihara's licensed numbers in Alaska and California. There was nothing suspicious in the call letters and numbers. He picked up the needle and started the turntable again, turning up the volume to hear more clearly.

This is Mark, is that you father?

It is me Michi, your mother and I are well.

As am I father.

My old friend's fleet will stay in port until next winter.

You are safe from the war in grandfather's summerhouse.

Mary, the gardener now lives with us as our maid.

Will she be there when grandmother returns?

She will stay until November; she works each day from seven to nine.

Our weather is so bad that I have little to do.

When the storms come stay home.

Tell mother everyone she loves is fine, good-bye.

Goodbye son, I do not want to burden you with our calls.

The clarity of the recording surprised Ito. The only sentence that concerned him was the last one. He made a note to question Michi about why a father would worry about becoming a burden to a son. He scribbled out a message confirming that the message had been sent for the general. Then he flipped open the file on the Korean worker who had been caught trying to cross the line into the Russian held end of the island. She was on her way to his office that afternoon, in custody of the border police. He would see if she was pretty before figuring out when she would be shot for spying.

CHAPTER 18

SEA OF CORTEZ, MEXICO, MARCH 1942

Chad worked the striped marlin next to the boat where the Mexican captain buried a long handled gaff hook under the jaw of the fish and pulled it over the side of the boat. The captain clubbed the fish and added it to the three already taking up most of the room in the boat. The smile on Chad's face brought a smile to Carmen's. She would have done almost anything for the man nursing his last cerveza, flexing sore arms. Almost anything was the operative thought.

The captain looked at Chad, expecting approval to put the fishing rods in their rack and head back to the small harbor only five miles away. Chad, watching a line of pelicans soar over the waves only a few feet from the boat, ignored him.

"I have to draw the line at blood that almost reaches my ankles," Carmen spumed. "I am ready for a swim, a shower and a drink."

Chad smiled and nodded his head. Carmen looked over at the smiling captain who didn't speak a word of English but hoped the conversation meant that his day was done before the afternoon heat.

Carmen looked at the captain. "Vamanos!"

The captain wrenched the heavy lever that shifted the crude transmission from neutral to forward and pushed the throttle full forward. The tiny ten-horse gasoline engine under the box in the middle of the boat surged, as Jorge spun the wheel toward the sleepy village.

Jorge slipped the engine into neutral as the boat neared the sand beach. Carmen tugged the yellow linen sundress over her head and folded it into the bag at her feet, then dove over the side. She surfaced and pushed hard swimming away from the boat, then turned back to the boat and stood up.

"Strip off your shirt and throw it in the bag, then hand it to me."

Chad finished helping Jorge slip the last of the marlin over the side where a dozen villagers waited to pull them ashore. "I am so burned, I don't want to take off my shirt," he answered.

"It's just for a minute and it really feels good," coaxed Carmen.

He pulled the sweaty shirt off and rolled it up, dropping it on top of her dress. He handed her the bag, which she balanced on her head, holding it with her left hand. He shook bloody hands with the captain, slipping him a ten-peso tip. He looked back at Carmen who stood staring at him.

"Are you coming or not?"

"I was just admiring the view," he replied, fully appreciating how the young woman filled the bright yellow swimsuit.

"Go ahead, dive. You have learned to swim enough in the last four days to keep your head above water. If it goes under hold your breath while I run the bag up to the beach, then I will save you," she laughed.

Chad's entry into the warm water looked a lot like an anchor dropping from a ship, but he managed to keep his face down and breath only when he took a stroke as he swam away from the boat.

"Another week and you will be ready for the swim team," she chortled.

"I grew up where the ocean temperature seldom gets much past the mid-forties," he managed, trying to shake the water from his nose. "We swam in a lake only a couple of miles from the house, but mostly we just cooled off on the few summer days when it was hot."

"Ayudarme con las canas de pascar," came a call from the boat. "Jorge wants some help carrying the fishing rods to shore."

Chad did his best imitation of a wounded baitfish swimming back to the boat. A minute later he and Carmen trudged up the sand where a graying woman with skin the color of cocoa framing pale blue eyes waited.

"That is pretty good fishing for only two hours out on the boat." Mildred Reed picked up the old camera from the beach chair in front of her and took a picture. "Now you two, go kneel down next to those fish and I will get a picture. I can't develop this film down here, but when you leave you can take it back to California with you. If there is anything good on the roll, make me a print."

Carmen stood and dusted the sand from her knees. "I don't know how we will ever be able to thank you Mrs. Reed."

"Don't try," answered Mildred. "I admit, when I saw the Beechcraft circle the house, I thought it might be Alex making a surprise trip, but I have enjoyed the company of you two more that you will ever know."

Chad picked up the bag and headed up the beach toward the noise of the outdoor cantina.

"You need to wait a minute, Chad," called Mildred. "You need to see why the people of the village love to host sport fishermen."

Chad turned just as a young priest slipped a huge machete from the wheelbarrow that he had parked next to the fish. There was a stir in the dozens of village children who had gathered on the beach. The priest pointed to one boy who came forward laying a large piece of canvas on the sand. The priest cut off a three-foot section of one of the marlin and dropped it on the canvas. A minute later a young girl pushed away through the crowd with a two-foot piece sticking out of her woven basket. In ten minutes, the marlin had been reduced to heads and tails that went into the wheelbarrow along with a small rasher of fish.

"The priest knows every family. Everyone in the village will eat your marlin for the next two days," giggled Mildred. The smallest piece in the wheelbarrow will be dropped off with Maria for our dinner tonight. The rest will go to the old people who cannot get here themselves."

"Will the priest keep any for himself?" asked Carmen.

"He doesn't need to. He will choose from a half-dozen dinner invitations tonight. Now let's get you two up to the shower and into some clean clothes. All that salt on your skin must be getting sticky." Mildred turned toward the two-story house just down the beach. "I had the boy refill the tank on the guest house this morning, I hope the water is still cool. I suggest a siesta and then Maria will have ceviche and a chilled bottle of Tequila on the patio."

The breeze stirred the tops of the palms that provided shade, and the generous application of aloe kept Chad's burn bearable as the three watched the sun disappear behind the mountains overlooking the village. Before them, the Sea of Cortez settled into a mirror, framed by white sand in front and the first stars in the distance. "I can't thank you and your husband enough for the hospitality and the loan of the Beechcraft to get here," said Chad. "I never dreamed that a trip like this could be arranged so quickly."

"You two seem to have made some very special friends," responded Mildred. Alex worked for years with Rocky Roads and his best friend is Walt Wilson. Rocky built the infrastructure in every oil field that Alex developed. They have been partners for years; even now that Rocky and Walt went back into the Navy. When Walt called Alex and asked if he could help, he was happy to oblige. His note to me indicates that you will be seeing his old partner in the near future. Those three old men have mentored a lot of young men in the last twenty years, you are lucky to be one of them."

"I am figuring that out real quick," smiled Chad. He sipped a tiny amount of liquid from the heavy green glass in front of him, looking up into the star filled sky.

"You don't like your tequila? You have been nursing that drink for two hours. I can have Maria bring out a bottle of scotch."

"No thanks Mrs. Reed. I have to fly tomorrow, and I would like to get out of here before dawn while it is still cool," said Chad.

"That makes sense. Twelve hours and two fuel stops in any airplane makes for a tough day. Alex says that if you stay out over the water there are fewer thermos, whatever those are. Anyway, he says the flight is smoother," finished Mildred.

"He's right, ma'am," agreed Chad. "Until the flight down here, Carmen had never been an airplane. They are part of my life, so I want flying to be fun for her."

"I'm going up to bed now and leave you two alone for your last night." Mildred rose, wrapping her long blue shawl around her shoulders.

"One question, Mrs. Reed, if you don't mind," interrupted Carmen.

"I don't mind. At sixty-five the only questions that could embarrass me would be about things that I have already given up," laughed Mildred.

"How is it that you are here in Mexico and your husband is still in California? I mean, don't you miss him?"

"Of course, I do. We bought this place five years ago to retire. Alex owns the boat that Jorge took you out in. He will die fishing. If he never sees a tie again, he will be as happy as a bass in a pond full of frogs. But when the war started, he decided that it was important to get his newest oil field producing. The country will need a lot of fuel. He also wanted me out of Los Angeles where he thought there was a real risk of a Japanese attack. On December 10th, he loaded me in that fancy airplane he bought and hauled me down here. In forty years, he had never given me an order before, so I figured he was serious."

The couple watched Mildred disappear into the house behind the patio.

"I am really happy you could get the time off to come down here," offered Chad.

"I have a confession," replied Carmen taking his hand. "You are going to sleep tonight with an Army officer. I quit my job and signed up. I am officially Second Lieutenant Carmen Alvarez, and

I report for duty at the end of the month. When we get back, I will go visit my folks in New Mexico. I report in San Francisco, and from there, who knows." Carmen's smile faded in the soft light, a more pensive look replacing it. "I promise that while there will be a lot of soldiers around, I will go to sleep every night saying a prayer for only one man."

Chad sighed. And if you don't mind, I will keep a copy of that picture of you in the swimsuit that Mrs. Reed took above my bunk. The other guys will look until they realize that it just makes them jealous."

Carmen kissed him on the cheek. "We have to be up at five for Jorge to drive us to the airstrip. I think we should head for bed," she added. Chad wondered if she had gotten a bit too much sun that day as he noticed the red in her cheeks as she leaned over to blow out the candle.

The two were surprised to find the village priest waiting at the side of the car in the morning. "Me gustaria que no ibas a la Guerra. Cuidate e gracias."

"He says he wishes you were not going off to war. Be safe and thank you," translated Carmen. "Why is he thanking you?"

"I will tell you when we get into the air. Let's get out of here."

It was getting dark, as Chad began his descent into the Burbank airport.

"You never did tell me why the priest thanked you," said Carmen, finally asking a question that had troubled her all day.

"It was nothing much. Last Monday was my twenty-first birthday. My family sent me a check for a thousand dollars. I cashed it and used the money to make this trip. What I had left over I had Mildred donate to the church."

Carmen ran through the expenses in her head. Including aircraft gas and tips the total was less than $300. "You didn't tell me it was your birthday. I owe you a kiss after we land. No, two, one for the village."

Their eyes were drawn out toward the setting sun by a bright flash on the horizon. Moments later, the Burbank tower ordered their Beechcraft to make an expedited landing. The military had ordered the skies emptied to clear the way for a dozen scrambling aircraft. They were responding to the destruction of a tanker, torpedoed by a Japanese submarine only miles from the coast.

CHAPTER 19

BRITISH COLUMBIA, CANADA, MARCH 1942

The newly formed squadron flew in formation from California to Great Falls Montana, where they sat for three days waiting for their one missing plane to arrive. Chad had ferried the modified P-38 to Seattle where Boeing worked feverishly to replace the radio that the Lockheed engineers had worked so hard to install. Walt Wilson had rejected the original after only two days of testing. He wanted something with more range, like the new radios being tested for the long range Boeing B-17 bomber.

That radio was three times the size of the original, which meant that one of the two fifty caliber machine guns in the nose had to go. This meant the cameras needed to move over two inches, which meant that the glass windows in the bottom of the nose had to move as well.

It had taken Lt. Colonel Jon Wayne nine years to make captain and finding that one of the pilots in his squadron had gone from West Point Cadet to captain in a year did not sit well with him. He was ready to move the squadron north without waiting until the base commander did a walk through inspection on his aircraft and wrote up a mandatory checklist on every one of them.

Only the ground crew and fueling truck met Gritt when he

arrived late the third day. He tossed his travel bag on one of the bunks in the barracks and made his way to the mess hall for a sandwich. Wayne found him there an hour later.

"Nice to see you could join us hotshot," said Wayne, as Gritt snapped to attention.

"The crew over at Boeing field didn't finish up until noon today, and they wouldn't release the airplane until one of their test pilots flew it and signed it off, Sir," replied Gritt. "From wheels up to landing only took me three hours, Sir."

"If it had been up to me, you would be going north with some of the girls ferrying planes to Alaska for the Russians," drawled Wayne. "We heard you were on the ground and waited in the officer's club, but evidently you are too special to drink with your squadron mates."

Chad noted just a tiny bit of slurring in his commander's speech. The conversation was a lot like walking on eggs. "I am sorry, Colonel. I worked side by side with the engineers all night, and I have only eaten a cheeseburger all day. I was really hungry, and I also knew that if I had a drink, I would probably fall asleep in my chair, Sir."

"Well, come on over when you finish your sandwich. We aren't going anywhere tomorrow; they have three of our planes in the hangar with the inspection plates all off, and the mechanics have gone home.

"They rolled the bird I was flying into a hanger when I got in. While I filled in their paperwork, a dozen guys showed up and began buttoning up three P-38s."

He had just finished the statement when a one star general strode through the door. "I was told to button up all of your airplanes this evening and get you on your way. I set up a weather briefing for 5 AM which should allow you to do your flight plan, get some chow and be off the ground by seven." The general didn't wait for an answer.

Wayne looked over at Gritt, "Finish up here and go find a bunk."

Chad wasn't sure whether the look in the colonel's eyes was anger or if he was just puzzled. Captain Wilson had warned him that he was going to be walking a tightrope reporting to two commanders, but until they reached Dutch Harbor there was nothing he could tell Colonel Wayne.

❀

The routing from Montana to Alaska was a carefully choreographed trip. The Canadian and American governments had built refueling air bases on a line from Montana north to Fairbanks. The bases were only a couple of hours apart with emergency airstrips in-between. Each month, dozens of aircraft made the trip north, most flown by women pilots. Since the attack on Pearl Harbor and the invasion of the Philippines, entire squadrons of planes destined for bases in Alaska were making the trip.

However, most of the planes flown by the transport command were on their way to Russia with the handover to Russian pilots in Fairbanks. With half of the Russian pilots women and almost all of the American transport pilots also women, Fairbanks had become a very popular base for military personnel.

"Aren't you the lucky ones," smirked the Army captain at the front of the room. "There is high pressure expected over the entire route of flight for the next couple of days. Skies should remain clear with winds from the north at no more than twenty knots at 12,000 feet. Surface winds will be variable, but I don't expect anything much higher than the same twenty knots. The only precaution I have for you gentlemen is for possible morning fog, as you get further north. Surface temperatures will decline all of the way to Fairbanks, where it will be in the negative ten-degree range for the daily highs and ten degrees colder at night. If for some reason you get delayed, there is a possibility of some really nasty weather from the Bering Sea making its way into Fairbanks three or four days from now."

The weatherman folded his briefing notes back into a file folder and skipped down the steps, walking past the sleepy eyed pilots on his way to the back of the hall. Colonel Wayne hauled his tall frame from the folding chair on the stage and waved at his number two in the back of the room.

"My deputy, Hill Billy will pick a couple of you to work out our flight plan with him. I suggest that you guys work on it over some chow. The rest of you are released for breakfast. We reconvene here in one hour. I want to be off the ground thirty minutes after that. Dismissed."

"Mr. Gritt, a moment please," ordered the colonel. "You have the only bird with extended range drop tanks. You have an hour and a half more range than the other men in this squadron. You will fly with the second group and you will be responsible for getting hard locations on any aircraft that may be forced down."

The hum of the twin Allison engines could almost put you to sleep, especially on a smooth day. Throttled back to the maximum cruise range settings, the sleek aircraft still cruised at 230 knots. From 12,000 in the air the country looked flat, and since their last refueling, it was all white.

The planners had decided to spend the night at Watson Lake on the border between British Columbia and the Yukon. Each leg of the trip was planned as a comfortable two-hour flight. Chad slid the plane out a bit from his normal formation position and began running through the frequencies on the radio installed in Seattle. Most of the time he found only static, but every once in a while, he came across chatter. He logged each frequency that had voices, noting ships running along the British Columbia coast and aircraft traffic from the middle of Canada. He was listening intently to a conversation in what he thought might be Russian, when the aircraft ahead and to his left began to rock his wings. Chad turned a switch on his instrument panel to switch to his regular radio.

"Where the hell are you hotshot?" came the voice of Wayne.

"Back on frequency, Sir," replied Gritt. I was testing the other radio."

"Well, while you were screwing around, we got a call from a transport group a hundred miles in front of us. It is a flight of eight P-39 Air Cobras. One in their group is having engine problems and is falling behind. They haven't been able to reach the pilot for the last ten minutes. Check your chart, they think she may have landed on the last emergency strip before Watson Lake. I want you to drop down and take a look, then climb back up and let us know what you see."

Chad clicked the microphone button two times, acknowledging that he understood, then tugged the throttles back. The map showed the strip in a wide valley, with a note that there was a road from a mine ten miles away. He watched the altimeter wind down as he approached the valley. Finding a tiny emergency airfield in all of the snow in front of him was a lot harder than he had anticipated. He made a pass down the valley without seeing anything and then turned for a second pass. He reached up and switched on the camera in front of him and set the adjustment for two thousand feet above ground level. He switched his radio to the emergency frequency.

"P-38 circling, this is Air Cobra seven-niner Kilo," came a woman's voice.

"November one-zero-one Eco X-ray, where the hell are you?" answered Chad.

"You will be over me in about thirty seconds," came the voice.

"I think I have you now. It looks like a lot of snow on that runway."

"About six inches is all. I think I found the problem. I switched fuel tanks on the ground, and the engine seems smooth. I have about a third left in the tank that still works; that will get me to Watson Lake."

Chad roared over the strip watching the pilot wave out of the open canopy, as the airplane taxied through the snow. "I will climb up to three thousand feet and watch your takeoff. I suggest that you taxi back and forth a few times to flatten out that snow. Dragging your wheels through powdery snow really slows your acceleration. Once you're airborne, I will climb back up and let the powers to be know that you are okay," added Chad. "Can I give them a message?"

"Tell them Linda should be there in less than an hour. I am going to stay low to avoid burning fuel to climb. I think spending ten minutes packing the snow will burn too much fuel. I'm light, so I should get off just fine."

Chad made a sweeping turn, pointing the nose of the airplane at the center of the runway well below, and dropped some flaps to slow his airspeed.

The Air Cobra was accelerating slowly, pushing through the snow. He was about to suggest that she abort the takeoff when he watched as the pilot added more flaps, bouncing the plane out of the snow, flying in ground effect only feet off the ground.

Chad watched as the plane barely cleared the low brush at the end of the runway, struggling to climb. Seconds later, the plane slammed into the tops of a stand of birch trees where the cleared area ended, and cartwheeled. For three seconds, Chad thought that the plane might remain intact, but that hopeful thought disappeared as a tiny orange spot grew into a ball of flame.

He made another turn, dropping to only a few hundred feet. There was nothing outside the flames except the wing tips. The heat from the fire bounced the heavy P-38 a couple of hundred feet as he flew over the site. He continued to circle until the flames disappeared. There was no movement.

"Colonel Wayne," called Chad climbing back through 10,000 feet, "are you still on frequency?"

"I'm up. What did you find?"

"I will have a full report. I even have photographs. Tell Watson Lake that they need to get a recovery team out to that strip. There is a lot of snow on the strip, so they will need skis. There is nothing recoverable from the plane, so this will be a body recovery mission, Sir."

The left engine of the P-38 began to sputter. He looked down and watched the fuel gage bouncing on empty. *Damn, Gritt you idiot, fly the airplane*, he thought as he switched on the pump that moved fuel from the axillary tanks to the main tanks for the first time on the trip.

The old pilot's adage rushed through his head. *Flying is not inherently unsafe, just terribly unforgiving to errors in judgment.*

An hour later, he worked in the bitter cold to remove the film from his camera and load new film. He and Wayne walked the film to the office of the base commander where Chad briefed the leader of the flight of Air Cobras on what he had watched.

"Would you like to see a picture of Linda?" asked her flight leader opening a file.

"No ma'am, I would prefer not to have her face in the dreams I am going to have for months."

CHAPTER 20

DUTCH HARBOR, ALASKA, MARCH 1942

The arrival of a dozen P-38s was received by those already stationed at the cold windy base with a yawn. Those commanding the Army, Army Air Corps and Navy personnel wrestled with three evils. The troops were tired of working around the clock to build a base and outlying bases in total wilderness and in weather that anywhere else would leave the populace sheltering at home. Second, the troops were bored, with no entertainment yet available on the base. And third, the troops felt worthless or at least wasted with the war in the Pacific being fought in Asia and the South Pacific.

Gritt had been able to spend no more than an hour with Mark since his arrival two weeks before. Lt. Colonel Wayne pressed the only pilot in the squadron with winter flying experience, to spend every daylight hour working with others trying to cram years of winter experience into their heads in weeks.

The winds screamed among the parked planes, scouring the wet snow off the upwind wings and piling it in the wind shadow of the fuselage on the downwind wings. In the bay, two Navy launches were busy retrieving a Navy PBY amphibious plane that had torn free from her mooring buoy. Chad stood in front of a group of pilots from several units, diagraming how turbulence from the mountainous islands they were operating in, could flip an aircraft inverted or turn it ninety degrees from its heading and how to anticipate and avoid that turbulence by studying the terrain. He glanced at the calendar. It was Tuesday somewhere that it mattered.

Since his arrival he had received only one message from Captain Wilson — sit tight while he worked through some chain of command issues.

Captain Roads had arrived back at the base after a four day unscheduled trip to Anchorage. He, Wayne, and the heads of intelligence from both the Army and Navy were waiting in the base commander's office, responding to an urgent message to drop everything for a meeting. Chad was the only junior officer summoned.

The Army general sat with his hands folded on his desk, a dour look on his face as Gritt saluted. "Take a seat Captain Gritt, since this meeting seems to be all about you and one of your friends."

The general turned to Captain Roads. "All right Rocky, read them the message you brought back from Anchorage."

Roads slipped a pair of wire-framed glasses on to his nose and opened a file. "From Captain Walter Wilson on behalf of the joint chiefs of staff," he started. "You have at your base an Army Captain by the name of Chad Gritt who has been trained in the use of a specialized aircraft capable of providing precise photographic recon, more accurate and detailed than normal air recon. He is also trained in the use of a specialized radio that can be of service in monitoring Japanese radio transmissions, including ground tactical. You are to extend every possible support to Captain Gritt in his assigned mission to monitor and define any and all Japanese activity in your area of operation and the mission of the Special Operations Group to use that information and information from all other sources available to determine Japanese Intentions." Roads took a sip of water. "With no command ranking officer from this office assigned to your theater of operations it is ordered that Navy Captain Rocky R. Roads shall in addition to his engineering duties act a liaison between the Special

Operations Group and Captain Gritt within the command structure of the Operations Theater."

Chad chanced a glance at the assembled officers, noting their demeanor. Collectively they could have frozen hot coffee in seconds.

"It is further ordered that the civilian in the employ of the Navy Seabees by the name of Mark O'Hara be extended the courtesy afforded the Special Operations Group. Mr. O'Hara is hereby transferred to the Military Intelligence Service (MIS) and assigned to the Special Operations Group. Captain Roads and Captain Gritt will interview Mr. O'Hara pertaining to specific intelligence that Mr. O'Hara may be able to offer about Japanese intentions and other matters of interest to the United States."

Roads flipped to the second page of the orders. "Those directly reporting to the Special Operations Group will coordinate their findings with this office to the greatest degree possible. When appropriate they will share their findings with the intelligence groups of the theater of operations. When possible, they will work with those intelligence groups to provide real time information to the commanders of the theater of operations. However, under no circumstances shall anyone risk compromising the mission or activities of the Special Operations Group. Their activities are deemed superior to all other considerations. Very Truly Yours…" Roads turned to Gritt. "You know more about this mission than I do. Give these fine officers as much briefing as you can."

Chad rose, a touch of sweat ran along his nose and chin in the cool room. "There are some very sketchy reports that the Japanese may have some interest in the Aleutians." He took a moment to organize his thoughts, making sure that he was not providing any information that might point to highly classified intelligence sources. "We all know how bad the winter weather is here, so the guess is that whatever is going to happen will be in the summer. No one knows whether that means this summer."

"As your briefings here have indicated, American long-range bombers are capable of inflicting serious damage along the islands of northern Japan from bases planned further out along the Aleutian island chain. The people I work with believe that the Japanese will act to keep American forces as far away as possible."

"Captain," replied Wayne, "our Navy already have airborne search planes scouring the skies. Those PBY's are covering possible approach routes out more than five hundred miles from here."

"Agreed, Sir," replied Gritt. "The Special Operations Group believes that the Japanese will land intelligence parties ashore before they commence any invasion. My job is to look for and listen for that type of activity. If they do land on one of the remote islands, I am to try to determine just how serious they are, and what additional threat they pose. Any information I pick up will be correlated with information from a number of additional classified sources."

"And what about your friend Ishihara?" snarled the Major in charge of Army intelligence. "It just doesn't make sense to have a Japanese spy watching everything we are doing."

Roads cleared his throat. "I assume Major that you are referring to my new employee, Mr. O'Hara."

"We have detected transmissions from his house, Sir. They have been in English, but seem to be aimed at his father, using a California call sign. His father has not been found. He should have reported for possible relocation to one of the camps, but when the Army checked his house, they found a bunch of American nurses living there." The major smiled smugly at Gritt.

"I personally leased the house," admitted Gritt. "I made it available to the nurses who helped me while I was in the hospital in order to free up needed rooms on the base. Michi and Kiko Ishihara were visiting his parents in Japan when the war broke out. They were detained."

"So, they were plants, placed by the Japanese years ago," snarled the Major. "Who knows what secrets they took back to Japan."

Chad watched, as most of the room warmed to the Major's narrative. He hadn't known that somehow Mark had reconnected with his parents. He didn't know about the radio. The direction of the conversation pissed him off. He closed his eyes, thinking of the shock that both he and Mark felt when they found their brothers' bodies not thirty miles from where they sat.

"Nanisore go imi suru koto wa, wareware wa wareware ga Nihon de shinraidediru hito kara no joho e no akusseu o motte iru to iu kotodesu," offered Gritt.

"I don't speak Japanese, Captain," snarled the Major.

"I said, what that means is that we have access to information from someone we can trust in Japan," replied Gritt. "The Ishihara's are my second family."

"They also appear to have access to information right here in Dutch Harbor from someone they trust, don't they Captain?" continued the major.

"That is enough, Bradbury," interrupted the General. "I don't like this much either, but we have orders from the offices of the joint chiefs. You continue to monitor and if you have concerns, take them to Captain Roads here."

"I don't like the entire idea of some rogue intelligence operation operating right under our noses," snarled Bradbury. "It's hard enough to work with the damned Navy."

"Dare mo karera no ricebowl kara taberu hito o sukide wa arimasen," whispered Chad.

"Speak up Captain. You have proven you speak Japanese," snarled the Major. "But I'll bite, just what did you just say?"

"I said, Major, that I don't blame you for your concerns, no one likes anyone eating out of their rice bowl."

Roads decided it was time to wrap up the meeting before the conflict in the room cost him what little good will he still maintained. "How long do you need to wrap up your morning briefing?" he asked Chad.

"Another hour, Sir."

"Good, that will give you time to go visit your old friend this evening. I will of course be going with you. I will have a messenger send a note that we will be there for dinner. I will pick you up at six."

Not ready to throw in the towel, Bradbury stood, throwing his notes into his battered briefcase. "The road to the other side of the bay is snowed in."

"When the time comes, I will invite you too, Major," spat Roads. "One great thing about commanding the Seabees is that we have road graders available."

Mark welcomed the two men at the door. "I haven't been able to get out fishing for the last three days," he started, so the best I can do is a stew from canned whatever."

"Then we won't be needing these pork chops," laughed Roads.

CHAPTER 21

SEA OF OKHOTSK, NORTH OF JAPAN, APRIL 1942

General Fumi had requested a water-powered generator and radio for the mission. What had arrived at the base had been a huge radio base station and a diesel generator that a dozen men could never move up a rugged mountain. The replacements would have to come from the Marines and clearing the red tape between the Army and the Navy had taken a week. Everything was starting behind schedule.

On the huge bridge of the transport submarine, Peter Yami stood next to the young commanding officer. Peter was fighting off the seasickness that had wrenched his insides all day. He had heard that travel by submarine was smooth with almost no sensation of motion, because the craft rode well below the effects of any surface storms. The speed underwater of eight knots meant that the trip from northern Japan to the waters off from Unalaska Island would take weeks under water. The speed on the surface of the streamlined vessel allowed travel at more than three times that speed.

More importantly, the diesel engines not only drove the craft across the surface, they also charged the batteries that allowed underwater maneuvering. At underwater cruising speed, the battery charge only lasted about six hours.

Peter moved away from the captain and the three other men on watch. He would have gone below to get out of the swirling spray, but the tiny bunk he had been assigned only amplified the bouncing and twisting of the vessel, and the faint smell of diesel exhaust made the sickness worse. He had decided to stay on the deck until either the captain dived the boat, or he was so tired that he collapsed.

The young captain handed Peter a small towel that he kept in his pocket to wipe the spray from the lenses of his binoculars and smiled. "Watashitachiha-sen o daibingu shimasu."

Peter had been on the bridge for twenty hours. *It's about time that the smart ass captain dove the boat*, he thought. He stumbled toward the hatch and the ladder to the interior where one of the marines assigned to help him with the mission waited to guide him toward his bunk.

Four more days of this, and they might as well just shoot me for all the good I will be, he thought rolling into his bunk. Eight hours later, he shrugged off the fatigue and remaining nausea and sat up, banging his forehead on the bunk above. He walked toward the head, delighted that the boat was still under water and the tossing had almost vanished. Only after pulling up his pants did he recognize the growl of the diesel engines throughout the boat.

He asked for permission to climb the ladder to the deck. The captain nodded toward him without dropping the binoculars that studied the sea in front of them. "Watashi wa kitataiheiyonode, namerakana o mita koto ga arimasen," he advised.

Peter stood watching what he admitted was the smoothest Pacific Ocean that he could imagine. "Kono tenki go tsudzukimasu?"

Peter prayed that the captain would confirm that the smooth seas would continue. The night before he had been afraid that he was going to die and by the time he reached his bunk thought he had. He paused to think about the captain's answer. He agreed that the clear flat weather probably made it much easier for an enemy ship or plane to see them. Still, he hoped the captain's prayer for rough weather went unanswered.

In the distance, the small Chidori class torpedo boat assigned to escort the submarine until it reached the waters near Unalaska Island, ran in a straight line toward the target. That small ship ran five miles in front of the submarine, a more obvious target than the submarine. From the air, the torpedo boat would appear the size of an aircraft carrier compared to the tiny submarine profile.

The torpedo boat would refuel the submarine from tanks strapped to her aft deck. That had to be completed before the vessels reached the patrol limits of the enemy scout planes that intelligence had identified at the Dutch Harbor base.

Aboard the large submarine, Peter and the two marines who would join him on the island, crowded into the forward storage hold where they began inventorying the equipment and supplies provided for the mission.

The Ha-112 would creep along just underwater only a hundred miles from where the three men would be relaying messages from Mark. A special antenna attached to the periscope would allow them to remain underwater during the daylight hours, maintaining a constant watch for messages. At night, she would move further out to sea where she could run on the surface to recharge batteries.

The captain's face was drained of color as the two vessels reached the refueling point. The surrounding sea was flat, the sky almost clear. The twilight partially hid the boats, but also their enemies. "One more night and a day and we will be there," laughed Peter to the marines, specially selected because they spoke English. "We will go ashore under the cover of darkness with only the moon for light. It will take us all night to move our equipment and supplies to the hiding place."

The refueling finished just as the half-moon climbed above the horizon. The Ha-112 surged away from their escort, her captain pumping water into the ballast tanks, allowing the submarine to settle into the water until just the air intakes and the tower rose above the sea. The ballasting slowed their speed, but made the boat much harder to detect, especially from the air.

They continued north while the torpedo boat turned southwest. The night was cold, with just enough riffle to make their wake difficult to detect. They were only thirty minutes from the refueling when a man clambered from the hatch, handing the captain a message. "Nani go mondaidesu ka?" asked Peter, watching the captain.

The man handed Peter the folded message from the escort ship, now about thirty miles away. A loud klaxon sounded throughout the ship just as the lookout at the rear of the tower began to scream. Peter chanced a glance to the rear before the captain pushed him toward the ladder. The hatch was sealed and the ship tilted downward, the sounds of water flowing over the deck growing louder.

"What is going on?" asked Monzu, one of the Marines.

"Our escort is being bombed by an American flying boat," said Peter. "There is a large fire on the horizon."

The submarine stayed down for a half-hour before creeping to the surface. Her tower barely broke the surface as the captain and four lookouts raced to the bridge. Peter felt like a piece of furniture as all around him people concentrated on their jobs, all now more serious. The boat's executive officer read a signal from the radio room, and then communicated it to the captain.

The man handed the message to Peter. A single bomb had struck the escort ship, and her decks were shredded by machine gun fire, as the big American aircraft had made a single pass. The ship was desperately calling for help.

"Wareware wa seizon-sha o sagashi ni modorimasu?" asked Peter.

Peter could see the strain in the officer's face as he shook his head. "Te."

A knot formed in Peter's stomach as he realized that they would not go back to assist the survivors of the damaged ship. He had not expected "no."

"Our mission is too important, Lieutenant, to risk this submarine to save one hundred men," barked the older marine sergeant, Yumi.

Peter could tell that the marine was not happy with his show of emotion. "I cannot help but feel concern for those men hundreds of miles from any help."

"Maybe their captain will save the ship," replied Yumi.

"The Americans know where they are," replied Peter. "Maybe they will send out a rescue ship."

"Those sailors will die before accepting help from the enemy," snarled Yumi.

Peter turned toward the galley where he hoped to find a cup of tea to give him something to hold with his trembling hands. "There is no report of American long-range flying boats up here."

Yumi watched him, worried by his commander's response to the attack. "That is why we were sent here, Sir."

The following night the large submarine crept toward the coast of Unalaska Island, her captain searching for landmarks given him in the pre-mission briefing. The seas were running from the west, making the target, a small bay behind the point, an ideal place to land Peter's group. The moon showed through the thin overcast, providing light to work.

Yumi led the first of three rafts toward the shore. Monzu would go with the second and Peter with the last.

"Anata wa watashi ni busshi o hakobu no ni yakudatsu ikutsuka no dansei o teikyo shimash ka?" asked Peter.

The captain handed him the mission orders. Not only was the captain not going to provide any help moving the hundreds of pounds of supplies to their hiding spot, he had already given the men paddling the boats orders to return within one hour or they would be left.

The three scouts watched as the rafts returned to the sub, their air chambers emptied for storage. It took only a quarter-hour before the submarine disappeared under the growing waves.

"Move everything further into this cove and hide it," ordered Peter. "We will take the radio and generator and make contact with our man in the harbor. Everything else we will move tomorrow night."

"May I ask a question, Sir?" asked Monzu.

"Of course," laughed Peter, a little nervous and relieved to be off from the submarine.

"How long have you been in the service?"

Peter realized that this was the kind of question no Japanese service man would normally ask an officer. He looked down at the heavy pack he was filling. He could reprimand the man or even shoot him for such insolence, but there were only three of them and the mission required three.

"I went to an officers' summer camp two years ago before I went back to the United States to study. I received my commission then, but I have only been on active duty for six months," he growled.

"What the corporal is saying," offered Yumi, glaring at Monzu, "is stick closely to us and allow us to offer advice so that we may teach you."

Mark had been monitoring the frequency assigned to communicate with the scout party at ten in the morning and ten at night for days. His hope that the mission might have been canceled had lulled him into a sense of relief. That relief was shattered only five minutes after he switched on the radio. "Go Huskies," blared through the speaker above his head. He picked up the microphone and keyed it. "Go Trojans," he answered. "I haven't been fishing, but I have some great stories."

"I am looking forward to that," came an answer, followed by "end."

The entire exchange had taken only ten seconds. Mark picked up the new phone on his desk and depressed the disconnect button on top three times. In minutes, both Chad and Rocky were on the phone. "They are here," said Mark.

Rocky waited for Chad's response. "I need to take a run out west in the morning with a combat flight. I will stop by when I get back. We will fly right by their hiding place so that you can verify our flight. Maybe I can get some pictures."

"And I will be on a PT boat on the way over to the runway

construction at Fort Glenn," offered Roads, "back late. Be prepared to brief me tomorrow night."

Mark tossed all night, rising just before dawn when the throaty roar of the Packard engines on a PT boat rumbled across the bay. He stood in the kitchen stumbling through making coffee as he watched the glitter of the wake leave the harbor and turn west. He waited until he was sure that the scouts could hear the engines before switching on the radio, allowing it a couple of minutes to warm up.

He checked to make sure that the power on the radio was set as low as possible and keyed the microphone. "Husky, this is Trojan, did I tell you I used one salmon fly out east? End."

"Husky back, you did now. End."

Mark could imagine three men packed into the small rock hut on the side of a mountain only ten miles away. He sipped his coffee. *I have a better deal,* he thought. Still, his nerves were on edge.

An hour later, he was back at the radio. "Husky, this is Trojan. Did I tell you I caught six steelhead out east? End."

He sighed. *It is really starting.*

CHAPTER 22

DUTCH HARBOR, ALASKA, APRIL 1942

"The rest of the Army Air Corps will move over to Fort Glenn as soon as the runway is finished," offered Roads. All of the buildings will be up by the end of the month." Roads sat with the commander of the Naval Base in Dutch Harbor.

"Can't say that I will miss the Army much," snarled the commander. I will miss the cover their fighters provide though."

"I am pulling some strings to keep the P-38s here for at least the time being," laughed Roads. "I need their cover for that special P-38 snooper down on the runway. Most of the P-40s are already on the ground at Glenn."

"Got it Rocky, but you didn't set up this meeting to gloat over the Army moving. What do you need?"

"I need a submarine to sit fifty miles north of the harbor for a month. I need them to monitor and record some transmissions between this island and a Japanese submarine sitting where they can send coded messages back to Japan."

The commander poured a cup of tea from the pot on his desk. "Had to give up coffee," he spat. "Stomach just won't handle the acid anymore. My intel folks and the G-2 folks in the Army have been listening to transmissions coming from your pal O'Hara. It's all a bunch of gibberish. I will never get the admiral to approve a sub just sitting to pick up what we are getting right here."

"Tony, I can't give you the whole picture just yet. Maybe in a month or so," responded Roads. "Pass on only the bare minimum, but get me that sub, okay?"

The man sitting on the other side of the desk frowned. "That's not how the Admiral runs things. I can get in a hell of a jam if he thinks I am playing him."

Roads smiled his best New England smile. "I shared the joints chief orders with you Tony. This comes under those orders. When the time comes, I will work it out so you get credit for the final results. In the interim, you need to know that there is a Japanese Scout force on the island and they have been here for a couple of weeks. The gibberish that O'Hara is sending is coded information about the movement of our ships and planes. The scouts are passing it on to the Jap sub."

The shocked man at the desk spit the scalding tea he had just inadvertently sucked into his mouth back into his cup. "Your group is sending the enemy real time information about our movements?"

"Right O, Tony. And when the time is critical, we will be sending them all false information. That will be the right time to take out the scout team and the sub. In the interim, we need to find out just how the scouts are relaying the information we send. I need to know the frequencies used by the scouts and the sub as well as enough information to figure out their codes," said Roads.

"I still don't get it, Rocky. Why do you want to leave this enemy intelligence group in place until it isn't needed anymore? And why gather all this radio intel if we are going to shut them down?"

"Because, we intend to replace their assets with our own when they are gone."

"How much do they already know, Rocky, I mean about our strength?"

"Not a lot, at least from the codes they supplied Mark. For example, they have no code for B-17 because they don't think there are any in Alaska. Until we told them, they didn't know that there were any fighters out here. We have given them just enough information so they think that there might be a half-dozen P-40s and six P-38s. When the time comes, we will tell them that the fighters went east, back to the mainland. To the best of our knowledge, they know nothing about the base at Fort Glenn."

"Rocky, the admiral has a whole task force including a half dozen subs out blocking the way from Japan. Why don't we just go kill the Japs on the island and sink that sub out there?"

"Tony, I don't know how, but I can tell you the Japanese are coming. They can hide an armada in the lousy weather in the north Pacific unless we get really lucky," replied Roads.

"You have spent too much time making money in the oil fields, Rocky. We are better than that. If you string out six ships with radar, they can see anything coming over a swath of two-hundred miles."

"With all due respect to our old classmates and the men they command, you have a Japanese scout team not more than thirty miles from here, landed by submarine, and transmitting both toward the harbor and out to sea. If I had walked in here and asked you if that were possible just an hour ago, you would have laughed me out of your office."

"That was the kind of gotcha that got you suspended from the football team," laughed Tony. "I can still feel the muscle balm in my jock. All right, the admiral will be here late this week, I will see what I can do."

Roads headed for the door, slipping his heavy wool coat over an arm.

"One more question Rocky. Why it is important to replace the enemy assets after we kill them?"

"Imagine how the planners in Japan would feel if a source they trusted told them that we were building four new bases along the Aleutians and that we were staging a half-million men getting ready to invade northern Japan?"

"They sure couldn't send a bunch more reinforcements to where they are already operating. I will sweeten the message for the admiral by letting him know that your man Gritt gave us the direction of the radio chatter that allowed us to bomb that Jap ship a couple of weeks ago. We had hoped for survivors, someone to tell us why it was out there all alone, but there was nothing left but a handful of bodies and an oil slick."

CHAPTER 23

CHITOSE, JAPAN, MAY 1942

General Fumi smiled at his subordinate as Colonel Ito stepped from the staff car. "I wanted you here so that we can discuss how our disinformation campaign can assist Admiral Hosogaya's mission into the Aleutians. Admiral Kakuta is already at sea with carrier division four, practicing operations in the northern Kurile Islands. Admiral Hosagaya with the rest of the fleet will sail tomorrow along with the invasion force transport ships.

"Permission to speak freely, Sir," replied Ito.

"Granted."

"If you had summoned me here to shine your boots I would have gladly come. I am very pleased to be out of that northern hell hole."

"The Korean girl you commandeered from the border police does not please you, Haru?"

His boss seldom surprised Ito, but he had not considered that his personal life might be of interest. "She is just fine for a Korean."

"That is good, take a day off. Then you will be flying back to keep her company. When you finally leave Karafuto, will you have her shot like the other Koreans that your soldiers use for target practice?"

Ito was shaken for a minute by the anger in his commander's face. "Do you want me to refer every spy I encounter to you for judgment?" asked Ito.

"No Haru, that will not be necessary. I am too busy. Besides, who am I to interfere with what pleases you?"

Fumi opened a small folder on the table. He placed three pages above the folder and pointed to the first. "Please read these in order."

The first page laid out the strength of each force moving against the Aleutians. The second was the timetable for the attacks including the bombing attack at Dutch Harbor and other harassing attacks. The third was a schedule for the invasion of three islands, Adak, Kiska and Attu.

"These are not the same islands that we were briefed on last winter," observed Ito.

"Good, I knew that you were listening. I just hope that Michi and his son were also engaged. If they are truly helping us it will make no difference, but if they are supporting their new country, we must allow them to reveal what they saw."

"We must make sure they see dates different than the ones in the original plan and we must give them just enough information to confuse them on the strength we are sending north."

"They have already given us good information, have they not?" asked Ito. "They confirmed that there are a few fighters at Dutch Harbor. They seem to indicate that the fighters are actually based on the mainland at Cold Bay and rotate into the Unalaska base. They have also confirmed long-range Navy patrol planes in Dutch Harbor. The sitting duck we hoped for may have some teeth."

"Then we will help the Navy extract them," smiled Fumi.

❀

The ferry from Hokkaido slammed into the pilings that guided it to the ramp in Otomari. The inexperienced captain took three tries to dock the vessel. Haruku shook his head. There was no tide run or wind. He had not been back to Otomari since he and Airi had turned the summerhouse over to his son months before. It had been a blessing to have Michi there to work with Roku to open the fish plant and prepare it for the season. But that was not what brought him back to Karafuto.

His spring swing to the company fish processing plants allowed him to roam all over Hokkaido Island. The fishing boats the company operated had become a challenge. Half of the experienced captains he employed were now in the service, and he had been informed that he would be allocated only 40 percent of the fuel he had purchased the previous year. After watching the ferry landing, he made a mental note to buy up every used tire he could find to cushion the company docks.

Haruku found it hard to keep his head in the critical details of running the business when the country he loved was evolving into an armed camp. He picked up the small travel bag at his feet and headed for the passenger ramp.

Michi was pushing a pallet of empty cans from the warehouse to the cannery when he saw his father. "I didn't get the message that you were coming," he said, reaching out to shake hands with his father. The hug he got surprised him.

"Let's walk, son," suggested Haruku, setting his bag on top of the stack of cans.

The two men turned toward a small road that paralleled the harbor.

"You are troubled," whispered Michi.

"I am," responded Haruku. "I believe that I am about to become a spy against my own country, against the emperor. The reports about the glowing victory against the United States at Pearl Harbor were exaggerated. The Japanese bombers and torpedo planes sunk perhaps a dozen ships, including three or four battleships."

"That is what the reports indicated," said Michi solemnly.

"The American aircraft carriers were not even there. I have friends in the government who tell me that most of the ships sunk at their moorings have been raised and are being repaired. Only weeks ago, there was another sea battle in the Pacific. There, both sides seem to have lost an equal number of ships, including aircraft carriers. I cannot divulge the name of the man who told me, not even to you. Any mention of this would cost him his life."

"We both were very public with our concerns about the industrial might of Japan versus that of the United States. I don't know, but I would bet that for every ship the Americans have lost, they have three more under construction," guessed Michi.

"And Japan will be hard pressed to replace its losses for years," finished Haruku. "Remember in your American history classes at USC, how President Lincoln chose a general to command the union forces against the confederacy? General Grant, I think was his name. Do you remember how he fought the war?"

"No, I don't," laughed Michi. "I was probably studying for that test over a pitcher of beer."

Haruku laughed, shaking his head. "That is what I expect you did in a lot of your classes. You missed the dean's list two full years. Anyway, General Grant attacked and attacked. He knew that the North could replace soldiers and equipment at a rate four or five times faster than the South. He was willing to take casualties in order to bleed his enemy to death."

"And you think that is what the United States is doing to Japan, Father?"

"From what you told me about your meeting with this General Fumi and his staff, the plan was to hit America with such a blow that they would quit. That has not happened. Now there will be a second blow. This time against the Aleutians where my grandson has been sent by the warmongers of my nation. I, myself, saw that two aircraft carriers have already headed to sea. A dozen other ships will be ready for sea in days, including troop transports. The attack will come in days not months, and for what? For every airplane we destroy, America will build five; for every ship we sink, she will build three. Each time we kill a farm boy from Iowa or an auto mechanic from Nevada, four more will volunteer to take their place." Haruku picked a branch from a tree beside the lane and began plucking the leaves from it, one at a time.

"You know I can get coded messages to Mark don't you Father?" asked Michi.

"I do, and I must do everything to try to stop my country from committing suicide."

"Father, to the men leading Japan, especially the Army officers that the Prime Minister has surrounded himself with, suicide is not only acceptable, it is more honorable than life," Michi said with concern.

"Maybe if the strategy originally attempted by Japan was to work against Japan, they will stop. Maybe if they lose in such a hard and unmistakable way, the emperor will throw them out and bring back civilian leaders with common sense. The military's promise that Japan can never be attacked has already turned out to be a lie."

"What do you mean, father?"

"The reports from mid-April of sabotage by anti-war activists in the Tokyo area are a lie. My friend tells me that the Americans flew bombers all the way from the United States and bombed Japan. No one in Japan believed that the Americans could build a bomber with that range."

"Father, only weeks ago I was ordered to send a message to Mark by that scum Ito. I used the message to send Mark almost the opposite of what I was ordered to send. Every message that I send is recorded, but with the exception of that transmission I have only talked about family. Tomorrow is one of the days that I can try to reach Mark. I will pass on your message."

"Look who dropped in for dinner," spewed Michi, as Kiko and Mary met the old Ford pickup pulling up to the house. It took a moment to notice that neither was smiling.

"What is wrong?' asked Haruku, picking up on the mood more quickly than his son.

"Our minders in the gardener's house were here this morning. Colonel Ito has ordered that we not use the radio for any purpose without his personal permission. He will be here the day after tomorrow to explain. You are to remain home that day. In the interim, the minders have taken the microphone."

"Do you think we are under suspicion?" asked Michi.

"I don't know, but this is very sudden and cannot be good," replied Kiko.

"I agree."

"Then Father, you should spend the night and then go back to Sapporo tomorrow. There is no reason for you to get caught up in this. I know that Ito has nothing in his recordings that cannot be explained. In the interim, I will work on the wording for a message for Mark. I expect they will want us to transmit again or they would have taken the radio."

❉

Ito's driver had not improved much over the winter. The proof came when Ito was seen walking down the driveway toward the house. "After we agree on a message for your son, you will take that truck you drive and pull my car out of the ditch up the road," ordered Ito.

"I cannot send Mark a message. Your men confiscated the microphone for the radio," responded Michi.

"It will be returned in the morning in time for you to transmit. You have new instructions for contacting your son. We want you to send a message putting him at ease. We know the enemy is listening."

Ito opened his case and laid out three pieces of paper. He looked over at Mary, waiting at the kitchen in her apron. "Tell your Korean to bring us tea."

CHAPTER 24

SEATTLE, WASHINGTON, MAY 1942

Seattle is a beautiful city when the sun is shining, thought Carmen, as she watched a handful of sailboats slipping through the waves paralleling the ship. She still smiled at the shock on the face of her immediate commander. The doughty colonel at Madigan Hospital where she had just finished a crash course on how to be a soldier voiced the same sentiments.

"Well that's a first, young lady. You are the first to volunteer for duty in Alaska. I don't even know where the Aleutian Islands are, but I will note that as your first choice. I would ask you why you want to go there, but I have an idea that I already know the answer."

The ship's dash from Seattle to the naval base at Dutch Harbor would take eight days. A faster trip, routed through the Straights of Juan de Fuca to the southwest end of Vancouver Island and then straight to Dutch harbor was too risky. Too many Japanese submarines. Instead, ships headed north followed the inside passage along the British Columbia coast, each captain choosing one of the entrances to the archipelago for escape into the Pacific.

The cargo ship was only two years old; her captain, determined to keep her afloat. That night, Carmen and the other five nurses dined at the captain's table. "I thank all of you for going north to take care of our troops," offered the captain, a roly-poly man in his early fifties.

"We are happy to be doing our duty," replied Carmen, speaking for all of them. "The magazines all advertise Alaska adventures. We figured we would let Uncle Sam pay for ours," she laughed.

"No sightseeing on this trip, I hope," replied the captain. "Other than the ocean, the only parts of Alaska I want to see are the hills around Dutch Harbor. If the weather holds, we can make it in four days once we head into the Pacific." He fussed with his pipe. "But it never holds."

"If it takes five days, you expect to make port on June first?" she asked.

"I want to be there on the first and back at sea the night of the second," he replied.

Somehow, Carmen was the only nurse aboard who made it to dinner the third night, the first out in the open Pacific. By the fifth night, half of the nurses had shaken off their pale green complexions and joined the officers at the table. "I am sorry about the winds," smiled the captain. "The seas are actually better than I expected. We will make port ahead of schedule."

"Some of us probably won't be coming back with you," laughed Carmen.

"I don't know, miss," replied their quiet host. "There is no war up there. If you are careful around the water and take your cold weather training seriously, you should all be just fine."

"That's not what I mean," she giggled. "After the trip up, I suspect that about half of us will find someone to marry with roots in Alaska just so they don't have to cross the Gulf of Alaska again. It's either that or shoot themselves."

"Maybe that's why they don't issue nurses sidearms," laughed the captain finally getting used to Carmen's humor.

The ship slipped into the deep harbor late in the afternoon. A tall Army doctor with movie star looks and a ring a quarter inch wide on his ring finger met them. "I am sorry, ladies, we didn't expect you until tomorrow. Your quarters are being painted as we speak. If you don't mind, it would be better for you to remain aboard until tomorrow afternoon. Besides, the food is probably better than ours." He laughed. "I will personally escort you to the new nurses' quarters tomorrow afternoon."

The evening found all six nurses at the side of the ship where they could watch the hustle of the new base. To their front and rear, slings of supplies were hoisted out of the holds. The ship's captain trundled up with six cloth bags.

"I have a present for each of you. In the bags you will find a bottle of scotch and one of bourbon and two bottles of wine. You will find that the officers club here has cheap drinks, but once in a while you may need a drink in private; you know, just you and your thoughts. I spent some time in the hospital during the last war."

"Thank you," offered Carmen who had become the group's spokesperson. "I have a question. What are those funny crates of things that look like huge sausages that they are unloading right now?"

"Those, my dear, are 500- pound bombs for our bombers. The small crates on top are the fins they attach to stabilize them. We had a hundred of them in the holds." The captain smiled at the women and headed back to the bridge.

We just crossed more than 2,000 miles of ocean, in a war, with no escort, riding on 50,000 pounds of bombs, she thought. "I'll crack my bottle of Scotch tonight if anyone would like to have a drink to celebrate just getting here safely."

❊

It was noon the next day when two cars and two trucks stopped next to the gangway. The doctor they had met the previous day supervised the loading of the women's personal baggage and a small mountain of medical supplies. Carmen and her friend Cathy Hedlund were assigned a room on the second floor of a barracks, only steps from the new hospital building.

"Parece que mi antiguo dormitorio de la Universidad," rattled off Cathy, bouncing on the narrow metal cot with its thin cotton mattress.

Carmen smiled at the tall woman with jet-black hair and pale green eyes. "Where did you do your training?" asked Carmen.

"In Seattle," replied Cathy. "My mom was a singer and a dancer who traveled with a Latin band until one evening in Seattle when she met a handsome Swede who was a medical student. She broke up the band to become a doctor's wife."

"Anyway, you are right, this room needs some color," replied Carmen.

Cathy walked over to the window, pulling aside the heavy black curtain. "Here we are in one of the most beautiful places that God ever created, and we end up with a view of the hospital next door."

CHAPTER 25

THE NORTH PACIFIC, ONE HUNDRED SIXTY MILES SOUTHWEST OF DUTCH HARBOR, JUNE 1942

Admiral Kakuji Kakuta had been on the bridge of the small escort carrier all night. Since his graduation from the Imperial Naval Academy in 1911, he had risen steadily through the ranks through careful planning and flawless execution of every assignment given him. Thirty years of peacetime discipline had prepared him for his first taste of battle, supporting the Japanese invasion of the Philippines and raids against the British in India and Ceylon.

He sipped from a huge porcelain mug of tea, as he listened to the latest report from his weather officer. He was nervous, more than he had been in his previous combat operations. Here, the weather was as dangerous as the enemy, he reminded himself. Here, he could launch the three dozen planes scheduled to attack the lightly defended American base on Unalaska Island and lose all of them if the weather turned and they couldn't find their way home. He had no interest in sacrificing his naval aviators on a diversion attack. The attack on Dutch Harbor's only real purpose was to pull the American aircraft carriers north of Pearl Harbor where they could be destroyed.

If we are to decoy the Americans for our attack on Midway, we must strike today, he thought. It was time to believe the briefers. The weather was a gift to the emperor. *The weather over our tiny armada will be better than that over the enemy at Dutch Harbor. Still, it will be good enough for the planned strike, especially for low altitude attacks,* he noted in his journal. "Pairotto o samashimasu," he ordered.

His aide rushed from the bridge to wake the pilots. They would have just enough time for breakfast and a final briefing before launching.

An hour later, the admiral watched as plane after plane roared from the deck below him. In the distance, he could see the aircraft from his second carrier buzzing around the ship like bees. The aircraft carriers *Ryujo and Jun'yo* would launch half their aircraft, holding back a few dive-bombers and high-level bombers for a second strike and most of the Zero fighters to protect his small fleet.

The Americans are so punctual, he thought, *I hope they are all asleep, waiting for that silly man with the bugle to call them to work.* He looked at his watch. *This morning I will wake them. If we are successful, only some of them will need to be awakened tomorrow.*

❁

The first bomb struck next to the radio station just after the radio operators transmitted their scheduled early morning report. The operators raced from their small building to see what had exploded. "My God, it's the Japs," screamed a young lieutenant. He and the three men standing with him dove into a ditch next to the building as a Japanese fighter rolled up onto a wing and turned toward where they stood. The ground they had just vacated erupted into a curtain of dirt, as two lines of machine gun bullets ripped past the huddling men. The young lieutenant was up and running before the plane finished its strafing run. He swung the door into the radio building so hard that it ripped from the hinges. "We are being attacked by Japanese aircraft," he screamed into the phone. He dialed another number and repeated his warning just as the wall between him and the door erupted with machine gun bullets, cutting the building almost in half. The older sergeant at the radio console disappeared in the flying debris.

"The radio link to Fort Glenn is down," came a call from the other side of the room. "Let's get the hell out of here, lieutenant."

From the dust, the sergeant emerged, charging for the door. The ground shook from the impact of bombs. The two men ran from the building, as another Japanese fighter raked it with fire. Diving into a ditch, the lieutenant landed on top of the two privates. "I am going to recommend you two for a decoration," he gasped.

What about me, Sir?" came a call from just a few feet away. "I followed you back into the com shack."

"That you did, sergeant, and it was a brave thing. But these two showed exemplary common sense in the face of overwhelming enemy strength. That has to count for something. Hell, all we did was try to get ourselves killed."

Near the harbor, Captain Rocky Roads rushed from his quarters, tugging at his belt trying to secure his pants over a stomach that decades earlier had been rock hard. Seconds later, Spiff arrived panting, having run the three hundred yards from his quarters dressed in only his shorts, undershirt and shoes.

"Get the men out of the barracks and into the air-raid shelters. Then see what we can do to help the anti-aircraft guys." A Japanese plane passed over the men, heading out to sea, trailing a faint line of smoke. "See if you can find some men to go help at the tank farm." Roads pointed at the fuel tanks at the other end of the base where black smoke trailed into the sky. "They didn't hit any of the large tanks or there would be more smoke. Maybe we can save some of the fuel."

The two men watched as a bomb hit one of the barracks buildings at the Army base. "God, I hope the men got out of that building," called Roads who had started to run.

"Where are you headed, Sir?" asked Spiff.

"I am going to go get O'Hara and then I am off to find the base commanders and shove that note I told you about, the one from Mark's father right up their butts."

Roads drove the jeep up to the front of Mark's house. He found him standing in his pajamas with a pair of binoculars glued to his eyes. "Get dressed," yelled Roads. "Maybe now they will listen. Bring your notes on that message from your dad."

The raid was over before Mark and Roads fought their way through the small crowd in the Administration building. They found the two base commanders standing on the back porch, watching the retreating Japanese planes. "Give me just five minutes, gentlemen," barked Roads in a tone that only a citizen soldier could have gotten away with.

"All right, Rocky," one of the men answered, wiping nervous sweat from his forehead. Just give us a minute or two to set up a quick briefing on the damage and the casualties."

Five minutes later, the men sat as Mark scrawled the message on the chalkboard at the front of the room.

Your mother and I are well

The fleet is still in port, but fishing will start late.

We are having trouble recruiting fishermen

The storms are over until late December

I am happy you found people to run the canneries

After the war we can look at the islands we discussed

I am happy you are well

"Go ahead, Mark," said Roads.

"Gentlemen, my father gave us a clear warning about this only a couple of days ago. Ignore the first line in the message. Read the second but reverse its meaning. The fleet had just left port when he sent this. The attack will start soon. Now, ignore the third line.

The fourth line says the storm will come in early June. Remember the chart with the months listed with the first six on one side of the paper and the last six parallel on the other. June equals December and vice versa."

Mark watched, as the men finally began to really listen. In the fifth line he told me that the islands that we were told were targets were not the ones that were going to be hit. I told you that those islands were safe. They still are. We need to look at what islands make sense."

Roads spoke up. "The messages in the other lines are also important, but they can be taken at face value. The Japanese are having manpower problems. They are searching for people to even run canneries to feed the people. But the critical part is we knew this was coming. I know that we had other intelligence sources that told us this was going to happen, but Mark gave you specific information about when."

There was a knock at the door, and a tired looking major in a medical smock stepped into the room. "I don't know the totals yet, gentlemen, but we lost at least twenty men in the two barracks that were hit."

"I will not speak for the general here," offered the old Navy captain across the table; "but even my wife sometimes has to hit me between the eyes with a club to get me to listen. I guarantee you that she only has to hit me once."

The radio room at Fort Glenn had requested two confirmations of the attack on Dutch Harbor.

The transmissions had come in on low power settings and on frequencies different than normally used to communicate between the bases. The P-40 Warhawks began scrambling almost an hour after the attack, first flying over Dutch Harbor only sixty miles away to confirm the reports and then turning out to sea to the south of the island, looking for retreating enemy aircraft.

On the ground, Chad stood, shifting from one foot to the next as the mechanics put the last of the inspection plates back onto his airplane. *What a hell of a time for an inspection and an oil change*, he thought. He was airborne a half-hour after the fighters. The oil change would have to wait.

He climbed the P-38 to 10,000 feet, well above where he expected the retreating enemy to be and turned south, out over the ocean at a slow cruise. In front of him, he began to dial the radio searching known enemy frequencies. Fifteen minutes later, he picked up Japanese on a frequency used by Imperial Navy aviators. The conversation was from four scout planes from at least two Japanese cruisers. They were reporting nothing in a search for American ships. He began playing with another dial in front of him, waiting for a needle to stabilize on an instrument marked out with the 360 degrees of the compass. He marked the direction on a map clipped to a board strapped to his knee.

He reached up and switched to the communications radio and keyed his microphone. He relayed the direction of the Japanese planes to the fighters searching south of Unalaska. In seconds, one flight of Warhawks turned to a new heading. Chad switched back to the search radio and again dialed in the chatter from the scout planes. He again marked the direction on his map, the second reading giving him the direction of flight of the Japanese planes.

He relayed the new information to the fighters. It took only nine minutes for the American fighters to find the first Japanese plane and only minutes following it to determine its direction of flight, as it closed on a second scout seaplane. Before the Warhawks could attack, two more scout planes were sighted.

Chad listened on the radio as the P-40s maneuvered to attack all four enemy planes. He switched back to the frequency that the Japanese were using. He listened intently, as the pilots reported the attack to their ships and then as a first and then a second sent frantic calls as their aircraft began to disintegrate around them, torn to shreds by bullets from the American fighters. He knew that he should be rejoicing as he heard the Japanese pilots inform their comrades that they were ditching in the sea. He closed his eyes for just a moment, his brain filled with the image of Mark's little brother lying under a tarp, his face still and blue.

The P-40s chasing the remaining two scout planes damaged them, but running short of fuel, broke off the attack. Chad radioed the location of the two downed Japanese planes to an American patrol boat. He made a low pass over the sinking aircraft, the crews of each staring at him from sinking planes. He watched one man in each aircraft step onto a sinking wing, covered with bitterly cold water. Each tried to help a second man from their cockpit. The sea around the downed planes was turning red. He rocked his wings as he made a second pass and then turned toward home. In ten minutes, in the cold North Pacific, the Japanese would lose consciousness. In thirty they would be dead.

Moments later, he passed over a patrol boat bearing down on the sinking enemy aircraft. He would need fuel soon.

❈

The new nurses rushed to the hospital, most still wearing slippers. In the triage center, only a handful of patients lay on gurneys, most with superficial blast wounds. Three men pulled from the rubble of the barracks were wheeled into the center by a handful of firemen and their friends.

Carmen rushed to a man covered by a bloody sheet. She lifted the sheet, revealing a length of wood driven into the man's chest below his heart. "This man needs a doctor right away," she called, trying to smile. "What's your name?"

"Malcolm, ma'am," came the answer in a raspy voice.

"You with the Arkansas National Guard anti-aircraft unit? What about that doctor?" she called over her shoulder.

"Yup ma'am, I was on duty until after midnight. I slept right through the alarm sounding. My ma back in Arkansas says I can sleep right through a tornado."

The man's breathing was slowing as Carmen searched for anything she could do to help the critically wounded man. "How about that doc?"

The handsome doctor who had escorted the nurses from the ship quietly pushed her aside as he arrived to examine the wound. Carmen noticed that he still wore pajamas under his coat. Both were soaked in blood. The doctor turned to her. "Just hold his hand nurse. I need to see if I can save either of the other two."

"Malcolm, my name is Carmen. I am from a ranch down in New Mexico. Do you like horses?" she asked as she squeezed his hand.

"We," the man was wheezing now, "we never could afford a horse, ma'am."

A moment later Malcolm began to convulse, a huge push of air rising through his throat emerging as a rattle. She watched as his eyes started to glaze over. She struggled to control her shaking as she pulled the sheet up over his face, turning to look for something she might do that mattered.

CHAPTER 26

THE NORTH PACIFIC, TWO HUNDRED MILES FROM DUTCH HARBOR, JUNE 1942

Thirty hours without sleep made Admiral Kakuta truculent. He sat in the briefing thankful his conditioning helped him stay awake. Those around him guarded every word. The picture that the returning pilots painted was very different from the intelligence that he had been supplied. The hills around the harbor had been alive with air defenses. While there were only a few planes on the runway, a dozen or more P-40s had responded to the attack. Maybe the aircraft were patrolling somewhere when his planes struck. His attackers had only lost three planes in the raid, none of them to the Warhawks, but the four scout planes from the cruisers had all been destroyed. Two of them crash landing close enough to their ships to allow rescue of the crews.

The squadron leaders offered no excuses when they reported that they had destroyed little of real consequence. Kakuta accepted the responsibility for poor targeting. This was not like Pearl Harbor where the attacking planes found aircraft packed along the runways and a harbor full of warships. Even in this godforsaken place the Americans were learning to fight.

As briefed, they had ignored the handful of cargo ships in the harbor. They managed only to set a refueling truck on fire at the fuel tank farm. Three buildings were burning when the attack ended. The enemy had been surprised but escaped almost unharmed. Aerial photos showed a base three times the size that he had been briefed on. The enemy must be laughing at his incompetence.

That would change tomorrow. The enemy would never expect them to attack again. They would stand down when no attack occurred early. They would find their late breakfasts came with fireworks. He left orders for all of the commanders to get some sleep. The convoy would steam away from Unalaska until midnight and then turn to run back at the enemy base at flank speed. He would launch a second attack from only a hundred miles out, striking after the enemy figured that no attack was coming.

He hoped the news of the attack on Dutch Harbor would divert the enemy's attention from Midway Island where a massive attack was scheduled for the morning of the fourth of June. The intelligence he was getting from the enemy harbor included little about the defenses. The Army spy's reports on the comings and goings of ships and planes were important. The unexpected defenses his pilots had found meant that it was not enough. Before retiring to his cabin, he sent that information to General Fumi.

At Fort Glenn, the mechanics worked all night preparing the fighters. In spite of the weather, a screen of scout-planes had fanned out to the south of the base, finding nothing. At sea, a half dozen Navy ships found only empty ocean. The one plane equipped to find the enemy sat under a tarp as the mechanics scrambled to fashion inspection plates that had blown off from Gritt's P-38, their screws left untightened in the haste to get the plane airborne that morning.

At Dutch, there were two issues. The first was to prepare for a possible second attack and then there was the issue of where to put a cemetery. They had experienced less than one hour of combat and already had twenty-five body bags to take care of.

The engineers – both Seabees and civilian contractors – pitched in to help the anti-aircraft artillery units move most of their guns from the hillsides, repositioning them around the harbor. The low level dive-bombers and the strafing Japanese fighter planes had delivered most of the damage. Moving the guns massed the firepower closer to the ground. The other advantage was that the guns could be used to help defend against an invasion.

At the cannery, Mark sent a constant stream of messages as patrol aircraft and ships came and went. He even reported that six P-40s had taken off and turned immediately to climb over the mountains heading toward the mainland. It was the first false message he had sent, a critical piece of misdirection that explained where the fighters had come from.

At the hospital barracks, six nurses packed themselves into one tiny room to eat the cold meal delivered to them and polish off the scotch that Carmen had opened on the ship. In the corner sat Cathy, the head of one of the other nurses leaning against her shoulder.

"Nattily, you worked in an emergency ward," soothed Cathy. You treated car wreck victims. Today wasn't much different than that. We did really good work today. You did everything the doctors asked you to do. "

"I know I signed up for this," sobbed Nattily. "I knew that this is what war is going to be like. I just felt so helpless. Those boys were my age or maybe even younger. Look at my shoes. I have never liked red shoes. I don't think I can go back into a surgery or triage center again."

In the corner of the room, Carmen sat quietly ignoring the glass in her hand, her eyes focused on the other hand where she clutched a small piece of the timber that had killed the one man she had tried to help. She squeezed it as tightly as she had squeezed Malcolm's hand as he lost his battle to live. Finally, she stood, tossing the wood fragment into a wastebasket and slipped on her coat.

At the bottom of the stairs, she found one of the ambulance drivers scrubbing blood from the back of the ambulance. "Private," she started, "I need to get over to the cannery across the bay."

"I'm sorry, ma'am, but the base is mostly locked down just in case the Japs come back."

"An old friend lives in the house over at the cannery," she pressed. "No one has seen him since the attack. I need to see if he is all right."

The tall driver looked down at the shaken nurse who still clutched a drink in her hand. "Don't let the MP's see you with that drink out here, ma'am." The private watched as the nurse fought back the tears forming in her eyes. "If I had an old friend, here I would want to know if he is all right myself, ma'am. I might quit shaking if I could talk to an old friend for just a few minutes." He smiled. "But I could get in a lot of trouble if I try to take you to see the Jap."

"You know Mark?" asked a surprised Carmen.

"Everybody on both bases knows there is a Jap here. A while back, some guys beat him up."

"Mark is as American as you, private," said Carmen. "His family gave up their home to a bunch of nurses at the base I used to work at."

"I didn't mean nothing, ma'am. I suspect that after today he is as scared as a man can get. I had a friend back in Idaho who was a Chinaman."

Carmen changed her tactics. "I got a report that Mark might be injured. Don't you think we should go find out?"

"If that was an order from an officer, I couldn't rightly refuse it, ma'am."

The base was a hive of activity, as the ambulance worked its way around dozens of vehicles moving anything that would shoot toward the harbor. Carmen noticed a Jeep parked outside the house where the driver stopped.

"Give me fifteen minutes, Private," she asked, not yet comfortable giving orders.

Her knock on the door was met not by Mark, but by a graying Navy captain with a clipboard in his hand. "I'm sorry nurse, this house is off limits to military personnel."

"If I take off my uniform, you wouldn't know that I am military," she answered. "Then I could be an old friend here to see how Mark is holding up. I haven't seen him since I moved into his parents' house in California."

"If you took off your uniform young lady, it would probably land both of us in more trouble than it is worth," laughed the Captain. "Now, I'm Rocky Roads, and I am the Navy's liaison with Mark. Just who might you be?"

"My name is Carmen Alvarez. Mark is a very close friend of my boyfriend. That's how I met Mark."

There was movement behind Roads. "Carmen, what are you doing here?" choked Mark. "Does Chad know you are here?"

"I guess you are coming in then," laughed Roads. "Would that be Captain Chad Gritt?" Mark took Carmen's coat, hesitating as Roads returned to the table in the corner and jotted down a radio response to their last report.

Carmen wrapped her arms around Mark, her tears erupting. "I got here two days ago, on that ship moving out of the harbor." She continued, pointing at a ship racing toward the open ocean. "We had to spend the night aboard and only got into our rooms last night." She fought to shake off the tears. "What a horrendous welcome. I held the hand of a twenty-year-old kid from Arkansas today as he died. And no, Chad doesn't know that I am here."

Roads spiked a cup of coffee with a splash of brandy from Mark's stash and handed it to the young woman. "Chad is over at Fort Glenn. The enemy apparently doesn't know that it exists."

"Excuse me," offered Mark, as he picked up a microphone and mumbled something about fishing. "You don't want to know," he laughed watching Carmen's puzzled look.

"More importantly, you can't tell anyone that you just saw that," ordered Roads. "I mean anyone, not your CO or roommate, not even the general."

"I promise," nodded Carmen. "I hate the Japs for starting this war. I hate them for every man we will bury after their attack." She stopped, staring at Mark.

"It's okay," he replied, "I'm an American. I hate their leaders, not the people. I saw just how important ending this war is today."

"Mark, the driver who brought me here said that you had been beaten. How are you?"

"The captain here makes sure that I am fine. Is it true that all of the Japanese Americans in California are being herded into camps?"

"It's true, there and Washington and Oregon and it makes a lot of us sick," replied Carmen.

"At least here I can do some good for the war effort," answered Mark, shaking off a chill.

"Can you get a message to Chad for me?" she asked.

"Now would not be a good time to let him know you are on the island," interjected Roads. "The ships that launched the planes that hit us today are still out there. They can strike from anywhere within two hundred miles. That's forty thousand square miles that they can hide in. At most we can search a tenth of that."

"You don't think they have gone home then," observed Carmen.

"Maybe, but they only hit a few buildings today. They did nothing to hurt the combat capabilities of the Army or the Navy today. I can't imagine that they came all this way to knock down a few buildings."

"You make it sound like what happened today was some game, maybe bowling. A lot of people died today. I watched them come into the hospital. Some didn't even look like humans anymore," whispered Carmen.

"It's no game young lady," replied Roads. "I thank you for volunteering to become an Army nurse. I thank you for what you did today. Believe me, the commanders here and at Fort Glenn feel every loss personally. But this won't end until the enemy loses ten men for every one we lose. That's why you will not tell Captain Gritt you are here. He runs a one-man show that just might let us smack the enemy really hard. I need him thinking about finding the enemy, not worrying about you."

Carmen fought down her anger. The man was a senior officer and obviously trusted by Mark. "I hope he finds them all," she snarled.

She rose, slipping her coat on as she headed to the door. "Mark, thank you for a few minutes with a friendly face. I don't want to ever feel any different about what I saw today. I hope I never see enough of it to get used to it. I don't know how a soldier can go from one battle to another. But if I could, I would kill every man who attacked us today."

"Do you know what Chad named his plane?" asked Roads.

"No, I haven't talked to him since he got here. His letters are really short."

"Don't blame him; all mail is censored to make sure that it includes nothing that the enemy can use," smiled Roads. "He named it, CARMEN'S FURY."

Mark smiled at the woman. "If you can get away, and Captain Roads okays it, the Captain and a couple of friends all show up here on Friday evenings for dinner." He handed Carmen a slip of paper with a phone number. "We are all doing what we can to get by."

The entire base went on alert at three the next morning. Every gun was manned, and those not manning the guns sat in air raid shelters. Nothing happened. By 6:30, fifteen aircraft were in the air scouring the skies for Japanese planes. Every possible attack route was covered. Many of those in the shelters emerged to find something to eat or take a shower. Carmen and Cathy made their way back to their room, tumbling onto their beds, asleep instantly.

Somewhere in her dreams, Carmen heard the guns firing and sirens blaring from yesterday's raid. It was all so real. She rolled over fighting through the fog in her brain just as Cathy sat up shrieking. A second later, the window in their room exploded, most of the glass blocked by the heavy curtain. Both women tugged on their shoes, thankful that they were still dressed. From in front of the barracks they could see the hospital wing just outside their window burning and above them the sky was full of enemy planes and lines left by tracer ammunition and exploding shells.

Enemy Patriots

Carmen stopped as a truck between her and her shelter erupted into flames. A Japanese fighter roared over her head. She grabbed Cathy and pulled her in the other direction. "We need to get to the hospital."

"But it's on fire," replied Cathy, her eyes the size of a deer's in headlights.

"The firemen are already coming," called Carmen over the din of hundreds of guns firing and bombs dropping. "I don't think there was anyone in that wing, but if there is, we can't let them burn."

As the women ran, a massive fireball erupted from a direct bomb hit at the fuel depot. They arrived at the hospital to find it almost deserted.

The fighters at Fort Glenn scrambled within minutes of the attack beginning. They swept past Dutch Harbor trying to avoid the trigger-happy troops on the ground, searching for the retreating enemy planes. Below them were some small fires, including one on a ship that had been beached months before to act as a barracks. Smoke rolled from the tank farm, but everything else looked tranquil. Even the two ships in the harbor seemed to have escaped damage.

Five minutes behind the fighters, Gritt clawed for altitude to extend the range of his radio direction finder. The radio discipline that the Japanese had displayed all the way across the Pacific and on approach for each of their attacks had broken down. He switched frequencies to the combat frequency of the American fighters.

"Cap one," he called, "this is Snooper. I have enemy radio chatter to the northeast."

"Snooper, say again. The Japanese carriers have to be the other direction."

"Definitely chatter between Japanese planes, Cap One. Moving toward Otter Point. If they aren't retreating, they are a second attack formation."

"Roger Snooper, we will go check it out. Cap one out." The flight of six P-40s swung to a new heading finding the retreating enemy in minutes. Their attack crowded out their frequency. Chad switched back to the Japanese frequency he had monitored finding it so full of chatter that he could make little sense of what he heard. All he knew for sure was that Japanese Navy pilots and the American Army pilots were killing each other. On a hunch, he switched to the reported frequency used by the Japanese in emergencies.

He was surprised to hear two pilots talking calmly. One was in a damaged Japanese Zero fighter, and the other was a friend escorting the damaged plane.

"Watashi wa fusho shite imasu," called the pilot of the damaged plane. So the man might be wounded as well.

"Watashi wa, nenryo go fusoku shite imasu," called his wingman. The wingman was short of fuel.

"Watashi wa kono shima ni joriku shiyou to shimasu."

Chad looked at the map on his knee and calculated the direction of the island that the wounded pilot was trying to land on. The closest island was Akutan.

"Fune ni modorimasu," called the wounded pilot.

"Watashi ga iru kagiri watashi wa dekiru kagiri, anata to issho ni taizai shimasu," answered his friend.

The wounded pilot was going to crash land, thought Chad. *His friend doesn't want to go back to the ship, but he can't wait long.* A plan clicked into Chad's head. He knew Japanese submarines were in the area.

He jotted down a note on his pad. *This is the Japanese submarine H-42. We are sending a boat for your pilot.* Chad translated the message and clicked his microphone.

"Kare no hikoki go anzen ne teishi shite imasu. Arigato."

Chad rolled the P38 into a sweeping right turn and pulled the throttles back. The enemy plane had landed and his guardian angel was heading home. Akutan Island came into view. Chad lined up on the one flat spot on the island and descended to five hundred feet. He switched on the camera. There on the flat tundra was a Japanese Zero. The pilot had done an amazing job landing the plane on the soft ground. *He should have left his landing gear up, the plane wouldn't have flipped,* he thought. As he roared over the plane, Chad noticed no movement from the pilot still hanging upside down in his seat. He pulled up to make a second run.

Out of the corner of his eye, he caught a glint of silver and then the twinkle of the machine guns as a second Zero rolled from behind a mountain just inland attacking his plane. Chad poured the power to the huge twin-engine plane knowing he could outrun a Zero. The canopy above him shattered and something smashed into his right leg.

He had flown directly across the stream of fire from the Zero. The bullets had stitched his plane from front to back. He craned his neck to see the Japanese plane turning to follow. The power of the Allisons ratcheted the speed of his plane toward four hundred miles an hour. He headed straight north, hopefully leading the fuel short enemy plane away from its carrier.

He looked back over his shoulder. The Zero was directly on his six but falling behind.

"You speak good Japanese," came a call over the guard frequency.

"And your English is top notch too," answered Chad.

"That twin-tailed devil you fly is trailing smoke," offered the Japanese pilot.

"And you are out of gas," answered Chad.

There was no answer.

Chad reached up and dialed in the frequency he had earlier used to find the retreating Japanese attackers. He listened for just a moment before twisting in his seat to watch the plane behind him turn.

The Japanese pilot had been ordered to destroy the plane he had been trying to save. Whoever was ordering him to destroy the Zero that his friend had landed on Akutan didn't care if he ran out of fuel. All that mattered was that the plane not fall into American hands. Chad listened to the conversation long enough to realize that the only way the plane behind him could reach its target was to go to a slow cruise, preserving what little fuel remained.

"You will never get there," Chad called in English.

"Just watch me, round eye," came a reply.

He swung the nose of the P-38 around and locked onto the tail of the retreating plane, now more than ten miles away. He scanned his gauges and switches, recognizing that he had forgotten to jettison the external fuel tanks after he had been attacked. He hit the switch, transferring fuel from those tanks to the main wing tanks. The tank on the right wing went empty in seconds. *Thank you, God.* The Japanese did not put tracer ammunition in their fighter's machine guns. The shot that had holed his auxiliary tank would have blown the plane out of the sky if it had been a tracer round.

Chad watched as the oil pressure in the right engine began to drop. He bumped back the throttles just a bit to take some of the load off from the damaged engine. Having an intact Japanese Zero would be a major intelligence success. He keyed the air-to-air frequency on his radio looking for help to intercept the enemy plane now only minutes from Akutan.

"No can help," offered Cap one. "We got four of theirs, but they shot down four of ours. The two of us left are at critical fuel levels, and we are already west of Akutan."

Chad thought for a minute. He then pushed the throttles back to the stops. He had to try to stop the destruction of the downed fighter.

"Watch yourself Snooper," came a call. "Those Zeroes can turn on a dime and give you back a nickel. I have never seen anything like it."

Chad watched the plane in front of him grow larger and larger in the gun sight that he had never tested. He armed the single fifty-caliber gun in the nose, noticing blood all over his glove on the right hand. He looked down at his leg, watching a tiny spurt of blood splashing the side of the cockpit with every beat of his heart. He tugged a leather cord that held the gold cross around his neck from his shirt. With his teeth and the bloody hand, he worked the knot out of the cord allowing the cross to drop to the floor of the cockpit.

He worked the cord around his leg above the wound and risked releasing the stick between his legs to use both hands to retie it. From his boot, he pulled a long hunting knife and twisted its handle into the cord, tightening it until the bleeding stopped. He pushed the tip of the blade into the thin seat cushion.

When he looked up again, the Japanese plane filled the gun sight, and Akutan Island filled the windscreen. He waited until he was only thirty feet behind the enemy plane now only a half mile from the downed Zero. He pulled the trigger and watched a five second burst rip the plane from the tail right through the cockpit. The plane nosed over, crashing seconds later into the water just offshore.

I would like to have met that man, thought Chad, a strange headache taking over his brain. He turned for Dutch Harbor, the closest runway available and pulled the throttles back to preserve his damaged engine. As he did, the right engine coughed three or four times and then quit. The twin-engine airplane began to roll, the torque of the huge propeller on the left engine trying to turn the airplane inside out with the loss of the counter-rotating prop on the other side. The plane rolled through a full revolution and then a second, slamming him against the side of the cockpit. He pressed the right peddle as hard as he could to stop the roll, recognizing that he didn't have the strength in his wounded right leg to hold the pedal for long.

He began to reduce the power in the one good engine, and then added just enough back to keep the plane in the air. The plane stabilized as the torque was reduced. He wedged his right boot next to the right rudder pedal. The effort left that leg exhausted, but the P-38 was flying and controllable.

The mountains around the harbor at Dutch filled his windscreen as he prayed that there was enough blood in his body and life in his airplane to get him to the ground. He keyed the microphone.

"Mayday, Mayday this is Snooper. My P-38 is shot to hell and I am trying to make Dutch. I am about ten minutes out. I will need an ambulance."

"Roger that Snooper. We will have the runway clear. You are cleared for a straight in approach. Winds light and variable."

Chad passed the mountain marking the harbor entrance only three hundred feet above the water and fought to line up with the runway. He reached for the flap handle. *No more than ten degrees or this bird will invert. Already done that,* he thought.

The plane rolled down the runway, burying its nose in the mud at the end. In seconds, the rescue team was beside the plane. One of the men reached into the cockpit to unstrap the unconscious man, cutting himself on the razor sharp blade of the knife still buried in the seat. Seconds later, Chad was on a stretcher and only minutes later at the hospital where all of the wounded from the raid were either in rooms or released. Only one doctor and one nurse greeted the ambulance. "I don't know if I can do this doctor," cringed Nattily.

"We can discuss it later," replied the doctor.

She looked at the nametag on the wounded pilot's uniform. The wound in Chads leg was again pumping blood with the release of the tourniquet. Nattily plunged her index finger into the wound, pressing on the pumping artery. "If you die you son of a bitch, my friend Carmen will never forgive me. Do you hear me? You cannot die."

The doctor followed, shaken by the change in the nurse and her language. "Thank you, Lord," he prayed. "Thank you for sending us so few wounded today." He called to the orderly to find more help. "Just hold down that artery until I can get in and see what we are dealing with."

CHAPTER 27

THE NORTH PACIFIC, JUNE 1942

Admiral Kakuta's planning meeting was going well. The strategy to use the fighter's machine guns to attack the anti-aircraft guns at Dutch Harbor had worked. That had taken the pressure off from the bombers. His pilots reported that at least one ship was destroyed, and the fuel tanks were aflame. At least one large building was on fire. Without fuel, the enemy would be hard pressed to send out scout planes. The enemy was a sitting duck.

By running so close to the enemy base, his two small carriers had given his attack planes the range to swing around behind the base before attacking. The attack from the direction that American planes used to move to and from the mainland had worked perfectly. They were striking targets before the enemy even knew they were there. He had lost only a handful of planes, leaving him plenty for a third strike. This one would be late that same evening.

A young ensign from the communications department interrupted the meeting, wanting to be anywhere but standing in the doorway. He hung his head as he requested permission to pass on a communiqué from Admiral Yamamoto himself. Kakuta unfolded the message, his face turning the color of cream. On the back of the message he scribbled a note and handed it back to the young man.

"Ichido ni subete no senpaku ni kore o soshin shimasu," he ordered.

Turning to the men in the room, he barked, "Wareware wa koko de okonawa rete imasu." The admiral stood to leave. His official secretary, a graying man who in another life had been a teacher, took the note that the admiral handed him, and finished the entry in the official command diary. The Imperial Japanese Navy had been badly defeated in the battle at Midway Island. While the pilots claimed to have left two enemy aircraft carriers afire and a handful of other enemy ships damaged, their own fleet was now headed home with four fewer aircraft carriers, and at least that many more ships sunk. Many of those remaining were damaged and the Americans were continuing to harass them as they retreated.

The admiral had been ordered to steam toward the central Pacific to support the fleet. That was the order he had given to the ensign. The secretary struggled to find a way to soften the admiral's closing remark. "We are done here," would not read very well when historians studied the diary.

At Dutch Harbor, word of the victory north of Hawaii spread like wildfire. Still, Mark's intelligence had told them the Japanese were in the north Pacific to invade, so the base remained on full alert. Even the engineers and Seabees manned rifle and machine gun positions around the harbor. Kakuta had guessed correctly that the loss of the fuel tanks curtailed the search for his fleet by scout planes, but the long range Navy seaplanes that survived the attack were still fully fueled. They patrolled only fifty miles around the base, watching for an invasion force.

At the hospital, Chad struggled to dig out of the anesthesia-fueled haze. He noticed movement around him and felt the soft touch of a woman holding his hand. He finally focused. Carmen's face smiled down at him. "Shit," he mumbled, "all this time I thought God was a man."

Carmen leaned down to plant a kiss on his forehead. "We will talk later, soldier." She rose to leave, ushered from the room by Captain Roads, then turned.

"Can't I stay a few minutes more?"

"We will be done with the captain in a half-hour. Some things changed today, and we need to brief him and find out why in the hell he was shooting at enemy planes and getting shot at."

"That doesn't tell me very much," pointed out Carmen.

"Remember last night when we talked, and I suggested that to win this war we needed to take ten of theirs for every one we lost?"

"I remember," smiled Carmen, "but the scuttlebutt around the base is that we only shot down a half dozen of their planes today. We lost at least that many men here."

"But in the central Pacific there was a much larger battle today. There we killed a hundred for everyone we lost. Now I need to get back to the captain or you will never get your turn," offered Roads.

Carmen looked down the hall to see her commanding officer scowling at her.

Roads carried a chair from the hallway into the room and sat down. The look on his face could have scoured the paint off from a ship. The other two chairs in the room held Spiff and Gritt's other commander Lt. Col. Jon Wayne who had arrived from Fort Glenn.

Chad beat Roads to the punch. "Did you pull the film from my camera?"

"No, your plane has a tent over it. The mechanics figure they can repair all of the damage in a few days. Somewhere they even found a spare Allison engine with the right propeller governor to replace the one you got shot to shit."

"I know that I wasn't supposed to go anywhere near the enemy," stumbled Gritt. "I managed to vector some of our guys to the retreating enemy."

"Six of our guys jumped a dozen retreating Japanese planes, Kates and Zekes and some Zeros," offered Wayne. "We have confirmed four enemy kills, and we lost four of ours to the Zeros. We would have never found them without your help."

"That doesn't explain you violating a direct order to stay out of the fight," snarled Roads.

"While the fighters were attacking, I switched frequencies to monitor the Japanese emergency frequency. I got some chatter from a damaged Zero who was crash landing on Akutan. I called his escort and told him I was on a Japanese sub and that I was sending a landing party to rescue the downed pilot. I thought he bought it and headed for home. When I made a photo pass over the downed plane, his buddy jumped me."

Next to Roads, Spiff thumbed through the small box of materials that the mechanics had pulled from the damaged P-38. He handed Roads the note Chad had scribbled.

"Go on," ordered Roads.

"I led the guy out to sea, knowing he was short on fuel. I knew that I had been hit, but the plane seemed undamaged. My adrenaline was pumping so I didn't even know I was wounded. When the guy turned back, I started listening to him talk to his commander. He had been ordered to destroy the downed Zero. I told the pilot he would never make it."

"So, you were communicating with the pilot of the second Zero in Japanese," asked Roads.

Chad laughed. "That's one of the funny things, we were talking in English. Whoever that guy was, he spoke better English than I speak Japanese."

"Maybe that's how he figured out your ruse," commented Spiff.

"Or maybe he knew that there were no submarines in the area," added Roads. "That still doesn't explain you disobeying an order."

"Develop the film, Captain. The photo lab can do it in an hour. There is a completely intact Japanese Zero on that island. Even Navy mechanics could probably get it flying in a couple of days."

"I thought you said that the other Japanese pilot was ordered to destroy the plane?"

"I managed to get the bleeding in my leg stopped and then I shot him down. His plane is in the water just offshore from Akutan."

"Do you think he made it ashore?" asked Spiff.

"I was only yards behind him when I shot. The cockpit took most of the burst. He was only a hundred feet above the water and he went in hard."

"So, you are telling me that there is a Jap Zero in almost flyable condition only a few miles from here, and all we have to do is go get it," Roads said. "Maybe the pilot of the downed plane has burned it."

"Look at the film, Sir," offered Chad. "I think the pilot is still in the cockpit, dead."

"Well, hotshot," snapped Wayne, "if you had gotten to this hospital just a minute later you would be sitting next to him waiting to talk to the Big Man.

"How bad was I hit?"

"The nurse on duty managed to compress the bleeding, and the doc patched up a whole in a major artery in your leg. It will take a month before you are going mountain climbing, Captain," offered Roads. "The round that went through the edge of the oil cooler of your engine smacked the fuselage outside the cockpit. It hit a rivet hard enough to blow it into the cockpit; that's what the doc found in your leg. You are a very lucky man. If the bullet had penetrated the cockpit, the hole would have been four or five times larger and you would be taking harp lessons about now."

"You know, Captain, that because of your special status, you cannot claim credit for the kill of the Japanese Zero," snarled Wayne.

"I don't want any credit. Maybe if I can find out who that guy was, when the war is over, I can find his parents and tell them that he died very bravely. He knew that he couldn't destroy the downed plane and make it back to his ship," uttered Chad.

"I am satisfied, how about you Colonel?" smiled Roads.

"If there really is a Jap Zero out there that we can fly, we can learn how to defeat them. I just don't believe it."

"Maybe, then we should just keep this between us until I can confirm all of this," spat Roads.

"One more thing," said Chad. "What is Carmen doing here?"

"You had better ask her," smiled Roads.

"You work with the docs to get better. As soon as you can, I want you over at O'Hara's to help him until you can fly again. Things are going to get interesting very quickly now. Let me brief you on another battle today and then I will let you rest."

Roads stopped at the nurse's station. "The captain was wearing this when he was hit." He handed the dour Army major at the desk the blood-encrusted cross that the mechanics had recovered from Chad's plane. "Could you have someone clean it up and find a new cord? The young man this represents was riding with the captain today."

Three days after Chad had been wounded, the doctors reluctantly released him. He was ordered to stay off his feet as much as possible and to keep his leg elevated. Throughout the previous three days, Carmen had managed to check on him three or four times a day, but other nurses were assigned to care for him.

Roads had pressed for his release, anxious for Chad to move over to Mark's. Chad's presence freed him for a clandestine trip to take a look at the damaged Zero.

"I am not going to get myself between your girl and her commanding officer," laughed Roads in answer to a question about whether Carmen would be allowed to see him. "She probably didn't tell her boss why she volunteered to come out here. I can tell you that I personally hate surprises," added Roads.

The ambulance carrying Gritt pulled up to Mark's house, and two orderlies helped Chad up the stairs. Roads poured himself a cup of Mark's coffee from the pot on the pot-bellied stove in the main room. "You want one?" he called to Mark and Chad.

Neither man answered as Mark fiddled with the tuning on the radio. "The Japanese are invading Attu Island," said Mark. "The teachers sent an emergency message which your folks picked up an hour ago. I have been monitoring the frequency since they called.

The teachers taped the transmit key on the microphone down when they fled. All of the chatter is now in Japanese."

Roads poured two more cups, emptying the pot and carried it over to the two men huddled around the speaker. "Like I said, it is going to get a lot more interesting. I had hoped that after the drubbing the enemy took in the Coral Sea and at Midway they might just sit back and sue for peace."

"Captain Roads," started Mark, "I only met one officer in Japan who had any idea how bad an idea this war was. The rest are filled with the spirit of Boshido. They will die rather than admit defeat or even that they were wrong. And now they are occupying American ground, taking American civilians prisoners just like my folks."

Roads finished his coffee. "I better get back across the bay. This invasion is going to rattle everyone I work with and piss off the President. He will want us to do something about this, and we will have to tell him that with only a handful of Army troops at our disposal, no marines and no transport ships he will have to wait. It is not going to be what a President wants to hear, so we will have to figure out just how to tell him."

"If you can sell the President something he doesn't want to buy, maybe you can sell Carmen's boss on letting her come by once in a while," laughed Chad.

"Oh, I figured out how to do that on the ride over," responded Roads. "I will tell her that Carmen is the only member of the medical staff with clearance to come into this house. That ought to do it." Rocky slipped on his coat. "You remember this when I ask you to do the impossible the next time, all right Captain?"

Roads stood to leave.

"What about the downed Zero?" asked Chad.

"It will have to wait. I haven't told anyone, and I don't intend to until I can confirm that it justifies explaining how you got your plane shot to shit."

❃

On Attu, Charles and Etta Jones stood under guard as the Japanese rounded up the villagers. It took only minutes for a Japanese lieutenant to figure out that Jones was the radio operator and that the Americans had been informed of the invasion. The schoolteacher and her meteorologist husband watched, as the village's only means of communicating with the world was hauled from the home. Outside, the soldiers smiled and laughed, as they went about the work of chasing down the handful of local kids that had run into the barren hills. From a mile away, two older boys studied the invaders below. "W-w-we c-can't let them c-catch us," said one.

"How many are here?" asked the same Japanese officer who had taken the radio.

"Two," replied Etta, pushing her graying hair from in front of her eyes. "How many soldiers did you bring?"

"Two thousand," laughed the lieutenant. "Stay in your house. Have a good night." He posted a guard outside the door. Etta walked to the window, watching a guard being posted at every door in the village. The soldiers were joking and laughing as they made faces at the children who stood on the porches staring at them.

At the house next door, she watched as one of the soldiers tucked a cigarette into the corner of his mouth and then began patting every pocket looking for a match. Finally, he knocked on the door behind him and made a gesture to the man who opened it, pretending to light his cigarette. The villager returned to the door handing the young soldier a handful of matches. Etta watched as the soldier bowed slightly, "arigato," he muttered.

"Maybe this will all be okay," offered Etta to her husband who sat quietly in his rocking chair.

Their morning started early as the Japanese lieutenant ordered the couple to follow him to meet with his commander. "You go to that house," ordered the lieutenant. "They will ask questions. You answer."

Etta looked at her watch as the third interrogator wrapped up his questions. The couple had been sitting for six hours. Finally, the young lieutenant stepped into the room, motioning for them to follow him.

"You are only teacher," he snapped looking at Etta. "And you are weather person and operator of the radio," he continued pointing at Charles. "You not American Army, that is good." He led the couple back to their house where the same guard from the night before smiled at them. "Stay in your house. Have a good night," offered the lieutenant for the second night in a row.

He was back again the next morning. "You will come with me Mr. Jones," he ordered. "You will stay here Mrs. Jones."

They marched with four soldiers just as the night before. They passed the house where the interrogation was held the day before. They crossed the small stream that ran next to the village. They stopped at a large tent. "You go there," ordered the lieutenant. "The major will talk to you."

Charles shook the moisture from his gray hair as he entered the tent. A tall man with receding hair sat at a small table. "You send message when Japan man come?"

"Yes," replied Charles.

"Whom you send it to?"

"I transmitted in the blind."

"You did not answer my question."

"I didn't wait for an answer. I just told anyone who was listening that you were here."

"You told the American Army we were here?"

"I don't know who got the message."

The major threw the microphone from the radio on the table. The tape that held down the transmit button was still in place. "You are an American Army spy."

"No, no I am not. I work for the weather service and the Bureau of Indian Affairs."

"Ha, you lie," replied the major. "There are no American Indians here. There are no horses or tepees."

"The people of these villages are helped by the same people who help the Indians you have seen in the movies."

"You lie. You tell me who you sent radio message to."

"I told you, I sent it in the blind," offered Charles now sweating.

"I could kill you right now for your lies," snarled the major.

"That would not change the truth. I transmitted in the blind. I am a weatherman and radio operator for the Bureau of Indian Affairs."

"After you die, I could give your wife to my soldiers for some fun. You did not need to tell your Army we were here. Now, tell me the truth." The major called for the lieutenant who waited outside the door. "This man is not going to tell me the truth. Perhaps he needs a little coaxing. Hold out his arm."

The lieutenant held out Charles' arm, wrist up. The major drew the sword at his waist and in a single move ran it across the artery in Charles wrist and slipped it back into its sheath.

"You tell me the truth now Mr. Spy, and I will call a doctor. If not, I will let you bleed to death and then give your wife to my soldiers."

Charles stood watching his blood pump onto the ground, pooling at his feet. "I am sure the Army and the Navy both heard my call," he cried.

"So now you tell the truth," laughed the major. "Now I tell you the truth. We have no doctor."

He turned to the lieutenant and pointed toward the door. "Take this man out of my tent to die. His blood smells. After he dies, come back here for my orders."

Charles stumbled, trying to stop the bleeding with his other hand. He stumbled again just outside the tent. The lieutenant helped him to his feet and over to a bench by the stream. He held Charles shoulders upright. "I am sorry," offered the lieutenant. "I will try to take care of your wife. She is honored teacher."

Charles looked up at the man, his vision fading. He tried to speak. The lieutenant watched as Charles' left hand fell away from putting pressure on his right wrist. A minute later, the gurgle from the man's throat told him the fight was over. He laid Charles body down on the bench and returned to the tent.

"Anata wa kare go jisatsu shita to iudarou," ordered the major. He handed the lieutenant a small folding knife.

The lieutenant opened the blade and dropped it on the ground next to the body and then started up the hill toward the village. He composed himself and knocked on the door, waiting for Etta's answer.

"I am so sorry teacher san. Your husband cut his wrist. He died before my major could summon a doctor." He watched the woman collapse screaming. "I will summon friends," he whispered and started into the village.

He was awakened to the firing of the guns, as an American plane overflew Attu. At breakfast, he learned that the same plane had overflown the other occupied island, Kiska. The enemy was not supposed to have long-range aircraft.

A few days later, he watched as the schoolteacher was helped into the boat from the ship that would take her and the other villagers to a camp in Yokohama. Her clothes were mismatched and on her head she had tugged a blue knitted cap. The woman laughed hysterically as she boarded the boat. In the cemetery not far away only a single new grave marked the coming of the Imperial Army.

He turned, saddened by the woman's grief and the madness that came with it. That night, he lit incense and prayed that someday, someone would read the report of the death of the American Army radio operator and search out the truth.

CHAPTER 28

OTOMARI, KARAFUTO, JAPAN, JULY 1942

General Fumi's plane arrived unannounced. It took Colonel Ito twenty minutes to drive to the airstrip, clambering from the back of his staff car. The general waited, seated under a tree. Two of the general's aides hovered close by. Ito's driver and the sergeant commanding the soldiers who monitored the Ishihara's radio waited near the car.

"It is very pleasant here, Haru," started Fumi. "Come sit on the grass. The temperature at headquarters is unbearable now. You are very fortunate to serve in such a place. Look about you. I know that you appreciate the gardens of Tokyo, but man can never build something as pure as the woods around us now."

Ito realized that he would never understand his commander. "I am sure that you did not dedicate a day from your busy schedule to sit under a tree."

"You are quite right, of course," replied Fumi. "That sort of thing will not be possible again until this war ends. That is why I am here. The war is only seven months old, and Japan is losing."

Ito turned, glaring at his commander, not believing what he was hearing. "General, we have won every battle so far. We occupy American lands."

"You read too many Army newspapers, Haru. The naval battles in the Philippines and near Midway Island were not victories. At Midway, the Americans lost only a couple of capital ships including one carrier. We lost eight including four of our precious carriers. More importantly, we lost all of the flight crews from those four carriers. If we work with super-human effort, we can replace one of those carriers in the next two years. The Americans have four more that will be completed next year. They have hundreds of pilots in training, and most importantly they have experienced men to lead them. We just lost most of the experienced naval aviators we have spent years training."

"Damn the Navy, we knew that we could never trust them," spat Ito. "That is why our leaders are all from the Army."

"The head of the Navy, Admiral Yamamoto, argued against a war with the Americans. When he was ordered to plan the attack at Pearl Harbor, he did everything expected of him and more. In the central Pacific, he expected two American carriers to be steaming north to defend the Aleutians. Instead there were four and land-based fighters and bombers at Midway Island. We didn't even know that the enemy still had four carriers in the Pacific."

"That is a failure of the intelligence group of the Navy, is it not?" asked Ito.

"Haru, they are Japanese too, are they not? Yamamoto warned that any war in the Pacific would be a naval war, once we fought anywhere but China and Korea. He warned that the Americans could trade Japan ship for ship and within two years we would have nothing left to fight with."

Ito's face was red, his cheeks drawn tightly, his mouth barely open over tightly clenched teeth. "I still blame the Navy. We in the Army must hold on while they rebuild. We must defeat the enemy on land everywhere we fight so that their ships mean nothing."

"You are close to being right, Haru," replied Fumi, "come let's walk."

Fumi rose, dusting the dried grass from his creased trousers. He slipped his coat from his shoulders and handed it to an aide who rushed to his side. "Watashitachi go modotta toki, anata wa koko ni tsumetai biru no haitta baketsu o motte imasu," barked the general.

"Where will your man find cold beer?" asked Ito as they walked.

"Being a general still offers privileges," laughed Fumi. "We brought a cooler with us. We will work very hard to see that Japan gets a fair peace. But there is no task or plan that can now bring victory. We might as well enjoy ourselves before we die."

"Why are you here, General?"

"We need more information from our man in Dutch Harbor. Somehow, we need him to give us information on the overall defenses of the Aleutians. We need information about troop build-ups and supplies. Admiral Hosogaya is determined to harden the Islands of Attu and Kiska where our troops are now digging in. We all know that the Americans will do anything to reclaim American soil. The only fair peace we can expect will come if the Americans feel it is going to be too costly in men and materials to defeat us."

"I still do not trust that Ishihara boy or even his father," replied Ito. "The codes that your man Peter developed do not allow us to transmit that kind of information. Even if he wanted to," added Ito, rethinking his comments.

"We must get a message to Mark that he needs to meet with Peter. Peter's code allowed for setting up a meeting. We need for Michi to tell his son that it is critical."

Ito was growing angry, as he listened. "You have ordered me to babysit that traitor and his wife. Did you know that they now even allow their Korean gardener to live in the house with them?"

"Haru, Michi is an honorable man. You yourself know that he is also a warrior. I trust that a man with your lack of concern for our traditions of beauty and gentleness can find a way to convince Michi that his son must help more."

"Are you taking off all of the restrictions you have placed on me?" asked Ito.

Fumi stopped, forcing Ito to stop with him. "Colonel, you

may not harm either Michi or his wife in any way. You may not harm his parents. A man of your inventiveness can work around those two simple restrictions. Now, the afternoon is growing very warm. I suggest we walk back and see how well my aide has chilled the beer waiting for us. We can speak of more pleasant things like China where at least we are still killing more of the enemy than we are losing."

The next morning, Ito arrived at the summer home unannounced. The skies had turned cloudy and a much-needed rain was just starting as he and two of his men parked the truck. Mary, who by now knew that the next step would be to send her for tea, greeted him at the door. While she fussed in the kitchen, Ito relayed the general's instructions to Michi.

"That will put my son at great risk," snarled Michi after hearing the request.

"Everyone must do their duty," scolded Ito. "Everyone is at risk. Even our women and children are at great risk. You and your wife could find that your comfortable life here is interrupted. Your wife has maintained her youth. It must be the soft American life. She is too attractive to be at risk, don't you think?"

Mary carried the tray of tea and cups into the room. Ito rose, slapping the tray from her hands and grabbing her by the wrist. As Michi rose to intervene, one of the sergeants at the door barged into the room leveling his rifle at him. "From today until I am convinced that you and your son are helping, your Korean whore will move back to the gardener's house where she will entertain my soldiers. It is the responsibility of attractive women from other countries to entertain the troops, don't you agree?"

Michi seethed. He slipped his hand under the table next to him, reaching for the short sword that he had concealed there. Mary looked over quietly shaking her head, no.

"You threaten this girl who has served us faithfully," snarled Michi. "You threaten my wife, and you expect me to help?"

"I am not threatening anyone, Lieutenant. I am simply stating facts. The amount of risk you and your family assume is entirely up to you. I will be out of the area for ten days. When I get back, I want to see the message you will send to your son. I will wait ten more days after you send it for Peter to notify me that he is cooperating. If everything goes as planned, in a month your life will be back to normal."

"Who will clean the house?" spat Michi.

"This girl can still come each day and garden and clean. The two guards that will be stationed with you until I know you are cooperating will see that she goes home every night." Ito smiled, his teeth resembling those of a saw blade between his tight lips. "They will enjoy her, as well as the radiomen."

CHAPTER 29

DUTCH HARBOR, ALASKA, FALL 1942

Captain Roads read Michi's message.

"Damned sorry about your folks, son," scowled Roads. "I guess we should have anticipated this. The Japs..." He looked at Mark hoping that he had not offended him. "...the enemy must have some inkling by now that our intelligence is better than theirs. It is obviously time for them to step up their game."

"What does that mean, Captain?" asked Mark.

"It means that the men running the show over there now understand that they are in a bad position. They also know that we have the means to take back Attu and Kiska Islands and we are going to try. They want to stop us and the keys to that will be resupplying their troops and you tipping them off about our plans."

Chad stood, stretching the tight muscles from his damaged leg. He refilled his coffee cup. "Just what can we do, Sir, to help Mark feed the sharks enough information to keep his folks alive?"

"It may actually be easier than what we are doing now," laughed Roads. "From the time we start giving the enemy this new information, we will be free to make it all up. Since they have no way to verify, we can tell them what we want."

"I guess that's right," replied Mark. "But when it turns out that what we give them isn't the truth, my parents' lives will be in real danger."

"You set up a meeting with your cave dwelling friend out there," said Roads. "Work out the language for an expanded code. I am going to catch a flight down to Seattle to meet with Chad's buddy, Walt Wilson. When I get back, I will have a plan on just what information we can feed the enemy. Depending on weather, I should be back in ten days."

"Just tell me, Sir, that you aren't going on down to California to watch them put that Zero back together," laughed Chad, " you know, take a little victory lap."

"Why Captain Gritt, I am shocked that you don't give credit to the Navy patrol plane that just accidentally came across that downed Zero." Roads took a moment before continuing. "It's too bad that finding that plane is so important that we can't tell anyone. I saw pictures of the pilot. His name was Koga, and he looked like a fine young man. By the way, you were wrong about him being wounded. There wasn't a mark on his body. He must have broken his neck landing. But you were right about a submarine. One of our destroyers chased a sub away from Akutan that same day."

There was a knock on the door. Mark opened it to find two bedraggled native men standing on the steps. "Are you the new boss man?" asked one. "We work here every summer, but with the war it took us a month to get from the village to Unalaska. We figured that the supply ship wasn't coming. We came as soon as we could."

"Give me a minute," replied Mark, " I will be right back."

"Now what do I do?" he asked Roads who was standing behind him.

"Put the boys to work sprucing the place up and maybe even go out and catch a few fish. I will authorize the Seabee paymaster to provide you with enough to keep these guys busy. We may need their council on the villages. Hell, I thought we had evacuated all of them."

Mark turned to the two young men. "How did you get here?"

"We paddled. It should have only taken a couple of weeks, but every time we saw a boat or airplane, we hid."

"Go on down to the bunkhouse and settle in. I will be down later to get you started. By the way, which village did you come from?"

"We are from Attu," replied the tallest man.

"My God, that's almost a thousand miles from here," observed Mark.

The young man smiled, "Yup."

Ivan and his silent cousin Paul had worked for the Ivanoffs for two years. They were handpicked by the village to work for the cannery. Both were expected to save what they earned to be used to attend Sheldon Jackson College someday. They had been two of the handful of young men who fled the Japanese invasion, hiding in the hills and watching. They had slipped past the sleeping sentries after a ship hauled the villagers away, then stolen a small sailboat and headed east. They had traded the open boat for a two-man bidarka at the abandoned village on Adak Island.

Ivan's account of the taking of Attu and their observations of the occupied island of Kiska kept the military intelligence officers interviewing them glued to their seats. The exile of the captured villagers was a surprise, one that opened the possibility of attacking the invaders by air.

One week after Mark sent his coded message requesting a meeting with Peter, he finally got an answer. When the confirmation came, it was delivered with some urgency. "Need to talk about fall fishing right away," was his message. Marks reply of "too much work for the next five days," set the meeting for midnight five days in the future.

Mark crept up the rocky shore from where Paul beached the bidarka. A decade before, he had led his father ashore at that same spot to find his brother and their friend Woody. He worked his way through the rocks and into the cove that years before had changed his life.

"Who is that with you?" came a voice from a gulley above him.

"Just a kid who works for my dad's company. He paddled me out in one of the skin boats the local people are famous for," answered Mark. "We used the boat to creep along the shore where the lookouts couldn't see us."

"You were supposed to come alone."

"How in the hell am I supposed to do that?" replied Mark. "How can I row or sail out here without being seen? How do I keep the boat from being beached, or worse, keep it from floating away while we talk? If someone found it, there would be a search."

"I really don't like it," scowled Peter finally standing. Across the gulley, on the hillside one of Peter's guards stood, slinging the rifle he carried. "Just who is this man you brought?"

"I told you, a young man from one of the villages. He just arrived a few days ago to work in the cannery. Obviously, we are not going to operate this year, but with no supply boats, I can't send him back."

"But now someone other than you knows we are here," snarled Peter, finally walking down to the rocky shore where Mark was waiting. "He must not compromise this mission."

Mark was shocked by what he saw. Peter's clothes were torn and so dirty that if you threw them on the ground, in dim light you might never see them. His hair was hanging past his shoulders and so tangled that Mark expected a tiny bird to poke its head up looking for a meal. "So, this is what you volunteered for?"

"Shut up," snarled Peter. "Did you bring something to write on?"

Mark unfolded a dozen sheets of lined paper from his shirt pocket and a stub of a pencil. "Do you have a new code worked out?" he asked. "I assume that your orders were the same as mine – provide hard information on the defenses and on any information about troop movements or an effort to retake the two islands the Imperial Army occupies."

The guard on the hill slipped quietly up behind Peter. Peter's rusty revolver pressed against the man's stomach, as he whirled. He took several deep breaths before pocketing the weapon.

"Anata wa tabako o motte imasu?" asked the guard, squinting at Peter, shaking his head.

Mark reached into his pockets and produced ten packs of cigarettes. "I figured that you might be short of smokes." Mark handed them to Peter, who handed them to the guard.

"What did you expect after ten months out here? Every time they change submarines, they send us new supplies. They now come only every four months. The captains are so concerned about being close to an American base that they throw what they can in one small raft and row it to shore. They never want to be on the surface for more than twenty minutes."

The guard took the cigarettes and headed up the hill.

"You should be out of here by next summer," said Mark. "The Americans are planning an invasion to take back the islands. After that there will be little need for either of us."

"They will be stopped. It is up to you and me to make sure that they are," interrupted Peter. He began writing, using a flat rock for a lap desk. "Give me the names of some Alaska flowers. I need twelve, one for each month of the year."

Mark began listing, visualizing each as he did.

"Now, give me names of six towns in Alaska. We will use Juneau and Fairbanks to mean Attu and Kiska."

Mark listed off six more towns.

Peter developed codes for other critical information. He then made a second copy.

"Okay, so if you give me a sentence with Seward and Juneau in it, that means that a scouting force is going to Attu. If you say you picked twenty wild roses—that means that you expect them about the twentieth of October. If you say Juneau and Valdez, that will mean an invasion force is moving on Attu. Get it?"

"You realize," observed Mark, "that with Aleutian weather the dates could change. Any operation could even be cancelled."

"Don't talk down to me, asshole, just because you live in a house and can take a shower. Try living in that hole for a winter;

that will teach you about weather. This is my operation and I make the rules," snarled Peter.

Mark sighed. "I know who has the hammer here. In a way, you did me a favor. If I weren't here, I would be cooling my heels in some camp in Idaho or Arizona with the rest of the Japanese Americans."

"Don't ever forget what the country we were born in is doing to our own people," barked Peter. "Now tell me about other American bases along the Aleutians."

"There is Fort Randall on the mainland just before the islands start. Then there is a new base being planned for Adak. Then there is a base that the Army Air Corps is building, but I don't know where," lied Mark. "Engineers and workers are rolling into Dutch Harbor every day." It was almost like Captain Roads knew what Peter would ask when he prepared Mark for this meeting.

"You must tell me where they are going," ordered Peter.

"If I mention an island's name and you attack it or the ships heading there, it will only take the intelligence people a few days to figure out where the information is coming from."

"Then we need to think of something else that can mean which island. You know, some kind of sea animal or cloud."

"Peter, there are hundreds of islands. Maybe I can say the word sunshine and then a number. Sunshine will mean something is going on at some island and the number will be the approximate distance from here. Attu would be sunshine, ninety. That would mean an island nine hundred miles from here."

"That is good. You have obviously gotten the message that Colonel Ito has your parents' lives in his hands. I will send him a note when the submarine changes out next month. He will be pleased to know that you are cooperating."

"Now tell me about this skin boat you came in," directed Peter, his eyes wild.

"It is the traditional boat of the people who live here. It is long and narrow and fully enclosed, except for two small holes allowing the paddlers to sit in the boat. It is very seaworthy in the hands of a skilled paddler, but a death trap for someone without experience."

"That is all then, I will walk with you back to the boat," smiled Peter.

The young Aleut paddler saw them coming and began dragging the light boat back to the water's edge. Peter extended his right hand toward Mark and in the other produced the rusted pistol aiming it at Paul.

"I'm sorry, you will have to come up with a story about how he headed back to the village or drowned or something," spat Peter. He pulled the trigger. Nothing happened.

"Put that away," worried Mark. "If you had killed this young man, I would never have made it back to the harbor. Didn't you hear a word I said about these boats?"

Peter began to twist the cylinder of the revolver. Mark's right fist caught him under the chin, lifting Peter off from his feet. Mark reached down and grabbed the pistol from the ground and heaved it out into the water. "If you try to get up before we leave, I will cave in your skull with a rock. I am not going to get hung as a spy because you kill this boy and trigger a search party that finds you."

Peter was still sitting when the bidarka rounded the small headland to the west.

Paul tapped Mark on the shoulder. "T-t-t-thanks M-m-m-mister Ora. T-t-t-those men t-t- took m-m-my m-m-mother a-a-and sister. I w-w-w-want to help k-k-kill all o t-t-them."

"You don't know it, Paul, but you just did. Now don't tell anyone, not even Ivan about this trip or that man." Mark finally began to shiver as the adrenaline in his body gave way to fear.

❃

The next day, Mr. O'Hara was one of the observers at the airstrip as the special P-38 lightning launched itself after weeks of sitting idle. Chad rolled the plane into a tight turn and headed out of the harbor, rolling the plane three full revolutions before turning northwest toward Akutan.

"Is that fool trying to kill himself?" asked Spiff.

"Nope," answered Roads, "just happy to be back in his element." Roads turned to Spiff and Mark next to him. "Neither of you are old enough to realize that you are not bulletproof."

At the cannery, Ivan and Paul splashed more paint on the dock than they managed to get on the walls. "Maybe we should sign to become soldiers," laughed Ivan.

"I t-t-think w-w-w-we already are," answered Paul, w-w-we w-will guide t-t-them. Ora s-s-says w-we will k-k-k-kill those men."

Fall stretched into winter as the Japanese huddled in caves carved into the hillsides on Attu and Kiska. Long range Navy patrol planes wandered over the enemy encampments when the weather allowed, dropping bombs that plowed deep holes in the tundra and occasionally hit something of importance.

The Japanese resupplied the bases, launching quick dashes across the north Pacific by transport vessels escorted by screening war ships. American air power around Kiska Island forced the Japanese to resupply critical food, ammunition and fuel by submarine. The Americans worked feverishly on newer bases closer to the enemy, bases with longer runways. The B-17 long-range bombers would join the pounding of the Japanese.

Chad's P-38 was fitted with larger axillary fuel tanks and he was often in the area when Navy patrol aircraft or Army bombers bombed the two islands. His listening to ground radio allowed them to target ships trying to resupply the Japanese bases. On one run, he overheard orders being issued to concentrate Japanese anti-aircraft fire in an area where only a couple of large tents could be seen. For the next three days, he concentrated on that area, flying high altitude runs over the bases, taking pictures until he ran out of film. The film lab would take days to process the film, leaving Gritt with little to do coming into the weekend.

On a Friday evening, the usual crowd and Carmen crowded

into Mark's kitchen listening to a static filled Tommy Dorsey radio show from San Francisco and frying steaks.

"I wonder where Chad is?" laughed Carmen.

"I need all of you to be quiet for a minute," interrupted Mark. He switched channels on the radio and picked up the microphone. Outside, two transport ships and two destroyers were leaving the harbor. Mark depressed the transmit button on the microphone. "Went fishing with two plugs and two spoons. Nice sunshiny day, the temperature was about sixty. Didn't catch shit." He dropped the microphone on the desk and changed back to the music.

"Let me see if I got that one right," giggled Carmen. "You just told the men out in that cave that there were two destroyers and two transports headed west into the Aleutians. The only thing I haven't figured out is the temperature thing."

Mark stood looking at her like she had just picked a trifecta at the Kentucky Derby. "How do you know that?"

"Let's see, I have seen you transmit messages about five times, always watching out the window. When a destroyer goes out you say spoon and when a transport goes out you say plug. You say sunshine any time a ship is headed west. What's the sixty mean?"

Roads began to laugh. "The amazing thing is that the enemy hasn't figured out that anyone with a dime's worth of common sense would have broken this code already. Go ahead and tell her what the sixty stands for."

"Sixty means six hundred miles, you just add a zero. That means the ships who just left are headed to an island six hundred miles out on the chain."

Carmen smiled. "And just what island would that be?"

"Hell," answered Mark, refilling Carmen's wine glass, "I don't know if there is an island at that point along the chain. It doesn't really matter. The enemy will be sending their submarines out there looking for something and they won't be looking at Adak."

"We will have to end this when the fireworks really get close," commented Spiff. "It is going to be really hard to convince them that ships carrying tens of thousands of troops aren't really in the harbor at Attu."

Chad burst through the front door. "Wait until you see these, Captain."

He hurried to the table and flipped open a file folder and laid a half dozen photos out on the table. "This one with the pontoons was the key." He pointed to a photo with two large sausage looking things sitting in front of one of the tents. Over the next four photos he pointed out different pieces of airplanes moving under cover of the tents. "Now look at this," he offered pointing at a plane that looked a lot like a Japanese Zero sitting on the beach just in front of a tent.

"That looks a lot like a Zero on floats," observed Roads.

"That's what it is, or whatever the Japanese call that configuration. We are going to need to send some fighters with our bombers from now on."

"At least until we have accounted for those fighters," continued Roads.

"That P-38 squadron I came up with just moved over to the new base on Adak. With drop tanks they don't have to wait for the bombers. They can go hunting. A set of floats has to really screw up the speed and maneuverability of a Zero," sighed Gritt.

"You don't sound very happy about destroying those fighters," growled Spiff.

"I trained hard to fly fighters, and now if I am involved in the fight at all, it will be to direct them. I get to sit safely outside the fray while the squadron takes all the risks."

"Says the man who landed his last basic training solo upside down and was just released from the hospital after tangling with a Zero flying a camera plane," smirked Carmen. "Let's get dinner over with so that we can go for a nice romantic walk in a driving rainstorm." She leaned down and kissed Chad on the cheek.

"The office in the cannery is available you two," quipped Mark.

"Take time while you can," smiled Roads. "American air and

naval power are going to build up all winter. Winston Churchill is pressing to shift our focus to Europe, and the Navy brass says the real war is in the Central Pacific. In D.C., it's unacceptable to have American territory in enemy hands."

CHAPTER 30

THE NORTH PACIFIC, SPRING 1943

The enemy chatter on ground frequencies had come down to bitching about sitting in anti-aircraft positions, trying to stay dry in the rain, and trying to stay warm in the snow. The critical messages between the two Japanese bases and Japan were all now encoded. Life on the ground had become a lot like what Chad imagined life as a gopher with eagles for neighbors must be like.

The Japanese managed to build docks and even some buildings, but whenever there was the kind of day that made life in the Aleutians special, prowling American planes tried hard to destroy everything being built. Chad lifted off from the airfield on Adak Island where he had just refueled. He dropped to five hundred feet and turned for a camera run over one of the Japanese bases. At almost four hundred miles an hour he watched the Japanese anti-aircraft gun crews trying to man their guns as he screamed over their island base. Behind his P-38 the air buzzed with their fire. It was becoming a favorite game for him, filming their bases at the altitude of two football fields, the enemy scrambling to catch up. At full power, Chad was over the enemy base before they could hear him coming.

In spite of the coded messages, the American intelligence groups always seemed to know what the enemy was doing, which wasn't much. American pilots had given the float equipped fighters the Japanese had worked so hard to build, a short life. Still, every month Army and Navy aviators died, a few to enemy fire, but many more to weather. By February, it had become Chad's practice to monitor American frequencies while returning from a mission to try to help pilots lost in the weather soup of the Aleutians or who had crash landed.

Gritt had become the envy of the base, the only guy most of the men knew with a steady girl. Their routine had ground down to work, staying warm and dry, and finding some way to spend an hour or two together. That last item was something that few of the other people on the base shared.

The tiny rock hideout outside of the harbor was becoming unbearable. Peter no longer confirmed the messages that Mark sent, unless it reflected a major activity. To the Japanese, it was obvious that most of the pounding Attu and Kiska were taking came from bases that their spy at Dutch Harbor knew little about. Even the messages from Michi had become few and far between. The troops and sailors on both sides had begun calling the North Pacific campaign the forgotten war. Men were dying and few knew, fewer yet knew why.

Once in a while, something happened that recharged their batteries. American bombers would catch a Japanese supply ship at one of the two bases and sink it. American submarines and Japanese submarines disappeared. The Japanese gunners would manage to hit one of the bombers, turning their bases into what, from the air, looked like a golf course where no one replaced a divot. O'Hara was now free to roam around the base without an escort.

Among the people involved in the Special Operations effort, Roads' primary effort had become cheerleading, especially with Mark, who read the distress in his father's communiqués, as the situation in Japan crumbled.

Chad's mission had evolved into helping the Navy's cat and

mouse game, as they struggled to cut off the resupply lines to the islands. His P-38 was at 12,000 feet, above a heavy cloudbank that covered the Pacific south of the Japanese bases. He thumbed through a dozen frequencies, trying to find an enemy, who had learned that radio silence was good insurance. Suddenly his radio crackled to life. Some Japanese transport, being escorted by a destroyer or two, was requesting permission to slow down until the main convoy could catch up. Chad quickly spun the dial of the direction finder and scratched a line from his position to where the transmission had taken place. A minute later another ship transmitted its answer. "Anata wa jibun no ichi o iji shimasu." The ship was to maintain its position.

The transmission had lasted long enough for Chad to plot a line to the second ship and then estimate a line between them. Below him, an American task force was spread out looking to block just such a resupply convoy. Chad pushed the nose of the P-38 over, advancing the throttles from just-keep-it-in-the-air to let's-go-kick-some-ass. He chose the line to the first transmission and dropped through the clouds, concentrating on his compass and praying that the atmospheric pressure where he was patrolling was close to what it had been where he took off. If it was much lower or if the cloud cover reached close to the ocean's surface, he was going swimming.

His altimeter wound down; 8,000 feet became 6,000 feet, which quickly became 4,000 feet. At 2,000 feet, the screaming P-38 slipped below the clouds. In the distance, only five miles away, a transport ship flanked by two destroyers was churning northeast toward Kiska Island. Chad screamed over the ships forty-five seconds later, continuing on a straight course until he figured he was out of gunnery range before beginning a turn. He plotted the direction of the ships and then redrew a line back to where the other transmission had taken place. He fumbled with his radio, dialing in the frequency he hoped the Navy would be using. "Task Force One Six, this is Snooper. I have just passed over a Japanese transport and two destroyers and have been reading communications with another

Japanese vessel believed to be part of a larger convoy approximately twenty miles southeast of this position." He released the transmit button and waited for a reply.

"Who the hell is this and how did you get this frequency?" came the reply.

"I am a specially equipped Army P-38, and I was given this frequency this morning when I launched from Dutch," replied Gritt.

"Well stay off this frequency, Army. We are conducting a sweep looking for a Japanese resupply mission," came the answer.

"That's what I am trying to tell you," keyed Chad, "I just flew over three ships and can confirm other ships in trail."

"Look Pal, or Tojo, or whoever you are, just stay the hell off from this frequency."

"This is Snooper. A few nights ago I had a Scotch with Admiral McMorris. Tell him Snooper called and found what he is looking for about 180 miles southeast of Kiska on approximately a 225 degree line." Chad grimaced, as he waited for a reply, but got none. "Have a nice day, Snooper out."

Chad pushed the throttles and started a slow climb back through the clouds. He was halfway back to Adak when his radio crackled.

"Hey Snooper, if you are still on frequency, the admiral says to say thanks. We are engaging. I think you found the whole Japanese Navy."

Chad smiled, *finally something other than same old shit, different day.*

It was a couple hours before dark when he finally rolled to a stop on the runway at Dutch. The crosswinds had been horrible on approach, the kind of bouncing and twisting that got a pilot wondering if man is supposed to fly. If he hadn't been so tired, he might have been nervous, instead he stuck the landing and tucked the P-38 into its parking place. Normally as an Army plane, at a Navy airstrip he had to chalk his own wheels and put his own bird to bed.

As he unbuckled his seat belts, two Navy guys who worked for Roads, rushed to help him. "That was fine work, Captain," laughed one of them. The task force found the Japs right where you said they would be. I think they are still slugging it out, Sir."

Chad looked around; both Roads and Carmen were sitting in a car parked next to a hanger trying to stay out of the rain. *This is the way to debrief a mission,* he laughed, knowing his next stop would be the officers club.

Roads had been briefed on what the intel guys were calling the battle of the Komandorski Islands. The task force had found a much stronger enemy than intelligence had predicted. Outnumbered more than two to one and with no air support available, they had attacked, trying to get through the Japanese escorts to sink the transport ships. Both sides had damage, the worst probably the American cruiser Salt Lake City, which had been badly hit, but was still afloat. The Japanese had taken their hits and for some reason turned around.

"Of course, Captain," concluded Roads, "as usual, you were never there."

"I don't see why it matters anymore," quipped Chad. "My primary mission here is pretty well done. Today was the first time in a month that I earned my pay."

"Be patient, son, what you know about enemy radio will be very important when we decide to retake Kiska and Attu. Besides, you earned your pay for a lifetime when you found that Zero. Once our guys got a good look at it, and started to fly it, we developed tactics that have saved hundreds of lives. I'll buy another round if you two want to waste an evening with a gray old man."

The threesome had just received a third round at the table when sirens from the area of the harbor began to wail. Chad rose to look toward the harbor where it was just light enough to see the outlines of the surrounding mountains and a billowing fire. "Something burning down by the airstrip," he said, as sitting down again. "Looks like they have it under control."

They hadn't touched the drinks when one of the enlisted men who had helped him secure his plane waved from the door where the club manager was having none of his argument that an enlisted man should be allowed in to deliver an important message.

Finally, Roads skidded his chair back and made his way across the busy room. A moment later he yelled at Chad and Carmen. "Grab your coats and mine; we need to take a little ride."

Five minutes later, the three stood in the rain and watched the firemen douse the last of the flames from where a large two engine Dakota transport plane laid crumpled. "He lost it at touchdown," offered an officer standing with them. "All four men aboard got out before it burned. I am damned sorry about your plane Captain."

Under the crumpled wreckage of the transport, just the nose of the P-38 was still recognizable, as part of what was now a blob of melted aluminum and cinders.

"Maybe this means Chad can get some time away from here. Maybe he can meet me back in California when I rotate out in April," observed Carmen, hoping for a positive answer from Roads.

"Are you leaving?"

"Not yet, my hero. I volunteered to do some training for the Navy."

"How about a walk," suggested Chad?

"Why not, my shoes are soaked anyway." He slipped her coat over her shoulders, and then a raincoat and opened the door.

"I will miss you, Miss Alvarez," he started.

"Let's not start that until the day gets closer. I have other things in mind. For example, when I told Mark about the transfer, he offered his house for the weekend. I just happen to have both days off, and have been told by someone close to your CO that you do too."

"What about Mark's transmissions to the cave dwellers?"

"We both know the codes by now. You will just have to be Mark with a bad cold. I just hope you can keep your strength up while you are sick."

CHAPTER 31

THE NORTH PACIFIC, APRIL 1943

R oads sat quietly as the staff meeting of senior officers wound down. He had known for weeks that the combined American-Canadian invasion force was ready to retake Attu. Mark had been preparing the enemy without realizing what he was doing, while Chad was monitoring the Japanese and helping to stop reinforcements.

Since the battle of the Komandorski Islands, the Japanese no longer tried to resupply their bases by surface craft, instead relying on freight submarines. The large subs were in demand all over the Pacific where American forces now controlled the seas. The little chatter that Chad picked up on his sweeps over their bases revealed a force both dispirited and bored. Supplies were short. A few died every week from American bombs with no way of striking back. Worse, their commanders knew that across the Pacific, the allies, while at the beginning of the war outnumbered them two to one, now outnumbered the Japanese military by twice that. There would be no reinforcements, and the weather was improving, which meant the Americans were coming.

The enemy's boredom was about to end. As the meeting broke up, Roads made his way across the bay to brief the Special Operations team.

"Your new P-38 will not be ready until early June," he advised Chad. "Within the next few weeks we could really use your expertise on what the enemy is saying on the ground. I pulled every string I could, but they cannot have a new snooper plane ready in time. When it's ready, one of the women transport pilots will get it to Alaska."

"That has to mean the invasion is set for some time before June."

"The rumor mill is running all over the base," answered Roads. "Some rumors are close to reality. Anyway, it's time to shut down our communications between the cave dwellers and the submarine they are reporting to."

Mark knew this day would come, but still it was a shock. "What about my folks when they go off the air?'

"The sub's transmissions will continue, Mark." Roads pulled a binder from his briefcase and handed it to Mark. Here are the transcripts of last month's transmissions from the sub to Japan. Our cryptology guys in Hawaii have jotted down the codes they think the enemy is using, taking your messages to Peter, then his to the sub and finally the subs to their handler and decoding them. Once we shut down the sub and take out your friends across the bay, it will be your job to continue sending messages."

Mark didn't feel relieved. "Within days of the invasion starting, the intelligence guys in Japan are going to figure out that we are sending false information."

"But we won't be sending false information, just information that is a little outdated. In the interim, I have two tasks for you two. First, I need a plan to get real time information on what is going on with the enemy on Attu, including what they do once the attack starts. Second, I think it is time to see if you can come up with a plan to evacuate your folks from Karafuto." Roads smiled at Chad and Mark. "We have the full cooperation of the Admiral. Still, keep it simple and real. He isn't about to invade Japan."

❃

Carmen brushed her hair across Chad's naked back. "You can't tell me where you're going, and you know I am scheduled out on the ninth. Will you be back by then?"

Chad rolled over, wrapping her in his arms and squeezing. He ran his hands down her back, onto her bottom. "I can't say any more."

"Then I guess it's time to dress before Mark gets back to the house. I wouldn't want to embarrass him."

"Carmen, right now he isn't thinking about anything except how to try to get the cave dwellers out of their cave. He will be gone all day." He lifted her long brown hair with the back of his hand kissing her neck. My God, you feel good."

"Stop that," she giggled.

"Can I help it if you are ticklish in the only place my lips can reach with you on top of me."

From below the house the starting growl of a diesel generator drowned out her whispered answer. All over the base radio operators began calling their commanders, as a loud hiss filled the speakers of their radio sets.

❋

On the hillside below the rock house, a squad of American infantry worked its way toward the enemy post. The grass was slick, the terrain steep. Solid clouds rested at the tops of the surrounding mountains, thick and black, turning afternoon into twilight. The squad communicated with hand signals as Mark directed their climb from the end of the column. He checked his watch for the fifth time in a half-hour.

"Captain," he whispered to the officer next to him, "the radio interference started five minutes ago. It won't take long before the men in that house figure out that something is wrong."

"How much longer until we get there?" asked the captain.

"At the pace we are climbing, maybe fifteen minutes." Mark raised the binoculars he kept hidden under his raincoat to keep the lenses dry, scanning the hill above. "If we stay in this creek, we should be above them in twenty minutes."

"I put two good woodsmen out in front," smiled the captain. "I don't have a single soldier with combat experience, so we will take it slow. I don't want to walk into an ambush."

The main group found the two scouts waiting where a trail, only the width of a man's foot, led up the hillside from the small stream. From the air or the sea below, the trail was invisible.

"What is that good awful stench?" asked the captain, covering his mouth to keep his voice from traveling.

One of the scouts pointed at the small pool the unit had just worked their way around. "That, Sir, is their toilet," he whispered. "It flushes every time it rains hard. This small waterfall just uphill must be where they draw their water."

"Leave two men here to cut off any escape this way," ordered the captain. "The rest of you move it. We want to be above them before they get suspicious."

From above, the only thing distinguishing the roof of the small house was a thin chimney. There was a very faint trace of smoke rising.

The soldiers spread out above the house. The rain, driven by a steady wind masked their movement. The sea, only a mile below was invisible. The captain turned to Mark and nodded.

"Peter, it is Mark!" he yelled. "We need to talk. Wareware wa hanashi o suru hitsuyo ga dete kimasu."

"I thought there was something strange about all of the radio frequencies being jammed," called Peter. "How many soldiers are with you?"

"Twenty, but they are here to take you into custody, not to hurt you," answered Mark.

"I will be shot as a spy," called Peter.

"Not if you are in uniform. You will all be treated as prisoners of war."

The statement was answered by a long silence. "I will discuss it with my soldiers."

"Peter, I am a prisoner too," lied Mark. "They have figured out what we have been doing. They have even allowed me to stay in my house."

Through the rain there was movement from the front of the house. One of the Japanese soldiers crawled from the doorway, swinging a long rifle toward Mark's voice. He shot in Mark's general direction. All of his targets were in the tall grass or behind rocks. His shot was answered by a dozen. The man swiveled, his body jerking as each bullet found its mark.

"Peter," called Mark, "that was really stupid. That man died for nothing. He is wearing a uniform. He would have been a POW. We already have two Japanese Navy pilots living at the base. And, don't think that you can warn the submarine, they have recorded every frequency we both use and are jamming them."

"Mark, tell me the truth, what is really happening in the war?"

"Peter, in the air and on the ocean, Japan is losing. Already they have lost half of their aircraft carriers while the Americans have added more. The war on land is just starting," answered Mark honestly.

"I am ready to go. I am happy not to spend one more day in this hole. You will not have to shoot me," called Peter.

A moment later, a muffled explosion sent dirt and rocks flying from the front of the stone house. The captain waved to his squad to converge on the house. As they did, a rifle sounded from above them; the captain stumbled, blood running down the inside of his raincoat and onto his boots. Mark turned, looking up into the eyes of the soldier that he had given the cigarettes to. The man smiled as he sighted his rifle at Mark who stood unarmed, shaking, waiting to die, and then the soldier swung the rifle toward one of the other soldiers moving toward the smoking house. Before he could pull the trigger, two bullets toppled him into the grass.

The Navy corpsman who had climbed the hill with them rushed to the captain and began working to stop the bleeding.

Mark slid down the hill where half dozen soldiers stood in front of the stone hut. "Don't go in there, Mr. O'Hara," offered one of the scouts, a sergeant.

Mark leaned into the low door. In the gloom, Peter's body lay against the back wall, his chest blown open and his hand and lower arm missing.

"I heard that this has been happening all over the Pacific," said the sergeant. "Rather than surrender, they blow themselves up with a grenade."

Mark started to crawl into the hut.

"You can't help that man," barked the sergeant.

"I am looking for code books or notes," answered Mark. Four small bound journals flopped into the mud at the sergeant's feet. Pulling Peter's hand from below the body, Mark tugged a knife from a sheath on his belt and severed the finger with Peter's class ring on it. He wrapped the finger and ring in a white handkerchief and tucked it into his pocket. "Just a little token that I promised my father," he offered to the sergeant. "When you bury this man, I will piss on his grave."

❃

A hundred miles to the northwest, the American submarine SCORPION cruised at only four knots, its periscope barely above the water. In the distance, her captain could occasionally pick up the spray when a larger wave splashed across the periscope of the Japa- nese submarine they were trailing.

"Sir, engineering says we have only about a 30 percent charge left on the batteries," whispered the executive officer. "We have been on batteries for five hours now."

"I get it Scottie, but that sub out there has been on batteries all day. I need to know immediately if he tries to start his diesels, but I don't see a snorkel. I think he has to surface to recharge. The shot will be a lot easier if he is on the surface."

"Aye, Sir. He is steady on his course, range steady at one thousand yards."

The captain checked his watch. Another hour passed. *How long can he stay down*, he wondered.

The captain finished another cup of coffee. He desperately needed to get rid of a couple of the cups from hours before.

"You're up," he said to his executive officer. "I'll be right back."

He had just reached the head when one of the hands called. "Now, really, after four hours," he mumbled, as he turned around.

"Captain," said the exec, "ears reports the sub is blowing its tanks."

"Give me a solution."

"Range one thousand yards. Speed still four knots. Course still zero one zero."

"Set torpedo depth at five feet," ordered the Captain. "We are close enough I only want to shoot two fish." He swung the periscope, setting up the angle on the bow and confirming range. "Fire one," he ordered and before he received confirmation of that firing, "fire two."

"Number one running hot and steady," came a call. "Number two hot and steady."

Through the periscope, he watched the Japanese submarine emerging from the depths, and a second later watched as the center of the boat lifted out of the water with the explosion of his first torpedo. He didn't have to tell his crew the result of the attack on the submarine they had been tracking for days; they could hear for themselves. There was no cheer, only faint smiles, as everyone aboard visualized what was going on in the steel tube full of men just like them only a half mile away.

"It's better them than us," offered the exec watching his captain's face.

"Let's get up on top and see if there are any survivors," stammered the captain.

"Blow mains, rig for diesels, battle stations surface," called the exec. "We have new orders, Chet. We are to make flank speed back to Dutch to pick up a scouting party."

The sinking submarine was the first ship that the *Scorpion* had ever fired on. "Not before we see if there are any survivors. I saw hatches opening just before the torpedo hit."

The *Scorpion* slipped up to the main dock at seven the next morning. Two Navy captains stood waiting, as three injured Japanese sailors in stretcher baskets were pushed onto the deck of the sub. A medical staff waited. Next to the captains, Chad Gritt and the two men from Attu waited, a small mountain of equipment covered by a tarp at their feet.

"I still think I should do this mission alone," said Chad. "The fewer men on that mountain, the lower the chance of being seen."

Roads just smiled. "What about orders do you not understand Mr. Gritt?"

The stretcher-bearers dropped a stretcher a few feet away, racing to help lift the next stretcher to the dock. Chad looked over at the tortured face of a Japanese officer, graying at the temples, his hands tied to the sides of the stretcher. "Watch that one," called one of the crewmen from the *Scorpion*. "He has tried to kill himself and anyone else he can reach since the captain fished him out of the drink."

Chad knelt next to the man and smiled. "Anyone got a smoke?" he asked. One of the corpsmen tossed Chad a pack of cigarettes. He slipped the matches from under the cellophane wrap and tapped a cigarette from the pack, lighting it. He took a couple of puffs to make sure it was lit and slipped it between the officer's lips.

"Tokiniha sore go shinu yori mo, anata no kuni no tame ni ikiru koto oo susue shimasu," he said.

Chad looked over at Roads and the other captain. "Sometimes it is better to live for your country than die for it."

The wounded officer swiveled his head knocking ashes from the cigarette on the aluminum frame of the stretcher. He closed his eyes, a tear on his cheek.

All three stretchers were hoisted into the Dodge ambulance.

Two guards with side arms climbed in with them for the five-minute ride to the hospital. In seconds a larger truck with provisions replaced it on the wharf.

"Chet," laughed the younger captain, "you are going right back out. Get your guys busy loading these supplies and then move over to the fueling dock." He turned to Roads. "You have the honor of introducing the passengers and the mission, since even I don't know what is so important that you can commandeer one of my boats."

The lanky sub captain scowled his way to the dock. "Are you the one who took us out of the war to waste our time writing down messages? My guys have been at sea for a week now, tracking the enemy sub we just sunk. The only good part of the mission is that radio operator we inherited. That kid Chimo is a real kick."

"I am responsible," smiled Roads, returning the man's salute. "Chimo spent ten years in Japan growing up, we needed someone who spoke the language fluently." Roads introduced the three men standing with him before turning toward the empty end of the dock.

"You are going to take the men you just met, and land them on the back side of Attu. They are going to climb to the top of the mountain overlooking the Japanese camp and set up a radio to monitor what they are saying. They will relay coded messages to your boat, which will be close enough to shore to recover them if they are compromised. Chimo will resend the messages in Japanese back to my man here."

"I didn't spend fifteen years of my life at sea to be a nursemaid," spat Chet.

"Commander, in less than a month 30,000 Americans and Canadians are going to assault that island. The men you are transporting will be pinpointing where the enemy strong points are, and when the attack starts, they will switch to English and keep the commanders posted on what the enemy is saying and doing."

"I think my men would rather be shooting at the enemy than listening to them."

"You mean the men who risked their lives to rescue those three

Japanese sailors. The same men who tied down the captain of that sub to keep him from ripping open his own wrists. I think all of you would pass up the rest of the war entirely, if it would save a dozen American or Canuk kids."

Chet smiled. "I know how to take an order, and so do they, Captain Roads."

"I am happy to hear that. Now one more thing, when the landing troops are getting things in hand, you will need to get those three men off that island. We don't need any casualties from friendly fire. And, Commander, as far as your men know, this is a simple scouting mission, and that is how it will go into your logbook. No names, no mention of radios, no discussion of receiving or retransmitting messages."

"How do we communicate with them while they are on shore?"

"Work it out on the way. I want those men ashore four days from today."

CHAPTER 32

ATTU ISLAND, ALASKA, MAY 1943

The *Scorpion* slipped into Temac Bay, with its decks awash. A half-dozen men trained binoculars on the slopes above for any sign of the enemy. "There's no sign of men on that hillside, not even a trail," mumbled the submarine's captain.

The boat crept within fifty yards of the beach before a small army of men began hauling a thousand pounds of supplies to the deck, including a three-man bidarka that Ivan and Paul had fashioned in the Seabee wood shop the week before. In minutes, the two halves of the frame were bolted together, and a canvas cover was stretched over it. Three men were helped into the craft and began paddling toward the shore, looking for a likely spot to stash most of the supplies.

Ivan pointed to a gravel beach below where a ravine stretched toward the top of the mountain. Chad, sitting in the center seat, tugged the flashlight from his jacket and sent a signal. The submarine was already growing faint in fading light. Four sailors dug their paddles into the clear water next to their raft, headed toward where the bidarka was beaching.

With seven men to unload, the black rubber raft was back on the water in minutes, ready to move a second load.

"We take only the radio, tarps and camouflage netting on the first trip up the mountain," offered Chad.

"W-w-w-what about a-a r-r-r-rifle?" asked Paul.

"There are three of us and about three thousand of them," answered Chad. "If they are watching right now, we won't get halfway up this mountain. Once we pick a spot to observe from, we will come back for another load."

Ivan looked at the pile of batteries hidden under a tarp, covered by grass. "You mean Paul and I will be coming back."

"No, it is going to be tough, but I would like the three of us to pack enough up that mountain to supply us for three days," answered Chad. "After that, it will probably take one trip per day for food and two fresh batteries."

"When will the Navy come?" asked Ivan.

"I don't know. They don't want us to know. If one of us is captured we can't tell the enemy when the invasion will come. We have enough supplies for weeks."

Ivan helped Chad into the straps of a heavy pack board, and then Paul. Those two men held his pack steady as he struggled into a pack that almost buckled his knees.

The trip to the top of rolling mountain took two hours. The two young men led Chad to a small cleft where they could watch the base below. Chad pushed five short green stakes into the ground and ran out an antenna wire, while the other two worked to put together a painted aluminum frame. They stretched a green tarp over it. Each time they crested the mountain the men crawled to avoid silhouetting themselves.

Across the valley, a larger mountain dominated the plain below. While Chad helped Ivan spread the camouflaged netting over the tarp, Paul sat in the grass with a pair of binoculars glued to his eyes.

"Can you see observation posts on the mountain?" called Chad.

Paul held up three fingers. The photos from Chad's recon flights matched what the sharp-eyed Aleut man saw.

With the low power radio in place, Chad began searching the

frequencies he had identified over the previous months, finding little chatter. He switched off the radio to save battery. "Let's make another trip."

When the men crawled into their canvas wrapped sleeping bags it was after midnight. Below it was still light. Chad made a note in a journal he carried, reflecting the day's activity, then closed it and returned it to the waterproof bag. "Goodnight gents," he mumbled.

"S-s-s-should-n-nt one o-of us s-s-stay a awake?" asked Paul.

"We will set up a watch starting tomorrow," replied Chad. "For right now I am so tired I couldn't stay awake."

"I w-will w-w-watch n-now."

Chad never heard him, nor did Ivan. Both were snoring in seconds. Paul picked a book of Rudyard Kipling stories from his personal pack and began reading, stopping every few minutes to scan the mountain below for anything that had changed. *Perhaps someday I will write about this adventure,* he thought. *To be a writer; no one would think I am dumb.*

The communications schedule with the *Scorpion* called for a transmission every eight hours. The radio communications coming from the Japanese base was minimal, but the activity during the day was even less. On any day that American planes could fly, the movement in the valley ground to a halt. Chad watched with fascination as the Japanese divided their work into small areas, all close to underground air raid shelters.

The schedule of air attacks had become so repetitive that the shelters emptied about four in the afternoon and the base below turned into an anthill on a sunny evening. Even the men manning the air artillery had built a routine where only a few guns fired at the passing planes, and each fired only six rounds.

On the third day, Chad intercepted communications on a channel used by the Japanese to communicate with their Navy. The communications was routine – weather, winds and observations from the watchers on the high mountain across from where the snoopers hid. Five hours later, a huge submarine rose from the deep in the outer harbor, making its way to the often-repaired pier in the center of the camp.

A hundred men converged on the sub, as it tied up. Barrels and boxes were lifted from two gaping hatches. Simple man-powered lifts swung nets full of supplies onto the dock where it was whisked away. Chad watched, fascinated as the freight went into storage sites scattered across the plain and onto the hillsides above. The crates of ammunition were sent directly to where the huge anti-ship guns were sighted or close to the anti-aircraft artillery. After the supplies were unloaded, a small tractor with a tank on a cart rumbled onto the pier and began pumping diesel fuel from the subs own tanks while an ambulance arrived with four men on stretchers. The sub was on the surface for only two hours. Chad checked his watch; it was just after nine at night when the sub slipped from the harbor.

His 10 p.m. report was short and simple: "A sub delivered supplies between seven and nine this evening and is headed home," he said in Japanese. *Maybe,* he thought, *the Navy can use the information to find that sub.*

The next day, a heavy bomber raid tore more divots from the ground below, churning up small mountains of earth, leaving pools of muddy water and hitting nothing of importance. The way the enemy had spread out its supplies made even a direct hit on one supply site unimportant.

As Chad sat with a set of earphones most of the day, Ivan and Paul crawled from vantage points to lookout with maps of the island and binoculars studying the enemy base. While much of the native village survived, the Japanese had built camouflaged positions for virtually everything of importance. On the seventh day, Chad arranged for the two young men to paddle out to where the *Scorpion* waited. They delivered a map that showed the location of every heavy gun and strong point on the base. The *Scorpion* would meet another sub to hand off the map. It would be rushed to Dutch.

On May 9th, everything started to change. Air artillery was moved into armored positions that had been prepared months before. Hundreds of men began packing supplies from the main base up onto the hillsides above the base. "The invasion is coming, isn't it?" observed Ivan. "The men down there know it is coming."

Chad's report at two that afternoon reflected the activity. Six hours later, well after the normal routine, twenty-four heavy bombers flew over the base, pounding the area with hundreds of bombs. Many of the sites marked on the map were destroyed, but the guns had been moved. Unlike every other raid that Chad had witnessed, the enemy stayed in the open, working.

The next morning, there was little movement. For the first time that afternoon, small patrols fanned out onto the shoreline and the surrounding hills. Paul's sharp eyes tracked a patrol that made its way from a naval defense gun emplacement on the hill below. Six men were working their way up through the grass headed directly for where they hid.

"They c-come f-f-fast n now," he offered. "Do w-we g-g-go?"

Chad looked at the camp. On the backside of the hill, there was a pile of drained batteries. The site itself, while difficult to see from below, would be impossible to miss from right in front of them. He checked his watch. It was still hours until the *Scorpion* would be expecting a call.

Ivan watched him intently. "We can take the bidarka and move further down the island," he offered.

"Then we can never come back, and we have only done part of what we were sent here to do," answered Gritt. "No, I think we figure out exactly where those men are going. Maybe they won't come this far. If they do, we fight. If we cannot kill all of them, or if the people below figure out what has happened, then we run." He looked at the other two waiting for a response.

Paul smiled and picked up the M-1 rifle he 'borrowed,' stuffing his pockets with all of the ammunition he could. Ivan nodded his head and smiled nervously. *Two civilians with rifles and a Thompson sub-machine gun in the hands of someone who has never fired one against six trained soldiers,* he thought. "Where to?" he asked Paul.

"T-they c-c-c-come r right here." He pointed at the small draw just below where they were set up.

Chad's hands shook. Neither of the others seemed worried. He pointed to a rock outcropping below and to their right. "You two go find a good place where you cannot be seen and wait there. When they come up the draw, I will wait until I can see as many as possible and then cut loose with the Thompson. You two make sure none of the others escape down the hill."

Below them, the air raid sirens began blaring. Chad looked off to the west where two formations of bombers were turning to make a run over the base. Shadowing them were a dozen fighters, still too far away to identify. Below them, enemy guns began to spread flack into the sky in front of the bombers.

A roar startled all three men. From behind them, six P-38s ripped over the hill where they sat, screaming down into the valley, targeting the anti-aircraft artillery. Two of the guns went quiet, as the P-38s lifted from their runs, circling out over the bay.

Ivan and Paul sprinted for the rocks to their right, sliding down behind them just as the head of the first Japanese soldier rose above the terrain in front of them. Chad watched as the first enemy soldier climbed straight toward where he lay. The soldier stopped for a moment to watch, as the bombers began hitting the base, clobbering more sites that had been marked on the map.

Chad checked to make sure the safety on the Thompson was off as the head of a second and then a third Japanese soldier crested the hill. *They are really spread out,* he observed. *At best, I can get a clear shot at two of them.* He waited until the front soldier looked up straight into his eyes.

Chad raised the Thompson to his shoulder and squeezed the trigger, forgetting everything he had been told. He held the trigger down until the first man melted into the grass and watched as the second stumbled, lifting his rifle. The Thompson locked open as the last bullet in the clip was fired.

The second Japanese soldier grabbed at his leg, his hand covering a spreading red stain, and then he raised his rifle again and fired. He worked the bolt, as Chad pulled the empty clip from his submachine gun. He felt a second bullet crack by his ear as he picked up a second clip from the rock in front of him and jammed it into the Thompson, and then struggled to chamber a round.

He looked up to see the Japanese soldier sink to the ground, working the bolt in his rifle as he did. Chad could look right down the barrel of that rifle. He tugged the trigger of the Thompson, sending a stream of .45 caliber bullets over the man's head. He pulled the barrel down as he fired, emptying the second clip. The man in front of him had disappeared.

From his right, Ivan was sprinting toward where he sat staring at the empty gun. "We killed two, but two are running down the hill."

Chad could hear the methodical crack of Paul's M-1, as he tried to stop the men. Paul stood up and shouted, "They are too far away!"

Shit, thought Chad. "We're going to have the whole goddamned Jap Army on our doorstep in an hour," he stammered. Ivan sat staring at him.

Chad had been listening to the Japanese talk about their plan to move back from the bay, when Paul had warned him of the patrol. He adjusted the frequency dial on the radio and then picked up the microphone while cramming the earphones back on his head. "P-38s circling over the bay on Attu, this is Snooper, anybody copying me?"

"I heard you broke your bird, Snooper," came the reply."

"I did. I am on the ground on top of the small mountain to the southeast of the main base. I have just been discovered by a Japanese patrol. I killed four of them, but two are running downhill. If they get some help, I am toast."

"Okay hotshot, this is Colonel Wayne. You guys listening to this, that's one of ours down there in trouble, let go hunting."

Chad watched as the P-38s swung back toward his mountain. He scrambled from his position and dug two red towels from his pack. He handed one to each of the men with him. "Put one on either side of the tarp."

"Colonel, we just marked our position with two red towels. There are three of us here, anyone outside of those towels is fair game."

He listened as Colonel Wayne split his group into two plane flights and spread them out. "I have the two men running down the hill," he called. "One in–"

The men on the hill watched as the nose of the P-38 erupted in flame. Right behind him another plane followed, the rattle of machine gun and cannon fire echoing even over the sound of bombs exploding over the harbor.

Chad watched with amazement as a second section swung around from the other direction, unleashing a stream of death toward the ground.

"That should take care of the problem, Snooper," came a call. "If there were only two men down there, both are down."

"I owe you one, Sir," answered Chad. "We are going to haul the bodies of the men we killed down closer to where you were firing. Don't get trigger happy."

"Hell, Captain, you are on you own, it's time for us to head for home. You know, warm shower, a steak at the club, Scotch with ice cubes. When you get back to town, you can buy for the six of us until we say stop. Have a nice day."

The P-38s made a strafing pass along the waterfront, starting a fire and then they were gone. "We need to move the men we killed down toward where those planes were shooting, just in case someone decides to come up looking for them."

As the men started down the hill, Chad grabbed Paul's arm. "When you yelled at us you didn't stutter."

Paul smiled, as he and Ivan grabbed the legs of the first man that Chad had killed. Chad walked another twenty yards where the second man lay, stitched from the top of his head to his belly button. He grabbed the man's arms and began to drag just as the skies opened up, rain soaking the men in seconds.

The rain-slick grass mixed with a smattering of winter snow made it easy to drag bodies downhill. The effect of the .45 caliber rounds from the Thompson were gruesome, and the .30 caliber bullets of the M-1's Ivan and Paul carried had stopped the two men they shot right where they were hit. Killing the enemy didn't shake the three men, but the two bodies below did rattle them. The P-38s spitting hundreds of rounds had shattered the bodies beyond recognition.

"Put the four we pulled down the hill over here where we can partially cover them with the men killed by the planes. If they come up looking, hopefully they won't realize that the bottom ones were killed by smaller weapons."

"I a-a-a-am g glad t-t-they are d-dead," scowled Paul.

Ivan just stared at the cloth bags of torn meat that the soldiers had become. The air raid had come in the later afternoon, well after American aircraft normally returned to base. Chad struggled with the weight of the man he was dragging.

The midnight sun made it difficult to tell the time. By Chad's watch, it was after midnight when the men crawled back under the tarp of their hiding place. All three were soaked, reeking of blood and exhausted. Paul passed out three cardboard cartons of rations. The men popped the heating tablets from their wrappers and propped them under the small pots each carried. As hungry as they were, a hot drink was the only thing on their minds.

Later, they ate cold dinners and then changed out of their wet clothing, laying it out in the rain to soak away the blood. "I will take the first watch while I listen to the radio," offered Chad. "I will try to reach the sub since we missed our last radio check. You two get some sleep. Paul, I will wake you in three hours to take over.

Chad awoke, his body telling him he was still exhausted. Paul smiled down at the man trying to clear his head. Paul pointed toward the sea. He smiled from ear to ear but said nothing. Chad struggled from the warmth of his sleeping bag and followed the Aleut man to where he could look out over the ocean.

"W-w-wait. T-the f-fog moves t-t-through."

Chad felt cheated; his schedule gave him two more hours of

sleep. "Why in the hell did...." The fog swept up over the mountain revealing the sea and a dozen ships.

"More there a-and th-th-there," offered Paul, pointing at bays across the plain below. Th-the J-j-japan m-move up to th-th-the hills. M-maybe coming th-this w-way."

Seconds later, the sound of heavy Navy guns echoed across the hills and the sound of explosions on the plain rumbled from the fog.

Chad stumbled back to the radio. He dialed in the *Scorpion* and pressed transmit. "Snooper here, do you read?"

"Did those big nasty naval guns wake you up, Snooper?" came the response. "It is about time you woke up; we have been trying to reach you for two hours."

"Is this Chimo, or one of the officers I am talking with?" asked Chad.

"It's me as usual, Captain Gritt."

"Well put somebody on that I can call an asshole, without getting courts martialed."

"Well, Sir, that would be someone of equal rank, and we don't have any Navy lieutenant commanders aboard. I'll get the captain for you."

A new voice came on. "Go ahead Snooper. I guess you have figured out that the invasion fleet is sitting on your doorstep."

"No shit, Sir. Sorry we were hard to find. We were in a firefight here last night. Must have slept in after it ended. Anyway, I do not have any direct link to the commander of the fleet. Can you get him a message for me?"

"Fire away, Snooper."

"Tell him the Japanese have all pulled back from the waterfront. They have scattered their dug-in positions on the hillsides around the plain, maybe even the one we are on. The Navy is shelling empty positions. We will stay put until we can see if we are compromised, but we may be on a dead run for the boat soon. We will keep the radio up so that we can keep you posted."

"That's affirm, Snooper. We will see if we can get you a direct line to the commander and to the ground force. They are having trouble getting the boats away, so they might be a little late. *Scorpion* clear."

"Snooper clear."

Chad turned to his two companions. "Let's slip down the mountain and see what is going on just below us."

The three men started down the mountain to where a small knob allowed them to search the hillside below their hide. A half-mile away, a Japanese heavy gun fired, sending a shockwave through the valleys. Across the mountains in front of them, other guns began lobbing shells toward the ships below.

Not far below the gun position, Japanese infantry were busy shoveling dirty mud and snow from lines of zigzag trenches cut into the sides of the mountain. Chad watched the enemy gun crew reloading, taking minutes to do what should have been done in seconds. It occurred to him that in days of watching, he had never seen a single practice round fired by the anti-ship artillery. Near the water, American naval gunfire was finishing what the bombers started, reducing the native village to splinters.

Chad reached into his jacket, retrieving the small notebook and pencil jotting down his observations.

Next to him, Paul sat anchored, binoculars glued to his face, pointing out enemy positions all around the valley. "B-B-B-Big g-gun," he managed, pointing to where a small group of men struggled to load another shell. "M-Machine g-g-g-guns on b both ends of t-t-t-that d-ditch."

Chad quickly found what the eagle-eyed young man was looking at by studying where his binoculars were sighted. "There are no Japanese down by the water that I can see."

Paul swung his binoculars toward the bay, saying nothing for five minutes. "Nope," he finally agreed.

Both men received a sharp rap on the head. Looking up into Ivan's face, he gave them the sign for silence. He pointed toward where the bodies from the fight on the hill were stacked only the length of a football field from where they hid. A dozen Japanese soldiers were dragging the bodies down the hill, an officer turning to look up toward the top of the hill. The men lay quietly until the soldiers disappeared below.

"Let's get back to the radio. We will monitor the frequencies they normally use for a couple of hours and then see if we can reach the invasion ships to report what we have seen." Chad began a hunched run through the soggy grass."

By the time the men slipped under the tarp at their camp, the first boats from the invading forces were on the beach below. Only a few dozen men spilled out of the boats and took cover as the boats backed away, returning for more troops.

"Why don't the Japanese attack those men?" asked Ivan. "They could kill all of them in minutes."

Chad began tuning the radio, finding continuous chatter.

"W-what d-d-do they s-say?" asked Paul sitting next to Chad.

"Their commander has ordered them to stay in their positions on the hillside and fight the Americans as they try to move away from the beaches. He is telling them that this is what they prepared for. They are to bleed the Americans, make them pay with their lives. He just told them that he requested reinforcements, but they might have to hold out for a month."

Chimo was ready when Chad called. ""Don't ask me why, but the radio operator I talked to said that you were to refer to him as breadbox." Chimo gave Chad the frequency he had been given by the invasion commander.

Ten minutes later, Chad signed off, the nature of the defenses they had seen and the orders from the Japanese commander passed on. Below, only a hundred Americans had made it to shore, finding little resistance. "The Japanese commander must believe help is coming," observed Chad.

"Or maybe he just made a big mistake," laughed Ivan. "Anyway, the men coming ashore must thank God that their boats aren't being met by machine guns."

"That's because the men with machine guns are coming up here," offered Paul, pointing at dozens of men spread out climbing the mountain.

"Time to close up shop," sighed Chad.

"*Scorpion*, this is Snooper, do you copy?"

"It's so good to hear your voice again," came the reply. "I figured that since you had a new girlfriend I might never hear from you again."

"Can the nonsense, Chimo," replied Chad. "We have been discovered and at least a company of enemy troops are climbing our mountain right now. It's time to get out of Dodge."

"The captain is listening, Snooper; does the enemy have any heavy weapons with them?"

"No, just rifles and it looks like at least two Nambu light machine guns," answered Chad, passing on information from the men intently watching the enemy beside him."

"How much time do you have?" asked Chimo.

Paul held up his hand and flashed the five fingers three times.

"Looks like we have about fifteen minutes before they are here."

"The captain says he can have the taxi waiting where it dropped you off in an hour."

"It will probably take us a half-hour to get to the beach. We will wait there for your signal unless these guys get too close. I am destroying the radio now. Snooper out."

Chad pried the back off from the radio, removing two tubes and dropping them into a pocket before replacing the back.

"Does that destroy the radio?" asked Ivan.

"No, but it will make it useless unless they have some spare tubes that will fit." Chad slipped a grenade from the pack. He pulled the pin, making sure that he kept the lever depressed. "Gather up what you absolutely need and get moving. I will be right behind you. I am going to leave a little surprise for the men climbing the hill. If it works, it should slow them down a bit."

Chad turned the volume all the way up, leaving only a hiss

in the headset. He carefully held the lever tightly as he tipped the radio face down onto the grenade, not moving his hand until the weight of the radio held the arming lever down. Then he grabbed his pack and sub-machinegun and followed Ivan and Paul toward the top of the mountain. The large bay on the other side of the hill was mirror calm.

Below him the two Aleut men were jogging down the trail now well carved into the steep slope. Struggling under half the load of the others, it was all Chad could do to stay on his feet on the slick path. The beach was two miles below him.

Above he heard a muffled explosion. His trap had worked; some of those chasing them were now casualties. Perhaps the others would break off their pursuit to help their wounded comrades. He turned his head back toward the top of the mountain just as the first Japanese soldier sprinted into view. Chad tripped over a rock in the trail, tumbling. The pack over his shoulder launched itself down the mountain. The duffel in his left hand cushioned his fall. His Thompson disappeared into the grass.

Chad scrambled to his feet, sliding down the wet grass toward where the pack that included his notebook and codes had lodged against a boulder. He grasped it, throwing it over his shoulder again as the first bullet from above smacked into the duffel he had just picked up. He scrambled back to the trail, struggling to stay on his feet. He failed.

Rolling onto his stomach, he scrambled to his knees and looked up. A single Japanese officer raced down the hill, a quarter mile in front of the rest of his soldiers. Chad fumbled with his pack and the duffel, stacking them above him and then unbuttoned the holster protecting his pistol. He jacked a shell into the chamber and rested the weapon on the duffel with a two-hand grip. The Japanese officer careened down the hill, a pistol waving from side to side, as he fought to keep his balance. The man was only ten yards away when Chad's small fort appeared. Chad watched the confusion on the man's face turn to fear just as two .45 caliber bullets ripped into the officer. The man tumbled down the steep slope, stumbling over Chad's small fort, landing on top of the man who had just killed him. He grabbed Chad by the throat with one hand while slapping the .45 away with the other. Then he locked both hands around Chad's neck.

The man's knees slammed into Chad, as he furiously tried to choke the life out of his enemy. Chad grasped the man's wrists, trying to pry them apart. It felt like an hour since he had last drawn a breath. He pounded on the Japanese officer's head with both fists. Chad's body began to convulse, as it fought for a breath of desperately needed air.

Chad's hands searched the ground for a rock or some other weapon, his vision starting to blur. He struck out at the officer's groin with his left hand as he tried one more time to twist the man's fingers from his throat with the other. His left hand found the hilt of the Japanese officer's sword. He struggled to pull the long blade from its sheath. There was no conscious effort left in him, his oxygen starved brain leaving only the will to live.

He felt the sword slide free of its sheath. He tried to lift it to slash at the officer's arm just as the fingers around Chad's neck began to loosen. His lungs tugged a partial breath through the fingers. Chad looked up into the staring eyes of the man on top of him. He pried the fingers from his neck and pushed the dead officer away. As his lungs finally started to work again, he wiped his face, and his hand coming away covered in blood. He didn't know if it was his or not.

Chad grabbed the pack and duffel, consciously slowing his pace to stay on his feet. He could feel the eyes of the Japanese soldiers on the back of his neck, as he stumbled downhill.

At the bottom of the hill, Ivan and Paul waited, their rifles pointed uphill. "Let's stash this gear and find the bidarka," managed Chad, struggling to catch his breath.

"The soldiers have stopped to help the man you shot," answered

Ivan. "Are you shot too?" he asked, staring at the front of Chad's uniform.

"They will keep coming," managed Chad, "their officer is dead; and no, I don't think so."

"Then they will find our gear when they reach the beach," continued Ivan. "There is nowhere to hide it. They will realize it didn't fit in the boat."

Paul began dragging a small drift log toward the beach. He motioned for the others to bring the gear, which he tied to the log with a length of cord from his pocket. While he worked, Ivan dragged the bidarka from the grass and then went back for the paddles.

"T-The b-bags w-will b-be wet," struggled Paul. "B-But t-they will d-dry."

The three men began paddling out into the bay, the log riding a few feet behind them on what was left of the cord. They managed to get out onto the water more than 200 yards before the first Japanese soldiers reached the beach. Bullets skipped across the water around them as all three men dug their paddles into the sea with everything they had left.

Gritt concentrated on the ocean in front of them.

A quarter mile further out, the sea began to boil and then erupted as the hull of a submarine lifted itself from the deep. Before the cascading water from the hull stopped, men were rushing onto the sail and from a hatch below it. It seemed like forever before the cannon on the bow of the submarine belched and a shell rocketed over their heads, detonating on the hillside just above where the Japanese were firing. In less than a minute, the gun crew sent four shells screaming toward the shore, the last sending the body of one of the Japanese tumbling through the air, and the rest retreating up the mountain.

"You looked like you needed a little help," smirked the captain of the *Scorpion* as a half dozen of his crew pulled the men and then their gear onto the deck.

"Thank you, Sir," replied Paul.

CHAPTER 33

DUTCH HARBOR, ALASKA, JUNE 1943

"Is Carmen still here?" Chad plopped his exhausted body into the front seat of Captain Roads' Jeep. "I know she was supposed to leave by now, but I was just kind of hoping…"

"Whatever she volunteered for bumped her up on the priority list," laughed Roads. "She went out on an air transport ten days ago. They were in a hurry to get her wherever she was going. Bumped two full colonels to get her on the plane."

"Volunteered for? I thought this was some kind of normal rotation for Carmen," replied a puzzled Chad.

"I guess she figured that you shouldn't be the only one volunteering for special missions," sighed Roads, slipping the jeep into gear. "I will drop you at your quarters. Grab a shower and meet me at the club as soon as you can. We have another opportunity, young man."

"You call shivering under a tarp, constantly wet, eating cold rations, then shooting our way off the mountain an opportunity?" asked Chad.

"Well there's that and the new P-38 sitting under a tarp over in Anchorage," laughed Roads. "How rough was it up on that mountain?"

"The first ten days were like a scout camp but without the bonfire. After that, things got really antsy. The enemy knew the invasion was coming and began to move all of their troops. We ended up in two gun battles. It's different, shooting a man looking you in the eyes and shooting down a plane. I would never make a good ground pounder, Sir. All the time I was worried about Ivan and Paul, but they are better at this than me."

The club had changed. Most of the frontline officers were somewhere to the west, engaged in prying a tenacious enemy from every hole and crevasse of Attu Island, or part of the force screening the battle from Japanese reinforcements. In their place, a dozen or more officers relaxed over drinks, most looking like they had been there all afternoon.

"You can tell you are winning when the back-echelon clerks and storekeepers show up talking tough," laughed Roads.

Chad rubbed his neck where the tight shirt and tie felt like a choke collar. He ran a finger over the bruising on his neck, oddly shaped like a man's hand. He resented the crowd of loud newcomers. He turned back to Roads just as a bourbon, on the rocks arrived. "Does that mean we are moving forward?"

"I have no orders to move, but the entire Seabee unit has been ordered to prepare to mount up with enough equipment and supplies to build a new airfield."

"I was surprised that the Japanese didn't build an airfield on the flat next to the harbor on Attu," offered Chad. There appeared to be plenty of room for a runway. From Attu we could bomb the northern islands of Japan."

"If we can figure that out, the Joint Chiefs of Staff can as well," smiled Roads swirling the Scotch in its glass. "The Japanese also know the map. The question is, what are they going to do? That gets us to the next problem, Kiska Island."

"I am not volunteering to go sit on a mountain again, if that is what you have in mind, Sir."

"I don't think that will be necessary. If we can get you closer with enough fuel, we should be able to listen in on that garrison from the air just as we originally planned." Roads finally sipped a bit of his drink.

"There is something you aren't telling me isn't there?" asked Chad.

"Yes. Now that there is no danger of us being thrown back off of Attu and probably little danger of another Japanese offensive in the North Pacific, the powers to be want to send Mark to one of the camps in Arizona."

"That's pure horseshit, Sir. He has been part of this team since day one. How can they even consider it? Besides, there is no mandatory evacuation of Japanese Americans in Alaska."

"That too is changing. Anyway, they consider his home California, Chad. I think I have it stopped for now, at least until we take Kiska, but after that I don't know…"

"What about the effort to get his parents out of Japan?"

"We have the admiral's full cooperation, unless it requires any people or equipment," laughed Roads. "The feeling in D.C. is that the Japanese are already beaten, so all we have to do is take care of Germany first and then we will finish the job on Japan in a couple months."

"That, Sir, is also a load. We will still be mopping up the Japanese on Attu in two months." Chad looked around the room again. "What in the hell does that have to do with trying to rescue Mark's folks?"

"I know we thought we were going to get some help with planning and maybe even some men. Now, I think we are on our own; but the powers to be around here have gotten used to us calling our own shots, whether or not they approve. Every time they buck us, we make a phone call, and someone in D.C. explains the facts to them."

"With the changes here, will that continue?" asked Chad, tipping his glass and emptying it, then unsuccessfully waiving at the bar for another. "Will we still call our own shots?"

"It doesn't have to continue, the locals just have to believe it will," smiled Roads. "By the way, the boss gave us a Navy PBY. I told him that the Special Operations Group needed a seaplane to expedite the attack on Kiska. It has the range to reach Karafuto. I thought you might like to check out in the PBY."

"That sounds like fun. I have float experience, but no seaplane time." Chad started to order another drink but thought better of it.

Roads watched him intently. "I asked Mark to join us here about now, to welcome you back, and to see if we can come up with a plan to use what's available to go to Japan."

"You know how I feel about being responsible for other men."

Roads smiled. "For someone who objects to leadership, you are pretty good at it." The older Navy Captain ordered another root beer. "It's hard to stay on the wagon out here."

"In the interim, we have to come up with a plan to monitor what is happening on Kiska. Is that how things roll? You know Captain, I am still really uncomfortable having men's lives dependent on my judgment. I prefer missions where I am alone. But I think our little trip to Attu probably saved some lives."

"It did," replied Roads. We know that the enemy is not coming to the rescue of their troops trapped on Attu. Don't ask me how we know, but I am confident in the information. The Japanese on that island will either surrender or die." Roads finished his drink.

"We were monitoring their communications. Their commander talked about rescue but prepared them to die for the emperor."

Mark appeared at the door, creating a stir among all of the newcomers. He walked to the table, a dozen officers glaring at him.

"Maybe we should adjourn to your house for this conversation," suggested Chad.

The three men, enjoying one of the few evenings without wind and rain, decided to walk. "Can you arrange air transportation over to Anchorage so that I can pick up the new airplane?" asked Chad.

"No sweat," answered Roads.

"Could you get a seat for Mark?"

"That might be a bit more difficult, but I will see what I can do. Why?"

"My folks own a little house there, a rental. I want to arrange to sell it to Mark to establish his residency. It's worth a try."

Roads nodded. Mark looked puzzled.

CHAPTER 34

DUTCH HARBOR, ALASKA, JULY 1943

Chad stood next to the new P-38 waiting for a Dakota transport to land. The first person off the plane was Mark, followed by a dozen men watching his every move.

"Thanks for arranging the trip to Anchorage," offered Mark. "I figured out what that was all about on the way over. It was good to see some Japanese Americans who weren't sitting in camps. Most of them figured they were on borrowed time."

"My folks were happy to have us in their home. I can't believe how much Anchorage has changed," replied Chad.

"How's your new ride?"

"Faster, and the new radio package is easier to use. I just don't know how much use it will get."

"I guess I don't understand?"

"You will, we are meeting Roads for dinner."

Spiff picked up the two men in a blue pickup with the paint peeling off revealing the original army brown. He turned down toward the harbor, where a crew boat waited to take them out to a strange looking ship anchored not far from where a Navy PBY flying boat was tied to a mooring buoy.

Roads waited at the top of the ladder, a smile from ear to ear. "Like my new office?"

"What the hell is this ugly thing, Sir?" asked Chad.

"They call it a landing ship. We are going to move tons of construction equipment to Attu, and this will make it faster and a lot safer than hauling it on open barges behind tugs. In the interim, we have a mission based on the plan you two cooked up before your little jaunt to Anchorage."

"Are we moving then?" asked Mark.

"I can't order you to move; you're a civilian MIS volunteer," replied Roads, as he led the men into a cramped meeting room just below the ship's bridge. "But if we are going to finish kicking the enemy out of the Aleutians and maintain our communications links with Japan long enough to work out a rescue plan for your folks, this is what we have to do."

Mark smiled and shook his head. "You could just threaten to shoot me, Captain. We are back to where we were when the war first started. Everyone I run into just wants me gone, so no one would care."

"Not everyone. I just met a Canadian admiral who asked specifically about you. Like me, he was called back into the service. Seems you made quite an impression on his daughter, Victoria, and then disappeared. I told him you were one of mine and were undercover. When you can, just let the girl down gently, in the name of Allied cooperation. If there is something there, well, I just wanted you to know she was asking and you might want to send her a letter."

"Okay, you have actually gotten my blood brother to squirm, Captain," Chad said. "Now what are we doing and where?"

"While you two were taking a week off, Spiff had the boys in the shop put together a communications hut and equipped it with radio equipment that duplicates what you have been using. The new stuff is a lot more powerful and will allow you to amplify signals from Kiska. We are leaving tomorrow to install it on Amchitka Island, only eighty miles from the Japanese base at Kiska. It will take about a week to move it ashore and to run antennas up the mountain from the cove where we will set up. There is no reason to burn up a bunch of avgas to monitor the enemy when we can sit in a comfortable cabin and listen, then relay."

"Let me get this, Sir," started Chad, "that pretty new P-38 over on the runway is going to just sit?"

"No, you will continue to fly sweeps south of Kiska to monitor any resupply efforts. Mark, here, and the two boys from Attu will man the new monitoring station. The Navy is already on Amchitka, so you won't be alone."

"Sir, you shouldn't refer to Ivan and Paul as boys. They fought like soldiers on Attu," said Chad.

"And now they are. While you were gone, both volunteered to join the Alaska Territorial Guard. I heard a rumor that the CO of the Guards personally talked to them on the radio and welcomed them. They are getting a couple of weeks of training as we speak and have offered to help Mark, if he is going."

"Like I said, I don't have much choice. I just want your commitment to follow through on something to try to get my family out from under the thumb of the Japanese Army."

"You have that, but first we need to see how many lives we can save on Kiska. The enemy on Attu is fighting a war of attrition, and for every casualty they inflict, the weather is taking down two. The enemy will lose thousands for that rock and the Allies will sacrifice hundreds dead and thousands wounded, and more than that to weather related injuries."

"So, Sir, what is the plan?" asked Chad.

"Mark will continue to send out of date messages to Japan until we are ready with the new monitoring station. He will feed the Japanese information from his old logbooks here. If he picks pages at random, no one will notice that he is repeating himself."

"You will fly your missions out of Dutch Harbor with refueling at Adak. I want you to fly that PBU out there every chance you get. We should have the monitoring station up on Amchitka in a week, then I want you to fly Mark and the Territorial Guard men out to man the new monitoring station in the PBY."

"That bird usually has a three-man crew, plus gunners," answered Chad.

"We don't have any more men in our little unit. You will have to make do with Spiff here. I will have one of the men from the radio shop checked out as your radio operator."

"I don't know anything about airplanes," spat Spiff.

"No, but you are a competent navigator. The captain here will do the flying. I'm starving, how about some dinner?"

"Sound good, where is the galley?" asked Chad.

"What galley? In celebration of Mark's new digs, I thought we could all dine on K-rations," laughed Roads, picking up a cardboard box and handing it to Chad.

Chad flew his monitoring missions, alternating between morning and afternoon flights. The Navy pilots that came with the PBY were more than happy to give him as many hours of take offs and landings and emergency procedures as Chad could absorb. His flying experience made cruise and navigation exercises unnecessary.

Mark sent morning and evening communiqués to Japan just as the Japanese submarine had been doing. He carefully worked out coded messages to his father to begin fleshing in a rescue plan that he and Chad were cooking up.

Each evening, the two men shared dinner at Mark's house.

On the sixth day after their gourmet dinner with Roads, Spiff knocked on the door. "They are ready for us," he offered nervously. "I checked weather and tomorrow looks really good. Now, I am going to go have a drink and pretend it isn't my last."

Mark smiled over at Chad as Spiff walked back to the stolen Army truck. "You need to talk to me every time you fly out past Amchitka." Mark handed Chad a scrap of paper with two radio frequencies noted. "Use the first for morning and the second for afternoon, I will be monitoring them. I have never seen either used since I arrived."

"What is this about?"

"Two things. First, I am trying to keep my family alive. Second, I am taking the captain at his word, that the primary goal of the mission to Amchitka is to save lives."

CHAPTER 35

AMCHITKA ISLAND, ALASKA, AUGUST 1943

Roads' landing ship was anchored just off from the northwestern point on Amchitka. A small boat from the ship slid up to the PBY and anchored close to shore to avoid the huge swell coming in from the North Pacific Ocean. While Spiff helped Ivan and Paul into the boat, Chad turned to Mark. "I'll see you in a couple of months at most. That would be my guess."

"I hope so. I assume the guys and I will be holed up in that little shack I saw on the hillside. When you circled the ship I could see where the Seabees have planted three antennas. If we can see them from the air, the enemy can too."

"Mark, the Japanese don't have any planes left in the Aleutians. You can't see the antennas or the hut from the water. But just in case, remember that the Navy has a weather station on the island."

"I am just as worried about them as the enemy," replied Mark.

"Why? They know you are here. If anything, their little camp is the vulnerable one."

"The Navy might not be looking at this situation like I am."

"Is there some hidden message in this for me? Hell, Mark, we have been like brothers for years."

"Let's just drop it. I will see you when my job here becomes obsolete. I think the Japanese will be gone sooner rather than later."

"What do you have up your sleeve?" Chad twisted Marks shoulder forcing him to look into his face.

"Just drop it. Don't forget to call me on the frequencies I gave you." Mark gave Chad a punch on the shoulder. "Let's do some fishing when this is over," he called, as the boat turned for shore.

Mark watched, as the PBY lifted off from the water and turned east, passing over the landing ship getting ready to get under way. The small plywood shack had three windows, three bunks, three chairs and one crude table. Across one wall, the Seabees had constructed a counter. Two radios were ready for use, powered by a bank of heavy truck batteries. A set of heavy cables ran outside through a hole in the wall.

"Let's take a look around." Mark headed toward the door. Ivan continued cleaning the rifle issued to him by the Territorial Guard. Paul never looked up from the book he was reading.

Mark stepped out into grass that stood higher than a man's knee. Behind the cabin, a small stream raced down the steep hill, no more than three feet wide and only inches deep. Mark walked uphill to a spot where the Seabees had driven heavy steel pipes into the streambed, bolting planks to them to form a crude dam. From the center of the dam, a six-inch pipe carried a stream of water to a paddle wheel, connected to a shaft that ran into a tiny doghouse size structure. Mark lifted the hinged roof. Inside, the paddle wheel turned a pulley. An automotive fan belt turned a second pulley, driving a generator that still had a Dodge Truck Division label plate. He lowered the roof.

Below him the landing ship was underway, followed by a flock of birds. He looked up the hill and then in both directions. *I might as well be on the moon.*

Mark was sending his evening broadcast to Japan when Paul slipped through the door. T-T-they are a-all g-gone. W-w-we a-are o-on our o-o-own."

"I am about through sending. I just want to set up a call with my dad before we go exploring a bit." He picked up a pencil and began drafting a coded message. It would be his first completely accurate message. He just hoped that his father passed it on.

Four hours later, he took the time to decode the return message from his father. *So there are now guards stationed near the house. I figured that would happen.* "I didn't expect that the Japanese would be flying recon around the island. That seems like a real waste of a flying boat."

"What are you talking about, Mr. Ishihara?" asked Ivan.

"Just talking to myself. Feel free to listen in when I do that. Maybe you can figure out what I am talking about; I sure can't." The three men ate their first boxed dinner while sitting on a rock overlooking the endless ocean. Then it started to rain.

Mark expected Chad to contact him on each mission south of Kiska. He'd agreed to check in again as he turned for home. Some days the weather was so bad in Dutch Harbor that he never got off the ground, but at least it was summer and most of the snowstorms were over.

The monotony of flying day after day with nothing to report was wearing on him. He couldn't even remember the day of the month as he cruised high above the clouds over the little cabin on Amchitka Island. *Maybe it's the tenth of August. I know its August anyway,* he thought. He keyed the microphone in his hand.

"Mark, you got your ears on?" he called, violating every rule of radio conduct.

"Yup, how is the weather up there?"

"Lousy, from the surface to about ten thousand feet, it is really terrible."

"Why don't you just go home then?"

"Just like you, I have a job to do. I will keep it short. I will be back in a couple of hours."

"Do you have to go today?"

"Duty and all that crap," replied Chad.

"Maybe you can have radio problems, at least on that radio you monitor enemy naval chatter on."

"Okay, Mark, what is going on?"

"I can't tell you. Just promise me, you will report anything you hear to me before you call anyone else."

"Okay, you got it partner. Snooper clear."

Chad carefully poured a tiny measure of coffee from his Thermos into a tall cup, a difficult task, as the plane vibrated and bounced in the winds above the clouds. He sipped a bit, thinking about Mark's comments, then he turned the nose of the plane south and switched on the monitoring radio.

Chad was an hour and forty minutes into his planned two-hour sweep when he detected a radio transmission on a Japanese naval frequency. It didn't last long enough to get a direction fix on the transmission. He tried to get lower but broke off the descent when his altimeter showed a thousand feet and he was still blind. The Aleutians made their own weather, and the altimeter where he was, 400 miles from Amchitka, could be different enough to leave him swimming if he went any lower. Climbing back above the clouds, he continued to monitor the frequency, extending his flight thirty minutes. He caught only one additional transmission. It lasted three seconds. Then there was nothing. He continued his route back toward Amchitka before heading home.

"Mark, you there?" he called high over what, below the clouds, should have been the northern tip of Amchitka.

"I am up. You see anything through that soup, hear anything?"

"Funny, I did. I heard two very short transmissions, only a few seconds and then nothing."

"Probably just some static," replied Mark.

"No, I distinctly heard a voice. The transmissions were a single word, and a number, in Japanese, but I couldn't get a direction. I should report it to the fleet screening Kiska."

"Don't," replied Mark. "Just go home and have a drink. We are doing the job that Captain Roads gave us."

"What are you talking about?"

"We are doing everything in our power to get the enemy out of the Aleutians without sacrificing a bunch of lives."

"That sounds pretty damned cryptic to me, old friend."

"Chad, please do not report the static you heard until I can confirm that there is something out there. I will carefully monitor the Japanese. If there is anything going on, I will call it in. Have a great night. Cabin clear."

Strange, thought Chad. He turned the P-38 east and bumped up the throttles. He had enough fuel in the tanks to shorten hours of boring flight back to base through speed. He dialed the Navy frequency and picked up the microphone. Instead of transmitting, he slipped the microphone back into its sleeve and turned that radio off. *Maybe Mark is right, why get a bunch of people riled up over nothing? That transmission could have carried on atmospherics all the way from Japan.*

Eight hours later, five Japanese destroyers dashed into the harbor at Kiska. In a well-planned ballet, all of the Japanese troops on the island found space on the cramped ships. The destroyers were on the way south at flank speed, in three hours. Mark heard almost nothing from the base. He hadn't expected to. The one word broadcast in the clear brought a smile to his face. "Arigato" meant thank you.

A week later, Chad relayed a message from Roads. Mark and the Aleut men were being pulled out. They were to switch off all of their equipment, pack up the radios, secure all of their notes and codes, and wait for a boat from the Navy's weather station. There, they would be ferried out to the PBY, which would pick them up at noon the next day.

The men began packing their equipment to the beach at five the next morning. Offshore, they could see warships, probably the same ships that a day before had been screening Kiska. Now they were staging only eighty miles from the Japanese base. *I guessed right,* thought Mark. *The invasion is in the next few days.*

The drone of the two big radial engines of the ungainly seaplane, could put you to sleep. Spiff asked for a break to go knock down a couple of cups of coffee, in his battle to stay awake. The radio operator joined him. "I'll send Mark back if I need either of you," offered Chad, as the lanky Spiff gave up his copilot's seat.

"You probably figured out that the invasion of Kiska is going to happen in the next five days," offered Chad.

"I don't think there is anyone left on Kiska," replied Mark.

"What are you talking about?"

"The day you thought you heard something; well you did. I think the enemy evacuated the base. There has been no one there for a week."

"How in the hell do you know that?" asked Chad, turning to stare at his friend.

"Don't you think they knew an invasion was coming?"

"They had to, but they didn't know when."

"Maybe, they didn't feel like sacrificing three thousand more men," answered Mark.

"If you knew they were pulling out, why didn't you call the Navy? Why didn't you want me to report what I heard?"

Mark smiled a nervous smile at his oldest friend. "Our mission was to get the enemy out of Alaska with the fewest casualties."

"We need to report this to the Navy right away. We need to stop the invasion."

"We need to discuss my supposition with Capitan Roads first," suggested Mark. "We wouldn't want to compromise our intelligence capabilities."

Chad turned his worried look back toward the gray waters in front of the nose of the plane. "All right, go back and tell the radio operator to get a message to Roads that we need to see him as soon as we land. And Mark, I know there is more to this. Don't make me dig it out on my own."

The meeting with Roads went just as Mark hoped. "So, after Captain Gritt reported what might have been coded traffic from the Japanese Navy, you and Ivan began monitoring both the Navy and Army radio frequencies. You were monitoring the Navy frequencies on the backup radio while Ivan monitored the Army on the other. Is that correct?"

"That's about it, Captain. The normal Army chatter, what little of it there was, went away completely about ten hours after Chad headed home. A couple of hours later, I heard a very short transmission on the Navy frequency, one word, "Arigato," then nothing. Since that day there has been no chatter at all from the base on any frequency. They are gone, I am certain of that."

"Either that, or the enemy has started a very crafty cat and mouse campaign," answered Roads. "I would hate to see our boys walk onto, what we told them was an undefended beach, and get hammered."

Chad sat watching the two men. "And then there is the issue of us monitoring the enemy. Do we really want to tell the world out team exists by sending this on?"

He offered a weak smile to his friend then turned back to Roads. "You're the boss. You have Mark's report. I can confirm that I did not report anything when I heard perhaps five seconds of traffic on a frequency I was to be watching. Mark was right, it was thin."

"I think you both handled this just right. In the end, the troops going ashore the day after tomorrow need to be ready for a fight. I will pass this along as just what Mark calls it, educated supposition. I doubt that the brass will change anything in the invasion plans. I just hope our own guys don't end up shooting each other."

"Any chance of a decent meal for Paul and Ivan and me, Captain? We haven't eaten anything but rations for weeks."

"I just happen to have saved steaks for the whole team, dinner in a couple of hours. But there will be no Scotch; the Navy is really backward about having a drink on one of their vessels."

✤

Mark tapped on the door of the tiny officer's berth where Chad had folded his tired body for a nap before dinner. He handed Chad his pad, folded to reveal the message that he had sent to his father.

Chad read it and decoded it in his head. Then he read it again. "You told your father that the invasion was going to happen on the twelfth of August. You told him that the Allies were bringing fifty ships and 25,000 troops. How in the hell did you know that?" he finished, his face as red as the fire extinguisher above his bunk.

"I guessed. I knew that we already had a couple of dozen ships in the area, and I calculated how many more I thought it would take to bring as many men as went ashore on Attu with their equipment. I knew that we wouldn't have been sent out to monitor the enemy if the invasion wasn't coming soon."

"You tipped off the enemy. You let thousands of troops escape, to maybe kill American troops somewhere else."

Mark looked around the empty passageway, where he stood. "I was told our job was to get the Japanese out of the Aleutians with as little loss of life as possible. That is what I did. At the same time, I gave my father something to bargain with, to keep him alive."

Chad sat up on the bunk. He pulled the metal wastebasket over and dug out the Zippo lighter he carried in the pants pocket of his flight suit. He tore out the page and flipped open the Zippo. He spun the steel wheel. He then touched the flame to the sheet in his hand and dropped it into the wastebasket.

"Get the hell out of here," he barked. "Give me some time to process all of this. You may be right all the way around, but maybe not."

"That's what I expected from you, brother. Just promise me that before you kick this up the ladder, we finish our plan to get my family out of Karafuto. After that, I don't care if they shoot me."

CHAPTER 36

ABOARD SHIP IN THE NORTH PACIFIC, AUGUST 1943

"I just wish you had discussed your plan with Roads before you started sending messages." Chad's face no longer showed the anger of the night before.

The small galley was empty. The ocean sailors were all doing whatever they did to avoid the tedium of acting as a floating office and supply depot for the Seabees. Most of the Seabees were ashore, positioning heavy equipment.

"I probably should have, but I saw this as an opportunity to make a real difference. We've already won this war, but people like Colonel Ito, the man holding my family, will never quit. Anyway, why should a bunch of Americans get killed just to kill a bunch of Japanese over an island we can capture with a little brain power?"

"I think it's best if we just let it go. It wouldn't take much for some intel guy to decide that our interpretation of what we did, and the outcome is wrong. Now, tell me what you know about this house where your parents are." Mark smiled as the word 'we' sunk in.

Mark briefed his friend on the location, and on what he had learned. "Three things concern me. First, there are Japanese soldiers housed in the gardener's house next to the main house. Second, the son of a bitch colonel who started all of this visits the house every day.

Finally, the Japanese have put a long range flying boat at the airport only thirty miles from the house. They are using it to fly reconnaissance into the North Pacific and around the island. Our idea of hiding the PBY in the cove near my grandfather's house won't work."

"Maybe this is better," replied Chad, topping off his cup. "Let's go see if the captain is in his office."

Roads dropped his pencil into a desk drawer and waved at the young seaman across the passage. He sent the young man for any map the ship's captain might have of northern Japan. The man was back in the time it took for the three men to empty the last of the coffee from the galley.

"We have a short window, gentlemen," started Roads, spreading the map out on his desk. "Once the enemy is off American soil, this theater is going to be even more of a backwater than it is now. Finding resources is going to get tough."

"What if this mission became an effort to grab a senior Japanese Colonel, an intelligence officer, while recovering some of our own undercover assets, Sir?" asked Chad.

"How valuable is this hypothetical intelligence officer?" asked Roads, looking at Mark.

"He knows about all of the Japanese capabilities in the Kurile Islands and Karafuto."

Roads looked up from the map. "If we are going to start launching bombers against the northern Japanese homeland, what he knows could be valuable. Will he cooperate?"

"Not a prayer, Captain. But if we can get him off the island and put him into a position where he, for all intents and purposes, is dead to his superiors, we might be able to come up with a strategy to get him to open up. Colonel Ito's whole life is about being a big deal officer."

"I can try to sell this. Tell me what you need."

"First, we need a submarine to get us to the beach next to the house. We need a couple of troops who can handle themselves in a fight. We need an expert open ocean navigator with flight experience, and we need a radio operator who can rig up an emergency radio in an airplane that we plan to steal."

"You are going to steal a plane?" asked incredulous Roads.

"Not *just* a plane but one of the new Japanese Emily seaplanes. Think of it. Our small unit helps find a Japanese Zero, which allows the Allies to develop new tactics. Then we steal their most sophisticated long-range airplane, right before we begin attacking northern Japan directly."

"I have created a monster," laughed Roads. "I think this whole thing might be suicide, but it is just crazy enough to work. It might just get us a new assignment since our original mission is coming to an end. I would hate to stop all this fun and have to go back to being an engineer."

"Then you will take this to the admiral?" asked Mark.

"I will take it to D.C. first, but you will have to talk Ivan and Paul into helping. I assume you have Spiff in mind as the navigator and the same radio operator who has been flying the PBY with you. I will not order anyone to go on this mission. You need to find me volunteers. And we can't use anyone who hasn't been through our security check."

"Got it, Sir," answered Chad. "We will flesh in the plan this afternoon. We will put on our used car sales togs this evening and see what we can do."

The two young Aleut men volunteered the minute they heard the plan. Mark went out of his way to explain the danger, but both still jumped at the chance to go somewhere outside of Alaska. The radio operator saw it as an opportunity to escape the construction crew he was assigned to. They would be locked away in the Aleutians building airstrips for months. Only Spiff challenged the whole idea.

"Invade Japan with six men and capture a senior Japanese officer who will fight us tooth and nail. On the way, we take out at least three Japanese infantrymen and God knows how many bodyguards protecting this Colonel Ito. Then we steal a truck, drive to a Japanese airbase, and steal a plane that we have never seen, and fly 1500 miles across the Pacific, and land a plane with Japanese markings at one of our bases."

"I think he got it just about right," said Chad. "Do you have anything to add, Mark?"

"Just that we will have at least two additional passengers to protect."

"Weather – what about weather on the flight?" offered Spiff. "We could pick a day when the weather is terrible all the way."

"I think he is getting on board," offered Chad. "At least now he has us all in the airplane winging our way home."

"I did no such thing. It just seems that every step in this gets more dangerous. The enemy could detect the sub. We could drown getting onto the beach. The troops around your grandfather's house could be crack soldiers. There could be roadblocks on the way to the airfield, and the plane could be guarded. But, I admit, the hours over open water, with nowhere to land scares me more than anything else."

"The intelligence on the Emily says it is one hell of a plane," said Chad. "It has four engines and a range more than twice the distance we will fly. Sparks will get a radio installed in the first couple of hours we are in the air. We will be in communications with our own people."

"What if we get there and the plane is out of gas? We can't just taxi over to the fueling station and fill it up."

"All good points," replied Mark. "That's why having you on board to help plan this is really important."

"Maybe the war will end before we can get it planned."

"No, if this is going to happen, we need to be on our way this week." Chad walked over and plucked three Cokes from the cooler.

"You know, I have a downright beautiful fiancé waiting back home. She will be really pissed at you two if I get killed."

"Don't worry about that," offered Chad with a smile. "When the war ends, there will be hundreds of guys available to take her mind off of you."

Spiff finally smiled. "She will be really impressed when I get the Navy Cross, or something for this. Maybe we will win the Medal of Honor."

"Probably not," replied Chad. "My guess is that this mission will be classified just like everything we do. No, you had better bank on the hundreds of men to solve the girl back home dilemma."

The entire plan was reduced to two neatly typed pages. It was on Roads' desk the next morning. He handed the men a telegram from D.C. "This mission is authorized, but there is zero chance that anyone will come to help you if something goes wrong. As you can see, the only advice from D.C. is to try to make it across the frontier to the Russian side of the island and surrender yourself to our allies and hope they don't hand you back to the Japs."

"It will only take a day to get what we need together. I think Model 11 pistols for all and Thompson submachine guns that fire the same .45 round make sense for weapons," volunteered Spiff. We need a radio and tools to install it and Sparks will need the radio shop to figure out an antenna. That's about it."

"He's right, Sir," added Chad. "We will need two rubber rafts with paddles. If the sub gets us close enough to the beach, we will row ourselves, then sink the rafts. We won't be there long enough to need shelter or food."

Roads turned to his aide. Spiff was staring at some spot on the bulkhead above the desk. "You are going to need to procure the weapons and ammunition the same way you find us trucks. The Seabees have rafts. Figure out your own personal gear. I'll get you a sub."

"Any chance of getting the *Scorpion* again?" Chad said. "The biggest risk I see is the first hour, when we are getting ashore. I like how those guys come charging to the rescue."

"I'll see what I can do. Just remember that the sub will turn and head for home once they see you destroy the rafts."

"Try buying those guys some patrol time around Japan. They all trained to hunt ships. This would give them that opportunity."

CHAPTER 37

THE NORTH PACIFIC, SEPTEMBER 1943

For the next two days, Mark and his father fired coded messages back and forth. Mark arranged for his father to pass on that the Americans were investigating how the Japanese knew the invasion of Kiska was coming and that he was in jeopardy. More importantly, Michi managed to fill in enough missing information to make the plan real; that is, if real meant that you could expect to draw a card to fill an inside straight with a million dollars in the pot.

Chad and Spiff stood in the crowded control room of the *Scorpion,* as it raced across the Pacific. The six-man team had been ferried from Adak to the harbor at Kiska, where the sub had been called from rescue picket duty. The boat had drawn supplies and filled its water and fuel tanks and been underway to Karafuto in two hours.

"Thanks to you two gentlemen for rescuing us from floating around waiting for some air-dale to leave his plane out in the ocean," remarked the boat captain.

"Happy to help, Chet," replied Chad. "How long is the trip to the point we marked on your chart?"

"We can cover about 500 miles a day, if the weather stays good, and we aren't forced to submerge; maybe three, or three and a half days to reach the coast of that island. I never even knew that Japan and Russia shared an island. The Russians aren't fighting in the Pacific, so we should be able to stay on the surface until we approach your destination."

"We want to come ashore early in the morning. We have someone waiting to meet us."

"Man, I hope you can trust whoever it is. The *Scorpion* will get those rafts launched. But I am real happy I won't be joining you. Three of your team might blend in, but you two will stand out like strippers at a tent revival."

"Oh, it shouldn't be too dangerous," added Spiff. He brushed his shaggy hair back under the stocking cap he wore. If everything goes to hell, we will just jump on the local train up to the border and spend the rest of the war guzzling vodka."

The team traded off joining the lookouts and officers on the tower of the sub. Paul and Ivan struggled. Neither had ever been anywhere, where you couldn't look outside, before their Kiska mission with Chad. On that voyage, the submarine had remained on the surface all but four hours and Chad had been too busy to check on them.

"C-Chad, I d-don't k-know if I c-can s-sleep d-down in t-that t-tube."

"Just find a bunk and launch yourself into one of your books. If you read everything you brought, the sub has a small library. Paul, it is all mind over matter."

"I d-don't k-know w-what t-that m-means."

"You can do whatever you make up your mind to do."

"I c-can r-read, but Ivan d-doesn't r-read much."

"He can stay outside unless we have to submerge. But sometime before we get where we are going, he will need to sleep. How did you deal with sleeping the last time we were on a sub?"

"S-s-short n-naps in t-t-the a air, up above, sitting. M-maybe f-f-f-four hours."

Neither of the two guardsmen managed any sleep the first two days. The boat captain allowed only one of the team onto the crowded bridge at a time. Chad made his way to their bunk area. Ivan's eyes were glued to the hatch into the next compartment. Paul's eyes darted around the compartment, his head jerking and bobbing.

"You two going to be okay?" asked Chad.

Neither responded.

"Let's go get some coffee," added Chad.

"I never considered that they might have this much trouble surviving in a sub," said Mark, watching the two men at the galley table.

"They won't be worth the powder it would take to blow them to hell, if they don't get some rest," agreed Spiff. "Chad, and those two are the only ones on the team that have ever fired a weapon in combat."

"I think I have something that might help," came a voice from behind them. The two men turned to find the sub's captain watching. "I'll be back. Get those two to their bunks."

Five minutes later, he was back, a young seaman in tow. "Have those two roll up their sleeves. Tell them something to get them to relax while the pharmacist mate gives them something to sleep."

"And just what would I tell them to get them to relax, when a man they don't know leans over them with a syringe?" answered Chad. "I can't."

"Hell, I don't know. Did the Russian flu hit Alaska?" asked Chet.

"It clobbered Alaska. Entire villages disappeared because so many died."

"Tell them that since we are going so close to Russia that we are going to vaccinate them, to keep them from getting the Russian Flu."

In minutes, both men went back to their darting eyes as Mark sat on a bunk across from them. In a half-hour, both were sound asleep. Mark made his way to the galley.

The boat was entering the Sea of Okhotsk before either of the young men awoke. Ivan climbed the ladder to the bridge, just as Chad started down.

"How was your sleep?"

"You know I can't sleep down there."

"Why, what is bothering you?"

"I worry. You know that if I sleep, something will happen, and I will drown or something."

"But nothing has happened yet."

"I know, but I just need to watch. I feel like some big gas is inside of me. It's trying to make my chest explode. I close my eyes, but I don't sleep."

"Ivan, you have been asleep for the last twelve hours, maybe more. You see, nothing happened to you or Paul."

Ivan turned, anger on his face. "Mr. Ishihara tricked us, didn't he? There was no medicine for flu. He gave us medicine to sleep."

"You needed the sleep. It worked. Maybe now that you know that it is all right, you can sleep tonight. We will probably be going ashore early tomorrow."

Ivan relaxed. "That stuff worked. Maybe you should take some for that Japanese Colonel we are going to capture. Mr. Ishihara says he will be a lot of trouble, but not if he is sleeping."

At ten that night, Sparks, working with the help of the engineers from the sub, rigged a simple antenna that allowed Mark to send messages back and forth to his father. He prayed that the Japanese listening post, wouldn't notice that the transmission from "Alaska" was much stronger than usual.

The Sea of Okhotsk lies between Russia's Kamchatka Peninsula, Kurile Islands the Russian Mainland, Korea and China. It is one of the busiest waterways in the world. The *Scorpion* crossed the Sea, making a straight-line passage toward Karafuto. Submerging to avoid radar contacts, but only for an hour each time, the vessel ran at flank speed. The blacked out vessel, riding low in the water, was almost impossible to see on a dark rainy night.

On a dreary morning, the captain of the *Scorpion* swung the periscope in a final sweep of the seas around him. "Okay Scottie, let's get her on the surface. I want us ready, so sound battle stations surface and get the deck party ready to launch our passengers."

"Sonar reports no engine sounds at all," replied the second officer. "It's spooky. I hope it's not a trap."

"You got the lousy morning you were looking for, Captain Gritt. We will surface to run last few miles, but we will stay on battery power to maintain silence. Without major landmarks, this is my best guess at the location. It checks with the distance from that flashing buoy that marks the border. I want those rafts inflated and loaded before we stop."

"Thanks to you and the whole crew. I still can't tell you what we are up to, but if everything works out, we will beat you back to Alaska."

"I sure hope so. We will get you ashore, and standby for one hour after you sink the rafts, then we are heading back to sea. I wish we had some explosives on board, I would like to take a crack at one of the trains that runs along the shore."

"Fine with me, just give me two days before you bring out the entire Japanese Army looking for saboteurs."

"With you and your team out there, we will pass on the train. It's really easy getting close to this island. I'll put that in my action report."

"You still going hunting after we are gone?"

"Yup, we intend to run home with all of our torpedoes used up. This is our first real opportunity to do what we trained for, sink enemy ships."

A crewman spun the wheel, opening the hatch to the conning tower, then swung it open showering Chad, who didn't know enough to step out of the way. In seconds, three lookouts were up the ladder, followed by the captain and Chad.

Two fifty-caliber machine guns were mounted at the sides of the bridge and ammunition lockers were opened as four lookouts crowded onto the bridge. Below, on the deck, Chad watched another crew preparing the deck gun that had saved his life on Attu.

He watched as the five men who were going ashore began stacking the little gear they were taking next to the two rafts being inflated by sub crewmembers.

"Scottie, give me one revolution on the radar. If there is nothing out there you do not have to report," called the captain.

"The charts indicate that we should be able to run you within a quarter mile of shore, Captain. If we have enough water under the keel, we will get even closer. When I stop, get you and your men into the boats. I briefed my men to keep any chatter to a minimum. When you are in the rafts, we will submerge about ten feet. That should allow you to get away from the boat without the noise of dragging the rafts over the grates and down the hull."

Chad remained silent, watching as the deck crew loaded the last of the supplies into the rafts, then retreated, quietly closing the hatch behind them. One by one his team took a seat, leaving him the front spot in the second raft.

Over the bow, the shoreline appeared out of the mist. A few minutes later, individual trees appeared above the beach and then branches on the trees. He felt a tap on his shoulder. Turning, he extended his hand, mouthing thanks, then started down the ladder to the deck. Faintly behind him he heard, "All stop, flood down ten feet."

He barely had time to seat himself and pick up the paddle lashed next to his seat, when the sea slipped over the deck, floating the rafts. The two rubber boats were just clear of the sub, when he heard the sound of water rushing. He turned to see the sub backing straight out. The *Scorpion* had moved them to within three hundred yards of the beach.

Mark leaped from the first raft and pulled it ashore. Chad looked out to sea. He knew the sub was still watching, but from his seat in the raft, it was gone.

Mark and Ivan picked up their weapons and headed into the trees just north of the mouth of a small river. The rest of the crew started packing the radio and three canvas bags up the beach. A moment later, Chad and Spiff pushed the rafts back into the light surf and began puncturing the tubes, swinging their arms to demonstrate to the sub what they were doing.

As the two men trotted back to where the others waited, Mark and a man carrying a fly fishing rod emerged from the trees.

Michi Ishihara strode past the others and wrapped Chad in a bear hug. "I wish we were meeting under better circumstances, but God it is good to see my two boys."

"Thank you for all you have been doing," managed Chad. "Break down that rod and take it with us, we have some fishing to do, back in Alaska."

Mark introduced his father to the others in the team. The older man knelt in the center of a circle of men and briefed them. "Some things have changed. First, your grandfather and grandmother just showed up. Second, Colonel Ito sent word that he would be arriving late this afternoon. It appears that he was summoned to General Yamaguchi's office in Hokkaido. He is being recognized for providing the intelligence that allowed the evacuation of Kiska. He won't be back until sometime after three."

"What about the three guards in the garden house?" asked Mark. "I would hate to have them find us waiting for Ito."

Michi checked his watch. "It is 5:30 now. There is only one guard now; the other two men in the garden house are there to monitor the radio traffic we exchange. They have a radio link directly to Ito's office. You will have to capture and gag them. They come down to the river each morning about six to bathe."

"Father, we do not have room in the plane for prisoners, and we cannot leave them here to tell any rescuers how few of us there are, or where we went."

Michi frowned. "I have gotten to know my jailers. They are boys younger than you. I had not thought through what might happen to them. To me, the war is something I read about. It is something that you and I participate in, only through words."

"Father, we have no choice if we are to survive. I was there when that bastard Peter blew himself up rather than surrender. Chad and the two native men have been in two shootouts with our enemy. The three men, and all of Ito's guards, will have to die, and we will have to get rid of the bodies in a way that they aren't found until we are gone. It is best if the men who come looking for Ito, think everyone is missing."

"What about your grandfather and grandmother?"

"They need to go with us, or they need to be on the ferry back to Sapporo before any of this leaks out."

"Mark, what is really going on in the war?"

"The empire is being rolled back everywhere. Probably half of the ships of the Imperial Navy have been sunk, including all but two aircraft carriers. Almost all of the experienced carrier pilots are dead. North of Australia, Japan is losing islands that they seized only a year ago. The Allies will defeat Germany first, liberate Europe, and then turn all of their power against Japan."

"Your grandfather will want to stay here. He believes that Japan will need leaders after the war, leaders that opposed expansionism and militarism."

"Then he and Grandmother must be on the ferry back to Hokkaido today."

The older man seemed to age before their eyes. Michi nodded. "Follow me, gentlemen," offered Michi. "I will show you where to wait for the men from the garden house." Michi started for the mouth of the river.

"Mark, you and I will talk to your grandparents. The rest of you will have to kill the soldiers; I do not have the will. Please do it quietly, I do not want to disturb Mark's grandmother."

Spiff reached into the canvas bag at his feet. He handed a strange looking pistol to Chad, and then tucked a second into his belt. "They are High Standard .22 long rifle pistols fitted with one of Hiram Maxim's silencers. It shoots a small bullet, so the ordinance people who sent them to Captain Roads and me, recommend three bullets to kill a man. They give off about the same amount of noise as a fat dog farting. Each of us will need to shoot one of the soldiers, and then both concentrate on the third."

Michi pointed to the small dock along the river. "They will come here to bathe." He looked at his watch. "They are very punctual; they should be here in about ten minutes. After you are done here, wait at the garden house up the path for either Mark or me to come and get you. Mark's grandmother cannot know what you do here." Michi untied a small rope from one of the pilings on the dock, retrieving two fat salmon, and then led Mark toward the main house.

The four men heard the Japanese soldiers before they saw them. They ducked behind a row of flowering bushes. The first two soldiers walked side by side, wearing khaki trousers and white undershirts. Each carried a small mat, woven of grass, over his head to ward off the light mist. Both men had a towel thrown over a shoulder. Each carried a small canvas bag, one obviously telling a joke, the other laughing. The third man trailed them by twenty yards. He carried a rifle slung over his shoulder.

As they approached the dock, the man in the lead stopped. His partner began to ask a question, but the first man silenced him, as he studied the trail near the dock. He put his arm out, to block his colleague, who had started forward again, and raised his other arm, pointing at the ground next to the dock. Chad peered through a gap in the bushes. The canvas bag that Spiff had taken the pistols from, sat directly in front of where they were hiding.

He raised his pistol, focusing on the man pointing. In seconds, three red splotches appeared on the man's shirt. The soldier looked down, shocked, and then collapsed to the ground. Spiff hit the second man four times, but he still turned to run before a fifth then sixth shot toppled him.

The third soldier stood stunned. Finally realizing what was happening, the guard dropped his towel and bag at his feet. He pulled at the rifle slung over his shoulder, just as the running man's body slid into his feet. The rifle slid down his arm, flopping into the mud of the trail. He spun and sprinted back toward the garden house. Both Chad and Spiff fired at the sprinter, watching him stumble. Then he regained his feet again.

The guard stumbled through the door of the garden house, finding the Korean housekeeper filling a teakettle at the hand pump in the kitchen. "Wabasha we amerikahito go kokop ni iru, satsuei shite imasu!" he screamed.

Mary looked stunned. "Watashi wa niwa de anata o hi hyoji narimasu watashitoisshoni kimasu." Mary dropped the kettle into the sink. She picked up a towel wrapping something else. Wrapping one arm around the wounded man she walked him out behind the house. In an alcove of blooming vines, she helped him onto a bench. Slipping a huge fillet knife from behind her, she slit his throat. She smiled, watching the man die.

Back in the garden house, she put the tea water on. There were guests coming.

Two minutes later, Chad stood outside the back door, calling in Japanese for the soldier to come out, as he was surrounded.

"You will find Japan man dead in the garden," called Mary. "Please come in."

Chad pushed the door open to find a pretty Korean woman sitting at the table, spooning tea into a porcelain pot. "Who are you?"

"I am Mary, the Ishihara's housekeeper and gardener. When Oki ran into the house, bleeding, yelling about Americans, I walked him out to the garden. I told him I would hide him, then I cut the bastard's throat. Welcome American soldier. I will have fresh tea for you and your friends."

"We killed two down by the river. Are there more?"

"No, only three. Are you here to take Michi and Kiko home?"

"Yes, how do you know that?

"Michi told me you might come. Is Mark with you?"

"Just a second, what did you say your name was?" asked Chad.

"Mary."

"Just a second, Mary, let me get the rest of our small team in here, and we can discuss this. Mark is here; he is at the house."

Five men crowded into the tiny kitchen. Chad introduced them. Mary filled five cups with tea. "Are you hungry?"

"No ma'am," replied Chad. "We ate breakfast a couple of hours ago. Where did you learn your English?"

"I live with a missionary family back in Korea, after the Japanese killed my parents. I went to the church college in Pusan before I let myself get caught and sent to Japan as a common laborer."

"Why would you want to become a laborer with that education?" asked Spiff.

"I am part of the Korean resistance movement. We have been fighting to throw the Japanese out of Korea for a quarter century. My job was to work my way into a posting where I can learn Japanese Army codes and radio procedures. Most laborers are only here for three years. When I go back, I will help rid my country of soldiers who only see Koreans as work animals and Korean girls as prostitutes.

"How did the people who sent you know that you would get that kind of posting?"

"I was smart and pretty. They figured I would be selected by a Japanese officer or official."

The men sat quietly digesting the message. Mary fidgeted.

"Do you have any place to go when we leave?" asked Chad finally.

"No. I will stay here and hope that I get posted to another place where I can continue my work."

"Mary, you cannot stay here. When we go, it will appear that everybody at the house, along with Colonel Ito and his bodyguards, disappeared. If you stay, they will torture you until you tell them what happened."

"Then I will run away and try to cross the border to the Russian side of the island. I have enough money hidden to take a boat back to Korea."

"But, if you are caught, they will torture you and then shoot you, won't they?"

Mary sat studying tealeaves in the bottom of the cup she cradled in both hands. "If I die, everything I have learned will die. I will have been humiliated for nothing."

"You will have to go with us, then," replied Spiff. "Besides, the Japanese are being beaten all over the Pacific. When the war ends, they will be gone from Korea."

"I always dreamed of seeing America. It must be an amazing place. I can only dream of a country where everybody shares the kindness and forgiveness that the Bible teaches."

Chad looked around the room, watching the faces of the four men he had recruited. None of them offered a response. Finally Mary looked up from her cup.

"Mary, there are a lot of people in America who need a lot of forgiveness. Still, I think you will like it, at least until travel back to Korea can be arranged."

The men finished their tea, and then a second cup. After an hour of waiting they decided that there was work to be done.

"Ivan, Paul, would you go back to the river and drag the bodies of the two men we shot back to the garden behind this house. Put them where the body of their friend is. In this rain, the blood will be gone in a few hours. Sparks, you go with them."

"Mary, will you show Spiff here the radio system the soldiers used, and where they keep any logs and codes? I am going to take a walk around and see if I can find someplace to hide the bodies."

"Captain Gritt, if you will wait a minute, I have an idea." She led Spiff into a small communications room, returning moments later.

Mary led Chad out into the rain. While they watched, the three men sent to recover the bodies dragged the first man past the porch and into the garden. Mary pointed at the road coming down the hill toward the house.

"Along that road there is a place where local people have dug coal from a hill for centuries. There is a deep hole in the side of the hill where you could hide the dead Japanese and then shovel some rocks from the top down, to cover them."

"You really hate them, don't you?" asked Chad.

"Not the Japanese people. Michi and Kiko treat me very well. Mark's grandfather is a gentleman. Mostly I hate the Army and the soldiers." Mary looked up into Chad's face and smiled. "That is not very Christian, is it? Someday I will pray that I can forgive them, but not today. Someday I will pray to be forgiven for killing that man in the garden." She paused. "If you will let me, I will kill Colonel Ito for you."

"Mary, we don't want Ito dead, we want to take him with us. He knows about all of the defenses in the prefecture."

"That makes me sad, Captain Gritt. I would rather see his blood running away in the rain. Anyway, Ito will arrive in a large truck with a driver and two guards. We can load the dead Japanese in the truck and haul them to where the coal is. Since the commercial coal mines opened, no one goes there anymore."

Chad looked down at the petite, pretty, woman at his side. He feared the Japanese military, and he was sworn to defeat it. But that morning, he felt remorse, shooting three unarmed men. He wasn't sure he had ever hated anyone, at least not like this woman did. Maybe a little hate made war easier.

While they watched, five people walked from the summer home out to the driveway. They embraced, the women wiping tears as Michi helped a frail woman into the front seat of the old Ford pickup. The older man took the wheel. In minutes, the pickup disappeared, allowing those watching to get out of the rain.

CHAPTER 38

KARAFUTO, JAPAN, SEPTEMBER 1943

Mark trotted between the summer home and the garden house, skipping over a small ditch that drained the garden. The runoff was scarlet. "Come up to the house now, we must plan how we can capture Ito. My father also knows a lot more about the Japanese plane and the air strip."

Mary stepped forward, smiling at Mark. "It is good to see you again."

Mark smiled back. "My mother told me what has happened to you since you were ordered to come to the garden house. I am very sorry."

"I will live." Mary looked at the huge clock on the kitchen wall above the iron sink. "You have work to do before we go to the house. It is almost ten. You will have to report to Colonel Ito's office. Come, I will show you the procedure. I will whisper what to say into your ear as you transmit. I would do the broadcast myself, but they would recognize a woman's voice."

Mark nervously picked up the microphone and checked to make sure that the correct frequency was dialed in, and then he transmitted what Mary whispered, word for word. When he was done, he sighed, feeling the nervousness flow from his body. "If they suspected anything, they wouldn't have told me that Ito would be here between six and seven this evening."

Michi and Kiko gathered what little they would travel with, into two old suitcases. Mary added a small drawstring canvas bag containing her meager possessions. The luggage was stored in the small closet, on top of the cot that Mary slept on when she was in the house. Michi called Roku, the cannery manager on the radio, to ask him to ensure that his parents got aboard the ferry leaving that afternoon.

"I didn't understand why you asked your manager to arrange passage in the name of Yoshita," offered Mark as he sipped from the bottomless teacup his mother kept filling.

"Your grandparents arrived on one of the company boats. Roku gave them the pickup to come here. By traveling back under a false name, we leave no record of them being here. Once we leave, the Army will investigate, but Ito's boss, General Yamaguchi, doesn't like him very much, so I hope that they will not look beyond the obvious." Michi sat next to his wife, holding her hand. While the men were planning the reception for Ito, she slipped out the back door to take a last walk through the garden. The bodies of the young soldiers had shaken her more than anything in her life. She had seen dead soldiers before, when Japanese and Russian mercenaries invaded Alaska. But these enemies had lived with them for months.

"How did you know that the plane at the airport was a Kawanishi?" asked Michi.

"The code; you referred to silver salmon which was the code for PBY when I sent messages about American airplanes to the submarine and you," answered Mark. "You mentioned how hard it was to find four new engines for the boats that fished for silver salmon. We just put it together."

"The airport is a backwoods operation, but with the loss of the bases in the Aleutians, northern Japan is now at risk from American bombers. They are building places for a dozen fighters, but there are only four there now. There will be two guards at the entrance to the airport at night. Colonel Ito is well known so his truck will be waived through."

"Any anti-aircraft guns at the airport?" asked Spiff.

"There are positions with large-caliber cannons pointing into the air, but no full time men to man them. Japan is really short of men now. Most men under the age of forty are already serving, so the guns at the airport will be manned by mechanics and fuel truck drivers if there is an attack."

"That leaves the four fighters as the only real risk once we get into the air," replied Spiff. "How far from where they park the flying boat are the fighters?"

"They are all parked in the same area."

"Perhaps we can just shoot them up with the guns on the Emily, as we taxi for takeoff," suggested Chad.

"I assume Emily is the code name you have for the Kawanishi. That would probably work, but it would also bring the entire base alive. The Japanese Navy is not as arrogant as the Army," replied Michi. "They know how vulnerable Japan is. They will respond quickly, even if it is only with rifles stored in their barracks."

"Then we have to disable those fighters quietly." Spiff tugged the silenced pistol from a place in the small of his back. He had tucked it there after he had wiped it clean earlier. "We can't do much damage with the tiny bullets, but we can flatten the tires and shoot some holes in the cowling. Maybe we will hit some things that are important. Two of us can each shoot up four clips of ammunition, while the rest of you load the plane."

Chad nodded, and then turned back to Michi. "Mr. Ishihara, your messages said that the plane will be fueled and that there will be no one guarding it?"

"I think it is time for you to call me Michi, Chad. And yes, I am as sure as I can be. Colonel Ito gloats about how much he knows. He told me that the Kawanishi is always kept fueled and loaded with ammunition, even some bombs under the wings, in case an American submarine is sighted. When it flies, the airplane is normally gone for the whole day."

The six-wheeled truck, with a canvas cover over the back crept down the hill as the people at the house nervously took their places. Ito climbed from the cab, taking the time to slip on his raincoat. His guards and driver also reluctantly pulled on raincoats as they spread out along the short walk to the house. Ito required them to stand ten yards apart, between the truck and the house, waiting to salute him as he passed. On a nice day it was hot, and standing, sometimes for an hour or two, was hard on their feet. On a rainy day, they hated this tribute to the colonel's arrogance. They were expected to remain standing until they had saluted Ito on his way back to the truck.

Kiko greeted him at the door, advising that the house servant was busy in the kitchen making tea. Michi rose from the desk in the corner and nodded as Ito threw his raincoat over a priceless black lacquered table in the corner of the room and took the seat always reserved for him.

"You had a pleasant trip to headquarters?" asked Michi.

"I did. The information that your son provided allowed us to slip past the Americans and evacuate the entire base. We left no one, and no one was hurt."

"Perhaps then, you can help to rescue Mark," continued Michi. "He is in great danger now."

"Of course, that would please me, but it is impossible. I would like to see Mark again just to thank him personally. Still, you must prepare yourself to never see your son again, just as thousands of Japanese families have prepared."

Mary glided into the room, bowing to Ito, carrying a huge pot of tea and two cups. She poured Ito part of a cup and stood ready with the pot for his approval. She had learned that if the temperature were not perfect, he would throw what was left in his cup on the floor while demanding that she prepare another pot.

Ito stopped his gloating conversation with Michi. He absent-mindedly tossed the tea into the back of his mouth. The scalding tea launched him from his chair. Mary removed the cover from the teapot, waiting for this moment. She tossed the rest of the scalding tea at Ito's face.

Before he could recover, Mark bolted from the bedroom and along with his father wrestled the man to the floor. Kiko jabbed the needle of a sedative into his leg, pressing the plunger with all her strength. Ito's screams brought a sharp command in Japanese and then the rattle of automatic weapons fire, as Spiff, Ivan and Paul sprang from their hiding places, cutting down the guards and driver with their Thompsons before they could react.

Ito twisted his head in fury, finding Mark filling his vision. "Perhaps now would be an opportunity to thank Mark yourself," said Michi. Behind Mark, a tall American with blue eyes kneeled, looking into the fury that was Ito's face.

"Colonel Ito, my name is Chad Gritt, Captain U.S. Army Air Corps and blood brother to my friend Mark here. You are about to disappear, as if you never existed. You will be traveling with us back to the United States where you will tell us all you know about the defenses of northern Japan."

"I will tell you nothing. Ask your friends here, I will never be a traitor to my country like they are."

"We will see, Colonel." Chad reached into his coat pocket, carefully unfolding several sheets of paper. "We will be leaving evidence behind, evidence that indicates that you planned the escape of the Ishihara family and your own defection to the enemy by going with them."

"I will never b-betr-r-ay Ja..."

"He is going to sleep," smiled Kiko. How long will these sedatives last?"

"That one shot should keep him out for five or six hours. When he starts to come out of it, we will give him another shot," answered Chad. He looked at his watch. "How long a drive is it to the airstrip?"

"Just over an hour," replied Michi.

"So, if we allow a half hour to get rid of the bodies, we should stay here another couple of hours before leaving. We want to arrive a little before midnight when the base is asleep."

Chad stood and reached into the small canvas bag at his side. He slipped a photograph of the airstrip from a folder. "The American Navy photographed every airstrip it could find before the war. Michi, can you show me exactly where the flying boat is parked? I will need to get us onto the runway, probably without any runway lights."

Kiko walked over to the front windows and watched as the men outside dragged the bodies of Ito's guards and the driver behind the truck, leaving them in the rain. The same shiver that wrenched her body when she found the men in the garden shook her again. Turning, she nodded at Mary. "We will fix some dinner since we have time." She managed a smile. "We have fresh salmon."

The stop at the old mine took longer than planned. The six dead men and the canvas that kept them from bleeding all over the truck, were stuffed into the hole left by prying coal from a narrow seam. Only after the bodies were in place did it dawn on the team that they had forgotten shovels to cover them. It took almost an hour of kicking rocks and gravel into the hole to cover the corpses. The men rinsed their filthy hands and feet in a small stream. Sodden, they climbed back into the truck.

Mark drove, the hat and raincoat of the dead driver covering the khaki uniform he had worn since morning. Next to him was Ito, his head tilted onto Mary's shoulder. Crammed next to her was Michi, now dressed in a business suit, reading glasses, a felt hat pulled down to cover his face. He had shaved off a moustache that he had worn for thirty years. In the back, the rest of the team bounced in the dark as the truck tried to make up a little time on the terrible road.

It was hard to believe that the airstrip they approached was an active military base. The facility was almost completely blacked out. At the guard shack one guard stood, at present arms, recognizing Ito's truck while the other walked over to the cab.

"What is she saying?" whispered Spiff, fingering the safety on the submachinegun in his lap.

"She told the guard that she is the colonel's concubine, and that they were staying at a house by the ferry terminal when the colonel became very sick. She called Dr. Ogani, who thinks it is appendicitis. The doctor called the military hospital in Hokkaido and arranged to accompany Ito there for emergency surgery. She asked the guards to send Ito's own pilots to the flying boat when they arrive, since Ito's driver knows how to start and warm up the engines but isn't a pilot."

The truck passed a line of construction equipment parked where four old civilian aircraft sat becoming part of the tarmac. Five minutes later, Spiff and Ivan trotted off in the dark, toward four shadows that had to be fighter planes. Michi found a second flashlight in the cab of the truck. He handed one to Chad, who headed to the cockpit to familiarize himself with the controls. The rest of the group wrestled the radio equipment up to the radio deck and then began loading what little else they carried. Ito was left in the front of the truck until everything else was loaded and Chad was seated in the pilot's seat. Paul and Mark carried the man to the plane where Michi helped lift him. Minutes later, he sat in the seat of one of the blister gunners, tied hand and foot to the metal seat, a rag stuffed into his mouth.

The plane was not designed for carrying passengers, but it was engineered to carry a crew of eleven for missions that might last ten hours. Spiff and Ivan crawled aboard. Sparks led Ivan to a seat in the nose, where the gunner normally sat, and Spiff to the copilot's seat before strapping himself into the seat of the radio operator.

Behind Chad, Michi Ishihara stood translating the labels on the switches on the panel. "The one with the red box around it is the master power switch you are looking for. Below that, I think are four separate switches for the magnetos on each engine." Michi pointed at fuel flow valve controls that allowed or shut off fuel to each engine. "The switches next to them are the fuel pump boosters you are looking for, I think."

"I think I have enough of this figured out to get us airborne, except for how to switch on the intercom, so we go out of here screaming at each other until we get enough light to figure out the rest of the panel. Until light, all I can do is take off and climb. I can't figure out the oxygen system without some light, so we will set a compass course to the northeast and stay below fifteen-thousand feet."

"I doubt that 15,000 will get us into the clear," replied Spiff. "Until we can climb, I can't take a sextant reading."

"It is what it is," smiled Chad, trying to hide his nervousness. He had never before tried to ride a compass in the dark, for hours, in a strange airplane, over a stormy ocean. "Until we can figure out how much fuel we have and the fuel burn, I will set the cruise at about fifty percent power to conserve fuel. You ready?"

"No, but I would rather be out over the Pacific than sitting here when it gets light."

Chad switched on the battery power and the magnetos. A red glow from a light above and to his left indicated that the last man to fly the plane had illuminated the instrument panel. He checked the altimeter. That reading would be his base reading for his climb away from Karafuto.

He hit the fuel boost pump for what in an American airplane would be the number one engine. He pressed the starter switch, releasing it as the engine caught. He repeated the procedure for the second and the third engines. He was just starting the fourth engine when Paul, who had seated himself in the dorsal gun turret, burst into the cockpit.

"T-t-there's c-car lights c-c-c-coming f-f-f-from the b-buildings."

Chad released the brakes and started to taxi, as he hit the boost pump for the number four engine. He engaged the starter. The engine caught just as the flashlight Spiff was shining out the side window revealed the number and white lines at the end of the runway. Chad jammed on the left brake, swinging the heavy plane onto the runway and then crammed the throttles full forward, even that of the still sputtering number four motor. The heavy plane leaped forward, then it began to drive itself into the pavement in front of the nose.

"Shit, shit, shit," stumbled Chad, as he desperately looked for the trim control while trying to keep the plane on the dark runway. "Shine that light back in the cockpit."

With light, Chad found the flap lever and tugged it to what he thought was fifteen degrees of flaps. With the trim control, he rolled in trim to raise the nose of the airplane. The heavy plane's nose lifted from the runway. The main landing gear broke free from the concrete beneath them. The plane just hung there, flying in ground effect, building little airspeed. It dawned on Chad that he had no idea of what was at the end of the runway. He heard Spiff gasp, as the main landing gear bounced on the runway.

To their left, a small car raced from a taxiway onto the runway. A man in the passenger seat waved at the staggering plane, and then the car disappeared between the engines, under the left wing.

He rolled the trim control closer to a neutral setting and then reached up and bumped the flap control to reduce the flaps. The shaking in the plane stopped and the rate of climb indicator showed that the plane was not only airborne, it was climbing. The crunch of the left main landing gear colliding with the car would have brought everyone out of their seats if it weren't for seatbelts. He left the engines at full power as the altitude began to register, one hundred feet, two hundred feet, three and finally five hundred feet.

Chad reached up and reduced the flaps to only five degrees, and was rewarded by an airspeed indicator that finally pushed well up into the green arc on the dial. He checked the compass and began a turn to the northeast and settled into the seat. He heaved a sigh.

"I wondered how long you could hold your breath," quipped Spiff.

"Rummage around in here and see if you can find the operating manual for this monster," requested Chad.

It took ten minutes for Spiff to find what Chad was looking

for. Chad leaned back and yelled toward the tail. "Paul, can you hear me?"

"Yup."

"Go find Mark and have him come up here."

Mark made his way to the light that Spiff was shining on the deck just behind the cockpit.

"Give Mark the book," said Chad.

"Mark, find me the section of the book that tells me how to set this thing for cruise and that talks about fuel consumption. Take the flashlight."

Chad pulled the flap lever to zero. The airspeed climbed another twenty knots and the rate of climb indicator also moved from five hundred feet per minute up to just over seven hundred. Chad pulled the engine power back until the airspeed dropped back to where it had been, and the rate of climb slipped back to five hundred feet per minute. "This thing is a real dog."

"What are you doing?" asked a rattled Spiff as the plane slowed.

"If we leave the engines on takeoff power any longer, one or all of them are going to come apart. Think back to what we do in the PBY."

"Hell, I never really kept track of all that crap. You fly, I navigate and try hard to remember, me flying is for the good ol' USA. Maybe one of the lights that is on should be off, or the other way around. It feels like we are dragging a telephone pole behind us."

Chad took the flashlight from Spiff and scanned the panel in front of him, between the seats and the panel overhead. "This will help," he muttered, pushing a small lever all the way forward. "It helps to retract the landing gear."

Below on the left there was a grinding sound, followed by a clunk, but the plane was noticeably faster and more responsive.

It took thirty minutes to reach 15,000 feet. Chad pulled the engines back to the midpoint on their manifold pressure gauges and then adjusted the props. Mark was still not back with the manual, but Chad figured that a two hundred knot speed was close to the optimum cruise for a plane that big on a long flight. *Now if I just had a cup of coffee.*

It took Mark more than an hour to wander back to the cockpit. He had dog-eared a dozen sections in the manual. "I'll read the headings to you. You tell me whether it is something you need to know before morning."

It took another half-hour to finally learn enough to make Chad comfortable.

"You have any idea when it gets light around here?" asked Mark.

"It was light enough for the submarine to run on the surface about five in the morning," commented Spiff. "Were going further north, so sometime before five."

Mark looked at his watch. "Two plus hours until light. How far from Japan will we be when it is light enough for Japanese fighters to find us?"

"We should be halfway across the Pacific by then. I figure six hours of cruising to reach Adak. There won't be any Japanese fighters out that far. You might take the flashlight back to where Sparks is working on the radios. See if you can help. I am more concerned with American planes after it gets light. On the way, have everyone put on one of the masks and plug them into the outlets next to their seats."

"Why do we need those?" asked Mark.

"One of the things you helped me figure out is the oxygen and the intercom. We are going higher, where Spiff can get a star sighting to confirm our position. I will start the climb in ten minutes. Make sure someone puts one on Ito and tell Mary to keep an eye on him. It's almost time for his next shot."

CHAPTER 39

THE NORTH PACIFIC, SEPTEMBER 1943

With first light, Chad finally got a good look at the plane. The clouds around them offered visibility to the tips of the wings, but that was enough. "Take a look at the right wing and tell me what you see."

Spiff twisted in his seat, working to see the wing set well behind the cockpit. "Damn, are those bombs?"

"Yup, remember what Michi said. They normally leave this plane set up for anti-submarine searches. I can't think of any reason we need them."

"Agreed, the question is how do we drop them?"

Chad keyed the intercom. "Mark, can either you or Michi come up to the cockpit?"

It took less than a minute for Michi to stick his head up between the two men. "Could you take a quick look through the manual and figure out how to jettison the bombs we are carrying?"

The intercom and interior of the plane exploded with screams, as the bombs fell away into the gray. Only Mary remained calm, as she said, "There are parts falling off the plane."

Chad apologized, "I couldn't come up with anything good that would come with hauling a ton of bombs into an area patrolled by American aircraft."

"Thanks Mr. Ishihara," he offered, just as he would have done when he was twelve.

"No sweat," offered Michi, "I better get back and try to calm my wife."

The cockpit began to materialize as something vaguely familiar. Chad checked the fuel gauges. The wing tanks showed just under half full. He checked the gauges for the two internal tanks. One showed completely full and the second, empty. In minutes, Spiff calculated the fuel aboard, and the range at the optimum power settings.

"We have enough plus about eight hundred miles if we get lost," he said. "I figure we still have about nine hundred miles to Adak, and we have almost twice that much fuel."

"It's probably a bad time for the lesson," replied Chad, "but aircraft fuel gauges are notoriously unreliable."

"If you don't need me for a few minutes, I'll wander back and give those two tanks the old hammer test. If one is full, it should sound a lot deader when I beat on it than the other." Spiff unbuckled his seat belt and crawled out of the cockpit.

Chad laughed. That was exactly the right thing to do. "While you are up, check to see how the radio installation is going. We need to tell Roads we are airborne."

Spiff stopped in front of Sparks, who was fiddling with the dial of a radio set, lashed to the small counter in front of him. The man gave Spiff a thumbs up. "We are ready to send the coded message whenever our fearless leader says."

"Send it, then let's do a manual check on the fuel. The two men made their way past sleeping passengers, slipping into a passage between the nose and tail. There they used a wrench to check the two fuel tanks. They sounded just like the gauges said they should. Just in front of the tanks, Mary was curled up sleeping on a seat across from Ito, who sat, his head tilted forward onto his chest. He looked dead.

Sparks knelt next to the man, pressing two fingers under his chin, looking for a pulse. Before he could rise, Ito slammed his left knee into the side of Sparks' head, tumbling him against the corner of an ammunition locker. Somehow Ito had slipped his foot out of his boot tied to the leg of his chair.

Spiff leaned forward, cracking the Japanese colonel with the wrench he carried. Then he felt for a pulse. There was still a heartbeat. Mary grabbed his sleeve, as she pressed a syringe into his hand. "I am so sorry; I must have fallen asleep."

Spiff stabbed the drug-filled syringe into Ito's shoulder. Then he and Mary dragged Sparks forward to a flat place on the deck. The radioman had a steady heartbeat. A bump the size of a walnut was forming on his forehead, and a small cut seeped blood. Mary covered him with a blanket from her bag. She plugged another oxygen mask in and pulled it over his face. "Go back to where Captain Gritt is flying; I will stay here with this man."

"I will in a minute," responded Spiff. "I have a small task first." He made his way back to Ito just as Mark started forward. Together they tugged Ito's boots off and used the laces to lash his legs even tighter to the seat he sagged in.

"Don't you think you might have tied him too tightly?" asked Mark. "You may cut off circulation to his feet."

Spiff rose and turned back toward the cockpit. "You go talk to everyone on this plane. Call me if you can find someone who gives a goddamn."

The two men and Mary retreated to their seats, the minutes without adequate oxygen making them lightheaded.

As the light improved, Chad looked down on an endless expanse of clouds. Spiff's first star sighting allowed him to mark their exact position on the map he dug from his bag. The second, just as it started to get light, allowed him to calculate the wind drift aloft. Chad adjusted his compass heading to bring them back on course.

The clouds below began to fall away, as they often do when the air cools. Chad pulled a little power leveling off just over twelve thousand feet, the belly of the plane skipping across the tops of the clouds. He keyed the intercom. "At this altitude, you can remove your oxygen masks for a half-hour at a time." He turned to Spiff in the seat next to him. "Think you can hold this heading and altitude long enough for me to take a look around?"

"I can try. What are you looking for?"

"I just think, the more I know about this bird the better I can fly it. I am going to have to land this beast. Besides, I need to check on our radio operator. We are going to need him soon."

It felt good to stretch his legs. He stopped where Mary sat, an oxygen mask covering her face. Sparks was still unconscious. "How's he doing?"

"His pulse is strong, but he hasn't even wiggled. I hope that he isn't bleeding inside his head."

"I've flown with this man for months. He has a really hard head," offered Chad with a smile.

While they were talking, Michi made his way forward. "I can't believe that I slept," he started. "Kiko cried for a couple of hours before she finally went to sleep. We weren't ready for what comes with war."

"I don't think anyone is. I had to shoot a couple of men when I was relaying information for the invasion of Kiska Island. I had to call in a strike by some airplanes on the men I didn't shoot just to keep them from telling their officers where I was hiding. Ivan and Paul were there. They weren't even in the military then, and they were fighting for their lives."

Michi nodded his head. "Anyway, I found something on the side of the plane that I think you should see."

Michi led Chad to two inspection windows just above the main landing gear. The window on the right showed the gear fully retracted and the door closed tight. On the left, the gear door was open a couple of inches. "Let me show you what else I found."

Michi unlatched a metal door over the wheel well. The left landing gear and wheel were twisted inside the wheel well. The tire was still inflated, but the gear assembly itself was canted to one side.

"We hit a small car trying to stop us on the runway," observed Chad. "We must have damaged the gear leg then."

"Can we land on broken landing gear?'

"If it will come down and lock, we probably can, but we will have to land so that most of the stress is on the other side."

"Can you do that in a plane that you have never landed before? And don't give me that crap that you can do anything."

"I can try," replied Chad.

"W-w-what a-about m-m-m-mind o-over ma-ma-matter?" came Paul's voice from behind the two men.

"That only works if something isn't broken," laughed Chad.

"T-t-then w-we l-l-land in t-the w-w-water."

Chad looked at the jammed gear door. He was confident that he could get the hull of the plane smoothly onto the water, but he didn't know what would happen when the hull settled enough to slam the damaged door with tons of water. "No sweat, but let's try to get off this plane without getting our feet wet."

Chad found Mark asleep across from his mother. He gently shook him awake. "Mark, you are going to have to be our radio operator, at least until Sparks regains consciousness. We need to talk to Roads and find out what the weather is at Adak."

"Give me a few minutes to find a cup of tea, and I will call him," replied Mark. "Mom brought a huge jug of tea, and this plane has a small electric hotplate next to the head to heat things."

"This plane has a head? Thank God, that's why I really came back here," answered Chad. "Show me."

Fifteen minutes later, the intercom crackled as Mark passed on what he had learned. There was no rain and no wind in Adak that morning, but there was fog right to the ground. The forecast was for improvement before noon. Chad sighed. So far everything was working, mostly according to plan. Hopefully, the weather gods wanted them to land safely in Adak. In front of the plane the clouds slipped closer to the sea, allowing Chad to follow them down until he was level at ten thousand feet.

"Okay everyone, you don't need the oxygen masks," he called.

A few minutes later, Kiko stuck her head into the cockpit. She handed each of the men a napkin with some sweet rolls and a cup of coffee. "It's not tomato soup and a grilled cheese sandwich, but it is the best I have," she laughed.

"Where did you get the coffee?" asked Spiff.

"It is instant coffee. Michi brought it with us when we came to Japan two years ago. We couldn't get more, so we only used it for special occasions. Enjoy, this is the last of it."

CHAPTER 40

THE NORTH PACIFIC, SEPTEMBER 1943

Road's plan was for Chad's old P-38 squadron to escort them the last two hundred miles into Adak, but while it looked like the fog was starting to break up, it was still too low to allow the escorts to take off. In front of the flying boat, the clouds ended and the blue of the North Pacific on a sunny morning spread before them. Here and there, huge patches of fog clung to the surface.

Where the water was clear of mist, the surface was as smooth as it ever was along the Aleutian chain. Below, the huge swell was missing its normal whitecap cover. Spiff tapped Chad on the shoulder, pointing at the map in his hand. If his navigation was right, they were passing south of Kiska Island. Adak was less than two hours in front of them.

They could hear the chatter of the other people over the intercom. The sunshine and open ocean below had raised everyone's spirits. *I still have to land this beast, but so far so good,* thought Chad. A hand on his shoulder interrupted his thoughts. He turned and looked into Mary's tear filled eyes.

"Your man, the one who runs the radio is not breathing. I was talking with Kiko for a few minutes and when I got back, he had no pulse. I am so sorry."

Chad managed a forced smile. "It is not your fault. That SOB who started all of this two years ago, Ito, killed Sparks."

"I would enjoy slitting his throat," offered Mary. "I could have done it fifty times in the last year. I wish I had."

"No, the only way we can make Sparks' death make sense is if we learn enough from Ito to save American lives." Chad realized that he really didn't mean a word of that.

For the next hour, everyone except Ito continuously checked their watches just to make sure time hadn't stopped.

In the distance, Chad could see the top of the mountains on Adak above the fog. Below, Mark relayed his questions to the air traffic controllers at the landing field. The fog was moving up and down with each small movement of a slight breeze coming from the south. At its best, the ceilings reached two hundred feet above the ocean, only about a hundred feet above the highest point on the airstrip.

Put me in a P-38 and I would be sitting in the officers' club in an hour, thought Chad. "Okay everybody, I am going down to take a look. Everyone find a seat and buckle up."

Chad swung out past the mountaintops that had become familiar over the past year. He lowered the flaps to 10 percent after he pulled back the power on the engines, running the fuel mixture to full rich, and the props to almost full power, in case he needed to pour the power to the plane to climb back out. The altimeter indicated that the fog started less than a thousand feet from the surface. If it ended 200 feet above the ocean, they were home.

He slowed the plane to 150 knots then lowered the flaps to 15 percent, which slowed them another 25 knots. He reached up and pulled the landing gear handle down. The sound of the gear doors opening, and the landing gear dropping was like a favorite old song to his ears. He watched the lights on the panel as the front gear and the right gear lights illuminated, but the left light stayed dark.

"Michi, can you take a look at the damaged landing gear through the window and the hatch and let me know what you see?" called Chad. He turned out over the ocean, to the north of the island, where the fog seemed to go on forever.

"The landing gear looks like it is all the way down, but it isn't completely straight," came the answer.

"How crooked is it?"

"Not much, maybe an inch from front to back."

"Okay, were going to try it. Go sit down."

"Mark," he called over the intercom, "tell the controllers that we have damaged landing gear. They need a crash truck standing by."

Chad swung the huge plane back towards Adak, lining it up at an angle with the mountains, a technique he had used before to descend below bad weather. He reduced the power a bit more. He was at twelve hundred feet and he needed to have visibility at least 200 feet above the water's surface to line up on the runway.

Chad defined his course on the compass. "Call my descent every fifty feet, Spiff."

Spiff read off the altimeter, as Chad stayed on the compass heading and tried to bore a hole in the fog with his eyes. He didn't get really nervous, at least nervous to where he had to dry his hands on his pants every few seconds, until they dropped below five hundred feet.

"Three hundred," called Spiff. "Two-fifty…two-hundred."

There was still nothing in front of the plane but gray. Worse, looking down, where he should have been able to see water, there was still only Gray.

"Let's go to one fifty," called Chad.

"It took Spiff less than fifteen seconds to call out, "one-fifty."

Chad crammed full power onto all four engines and tugged the landing gear lever into the up position. He began a missed approach turn, as the huge plane's four 1800 horsepower engines launched the plane into the sky. In less than twenty seconds, the blue sky appeared through the windscreen.

"No go," called Chad.

"No shit," called Mark.

"Knock it off and tell Roads that we want to make a water landing out where the fog ends. Tell him we need a ship standing by. Tell him we might have hull damage where our landing gear was damaged on takeoff. If we do, this plane could roll over on landing."

Chad sat, wishing he had a cigarette, and he didn't smoke. He pulled the power back and stabilized the plane at two thousand feet.

Mark was back in less than a minute. "Roads has no ships in the area. Everyone has moved over to Kiska. They are already building an airstrip there. He suggests we head for Kiska harbor where what little of the Navy left in the Aleutians is anchored up. The weather there is clear."

Chad pointed at the fuel gauges. Spiff nodded yes. "Tell the Captain we are on the way to Kiska. We are probably about two hours out. Tell them what is going on, I don't want a dozen Navy ships opening up on us while I am trying to land."

"Spiff, just how much fuel do we have?"

"Enough to make Kiska and maybe another half-hour. That assumes the estimates and fuel consumption guess we made in the beginning is accurate." He pointed at the fuel gauges in the instrument panel. "When we transferred the fuel from the internal tank to the wings the gauges ran up to three-quarters. They have been at one-eighth for over an hour. I don't think they are moving."

Chad called Mark. "Now is when all of those flights over Kiska pay off. I remember the bay. See if Roads can get us some radio frequencies and contacts over there."

"Paul," he called, "go rummage around and see if there are any life preservers stashed anywhere."

Chad throttled back the huge engines to conserve whatever fuel remained. Kiska was now just over an hour away. They would burn less fuel at altitude, but it would take a lot of fuel to climb. "We will stay at two thousand feet," he mumbled to anyone listening.

They had been on course for thirty minutes when Mark made his way to the cockpit and tapped Chad on the shoulder. "Roads says a couple of your P-38 buddies just lifted off the strip at Adak.

They should catch up to us to escort us in. The fog is still terrible there, so they put enough fuel on to make it to the new strip at Attu after we land."

"It will be nice to have the company. Let me know when they check in with you."

The mountains of Kiska were barely visible when two P-38s screamed by the lumbering seaplane only a few feet from each wingtip. Both turned in front of the plane and then took up stations off from the wings, so close that Chad could see the faces of old friends smiling at him.

"Colonel Wayne says he is damned happy not to be trying to shoot us down. He says with all of the guns sticking out of the fuselage, this thing looks like a flying porcupine."

"Tell him he would have never caught us if this were combat. This thing can really scream when you pour the coal to these huge engines. Thank him for the escort. Tell him I am going to ask Captain Roads if I can keep it."

Chad looked out the window at his official commanding officer flying his P-38 on his left wingtip, watching him laugh. In the distance the island began to emerge from the haze.

Chad swung the lumbering plane out to the north to set up a long approach into the wind.

Paul stuck his head into the cockpit and held up six life preservers. "F-found t-t-t-them w-with a r-raft, u under t-t-t-the f-f-f-flour n near the d-door."

"Give one to each of the women and one to Michi and Mark. Put one on Colonel Ito. You and Ivan figure out which of you gets the last one."

"I w-w-will p-put o-one o-on the r-r-radio m-man. He c-can't s-swim n-n-now."

Chad nodded. "Go ahead and move Sparks and Ito back to the door, and then find a place to buckle in."

Below, a dozen ships sat in the shelter of the peninsula that jutted out of Kiska to the east, blocking the Pacific swell. "Mark, see who you can raise on the radio. Tell them we are starting out descent for landing."

Chad began the landing ritual again, this time leaving the landing gear in the up position for a water landing. He watched as the two escorts peeled off and circled behind him. With ten miles to land, he set up a shallow descent that would allow him to touch down about halfway through the scattered ships.

He slowed the plane, adding flaps. The picket ship, a destroyer, flashed by the wing only three hundred feet below. The two P-38s screamed by the plane. Each fired a short burst from their guns as a tribute and then pulled high G turns before climbing.

The flying boat began to drop toward the water, finding a clear path between the anchored ships.

"I thought that plane was one of ours," screamed the young gun captain manning an anti-aircraft gun on a landing ship. Those fighters just shot at it. It is headed right at the hospital ship." He ratcheted the bolt on the twin .50 caliber machine guns in front of him and opened fire. In seconds, gun mounts on two other ships joined in. The huge plane, with the rising sun painted on the side, was an impossible target to miss.

Bullets stitched the plane from the nose to the tail. The two engines on the port side belched smoke, and then fire erupted from the wing. Inside, the armor deflected many of the bullets, but many more punched holes through the light aluminum making up the plane's skin. The two empty internal fuel tanks rumbled as a dozen heavy rounds slammed into them, some ricocheting around the inside of the tanks. Chad pulled the power, slamming the plane onto the water where it bounced and then began skipping across the water like a porpoise.

He pulled on the controls with all of his strength to keep the plane from diving nose first into the water. The maneuver worked, but instead of smoothly settling onto the water, the plane twisted sideways, smacking the water at an angle. Chad felt a blow to his side, as the plane skidded and then tipped up onto its right wing and splashed to a stop.

Chad threw off his seat belt but couldn't get out of his seat. The firing had stopped.

Across from him, Spiff wiped at a bloody nose and stared across at Chad. There was blood all over the cockpit on the pilot's side. "You hit bad?"

Chad tilted his head back; his eyes glued shut in pain. He didn't answer.

Spiff released his seat belt, climbing across the cockpit. He checked Chad's belt, then lifted the wounded pilot from his seat and began dragging him toward the rear door.

At the door, Mark and Ivan heaved Sparks' body from the sinking plane, and then Ito's limp body. Mary jumped into the brutally cold water.

Mark screamed for his parents, just as Spiff handed the now limp body of Chad to Ivan. "Your mom is helping your dad forward. I think he was wounded. Come on."

He and Mark made their way through the water inside the fuselage, seawater already above their shoes. They found Kiko trying to carry her husband who was bleeding from his left arm and hip. The two men picked up the wounded man and carried him toward the door just as Paul lifted the life raft from the hatch in the floor where he had found the life preservers. He pushed the raft out the door and pulled the cord with the bright red ring on the end. The raft began to inflate.

Mark pushed his mother into the raft and then he and Spiff lowered his father next to her. "Thank you, thank all of you for what you have done for us," managed Michi.

Mark threw a canvas wrapped package into the raft.

Three of them worked to slide Chad's dead weight into the raft. Seconds later, the four remaining men dove into the water as the raft began to drift away. Each managed to grab the rope around the edge of the raft. Ivan and Paul crawled over the inflated tube. They found a rope coiled in the bottom and threw it to Mary who clung to it as they dragged her to the rafts side. Spiff and Mark pushed her into the raft just as the first rescue boat from the fleet arrived.

Behind them, the Japanese seaplane was submerged down to its wings. From below the raft, bubbles drifted to the surface as the raft also began to settle. The two men drifting in life jackets were the first picked up by the rescue boat. Then the boat maneuvered next to the raft, to pluck Spiff and Mark from the water. Mark looked up into the face of a young sailor as he was pulled over the side. "Watch out for the Jap Colonel there, he is very dangerous." The young sailor looked into Mark's Asian face with a stunned look.

A second boat arrived just as the flying boat slipped beneath the surface. In moments, the people in the raft were lifted into the boat and it was on its way to the hospital ship anchored only a half mile away.

CHAPTER 41

KISKA ISLAND, ALASKA, SEPTEMBER 1943

The hospital ship had been part of the invasion fleet. While there were no Japanese troops left on Kiska, friendly fire and weather-related casualties kept the medical personnel busy. On shore, the soldiers were continuing their sweeps to make sure that there were no enemy troops hidden somewhere, even as the Seabees worked to build a dock system and an airstrip.

In the surgery, Michi's left arm was amputated, and shrapnel from the seat he was sitting in was removed from his hip. If the tubular metal seat hadn't absorbed most of the impact of the bullet, he would have been a dead man. Outside of the surgery, Kiko and Mark waited. Normally, civilians would have never been allowed into the bowels of the huge white ship with the Red Cross painted on the side, but the commanding admiral of the fleet had intervened.

"First your father loses the finger that that Peter boy cut off and now his arm," whispered Kiko.

"At least it is the same arm, Mother," answered Mark trying to smile. He reached into his pants pocket and retrieved Peter's class ring. "I saved this for father." He handed it to his mother.

Only steps away, that admiral stood with Spiff, shaking his head. "God, I am sorry. I'll get to the bottom of this. I had every ship's captain respond personally that they had briefed their gun crews that a seaplane with Japanese markings was going to land, and no one was to fire on it."

"At least Captain Roads' message got through," Spiff said. "If anyone of the combat ships had opened up with their heavy caliber guns, we would all be dead."

"Captain Roads will be here in a couple of hours. The PBY crew heard what happened and decided that they didn't need to wait for the fog to clear to take off."

A nurse just coming on duty dropped the tray and clipboard she was carrying. She froze as she looked at Spiff, and just down the hall, Mark. "Oh God, oh God, oh God," she mumbled as she crept toward the Admiral.

"Spiff, where is Chad?" mumbled Carmen.

"Miss," snapped the admiral, "that is not how you address a superior officer."

Both Spiff and Carmen ignored the man, as Spiff pulled the woman into his arms. "He is in surgery now. We were flying that Japanese boat that stirred up all of the excitement earlier. We stole it in Japan and used it to get Mark's parents out of Karafuto."

"How bad is he?"

"Hell, Carmen, I don't know. One of the bullets hit the metal in his seat and exploded. His whole left hip was blown open from what I could see. Thank God it happened right next to this ship. We had him in surgery in fifteen minutes."

Carmen walked down the passage where Mark introduced her to Kiko. The two women conversed in hushed voices, discussing Michi. In minutes, she was back. The admiral, with little experience being ignored, swallowed his pride and just watched. "Did you lose anyone?" asked Carmen.

"Yeah, that cocky kid who ran the radios for us on the PBY was with us. We had a Japanese colonel on board, a prisoner. Somehow, he got a foot loose. Sparks thought he might be dying, so he leaned over to see if he could help. That SOB smashed him in the head. He didn't make it, but we got his body out of the plane before it sunk."

Carmen disappeared for a couple of minutes and then reappeared in a surgical cap and gown, tears streaming down her face. "Lieutenant," started the admiral, but Carmen was already through the doors into the surgery.

The admiral was in and out all afternoon, checking on the men in sickbay. It was late in the afternoon when Captain Roads was ushered, by the admiral, into what had become a waiting room. "I guess Alaska just creates cowboys, Admiral," offered Roads. "Gritt is just the latest. Jimmy Doolittle and Billy Mitchel both have some roots in Alaska. They all are a little unorthodox, but they seem to get the job done. Anyway, thanks for helping my people. And I can understand how some young kid could lose it if he thought the hospital ship was threatened. I'm glad that I don't have to figure out what to do about it."

Kiko stopped her son as they waited for the boat that would take them over to the landing ship that Roads used as an office. "I want this to be over for your father and me."

"I hope it is," replied Mark.

"It began with that awful Peter fellow. It is best if we forget that he ever lived." Kiko pulled the class ring from her pocket. She threw it as far as she could, watching it splash into the ocean. "You will have to help your father learn to fish with only one arm."

A short time later, a half-dozen exhausted people climbed the ladder of the landing ship that was the office for the construction of the runway on Kiska. Roads led them to a room where the ship's galley had prepared a meal. Roads locked the doors to the room and produced a bottle of Scotch. "He is going to live, but he is going to take a lot of rehab to get that left leg working again. The doctor put more pins and screws into Chad's hip and leg than you find in a hardware store. He sewed up the muscle, but he had to take out a bunch that was too torn to repair," explained Carmen. "It may take years of rehabilitation to see how much use he will have of the leg."

Roads circled the room, pouring Scotch for all present. "The mission was worth it." He smiled at Kiko, who sat quietly looking into her glass.

"Yes, I guess it was," she answered. "I believe that Colonel Ito would have killed both Michi and me when we were of no further service."

"You will want to talk to Mary here too. She has been studying the radio operations of our enemy for a year. She heard or saw almost every communiqué from Ito," added Kiko.

"He will give us more; it will just take time. In the interim, he has already given us more than we could have ever expected," offered Roads. "That briefcase you threw into the raft is full of information about northern defenses and intelligence operations."

"It also discusses several places in Alaska where the Japanese have landed teams. They were seriously considering a major invasion. Ivan, you and Paul will be asked to visit each of those sites to make sure they didn't leave anyone behind and to figure out what they were looking for."

"What about our team?" asked Mark.

"For now, we are to stand down. I have arranged for your parents to be flown into Anchorage where they can live in the house that Chad arranged. They should stay there until this country gets its head screwed back on and ends its confinement of Japanese Americans. They will be free to operate the company business, but I wouldn't jump on any ships to the states until confinement is lifted. When did they say your father would be ready to leave?"

"He should be well enough to travel in a week," answered Kiko.

"Sir," came a soft voice, "can you arrange for me to travel back to Korea?"

"That would be a very bad idea right now. The reports are, that the Japanese have started arbitrarily shooting people that they think oppose the occupation; no charges, no trials."

"You can come with us," offered Kiko.

"And you, Mark, the government would be interested to have

you join me and Spiff on a trip back to D.C. There is a new intelligence unit that operates mostly in Europe. They are interested in exploring how to expand into Asia," offered Roads. "We aren't going for a month or so."

"Maybe it would be a good idea to take Mary with us. She has been fighting the Japanese longer than any of us."

"I don't know," responded Roads, "this is very dangerous work."

"Captain, that should be the least of your worries about Mary," replied Mark.

"Let's get on to some dinner, folks. I bet you are all exhausted. I will arrange for a boat back to the hospital ship in the morning."

A messenger tapped on the door. "Hide the Scotch," said Roads, as he unlocked the door. The young seaman handed him a sealed envelope and saluted before disappearing. Roads closed the door and ripped the end off from the envelope.

"I asked the *Scorpion* to continue to monitor the frequency you and your dad used. Their radio operator intercepted a message sent in the clear about an hour ago in English. Let me read it. *Mark, if you were responsible for rescuing your parents, congratulations. I wish them a long, healthy life. The Tokko have detained your grandfather. He was one of only eleven people rescued after an American submarine torpedoed it. I am sorry, your grandmother was not found. I am sorry. I am working to get Haruku released. The foreman at your plant told me that your grandparents had just delivered one of the company boats to Karafuto. Also thank you for helping me with a decades old problem. Fumi.*"

Now, what does that all mean?"

Mark turned to his mother; whose shoulders sagged. She wiped her eyes with her sleeve. "You will have to ask my husband."

Chad was awake, but drugged heavily when Roads, Spiff and Carmen slipped into the private room that the admiral had arranged. "What are you doing here?" he asked Carmen.

"This is what I volunteered for," she answered. "I trained nurses on what to do with cold weather injuries on the way up from Seattle."

"The doc says I am in for a fight just to walk again," he managed.

Carmen leaned over Chad and wrapped her arms around him, tears staining the crisp white sheets pulled up around his neck. She kissed him, holding her kiss as long as she could. "We will get through this. You will fly again. Nothing will keep you out of the sky."

Behind Roads and Spiff a graying doctor with bifocals slipped into the room, waiting to talk to his patient.

Chad managed a smile through lips that didn't work normally. "I wish you could be there while I work out the kinks."

"I would like that, too, but I still have the responsibilities that come with the commission. What's important is that your son or daughter is going to have a father."

The doctor smiled. "You know Lieutenant, that the military does not allow pregnant nurses in combat zones."

ACKNOWLEGEMENTS
ENEMY PATRIOTS

With the full encouragement of my wife, Carmen, I walked away from a successful business and political consulting career to follow my passion for writing.

Perhaps three dozen different websites and online papers contributed to the preparation of writing ENEMY PATRIOTS. Additionally, I would like to acknowledge the extensive materials made available to me by both the POBEDA MUSEUM and the MUSEUM OF LOCAL LORE, both in Sakhalin, Russia. Prior to World War II, the island now known as Sakhalin was split in the center, with the northern half Russian and the southern half called Karafuto by the Japanese.

In Alaska, the wonderful small ALASKA VETERANS MUSEUM in Anchorage and the excellent small PRINCE WILLIAM SOUND MUSEUM in Whittier provided great visual research.

Numerous books read over the two decades offered insight for this story. I want to acknowledge three for their contribution. The first is John Haile Cole's little read but excellent book on air combat in Alaska, MISSION TO THE KURILS. The second is Brian Garfield's best seller, THE THOUSAND-MILE WAR: WORLD WAR II IN ALASKA AND THE ALEUTIANS, which describes the military theater and fight superbly. Last is James C. McNaughton's book, NISEI LINGUISTS: JAPANESE AMERICANS IN THE MILITARY INTELLIGENCE SERVICE DURING WORLD WAR II, that acknowledges the contribution of Japanese Americans recruited into the Military Information Service who fought and died next to the Marines and Army in the Pacific. Their story has been ignored, or worse, covered up for decades.

For writing help, I would like to thank Gabrielle Raffuse, PhD., who tore herself away from her passion for literary writing, to help this storyteller refine a sparse, 'just the facts' writing style used in my involvement in business and political writing.

Bestselling author Marc Cameron's encouragement in the first couple of years that I turned to writing full time helped me stick with the program. Best selling author, Sheldon Siegel's coaching and mapping offered a faster and less restrictive path to my readers. Senior Editor Grace Doyle at Thomas and Mercer, who could never fit my stories into her publishing list, but who tried, offered her direction.

Finally, with the greatest appreciation and admiration, I want to thank bestselling author and friend Robert Dugoni for his constant encouragement, plot and editorial coaching, and willingness to kick me when I was not listening.

The technical support of Rob Bignell, my editor helped make the book more concise. The team at Damonza who provided cover and formatting support, turned a manuscript into a book. Finally, thank you DERRICK for helping launch *www.rodgercarlyle.com* and Dacia for social media help.

THE POLITICS: On every front of World War II, armies, air forces and navies clashed. Deeply imbedded in the conflict was racial prejudice. The Nazi concentration camps are notorious. The Japanese brutality towards the Chinese and Koreans is still felt today. The United States interred their Japanese American citizens and then later allowed for an all Japanese-American unit to fight in Europe. Only in the United States were the racial barriers breached during the war. Many know of the highly decorated 442nd regimental combat team's heroics in Europe, a unit made up of Japanese Americans. Few know of the combat experiences and sacrifices of Japanese Americans who risked automatic death sentences as intelligence operatives against Japan. They served side by side with the troops island hopping across the Pacific. Others were spies, helping the 'new country' against the 'old.'

One other note, every nation had some deeply flawed, inhumane officers, some more than others. But each, also had highly principled men and women, people who could be your friend, whose only crime was national patriotism. Introducing them in my stories is an important part of defining the 'enemy.'

If you liked ENEMY PATRIOTS, please consider posting a review on Amazon or Goodreads so other readers can find my stories. Thank you for reading my story!

Leave a review on Amazon

www.rodgercarlyle.com

Goodreads Author Rodger Carlyle

Amazon Author Rodger Carlyle

ABOUT THE AUTHOR

RODGER CARLYLE is a storyteller who draws on an enormous personal library of experiences. An adventurer, political strategist, and ghostwriter whose love of flying began in the Navy, his experiences stretch from New York to Los Angeles, from Amsterdam to Khabarovsk in the Russian Far East, and from Canada into Latin America.

Through his passion for research, he treasures finding those events that are ignored or covered up by the powerful when some strategy or plan goes completely to hell. From there, he creates a fictional adventure narrative that tells a more complete story.

Rodger is comfortable in black tie urban settings, but he is never happier than in the wilderness. He has faced down muggers in San Francisco, intimidation by the Russian Mafia, and charging grizzly bears. Most of his stories take his readers to places they will never visit. He likes to think that he is there with them.

Visit Rodger Carlyle's website at www.rodgercarlyle.com.